The King
of Dreams

The King
of Dreams

BOOK THREE OF THE PRESTIMION TRILOGY
THE CONCLUDING VOLUME OF THE MAJIPOOR CYCLE

ROBERT
SILVERBERG

EOS
*An Imprint of*HarperCollins*Publishers*
10 East 53rd Street
New York, New York 10022-5299

Copyright © 2001 by Agberg, Ltd.
Interior design by Kellan Peck
ISBN: 0-06-105171-3

Library of Congress Cataloging-in-Publication Data

Silverberg, Robert.
The king of dreams / Robert Silverberg.
p. cm.
"Book Three of the Prestimion trilogy."
ISBN 0-06-105171-3 (hardcover)
1. Majipoor (Imaginary place)—Fiction. I. Title.

PS3569.I472 K55 2001
813'.54—dc21   00-046648

First Eos hardcover printing: June 2001

Eos Trademark Reg. U.S. Pat. Off. and in Other Countries,
Marca Registrada, Hecho en U.S.A.
HarperCollins® is a trademark of HarperCollins Publishers Inc.

Printed in the U.S.A.

FIRST EDITION

10 9 8 7 6 5 4 3 2 1

www.eosbooks.com

For Jennifer and Peter

—such twists, such turns!

And Lord Stiamot wept when he heard them singing the ballad of his great victory at Weygan Head, because the Stiamot of which they sang was not the Stiamot he knew. He was not himself any more. He had been emptied into legend. He had been a man, and now he was a fable.

—AITHIN FURVAIN
The Book of Changes

I

The Book of Waiting

1

"That has to be what we're looking for," said the Skandar, Sudvik Gorn, standing at the edge of the cliff and pointing down the steep hillside with harsh jabbing motions of his lower left arm. They had reached the crest of the ridge. The underlying rock had crumbled badly here, so that the trail they had been following terminated in a rough patch covered with sharp greenish gravel, and just beyond lay a sudden drop into a thickly vegetated valley. "Vorthinar Keep, right there below us! What else could that building be, if not the rebel's keep? And easy enough for us to set it ablaze, this time of year."

"Let me see," young Thastain said. "My eyes are better than yours." Eagerly he reached for the spyglass that Sudvik Gorn held in his other lower arm.

It was a mistake. Sudvik Gorn enjoyed baiting the boy, and Thastain had given him yet another chance. The huge Skandar, better than two feet taller than he was, yanked the glass away, shifting it to an upper arm and waving it with ponderous playfulness high above Thastain's head. He grinned a malicious snaggletoothed grin. "Jump for it, why don't you?"

Thastain felt his face growing hot with rage. "Damn you! Just let me have the thing, you moronic four-armed bastard!"

"What was that? Bastard, am I? Bastard? Say it again?" The Skandar's shaggy face turned dark. He brandished the spyglass now as though the tube were a weapon, swinging it threateningly from side to side. "Yes. Say it again, and then I'll knock you from here to Ni-moya."

Thastain glared at him. "Bastard! Bastard! Go ahead and knock me, if you can." He was sixteen, a slender, fair-skinned boy who was swift enough afoot to outrace a bilantoon. This was his first important mission in the service of the Five Lords of Zimroel, and the Skandar had selected him, somehow, as his special enemy. Sudvik Gorn's constant maddening ridicule was driving him to fury. For the past three days, almost from the beginning of their journey from the domain of the Five Lords, many miles to the southeast, up here into the rebel-held territory, Thastain had held it in, but now he could contain it no longer. "You have to catch me first, though, and I can run circles around you, and you know it. Eh, Sudvik Gorn, you great heap of flea-bitten fur!"

The Skandar growled and came rumbling forward. But instead of fleeing, Thastain leaped agilely back just a few yards and, whirling quickly, scooped up a fat handful of jagged pebbles. He drew back his arm as though he meant to hurl them in Sudvik Gorn's face. Thastain gripped the stones so tightly that their sharp edges bit into the palm of his hand. You could blind a man with stones like that, he thought.

Sudvik Gorn evidently thought so too. He halted in mid-stride, looking baffled and angry, and the two stood facing each other. It was a stalemate.

"Come on," Thastain said, beckoning to the Skandar and offering him a mocking look. "One more step. Just one more." He swung his arm in experimental underhand circles, gathering momentum for the throw.

The Skandar's red-tinged eyes flamed with ire. From his vast chest came a low throbbing sound like that of a volcano readying itself for eruption. His four mighty arms quivered with barely contained menace. But he did not advance.

By this time the other members of the scouting party had noticed what was happening. Out of the corner of his eye Thastain saw them coming together to his right and left, forming a loose circle along the ridge, watching, chuckling. None of them liked the Skandar, but Thastain doubted that many of the men cared for him very much either. He was too young, too raw, too green, too pretty. In all probability they thought that he needed to be knocked around a little—roughed up by life as they had been before him.

"Well, boy?" It was the hard-edged voice of Gambrund, the round-cheeked Piliplok man with the bright purple scar that cut a vivid track across the whole left side of his face. Some said that Count Mandralisca had done that to him for spoiling his aim during a gihorna hunt, others that it had been the Lord Gavinius in a drunken moment, as though the Lord Gavinius ever had any other kind. "Don't just stand there! Throw them! Throw them in his hairy face!"

"Right, throw them," someone else called. "Show the big ape a thing or two! Put his filthy eyes out!"

This was very stupid, Thastain thought. If he threw the stones he had better be sure to blind Sudvik Gorn with them on the first cast, or else the Skandar very likely would kill him. But if he blinded Sudvik Gorn the Count would punish him severely for it—quite possibly would have him blinded himself. And if he simply tossed the stones away he'd have to run for it, and run very well, for if Sudvik Gorn caught him he would hammer him with those great fists of his until he was smashed to pulp; but if he fled then everyone would call him a coward for fleeing. It was impossible any way whichever. How had he contrived to get himself into this? And how was he going to get himself out?

He wished most profoundly that someone would rescue him. Which was what happened a moment later.

"All right, stop it, you two," said a new voice from a few feet behind Thastain. Criscantoi Vaz, it was. He was a wiry, broad-shouldered graybearded man, a Ni-moyan: the oldest of the group, a year or two past forty. He was one of the few here who had taken a liking of sorts to Thastain. It was Criscantoi Vaz who had chosen him to be a member of this party, back at Horvenar on the Zimr, where this expedition had begun. He stepped forward now, placing himself between Thastain and the Skandar. There was a sour look on his face, as of one who wades in a pool of filth. He gestured brusquely to Thastain. "Drop those stones, boy." Instantly Thastain opened his fist and let them fall. "The Count Mandralisca would have you both nailed to a tree and flayed if he could see what's going on. You're wasting precious time. Have you forgotten that we're here to do a job, you idiots?"

"I simply asked him for the spyglass," said Thastain sullenly. "How does that make me an idiot?"

"Give it to him," Criscantoi Vaz told Sudvik Gorn. "These games are foolishness, and dangerous foolishness at that. Don't you think the Vorthinar lord has sentries aplenty roving these hills? We stand at risk up here, every single moment."

Grimacing, the gigantic Skandar handed the glass over. He glowered at Thastain in a way that unmistakably said that he meant to finish this some other time.

Thastain tried to pay no attention to that. Turning his back on Sud-vik Gorn, he went to the very rim of the precipice, dug his boots into the gravel, and leaned out as far as he dared go. He put the glass to his eye. The hillside before him and the valley below sprang out in sudden rich detail.

It was autumn here, a day of strong, sultry heat. The lengthy dry sea-son that was the summer of this part of central Zimroel had not yet ended, and the hill was covered with a dense coat of tall tawny grass, a sort of grass that had a bright glassy sheen as though it were artificial, as if some master craftsman had fashioned it for the sake of decorating the slope. The long gleaming blades were heavy with seed-crests, so that the force of the warm south wind bent them easily, causing them to ripple like a river of bright gold, running down and down and down the slope.

The hillside, which descended rapidly in a series of swooping de-clines, was nearly featureless except where it was broken, here and there, by great jagged black boulders that rose out of it like dragons' teeth. Thas-tain could make out a sleek short-legged helgibor creeping purposefully through the grass a hundred yards below him, its furry green head lifted for the strike, its arching fangs already bared. A plump unsuspecting blue vrimmet, the helgibor's prey, was grazing serenely not far away. The vrimmet would be in big trouble in another moment or two. But of the castle of the rebellious lordling, Thastain was able to see nothing at all at first, despite the keenness of his vision and the aid that the spyglass pro-vided.

Then he nudged the glass just a little to the west, and there the keep was, snugly nestling in a deep fold of the valley: a long low gray curving thing, like a dark scar against the tawny grassland. It seemed to him that the bottommost part of the structure was fashioned of stone, perhaps to the height of a man's thigh, but everything above that was of wood, ris-ing to a sloping thatched roof.

"There's the keep, no doubt of it," Thastain said, without relin-quishing the spyglass.

Sudvik Gorn was right. In this dry season, it would be no great chal-lenge whatever to set the place on fire. Three or four firebrands hurled from above and the roof would go up, and sparks would leap to the parched unmown grass that came clear up to the foundations of the building, and the gnarled oily-looking shrubs nearby would catch. There would be a roaring holocaust all around. Within ten minutes the Vorthinar lord and all his men would be roasted alive.

"Do you see sentinels?" Criscantoi Vaz asked.

"No. Nobody. Everybody must be inside. No—wait—yes, someone's there!"

A strange figure, very thin and unusually elongated, coming into view around the side of the building. The man paused a moment and looked upward—straight at Thastain, so it seemed. Thastain dropped hastily to his belly and signalled with a furious sweep of his left hand for the men behind him to move back from the ridge. Then he peered over the edge once more. Cautiously he extended the glass. The man was continuing on his path, now. Perhaps he hadn't noticed anything after all.

There was something exceedingly odd about the way he was moving. That swinging gait, that curious flexibility of movement. That strange face, like no face Thastain had ever seen before. The man looked weirdly loose-jointed, somehow—rubbery, one might say. Almost as though he were—could it be—?

Thastain closed one eye and stared as intensely as he knew how with the other.

Yes. A chill ran down Thastain's spine. A Metamorph, it was. Definitely a Metamorph. That was a new sight for him. He had spent his whole short lifetime up here in northern Zimroel, where Metamorphs were rarely if ever encountered—were, indeed, practically legendary creatures.

He took a good look now. Thastain fined the focus of the glass and was able to make out plainly the greenish tint of the man's skin, the slitted lips, the prominent cheekbones, the tiny bump of a nose. And the longbow the creature wore slung across his back was surely one of Shapeshifter design, a flimsy, highly flexible-looking thing of light wickerwork, the kind of weapon most suitable for a being whose skeletonic structure was pliant enough to bend easily, to undergo almost any sort of vast transformation.

Unthinkable. It was like seeing a demon walking patrol before the keep. But who, even someone who was in rebellion against his own liege lords, would dare ally himself with the Metamorphs? It was against the law to have any traffic with the mysterious aboriginal folk. But, thought Thastaine, it was more than illegal. It was monstrous.

"There's a Shapeshifter down there," Thastain said in a rough whisper over his shoulder. "I can see him walking right past the front of the house. So the story we heard must be true. The Vorthinar lord's in league with them!"

"You think he saw you?" said Criscantoi Vaz.

"I doubt it."

"All right. Get yourself back from the edge before he does."

Thastain wriggled backward without rising and scrambled to his feet when he was far enough away from the brink. As he lifted his head he became aware of Sudvik Gorn's glowering gaze still fixed on him in cold hatred, but Sudvik Gorn and his malevolence hardly mattered to him now. There was a task to be done.

2

Morning in the Castle. Bright golden-green sunlight entered the grand suite atop Lord Thraym's Tower that was the official residence of the Coronal and his consort. It came flooding in a brilliant stream into the splendid great bedroom, walled with great blocks of smooth warm-hued granite hung with fine tapestries of cloth of gold, where the Lady Varaile was awakening.

The Castle.

Everyone in the world knew which castle was meant, when you said "the Castle": it could only be Lord Prestimion's Castle, as the people of Majipoor had called it these twenty years past. Before that it had been called Lord Confalume's Castle, and before that Lord Prankipin's, and so on and so on back into the vague mists of time—Lord Guadeloom's Castle, Lord Pinitor's Castle, Lord Kryphon's Castle, Lord Thraym's Castle, Lord Dizimaule's Castle, Coronal after Coronal across the endlessly flowing centuries of Majipoor's long history, the great ones and the mediocre ones and the ones whose names and achievements had become totally obscure, king after king all the way back to the semi-mythical builder himself, Lord Stiamot of seventy centuries before, each monarch giving his name to the building for the duration of the time of his reign. But now it was the Castle of the Coronal Lord Prestimion and his wife, the Lady Varaile.

Reigns end. One of these days, almost certainly, this place would be Lord Dekkeret's Castle, Varaile knew.

But let that day not come soon, she prayed.

She loved the Castle. She had lived in that unfathomably complex array of thirty thousand rooms, perched here atop the astounding thirty-mile-high splendor of Castle Mount that jutted up like a colossal spike out of the immense curve of the planet, for half her life. It was her home. She had no desire to leave it, as leave it she knew she must on the day that Lord Prestimion ascended to the title of Pontifex and Dekkeret replaced him as Coronal.

This morning, with Prestimion off somewhere in one of the down-slope cities dedicating a dam or presiding over the installation of a new duke or performing one of the myriad other functions that were required of a Coronal—she was unable to remember what the pretext for this journey had been—the Lady Varaile awoke alone in the great bed of the royal suite, as she did all too often nowadays. She could not follow the Coronal about the world on his unending peregrinations. His boiling restlesness kept him always on the move.

He would have had her accompany him on his trips, if she could; but that, as both of them realized, was usually impossible. Long ago, when they were newly wed, she had gone everywhere at Prestimion's side, but then had come the children and her own heavy royal responsibilities besides, the ceremonies and social functions and public audiences, to keep her close to the Castle. It was rare now for the Coronal and his lady to travel together.

However necessary these separations were, Varaile had never reconciled herself to their frequency. She loved Prestimion no less, after sixteen years as his wife, than she had at the beginning. Automatically, as the first dazzling shafts of daylight came through the great crystal window of the royal bedroom, she looked across to see that golden-green light strike the yellow hair of Prestimion on the pillow beside hers.

But she was alone in the bed. As always, it took her a moment to comprehend that, to remember that Prestimion had gone off, four or five days ago, to—where? Bombifale, was it? Hoikmar? Deepenhow Vale? She had forgotten that too. Somewhere, one of the Slope Cities, perhaps, or perhaps someplace in the Guardian ring. There were fifty cities along the flanks of the Mount. The Coronal was in ever-constant motion; Varaile no longer bothered to keep track of his itinerary, only of the date of his longed-for return.

"Fiorinda?" she called.

The warm contralto reply from the next room was immediate: "Coming, my lady!"

Varaile rose, stretched, saluted herself in the mirror on the far wall. She still slept naked, as though she were a girl; and, though she was past forty now and had borne the Coronal three sons and a daughter, she allowed herself the one petty vanity of taking pleasure in her ability to fend off the inroads of aging. No sorcerer's spells did she employ for that: Prestimion had once expressed his loathing for such subterfuges, and in any case Varaile felt they were unnecessary, at least so far. She was a tall woman, long-thighed and lithe, and though she was strongly built, with full breasts and some considerable breadth at the waist, she had not grown at all fleshy with age. Her skin was smooth and taut; her hair remained jet-black and lustrous.

"Did milady rest well?" Fiorinda asked, entering.

"As well as could be expected, considering that I was sleeping alone."

Fiorinda grinned. She was the wife of Teotas, Prestimion's youngest brother, and each morning at dawn left her own marital bed so that she could be at the service of the Lady Varaile when Varaile awoke. But she seemed not to begrudge that, and Varaile was grateful for it. Fiorinda was like a sister to her, not a mere sister-in-law; and Varaile, who had had no sisters of her own nor brothers either, cherished their friendship.

They bathed together, as they did every morning in the great marble tub, big enough for six or eight people, that some past Coronal's wife had found desirable to install in the royal chamber. Afterward Fiorinda, a small, trim woman with radiant auburn hair and an irreverent smile, threw a simple robe about herself so that she could help Varaile with her own costuming for the morning. "The pink sieronal, I think," said Varaile, "and the golden difina from Alaisor." Fiorinda fetched the trousers for her and the delicately embroidered blouse, and, without needing to be asked, brought also the vivid yellow sfifa that Varaile liked to drape down her bosom with that ensemble, and the wide red-and-tan belt of fine Makroposopos weave that was its companion. When Varaile was dressed Fiorinda resumed her own garments of the day, a turquoise vest and soft orange pantaloons.

"Is there news?" Varaile asked.

"Of the Coronal, milady?"

"Of anyone, anything!"

"Very little," said Fiorinda. "The pack of sea-dragons that were seen last week off the Stoien coast are moving northward, toward Treymone."

"Very odd, sea-dragons in those waters at that time of year. An omen, do you think?"

"I must tell you I am no believer in omens, milady."

"Nor I, really. Nor is Prestimion. But what *are* the things doing there, Fiorinda?"

"Ah, how can we ever understand the minds of the sea-dragons, lady? —To continue: a delegation from Sisivondal arrived at the Castle late last night, to present some gifts for the Coronal's museum."

Varaile shuddered. "I was in Sisivondal once, long ago. A ghastly place, and I have ghastly memories of it. It was where the first Prince Akbalik died of the poisoned swamp-crab bite he had had in the Stoienzar jungle. I'll let someone else deal with the Sisivondal folk and their gifts. —Do you remember Prince Akbalik, Fiorinda? What a splendid man he was, calm, wise, very dear to Prestimion. I think he would have been Coronal someday, if he had lived. It was in the time of the campaign against the Procurator that he died."

"I was only a child then, milady."

"Yes. Of course. How foolish of me." She shook her head. Time was flowing fiercely past them all. Here was Fiorinda, a grown woman, nearly thirty years old; and how little she knew of the troublesome commencement of Lord Prestimion's reign, the rebellion of the Procurator Dantirya Sambail, and the plague of madness that had swept the world at the same time, and all the rest. Nor, of course, did she have any inkling of the tremendous civil war that had preceded those things, the struggle between Prestimion and the usurper Korsibar. No one knew of that tumultuous event except a chosen few members of the Coronal's inner circle. All memory of it had been eradicated from everyone else by Prestimion's master sorcerers, and just as well that it had. To Fiorinda, though, even the infamous Dantirya Sambail was simply someone out of the storybooks. He was a thing of fable to her, only.

As we all will be one day, thought Varaile with sudden gloom: mere things of fable.

"And other news?" she asked.

Fiorinda hesitated. It was only for an instant, but that was enough. Varaile saw through that little hesitation as if she were able to read Fiorinda's mind.

There was other news, important news, and Fiorinda was concealing it.

"Yes?" Varaile urged. "Tell me."

"Well—"

"Stop this, Fiorinda. Whatever it is, I want you to tell me right now."

"Well—" Fiorinda moistened her lips. "A report has come from the Labyrinth—"

"Yes?"

"It signifies nothing in the slightest, I think."

"Tell me!" Already the news was taking shape in Varaile's own mind, and it was chilling. "The Pontifex?"

Fiorinda nodded forlornly. She could not meet Varaile's steely gaze.

"Dead?"

"Oh, no, nothing like that, milady."

"Then *tell* me!" cried Varaile, exasperated.

"A mild weakness of the leg and arm. The left leg, the left arm. He has summoned some mages."

"A stroke, you mean? The Pontifex Confalume has had a stroke?"

Fiorinda closed her eyes a moment and drew several deep breaths. "It is not yet confirmed, milady. It is only a supposition."

Varaile felt a burning sensation at her own temples, and a spasm of dizziness swept over her. She controlled herself with difficulty, forcing herself back to calmness.

It is not yet confirmed, she told herself.

It is only a supposition.

Coolly she said, "You tell me about sea-dragons off the far coast, and an insignificant delegation from an unimportant city in the middle of nowhere, and you suppress the news of Confalume's stroke so that I need to pull it out of you? Do you think I'm a child, Fiorinda, who has to have bad news kept from her like that?"

Fiorinda seemed close to tears. "Milady, as I said a moment ago, it is not yet known as a certainty that it was a stroke."

"The Pontifex is well past eighty. More likely past ninety, for all I know. Anything that has him summoning his mages is bad news. What if he dies? You know what will happen then. —Where did you hear this, anyway?"

More and more flustered, Fiorinda said, "My lord Teotas had it from the Pontifical delegate to the Castle late last night, and told me of it this morning as I was setting out to come to you. He will discuss it with you himself after you've breakfasted, just before your meeting with the royal ministers. —My lord Teotas urged me not to thrust all this on you too quickly, because he emphasizes that it is truly not as serious a matter as it sounds, that the Pontifex is generally in good health and is not deemed to be in any danger, that he—"

"And sea-dragons off the Stoien coast are more important, anyway," Varaile said acidly. "Has a messenger been sent to the Coronal?"

"I don't know, milady," said Fiorinda in a helpless voice.

"What about Prince Dekkeret? I haven't seen him around for several days. Do you have any idea where he is?"

"I think he's gone to Normork, milady. His friend Dinitak Barjazid has accompanied him there."

"Not the Lady Fulkari?"

"Not the Lady Fulkari, no. Things are not well between Prince Dekkeret and the Lady Fulkari these days, I think. It was with Dinitak he went, on Twoday. To Normork."

"Normork!" Varaile shuddered. "Another hideous place, though Dekkeret loves that city, the Divine only knows why. And I suppose you have no idea whether anyone's tried to inform him yet, either? Prince Dekkeret might well find himself Coronal by nightfall and yet nobody has thought of letting him know that—"

Varaile realized that she was losing control again. She caught herself in mid-flight.

"Breakfast," she said, in a quieter tone. "We should have something to eat, Fiorinda. Whether or not we're in the middle of a crisis this morning, we shouldn't try to face the day on an empty stomach, eh?"

3

The floater came around the last curve of craggy Normork Crest and the great stone wall of Normork city rose up suddenly before them, square athwart the highway that had brought them down from the Castle to this level on the lower reaches of the Mount's flank. The wall was an immense overbearing barrier of rectangular black megaliths piled one upon another to an astonishing height. The city that it guarded lay utterly concealed from view behind it. "Here we are," Dekkeret said. "Normork."

"And *that*?" Dinitak Barjazid asked. He and Dekkeret traveled together often, but this was his first visit to Dekkeret's native city. "Is that little thing the gate? And is our floater really going to be able to get through it?" He stared in amazement at the tiny blinking hole, laughably disproportionate, tucked away like an afterthought at the foot of the mighty rampart. It was barely wide enough, so it would seem, to admit a good-sized cart. Guardsmen in green leather stood stiffly at attention to either side of it. A tantalizing bit of the hidden city could be seen framed within the small opening: what appeared to be warehouses and a couple of many-angled gray towers.

Dekkeret smiled. "The Eye of Stiamot, the gate is called. A very grand name for such a piffling aperture. What you see is the one and only entryway to the famous city of Normork. Impressive, isn't it? But it's big enough for us, all right. Not by much, but we'll squeak through."

"Strange," Dinitak said, as they passed beneath the pointed arch and entered the city. "Such a huge wall, and so wretched and paltry a gate. That doesn't exactly make strangers feel that they're wanted here, does it?"

"I have some plans for changing that, when the opportunity is at hand," said Dekkeret. "You'll see tomorrow."

The occasion for his visit was the birth of a son to the current Count of Normork, Considat by name. Normork was not a particularly important city and Considat was not a significant figure in the hierarchies of Castle Mount, and ordinarily the only official cognizance the Coronal would be likely to take of the child's birth would be a congratulatory note and a handsome gift. Certainly he would not make it the occasion for a state visit. But Dekkeret, who had not seen Normork for many a month, had requested permission to present the Coronal's congratulations in person, and had brought Dinitak along with him for company. "Not Fulkari?" Prestimion had asked. For Dekkeret and Fulkari had been an inseparable pair these two or three years past. To which Dekkeret had replied that Count Considat was a man of conservative tastes; it did not seem proper for Dekkeret to visit him in the company of a woman who was not his wife. He would take Dinitak. Prestimion did not press the issue further. He had heard the stories—everyone at the court had, by now—that something had been going amiss lately between Prince Dekkeret and the Lady Fulkari, though Dekkeret had said not a word about it to anyone.

They had been the closest of friends for years, Dekkeret and Dinitak, though their temperaments and styles were very different. Dekkeret was a big, deep-chested, heavy-shouldered man of boundless energy and unquenchable robust spirit, whose words tended to come booming out of him in a cheerful resounding bellow. The events of his life thus far had predisposed him to optimism and hope and limitless enthusiasm.

Dinitak Barjazid, a man a few years younger with a lean, narrow face and dark, glittering, skeptical eyes, was half a head shorter and constructed on an altogether less substantial scale, compact and trim, with an air of taut coiled muscularity about him. His skin was darker even than his eyes, the swarthy skin of one who has lived for years under the frightful sun of the southern continent. Dinitak spoke much more quietly than Dekkeret and took a generally darker view of the world. He was a shrewd, pragmatic man, raised in a harsh sun-baked land by a tough and wily scoundrel of a father who had been a very slippery sort indeed. Often there was a questioning edge on what Dinitak said that caused Dekkeret to think twice about things, and sometimes more than twice.

And he was governed always by a harsh, strict sense of propriety, a set of fierce moral imperatives, as though he had decided early in life to build his life around a philosophy of doing and believing the opposite of whatever his father might have done or thought.

They held each other in the highest estimation. Dekkeret had vowed that as he rose to prominence within the royal government of Majipoor, Dinitak would rise with him, although he did not immediately know how that would be accomplished, considering the clouded and notorious past of Dinitak's father and kinsmen. But he would find a way.

"Our reception committee, I think," said Dinitak, pointing inward with a jab of his upturned thumb.

Just within the wall lay a triangular cobblestoned plaza bordered along each side by drab wooden guardhouses. The emissary of the Count of Normork was waiting for them there, a small, flimsy-looking black-bearded man who seemed as though he could be blown away by any good gust of wind. He bowed them out of their floater, introduced himself as the Justiciar Corde, and in flowery phrases offered Prince Dekkeret and his traveling companion the warmest welcome to the city. The Justiciar indicated a dozen or so armed men in green leather uniforms standing a short distance away. "These men will protect you while you are here," he declared.

"Why?" Dekkeret asked. "I have my own bodyguard with me."

"It is Count Considat's wish," replied the Justiciar Corde in a tone that indicated that the issue was not really open to discussion. "Please— if you and your men will follow me, excellence—"

"What is that all about?" said Dinitak under his breath as they made their way on foot, escorted fore and aft by the black-clad guardsmen, through the narrow, winding alleys of the ancient city to their lodging-place. "I wouldn't think that we'd be in any danger here."

"We're not. But when Prestimion was here on a state visit not long after he became Coronal, a madman tried to assassinate him right out in front of the Count's palace. That was in the time of Count Meglis, Considat's father. Madness was a very common thing in the world back then, you may recall. There was an epidemic of it in every land."

Dinitak grunted in surprise. "Assassinate the Coronal? You can't be serious. Who would ever do a wild thing like that?"

"Believe me, Dinitak, it happened, and it was a very close thing, too. I was still living in Normork then and I saw it with my own eyes. A lunatic swinging a sharpened sickle, he was. Came rushing out of the crowd in the plaza and ran straight for Prestimion. He was stopped just in time, or history would have been very different."

"Incredible. What happened to the assassin?"

"Killed, right then and there."

"As was right and proper," Dinitak said.

Dekkeret smiled at that. Again and again Dinitak revealed himself as the ferocious moralist that he was. His judgments, driven by a powerful sense of right and wrong, were often severe and uncompromising, sometimes surprisingly so. Dekkeret had taken him to task for that, early in their friendship. Dinitak's response was to ask Dekkeret whether he would prefer him to be more like his father in his ways, and Dekkeret did not pursue the issue after that. But often he thought that it must be painful for Dinitak, forever seeing sloth and error and corruption on all sides, even in those he loved.

"Prestimion was unharmed, of course. But the whole event was a tremendous embarrassment for Meglis, and he spent the rest of his days trying to live it down. Nobody outside Normork thinks about it at all, but here it's been a blemish on the reputation of the entire city for almost twenty years. And even though it's hardly likely that such a thing would happen again, I suppose that Considat wants to make absolutely certain that nobody waving a sharp object gets anywhere near the Coronal-designate while we're here."

"That's imbecilic. Does he seriously think his city is a hotbed of crazed assassins? And what a damnable nuisance, having these troops marching around with us everywhere we go."

"Agreed. But if he feels he has to bend over backwards in the name of caution, we'll have to humor him. It would give needless offense if we objected."

Dinitak shrugged and let the matter drop. Dekkeret was only too well aware of how little tolerance there was in his friend's makeup for folly of any sort, and plainly this business of providing unneeded guards for the visitors from Castle Mount fell into that category. But Dinitak was able to see that having the guards around would be just a harmless annoyance. And he understood when to yield to Dekkeret in matters of official protocol.

They settled quickly into their hostelry, where Dekkeret was given the capacious set of rooms that was usually reserved for the Coronal, and Dinitak a lesser but comfortable apartment one floor below. In early afternoon they set out on their first call, a visit to Dekkeret's mother, the

Lady Taliesme. Dekkeret had not seen her in many months. Although her son's position as heir-designate to the throne entitled her to a suite of rooms at the Castle, she preferred to remain in Normork most of the time—still living, actually, in the same little dwelling in Old Town that their family had occupied when Dekkeret was a boy.

She lived there alone, now. Dekkeret's father, a traveling merchant who had had indifferent success plodding to and fro with his satchels of goods amongst the Fifty Cities, had died a decade earlier, still fairly young but worn out, defeated, even, by the long laborious struggle that his life had been. He had never been able quite to make himself believe that his son Dekkeret had somehow attracted the attention of Lord Prestimion himself and had found his way into the circle of lordlings around the Coronal at the Castle. That Dekkeret had been made a knight-initiate was almost beyond his capacity to comprehend; and when the Coronal had raised him to the rank of prince, his father had taken the news merely as a bizarre joke.

Dekkeret often wondered what he would have done if he had come to him and announced, "I have been chosen to be the next Coronal, father." Laughed in his son's face, most likely. Or slapped him, even, for mocking his father with such nonsense. But he had not lived long enough for that.

Taliesme, though, had handled her son's improbable ascent, and the stunning elevation of her own position that necessarily had accompanied it, with remarkable calmness. It was not that she had ever *expected* Dekkeret to become a knight of the Castle, let alone a prince. And undoubtedly not even in her dreams had she imagined him as Coronal. Nor was she the sort of doting mother who blandly accepted any success that came to her son as nothing more than his proper due, inevitable and well deserved.

But a simple and powerful faith in the Divine had been her guide throughout all her life. She did not quarrel with destiny. And so nothing ever surprised her; whatever came her way, be it pain and sorrow or glory beyond all measure, was something that had been preordained, something that one accepted without complaint on the one hand and without any show of astonishment on the other. Plainly it must have been intended from the beginning of time that Dekkeret would be Coronal someday—and therefore that she herself would finish her days as Lady of the Isle of Sleep, a Power of the Realm. The Coronal's mother was always given that greatly auspicious post. Very well: so be it.

She had not anticipated any such things, of course; but if they happened anyway, well, their happening had to be viewed in retrospect as something as natural and unsurprising as the rising of the sun in the east each day.

What surprised Dinitak was the meanness of the Lady Taliesme's house, a lopsided little place with sagging window-frames amidst a jumble of small buildings that might have been five thousand years old, on a dark, crooked street of uneven gray-green cobbled pavement close to the center of Old Town. What sort of home was this for the mother of the next Coronal?

"Yes, I know," Dekkeret said, grinning. "But she likes it here. She's lived in this house for forty years and it means more to her than ten Castles ever could. I've bought new furniture for her that's costlier than what was here before, and nowadays she wears clothing of a sort that my father could never have afforded for her, but otherwise nothing in the least has changed. Which is exactly as she wants it to be."

"And the people around her? Don't they know they're living next door to the future Lady of the Isle? Doesn't she know that herself?"

"I have no idea what the neighbors know. I suspect that to them she's just Taliesme, the widow of the merchant Orvan Pettir. And as for herself—"

The door opened.

"Dekkeret," said the Lady Taliesme. "Dinitak. How good to see you both again."

Dekkeret embraced his mother lovingly and with great care, as though she were dainty and fragile, and might break if hugged too enthusiastically. In fact he knew she was not half so fragile as he fancied her to be; but none the less she was a small-framed woman, light-boned and petite. Dekkeret's father had not been large either. From boyhood onward Dekkeret had always felt like some kind of gross overgrown monster who had unaccountably been deposited by prankish fate in the home of those two diminutive people.

Taliesme was wearing a gown of unadorned ivory silk, and her glistening silver hair was bound by a simple, slender gold circlet. Dekkeret had brought gifts for her that were of the same austere taste, a glossy little dragonbone pendant, and a cobweb-light shimmering headscarf made in distant Gabilorn, and a smooth little ring of purple jade from Vyrongimond, and two or three other things of that sort. She received them all with evident pleasure and gratitude, but put them away as swiftly as politeness would permit. Taliesme had never coveted treasures of that sort in the days when they had been poor, and she gave no sign of having more than a casual interest in them now.

They talked easily, over tea and biscuits, of life at the Castle; she inquired after Lord Prestimion and Lady Varaile and their children and— briefly, very briefly—mentioned the Lady Fulkari also; she spoke of Septach Melayn and other Council members, and asked about Dekkeret's current duties at the court, very much as though she were of that court herself in every fiber of her body rather than the mere widow of an unimportant provincial merchant. She referred knowingly, too, to recent events at the palace in Normork, the dismissal of a minister who was overfond of his wine and the birth of Count Considat's heir and other matters of that sort; twenty years ago she would have had no more knowledge of such things than she did of the private conversations of the Shapeshifter wizards in their wickerwork capital in distant Piurifayne.

It gave Dekkeret great delight to see the way the Lady Taliesme was continuing to grow into the role that destiny was forcing upon her. He had spent almost half his life, now, among the princes of the Castle, and was no longer the provincial boy he had been, that long-ago day in Normork, when he first had come to Prestimion's notice. His mother had not had an opportunity for the same sort of education in the ways of the mighty. Yet she was learning, somehow. Essentially she remained as artless and unassuming as ever; but she was nonetheless going to be, at some time not very far in the future, a Power of the Realm, and he could see how capably she was making her accommodation to the strange and altogether unanticipated enhancement of her life that was heading her way.

A pleasant, civilized chat, then: a mother, her visiting son, the son's friend. But gradually Dekkeret became aware of suppressed tensions in the room, as though a second conversation, unspoken and unacknowledged, was drifting surreptitiously in the air above them:

—*Will the Pontifex live much longer, do you think?*

—*You know that that is something I don't dare think about, mother.*

—*But you do, though. As do I. It can't be helped.*

He was certain that some such secret conversation was going on within her now, here amidst the clink of teacups and the polite passing of trays of biscuits. Calm and sane and stable as she was, and ever-tranquil in the face of destiny's decrees, even so there was no way she could avoid casting her thoughts forward to the extraordinary transfor-

mation that fate would soon be bringing to the merchant's son of Normork and to his mother. The starburst crown was waiting for him, and
the third terrace of the Isle of Sleep for her. She would be something
other than human if thoughts of such things did not wander into her
mind a dozen times a day.

And into his own.

4

*A*lready, in his mind's eye, Thastain could see the blackened timbers of the house of the Vorthinar lord crumbling in the red blaze of the fire they would set. As it deserved. He could not get his mind around the enormity of what he had seen. It was bad enough to have rebelled against the Five Lords; but to consort with Metamorphs as well—! Those were evils almost beyond Thastain's comprehension.

Well, they had found what they had come here to find. Now, though, came disagreement over the nature of their next move.

Criscantoi Vaz insisted that they had to go back and report their discovery to Count Mandralisca, and let him work out strategy from there. But some of the men, most notably Agavir Toymin of Pidruid in western Zimroel, spoke out passionately in favor of an immediate attack. The rebel keep was supposed to be destroyed: very well, that was what they should set about doing, without delay. Why let someone else have the glory? Assuredly the Five Lords would richly reward the men who had rid them of this enemy. It was senseless to hang back at this point, with the headquarters of the foe right within their reach.

Thastain was of that faction. The proper thing to do now, he thought, was to make their way down that hillside, creeping as warily as that sharp-toothed helgibor, and get going on the job of starting the fire without further dithering.

"No," Criscantoi Vaz said. "We're only a scouting party. We've got no authority to attack. Thastain, run back to the camp and tell the Count what we've found."

"Stay where you are, boy," said Agavir Toymin, a burly man who was notorious for his blatant currying of favor with the Lord Gaviral and the Lord Gavinius. To Criscantoi Vaz he said, "Who put you in charge of this mission, anyway? I don't remember that anybody named you our commander." There was sudden sharpness in his tone, and no little heat.

"Nor you, so far as I know. —Run along, Thastain. The Count must be notified."

"We'll notify him that we've found the keep and destroyed it," said Agavir Toymin. "What will he do, whip us for carrying out what we've all come here to do? It's three miles from here to the Count's camp. By the time the boy has gone all the way back there, the wind will have carried our scent to the Shapeshifters down below, and there'll be a hillside of defenders between us and the keep, just waiting for us to descend. No: what we need to do is get the job over with and be done with it."

"I tell you, we are in no way authorized—" Criscantoi Vaz began, and there was heat in his voice too, and a glint of sudden piercing anger in his eyes.

"And I tell *you*, Criscantoi Vaz—" Agavir Toymin said, putting his forefinger against Criscantoi Vaz's breastbone and giving a sharp push.

Criscantoi Vaz's eyes blazed. He slapped the finger aside.

That was all it took, one quick gesture and then another, to spark a wild conflagration of wrath between them. Thastain, watching in disbelief, saw their faces grow dark and distorted as all common sense deserted them both, and then they rushed forward, going at each other like madmen, snarling and shoving and heaving and throwing wild punches. Others quickly joined the fray. Within seconds a crazy melee was in progress, eight or nine men embroiled, swinging blindly, grunting and cursing and bellowing.

Amazing, Thastain thought. Amazing! It was ridiculous behavior for a scouting party. They might just as well have hoisted the banner of the Sambailid clan at the edge of the cliff, the five blood-red moons on the pale crimson background, and announced with a flourish of trumpets to those in the keep below that enemy troops were camped above them, intending a surprise attack.

And to think of the calm, judicious Criscantoi Vaz, a man of such wisdom and responsibility, allowing himself to get involved in a thing like this—!

Thastain wanted no part of this absurd quarrel himself, and

quickly moved away. But as he came around the far side of the struggling knot of men he found himself suddenly face to face once again with Sudvik Gorn, who also had kept himself apart from the fray. The Skandar loomed up in front of him like a mountainous mass of coarse auburn fur. His eyes glowed vengefully. His four huge hands clenched and unclenched as if they already were closing about Thastain's throat.

"And now, boy—"

Thastain looked frantically around. Behind him lay the sharp drop of the hillside, with a camp of armed enemies at its foot. Ahead of him was the infuriated and relentless Skandar, determined now to vent his choler. He was trapped.

Thastain's hand went to the pommel of the hunting knife at his waist. "Keep back from me!"

But he wondered how much of a thrust would be required to penetrate the thick walls of muscle beneath the Skandar's coarse pelt, and whether he had the strength for it, and what the Skandar would succeed in doing to him in the moments before he managed to strike. The little hunting knife, Thastain decided, would be of not the slightest use against the huge man's great bulk.

It all seemed utterly hopeless. And Criscantoi Vaz, somewhere in the middle of that pack of frenzied lunatics, could do nothing to help him now.

Sudvik Vorn started for him, growling like a mollitor coming toward its prey. Thastain muttered a prayer to the Lady.

And then, for the second time in ten minutes, rescue came unexpectedly.

"What is this we have here?" said a quiet, terrifying voice, a controlled, inexorable voice that seemed to emerge out of nowhere like a metal spring uncoiling from some concealed machine. "Brawling, is that it? Among yourselves? You've lost your minds, have you?" It was a voice with edges of steel. It cut through everything like a razor.

"The Count!" came an anguished sighing cry from half a dozen throats at once, and all fighting ceased instantaneously.

Mandralisca had given no indication that he intended to follow them to this place. So far as anyone knew, he planned to remain behind in his tent while they went in search of the Vorthinar lord's stronghold. But here he was, all the same, he and his bandy-legged little aide-de-camp Jacomin Halefice and a bodyguard of half a dozen swordsmen. The men of the scouting party, caught like errant children with

smudges of jam on their faces, stood frozen, staring in horror at the fearsome and sinister privy counsellor to the Five Lords.

The Count was a lean, rangy man, somewhat past middle years, whose
every movement was astonishingly graceful, as though he were a dancer.
But no dancer had ever had so frightening a face. His lips were hard and
thin, his eyes had a cold glitter, his cheekbones jutted like whetted blades.
A thin white vertical scar bisected one of them, the mark of some duel of
long ago. As usual he wore a close-fitting full-body garment of supple,
well-oiled black leather that gave him the shining, sinuous look of a serpent. Nothing broke its smoothness except the golden symbol of his high
office dangling on his breast, the five-sided paraclet that signified the
power of life and death that he wielded over the uncountable millions
whom the Five Lords of Zimroel regarded, illicitly, as their subjects.

Shrouded in an awful silence now did Mandralisca move among
them, going unhurriedly from man to man, peering long into each one's
eyes with that basilisk gaze from which you could not help but flinch.
Thastain felt his guts churning as he awaited the moment when his turn
would come.

He had never feared anyone or anything as much as he feared Count
Mandralisca. There always seemed to be a cold crackling aura around
the man, an icy blue shimmer. The mere sight of him far down some
long hallway inspired awe and dread. Thastain's knees had turned to
water when Criscantoi Vaz had told him, after selecting him for this
mission, that it would be headed by none other than the formidable
privy counsellor himself.

It was unimaginable, of course, to decline such an assignment, not
if he hoped to rise to a post of any distinction in the service of the Five
Lords. But throughout the whole of the journey out of the Sambailid
domain and up into this region of forests and grassland where the rebels
held sway he had tried to shrink himself down into invisibility whenever
the Count's glance ventured in his direction. And now—now—to be
compelled to look him straight in the eye—

It was agonizing, but it was over quickly. Count Mandralisca paused
before Thastain, studied him the way one might study some little insect
of no particular interest that was walking across a table in front of one,
and moved on to the next man. Thastain sagged in relief.

"Well," Mandralisca said, halting in front of Criscantoi Vaz. "A little
bit of knockabout stuff, was it? Purely for fun? I would have thought better of you, Criscantoi Vaz."

Criscantoi Vaz said nothing. He did not flinch from Mandralisca's gaze in any way. He stood stiffly upright, a statue rather than a man.

A sudden gleam like the flicker of a lightning-bolt came into the Count's eyes and the riding crop that was always in Mandralisca's hand lashed out with blinding speed, a scornful backhand stroke. A burning red line sprang up on Criscantoi Vaz's cheek.

Thastain, watching, recoiled from the blow as if he himself had been struck. Criscantoi Vaz was a sturdy-spirited man of much presence, of great sagacity, of considerable quiet strength. Thastain looked upon him almost as a father. And to see him whipped like this, in front of everyone—

But Criscantoi Vaz showed scarcely any reaction beyond a brief blinking of his eyes and a brief wince as the riding crop struck him. He held his upright stance without moving at all, not even putting his hand to the injured place. It was as if he had been utterly paralyzed by the shame of having been discovered by the Count in such a witless fracas.

Mandralisca moved on. He came to Agavir Toymin and struck him quickly with the crop also, almost without pausing to think about it, and, reaching the end of the row where Stravin of Til-omon stood, hit him also. He had put his mark on the three oldest men, the leaders, the ones who should have had enough sense not to fight. To the others it was a sufficient lesson; there was no need actually to strike them.

And then it was done. Punishment had been administered. Mandralisca stepped back and scrutinized them all with unconcealed disdain.

Thastain once more tried to shrink himself down into invisibility. The intensity of Mandralisca's frosty glare was a frightful thing.

"Will someone tell me what was happening here, now?" The Count's gaze came to rest once again on Thastain. Thastain shivered; but there was no recourse but to meet those appalling eyes. "You, boy. Speak!"

With extreme effort Thastain forced a husky half-whisper out of himself: "We have found the enemy keep, your grace. It lies in the valley just below us."

"Go on. The fighting—"

"There was a dispute over whether to go down to it immediately and set it on fire, or to return to your camp for further orders."

"Ah. A dispute. A *dispute*." A look that might almost have been one of amusement came into Mandralisca's stony eyes. "With fists." Then his visage darkened again. He spat. "Well, then, here are the orders you crave. Get yourselves down there at once and put the place to the torch, even as we came here to do."

"It is guarded by Shapeshifters, your grace," Thastain said, astonishing himself by daring to speak out unbidden. But there it was: his words hung before him in the air like puffs of strange black smoke.

The Count gave him a long slow look. "Is it, now? Guarded by Shapeshifters. What a surprise." Mandralisca did not sound surprised, though. There was no expression whatever in his tone. Turning toward Criscantoi Vaz, he said, "Well, they will burn along with everyone else. You: I place you in charge. Take three men with you. The enemies of the Five Lords must perish."

Criscantoi Vaz saluted smartly. He seemed almost grateful. It was as though the blow across the face had never occurred.

He glanced around at the group of waiting men. "Agavir Toymin," he said. Agavir Toymin, looking pleased, nodded and touched two fingers to his forehead. "Gambrund," said Mandralisca next. And, after a brief pause: "Thastain."

Thastain had not expected that. Chosen for the mission! Him! He felt a great surge of exhilaration. The thumping in his chest was almost painful, and he touched his hand to his breastbone to try to still it. But of course he would have been chosen, he realized, after a moment. He was the quickest, the most agile. He was to be the one who would run forward to hurl the firebrands.

The four men descended in a triangular formation, with Thastain at the apex. Gambrund, just behind him, carried the bundle of firebrands; flanking him were Criscantoi Vaz and Agavir Toymin, armed with bows in case the sentries saw them.

Thastain kept his head down and went forward with great care, mindful of the helgibor he had seen and such other low-slung predators of the grassland that might be lurking hidden in all this thick growth. The bright glassy sheen of the tawny grass, he realized now, was not just a trick of the eye; the blades did not simply *look* glassy, but actually felt like glass, stiff and and sharp-edged, unpleasant to move through, making a harsh whispering sound as he pushed them aside. They provided a slippery surface to walk on when they were crushed underfoot. Every step Thastain took was a tense one: it would be all too easy, sliding and slithering as he was, to lose his footing and go stumbling headlong down into the enemy camp.

But he negotiated the slope safely, halting when he reached a position that he judged was within throwing range. Moments later the other three came up behind him. Thastain pointed toward the keep. No sentinels were in sight.

Criscantoi Vaz indicated what he wanted done with quick urgent gestures. Gambrund held out a firebrand; Agavir Toymin produced a little energy-torch and ignited it with a quick burst of heat; Thastaine took it from him, ran forward half a dozen steps, and threw it toward the keep, turning himself in a nearly complete circle for greater velocity at the moment of release.

The blazing brand flew in a high, arching curve and landed in a bed of dry grass no more than five feet from the keep. There was the crackling sound of immediate ignition.

Burn! thought Thastain jubilantly. Burn! Burn! So perish all the enemies of the Five Lords!

Criscantoi Vaz followed Thastain's brand a moment later with a second, throwing it with less elegance of form than Thastain but with greater force: it soared splendidly through the air and came down on the thatched roof itself. A pinkish spiral of flame began to rise. Thastain, flinging the next firebrand more emphatically, reached the group of black-trunked glossy-leaved shrubs closest to the building's wall: they smoldered for a moment and burst into vivid tongues of fire.

The occupants of the keep, now, were aware that something was up. "Quickly," Criscantoi Vaz cried. They still had two firebrands left. Thastain seized one with both hands as soon as Agavir Toymin had it lit, ran a few steps, whirled around, and flung it: he too reached the roof this time. Criscantoi Vaz placed the last one in a patch of dry grass outside the door, just as three or four men began emerging from it. Several of them set to work desperately trying to stamp out the blaze; the others, shouting in a kind of frenzy, started to make their way up the slope toward the attackers. But the climb from the valley floor was practically a vertical one and they had brought no weapons with them. After a dozen yards or so they gave up and turned back toward the keep, which with astonishing swiftness was being engulfed by fire. Like madmen they ran inside, though the whole entranceway was already ablaze. The front wall fell in after them. They would all roast like spitted blaves in there, the rebels and their tame Shapeshifters as well. Good. Good.

"We've done it!" Thastain cried, exulting at the sight. "They're all burning!"

"Come, boy," said Criscantoi Vaz. "Get yourself moving."

He planted himself solidly and covered the retreat of the other three with drawn bow. But no one emerged now from the burning building. By the time Thastain had reached the safety of the crest, the rebel keep and much of the surrounding grassland were on fire, and a black spear of smoke was climbing into the sky. The blaze was spreading with awesome rapidity. The whole valley was sure to go up: there would be no survivors down there.

Well, that was what they had come here to accomplish. The Vorthinar lord, like so many of the little local princelings across the vast face of the continent of Zimroel, had defied the decrees of the five Sambailid brothers who claimed supreme authority in this land; and so the Vorthinar lord had had to perish. This continent was meant to be Sambailid territory, had been for generations until the overthrow of the Procurator by Lord Prestimion, now was Sambailid again. And this time must remain so for all eternity. Thastain, born under Sambailid rule, had no doubts of that. To permit anything else would be to open the door to chaos.

Count Mandralisca seemed mightily pleased with the work they had done down there. There was something almost benign about his quick frigid smile as he greeted them on the crest, his brief, fleeting handclasp of congratulation.

They stood together for a long while at the cliff's edge, gleefully watching the rebel keep burn. The fire was spreading and spreading, engulfing the dry valley from end to end. Even when they were back at camp, miles away, they could still smell the acrid tang of smoke, and black drifting cinders occasionally wandered toward them on the southward-trending wind.

That night they opened many a flagon of wine, good coarse red stuff from the western lands. Later, in the darkness, feeling as tipsy as he had ever been though he had taken care to stop drinking before most of the others, Thastain went stumbling toward the ditch where they relieved themselves, and discovered the Count already there, with his aide-de-camp, that stubby little man Jacomin Halefice. So even the Count Mandralisca needed to make water, just as ordinary mortals did! Thastain found something pleasantly incongruous about that.

He did not dare approach. As he hung back in the shadows he heard Mandralisca say in quiet satisfaction, "They will all die the way the Vorthinar lord died today, eh, Jacomin? And one day there will be no lords in this world other than the Five Lords."

"Not even Lord Prestimion?" the aide-de-camp asked. "Or Lord Dekkeret, who is to come after him?"

Thastain saw Mandralisca swing about to face the smaller man. He was unable to see the expression on the Count's face, but he could sense the bleak icy set of it from the tone of Mandralisca's voice as he replied:

"Your question provides its own answer, Jacomin."

5

―――――

*A*sleep in his bed in the royal lodging-house in the Guardian City of
Fa, Prestimion dreamed that he was back in the swarming, incom-
prehensibly vast collection of buildings atop Castle Mount that went by
the name of Lord Prestimion's Castle. He was wandering like a ghost
through dusty corridors that he had never seen before. He was taking
unfamiliar pathways that led him down into regions of the Castle that
he had not even known existed.

A little phantom led him onward, a small floating figure drifting
high up in the air before him, beckoning him ever deeper into the maze
that was the Castle. "This way, my lord. This way! Follow me!"

The tiny phantom had the form of a Vroon, one of the many non-
human peoples that had dwelled on Majipoor almost since the earliest
days of the giant planet's occupation by humans. They were doll-sized
creatures, light as air, with a myriad of rubbery tentacular limbs and
huge round golden eyes that stared forth on either side of sharply
hooked yellow beaks. Vroons had the gift of second sight, and could
peer easily into minds, or unerringly determine the right road to take in
some district altogether unfamiliar to them. But they could not float ten
feet off the ground, as this one was doing. The part of Prestimion's slum-
bering mind that stood outside itself, watching the progress of his own
dreams, knew from that one detail alone that he had to be dreaming.

And he knew also, taking no pleasure in the knowledge, that this was
a dream he had dreamed many times before, in one variation and another.

He *almost* recognized the sectors of the Castle through which the Vroon was leading him. Those ruined pillars of crumbling red sandstone might belong to Balas Bastion, where there were pathways leading to the little-used northern wing. That narrow bridge could perhaps be Lady Thiin's Overpass, in which case that spiraling rampart faced in greenish brick would lead toward the Tower of Trumpets and the Castle's outer facade.

But what was this long rambling array of low black-tiled stone hovels? Prestimion could put no name to that. And that windowless, freestanding circular tower whose rough white walls were inset with row upon row of sharpened blue flints, sharp side outward? That diamond-shaped desert of gray slabs within a palisade of pink marble spikes? That endless vaulted hall, receding into the infinite distance, lit by a row of giant candelabra the size of tree-trunks? These places could not be real parts of the Castle. The Castle was so huge that it would take forever to see it all, and even Prestimion, who had lived there since he was a youth, knew that there must be many tracts of it that he had never had occasion to enter. But these places where his sleeping self was roaming now surely had no real-world existence. They had to be dream-inventions and nothing more.

He was going down and down and down a winding staircase made of planks of some gleaming scarlet wood that floated, like the Vroon, without visible means of support in the middle of the air. It was clear to him that he must be leaving the relatively familiar upper reaches of the Castle now and descending into the auxiliary zones lower on the Mount where the thousands of people whose services were essential to the life of the Castle dwelled: the guards and servitors, gardeners and cooks, archivists and clerks, road-menders and wall-builders and game-keepers, and so on and so on. Neither waking nor dreaming had he spent much time down there. But these levels were part of the Castle too. The Castle, big as it was, grew even greater from year to year. It was like a living creature in that regard. The royal sector of the great building nestled atop the uppermost crags of the Mount, but it had layer upon layer of subterranean vaults beneath, cutting deep into the stony heart of the giant mountain. And also there were the outer zones, sprawling downward for many miles along every face of the Mount's summit like long trailing arms, extending themselves farther down the slope all the time.

"My lord?" the Vroon called, singing sweetly to him from overhead. "This way! This way!"

Puffy-faced Hjorts lined his path now, bowing officiously, and great thick-furred Skandars made the starburst salute with all the dizzying multiplicity their four arms afforded, and whistling greetings came to him from reptilian Ghayrogs, and flat-faced three-eyed little Liimen acknowledged him also, as did a phalanx of pale haughty Su-Suheris folk—representatives of all the alien races that shared vast Majipoor with its human masters. There were Metamorphs here as well, it seemed, long-legged slinking beings who slipped in and out of the shadows on every side. What, Prestimion wondered, were *they* doing on Castle Mount, where the aboriginal species had been forbidden since the long-ago days of Lord Stiamot?

"And now come this way," said the Vroon, leading him into a building that was like a castle within the castle, a hotel of some sort with thousands of rooms arranged along a single infinitely receding hallway that uncoiled endlessly before him like a highway to the stars; but the Vroon was a Vroon no longer.

This was the version of the dream that Prestimion most dreaded.

There had been a transformation. His guide now was dark-haired Lady Thismet, daughter to the Coronal Lord Confalume and twin sister to Prince Korsibar, Thismet whom he had loved and lost so long ago. As buoyant as the Vroon and just as swift, she danced along before him with her bare toes a few inches above the ground, remaining always just out of his reach, turning now and then to urge him along with a luminous smile, a wink of her dark sparkling eyes, a quick encouraging flutter of her fingertips. Her matchless beauty speared through him like a blade. "Wait for me!" he called, and she answered that he must move more quickly. But, fast as he went, she was always faster, a slim lithe figure in a rippling white gown, her gleaming jet-black hair fanning out in back of her as she retreated from him down that unending hall. "Thismet!" he cried. "Wait, Thismet! Wait! Wait! Wait!" He was running with desperate fervor now, pushing himself to the last extreme of his endurance. Ahead of him, doors were opening on either side of the endless corridor; faces peered out, grinned, winked, beckoned to him. They were Thismet too, every one of them, Thismet again and again, hundreds of Thismets, thousands, but as he came to each room in turn its door slammed shut, leaving him only the tinkling laughter of the Thismet behind it. And still the Thismet who was guiding him moved forward serenely, constantly turning to lure him onward, but never letting him catch up.

"Thismet! Thismet! Thismet!"

His voice became a tremendous clamoring roar of agony and rage and frustration.

"My lord?"

"Thismet! Thismet!"

"My lord, are you ill? Speak to me! Open your eyes, my lord! It's me, me, Diandolo! Wake up, my lord. Please, my lord—"

"This—met—"

The lights were on now. Prestimion, blinking, dazed, saw the young page Diandolo bending over the bed, wide-eyed, gaping at him in shock. Other figures were visible behind him, four, five, six people: bodyguards, servitors, others whose faces were completely unfamiliar. He struggled to come fully up out of sleep.

The sturdy figure of Falco now appeared, nudging Diandolo aside, bending forward over Prestimion. He was Prestimion's steward on all his official travels, twenty-five or so, a fine strapping fellow from Minimool with an enviable head of thick glossy black hair, a wonderfully melodious singing voice, and a bright-eyed look of invincible good cheer.

"It was only a dream you were having, my lord."

Prestimion nodded. His chest and arms were drenched with sweat. His throat felt rough and raw from the force of his own outcries. There was a fiery band of pain across his forehead. "Yes," he said hoarsely. "It was—only—a—dream—"

6

*T*hree of Varaile's four children were waiting for her in the morning-room when she entered it. They rose as she entered. It was the family custom for them to take the first meal of the day with her.

Prince Taradath, the eldest, was accompanying his father on his current journey, and therefore it was the second son, Prince Akbalik, who formally escorted Varaile to her seat. He was twelve, and already tall and sturdy: he had inherited his father's yellow hair and powerful build, but he had his mother's height. In two or three years he would be taller than either of his parents. His soft eyes and thoughtful manner, though, belied his stature and heft: he was destined to be a scholar, or perhaps a poet, most definitely not any sort of athlete or warrior.

Prince Simbilon, ten years old, still round-faced in a babyish way, terribly solemn of demeanor—priggish, even—elaborately offered Varaile the tray of fruits that was her usual first course. But the Lady Tuanelys, who was eight and had a conspicuous lack of interest in the routines of politeness, gave her mother nothing more than the quickest of nods and returned to her seat at the table, and to the plate piled high with cheese covered with honey that she had already provided for herself. It was folly to expect courtesy from Tuanelys. She was a pretty child, with a lovely cloud of golden hair that she wore in a beaded net, and finely sculpted features that foretold the feminine beauty that would be hers in six or seven more years; but her lean little body was as straight and long as a strap, just now. She was a runner, a climber, a fighter, a tomboy in every way.

"Did you sleep well, mother?" Prince Akbalik asked.

"As ever. And yourself?"

But it was Tuanelys who answered. "I dreamed of a place where all the trees grew upside down, mother. Their leaves were in the ground and their roots stuck up into the sky. And the birds—"

"Mother was speaking to Akbalik, child," said Prince Simbilon loftily.

"Yes. But Akbalik never has anything interesting to say. And neither do you, Simbilon." The Lady Tuanelys stuck her tongue out at him. Simbilon reddened, but would not respond. Fiorinda, watching the family scene from one side, began to giggle.

Akbalik now said, as though there had been no interruption, "I slept very well, mother." And began to tell her of his schedule for the day, the classes in history and epic poetry in the morning and the archery lesson that afternoon, as though they were events of the greatest importance to the world. When he was done, Prince Simbilon spoke at length of his own busy day to come, punctuated twice by requests from the Lady Tuanelys to pass her serving-dishes of food. Tuanelys had nothing else to say at all. She rarely did. Her life just now seemed almost entirely focused on swimming; she spent hours each day, as much time as she could steal from her schooling, racing fiendishly back and forth in the pool in the east-wing gymnasium like a frenzied little cambeliot. There was something manic about the intensity with which she swam her laps. Her instructor said she had to be halted after a certain time lest she swim herself into exhaustion, because she would never stop of her own accord.

This morning her children's self-absorption seemed less amusing to Varaile than it usually did. The disturbing report from the Labyrinth cast a somber shadow over everything. How would they react, she wondered, if they knew that their father might suddenly be much closer than ever before to becoming Pontifex, and that they could all find themselves uprooted from their good life at the Castle and forced to move along to the grim subterranean Labyrinth, the Pontifical seat far to the south, before long?

Varaile forced herself to sweep all such thoughts aside.

That Prestimion would one day be Pontifex had been inevitable from the hour that he had been anointed as Coronal and they had placed the starburst crown upon his head. Confalume was very old. He might die today, or next month, or next year; but sooner or later, and more likely sooner than later, his time had to come. Beyond question Akbalik and Simbilon must understand quite well what that would mean for them all. As for Tuanelys, if she did not know now, she would have to learn. And to accept. With high rank comes the obligation to conduct oneself in a royal fashion, even if one is only a child.

By the time she had finished eating Varaile felt fully in command of herself again. It was time now for her morning conference with Prestimion's ministers: in his absence from the Castle, she served as regent in the Coronal's stead.

Teotas was waiting for her outside the morning-room.

His face was even more grave than usual today, and its folds and furrows looked as though they had deepened overnight. Once he had resembled his older brother Prestimion so closely that one who did not know them well might almost have taken them for twins, though in truth there was a decade's gap between them in age. But Teotas had a sharp, hot, brooding temper that Prestimion lacked, and here in his middle years it had carved gulleys in his face that made him seem much older than he was, whereas Prestimion's skin was still unlined. There was no mistaking Teotas for the Coronal any longer; but it was not easy to believe that Teotas was the younger brother.

"Fiorinda gave you the message from the Labyrinth?"

"Eventually. I think she would rather have hidden it from me altogether."

"We would all like to hide it from ourselves, I think," Teotas said. "But from some things there's no hiding, eh, Varaile?"

"Will he die?"

"No one knows. But this latest event, whatever it is, undoubtedly brings him closer to the day. I think, though, that we have a little more time left to us in this place."

"Are you saying that because you know that it's what I want to hear, Teotas? Or do you actually have some hard information? *Did* the Pontifex have a stroke or didn't he?"

"If he did, it was a very light one. There was some difficulty in one leg and one arm—his mind went dark for an instant—"

"Fiorinda told me about the leg and the arm. Not about the darkness in his mind. Come on: what else?"

"That is all. He has his mages treating him now."

"And also a physician or two, I hope?"

Teotas said, shrugging, "You know what Confalume is like. Maybe he has a doctor with him, and maybe not. But the incense is burning round the clock, of that I'm sure, and the spells are being cast thick and fast. May they only be efficacious ones."

"So do I pray," said Varaile, with a derisive snort.

They walked quickly down the winding corridors that led to the Stiamot throne-room, where the meeting would be held. The route took them past the royal robing-chamber and the splendid judgment-hall that Prestimion had caused to be constructed out of a warren of little rooms adjacent to the grandiose throne-room of Lord Confalume.

Every Coronal put his own mark on the Castle with new construction. The judgment-hall, that magnificent vaulted chamber with great arching frosted windows and gigantic glittering chandeliers, was Prestimion's chief contribution to the innermost part of the Castle, though he had also brought about the building of the great Prestimion Archive, a museum in which a trove of historical treasure had been brought together, along the outside margin of the central sector that was known as the Inner Castle. And he had still other ambitious construction plans, Varaile knew, if only the Divine would grant him a longer stay on the Coronal's throne.

Nevertheless, for all the stupefying grandeur of the glorious judgment-hall and Lord Confalume's throne-room beside it, Prestimion had preferred since the beginning of his reign to spurn those imposing settings and to hold as many official functions as he could in the ancient Stiamot throne-room, a simple, even austere, little stone-floored chamber that supposedly had come down almost unchanged from the Castle's earliest days.

As Varaile entered it now, she saw nearly all of the high peers of the realm arrayed within: the High Counsellor Septach Melayn and the Grand Admiral Gialaurys and the magus Maundigand-Klimd, and Navigorn of Hoikmar and Duke Dembitave of Tidias and three or four others, as well as the Pontifical delegate, Phraatakes Rem, and the Hierarch Bernimorn, the representative of the Lady of the Isle at the Castle. They rose as she came in, and Varaile signalled them back into their seats with a flick of her fingertips.

Of the potent figures of the kingdom only Prestimion's other brother, Prince Abrigant, was missing. In the early years of Prestimion's reign Abrigant had played an important role in government affairs—it was his discovery of the rich iron mines of Skakkenoir that had been the foundation of much of the great prosperity of the kingdom under Prestimion's rule—but more recently he had withdrawn to the family estates down-slope at Muldemar, the responsibility for which had fallen to him by in-heritance, and he spent most of his time there. But all of the others had gathered. The presence of so many great dignitaries here at the Council meeting today intensified the misgivings that Varaile already felt.

Quickly she crossed the room to the low white throne of roughly hewn marble that was the Coronal's seat, and today, with the Coronal away, was hers as regent. She glanced to her left, where Septach Melayn sat, the elegant long-limbed swordsman who had been Prestimion's dearest friend since his youth, and who was, next to Varaile herself, the adviser whose word he respected the most. Septach Melayn met Varaile's gaze uneasily, almost sadly. Gialaurys—Navigorn—Dembitave—they appeared to be uncomfortable too. Only the towering Su-Suheris magus, Maundigand-Klimd, was inscrutable, as always.

"I am already aware," she began, "that the Pontifex is ill. Can anyone tell me precisely *how* ill?" She turned her attention toward the Pontifi-cal representative. "Phraatakes Rem, this news comes by way of you, am I correct?"

"Yes, milady." He was a small, tidy, gray-haired man who for the past nine years had been the Pontifex's official delegate at the Castle—es-sentially an ambassador from the senior monarch to the junior one. The intricate golden spiral that was the Labyrinth symbol was affixed to the breast of his soft, velvety-looking gray-green tunic. "The message arrived last night. There have been no later ones. We know nothing more than what you surely have already heard."

"A stroke, is it?" said Varaile bluntly. She was never one for mincing words.

The Pontifical delegate squirmed a little in his seat. It was discon-certing to see that polished diplomat, always so unctuous and self-assured, show such a visible sign of distress. "His majesty experienced some degree of vertigo—a numbness in his hand, an uncertainty of sup-port in his left leg. He has taken to his bed, and his mages attend him. We await further reports."

"It sounds very much like a stroke to me," said Varaile.

"I can offer no opinion concerning that, milady."

Yegan of Low Morpin, a stolid, rather humorless prince whose pres-ence on the Council had long mystified Varaile, said, "A stroke is not necessarily fatal, Lady Varaile. There are those who have lived for many years after suffering one."

"Thank you for that observation, Prince Yegan." And to Phraatakes Rem: "Has the Pontifex been generally in good health thus far this season, would you say?"

"Indeed he has, milady, active and energetic. Making proper allowance for his age, of course. But he has always been an extremely vigorous man."

"How old is he, though?" Septach Melayn said. "Eighty-five? Ninety?" He left his seat and edgily began to pace the little room, his long legs taking him from side to side and back again in just a few quick strides.

"Perhaps even older than that," said Yegan.

"He was Coronal for forty years and then some," offered Navigorn of Hoikmar, speaking with a wheeze. He once had been a powerful figure of a man, a great military leader in his time, but lately was grown fat and slow. "And Pontifex, now, for twenty years after that, is that not so? And therefore—"

"Yes. Therefore he must be very old," said Varaile sharply. She struggled to rein in her impatience. These men were all ten and twenty years her senior, and their days of real decisiveness were behind them; her quick-spirited nature grew irritable easily when they wandered into these circuitous ruminations.

To the Hierarch Bernimorn she said, "Has the Lady been informed?"

"We have already sent word to the Isle," said the Hierarch, a slim, pale woman of some considerable age, who managed to seem at once both frail and commanding.

"Good." And, to Dembitave: "What about Lord Prestimion? He's in Deepenhow Vale, I think. Or Bombifale."

"Lord Prestimion is at present in the city of Fa, milady. A messenger is preparing at this moment to set out for Fa to bring him the news."

"Who are you going to send?" Navigorn asked. He said it in a thick, blunt, almost belligerent way.

Dembitave gave the old warrior a puzzled look. "Why—how would I know? One of the regular Castle couriers is going, I suppose."

"News like this ought not to come from a stranger. I'll bear the message myself."

Color flared in Dembitave's pale cheeks. He was Septach Melayn's cousin, the Duke of Tidias, a proud and somewhat touchy man, sixty years of age. He and Navigorn had never cared much for each other.

Plainly he took Navigorn's intervention now as some kind of rebuke. For a moment or two he proffered no response. Then he said stiffly, "As you wish, milord Navigorn."

"What about Prince Dekkeret?" Varaile asked. "One would think he ought to know too."

There was a second awkward silence in the room. Varaile stared from one abashed face to another. The answer was all too clear. No one had thought to tell the heir apparent that the Pontifex might be dying.

"I'm told he has gone off to Normork with his friend Dinitak to see his mother," Varaile said crisply. "He too should be made aware of this. Teotas—"

He snapped to attention. "I'll tend to it immediately," he said, and went from the chamber.

And now? What was she supposed to do next?

Improvising swiftly, she said to the Pontifical delegate, "You will, of course, communicate our deep concern for his majesty's health, our dismay at his illness, our overriding wish that this episode prove to be only a moment's infirmity—" She searched for some further expression of sympathy, found nothing appropriate, let her voice break off in mid-statement.

But Phraatakes Rem, deftly taking his cue, smoothly replied, "I will do that, have no fear. —But I beg you, milady, let us not overreact. There was no real urgency in the phrasing of the message I received. If the High Spokesman had felt his majesty's death to be imminent, he would have put matters in a very different way. I understand the distress that milady might feel over an impending change in the administration, and of course each of us here must feel the same distress, knowing that his role in the government may soon be coming to its end, but even so—"

The deep gravelly rumble that was the voice of the burly, ponderous Grand Admiral Gialaurys cut into the Pontifical delegate's measured tones. "But what if Confalume really is in a bad way? I point out that we have a magus among us who clearly sees all that is to come. Should we not consult him?"

"Why not?" cried Septach Melayn heartily. "Why should we leave ourselves in the dark?" His distaste for sorcery of all sorts was as well known as the Grand Admiral's credulous faith in the power of wizardry. But these two, who had been Prestimion's great mainstays in the war against the usurper Korsibar, had long since come to a loving acceptance of the vast chasms of personality and belief that lay between them.

"By all means, let's ask the high magus! What do you think, Maundigand-Klimd? Is old Confalume about to leave us or not?"

"Yes," said Varaile. "Cast the Pontifex's future for us, Maundigand-Klimd. His future and ours."

All eyes turned toward the Su-Suheris, who, as usual, stood apart from the rest, silent, lost in alien ruminations beyond the fathoming of ordinary beings.

He was a forbidding-looking figure, well over seven feet tall, resplendent in the rich purple robes and jewel-encrusted collar that marked his rank as the preeminent magus of the court. His two pale hairless heads rode majestically at the summit of his long, columnar, forking neck like elongated globes of marble, and his four narrow emerald-green eyes were, as ever, shrouded in impenetrable mystery.

Of all the non-human races that had come to settle on Majipoor, the Su-Suheris were by far the most enigmatic. Most people, put off by their wintry manner and the eerie otherworldliness of their appearance, looked upon them as monsters and feared them. Even those Su-Suheris who, like Maundigand-Klimd, mingled readily with people of other species never entered into any sort of real intimacy with them. Yet their undeniable skills as mages and diviners gave them entry into the highest circles.

Maundigand-Klimd had explained to Prestimion, once, the technique by which he saw the future. Establishing a linkage of some type between his pair of minds, he was able to create a vortex of neural forces that thrust him briefly forward down the river of time, a journey from which he would return with glimpses, however cloudy and ambiguous they could sometimes be, of that which was to come. He entered that divining mode now.

Varaile watched him tensely. She was no great believer in the merit of sorcery herself, any more than Prestimion or Septach Melayn were, but she trusted Maundigand-Klimd and regarded his divinations as far more reliable than those of most others of his profession. If he were to announce now that the Pontifex lay on the brink of death —

But the Su-Suheris simply said, after a time, "There is no immediate reason for fear, milady."

"Confalume will live?"

"He is not in present danger of dying."

Varaile let out a deep sigh and leaned back in relief against the throne. "Very well, then," she said, after a moment. "We have been given a reprieve, it seems. Shall we accept it without further question, and move on to other things? Yes. Let us do that." She turned to Belditan the Younger of Gimkandale, the chancellor of the Council, who kept the agenda for Council meetings. "If you will be good enough to remind us, Count Belditan, of the matters awaiting attention today—"

The Pontifical delegate and the Hierarch Bernimorn, whose presence at the meeting was no longer appropriate, excused themselves and left. Varaile now plunged into the routine business of the realm with joyful vehemence.

A reprieve indeed is what it was. A respite from the inevitable. They would not have to leave the sun-washed magnificence of the Castle and its lofty Mount and take themselves down into the dark depths of the Labyrinth. Not now, at any rate. Not yet. Not quite yet.

But at the end of the meeting, when they had finished dealing with the host of trifling matters that had managed to make their way this morning to the attention of these great and powerful figures of the world, Septach Melayn lingered in the throne-room after the others had gone. He took Varaile gently by the hand and said in a soft tone, "This is our warning, I fear. Beyond any doubt the end is coming for Confalume. You must prepare yourself for great change, lady. So must we all."

"Prepare myself I will, Septach Melayn. I know that I must."

She looked upward at him. Tall as she was, he rose high above her, a great lanky spidery figure of a man, whose arms and legs were extraordinarily thin and whose slender body had, even now when age was beginning to come upon him, wondrous grace and ease of movement.

Here in his later years Septach Melayn had grown even more angular. There seemed to be scarcely an ounce of unneeded flesh anywhere on his spare, attenuated frame; but still he radiated a kind of beauty that was rare among men. Everything about him was elegant: his posture, his way of dress, his tumbling ringlets of artfully arrayed hair, still golden after all these years, his little pointed beard and tightly clipped mustache. He was a master of masters among swordsmen, who had never come close to being bested in a duel and had on only one occasion ever been wounded, while fighting four men at once in some horrendous battle of the Korsibar war. Prestimion long had loved him like a brother for his playful wit and devoted nature; and Varaile had come to feel the same sort of love for him herself.

"Do you think," she asked him, "that Prestimion is ready in his heart to become Pontifex?"

"Would you not know that better than I, milady?"

"I never speak of it with him."

"Then let me tell you," said Septach Melayn, "that he is as ready for it as ever a man could be. All these many decades, living first as Coronal-designate and then as Coronal, he's known that the Pontificate must lie at the end of his days. He has taken that into account. He *fought* to become Coronal, remember. It wasn't simply handed to him. For two full years he battled against Korsibar, and broke him, and took the throne back from him that he had stolen. Would he have striven so fiercely for the starburst crown, if he had not already made his peace with the knowledge that the Labyrinth waited for him beyond his time in the Castle?"

"I hope you are right, Septach Melayn."

"I know I am, good lady. And you know it too."

"Perhaps I do."

"Prestimion would never see becoming Pontifex as a tragedy. It is part of his duty—the duty that was laid upon him in the hour Lord Confalume chose him to be the next Coronal. And you know that he has never shirked duty in any way."

"Yes, of course. But still—still—"

"I know, lady."

"The Castle—we have been so happy here—"

"No Coronal likes to leave it. Nor the Coronal's consort. But it has been this way for thousands of years, that one must be Pontifex after one is Coronal, and go down into the Labyrinth, and live there beneath the ground for the rest of one's days, and—"

Septach Melayn faltered suddenly. Varaile, startled, saw a mist beginning to form in his keen pale-blue eyes.

He would leave the Castle too, of course, when Prestimion's time to go arrived. He would follow Prestimion even to the Labyrinth like all the rest of them. There was pain in that realization for him as well; and for a moment, only a moment, it was evident that Septach Melayn had been unable to conceal that pain.

Then the dark moment passed. His bright dandyish smile returned, and he touched the tips of his fingers lightly to the golden curls at his forehead and said, "You must excuse me now, Lady Varaile. It is my hour for the swordsmanship class, and my pupils are expecting me."

He started to take his leave.

"Wait," she said. "One more thing. Your talk of your swordsmanship class puts me in mind of it."

"Milady?"

"Do you have room in that class of yours for one more disciple? Because I have one for you: a certain Keltryn of Sipermit, by name, who is newly come to the Castle."

Septach Melayn's expression was one of bafflement. "Keltryn is not generally thought to be a man's name, milady."

"Indeed it isn't. This is the *Lady* Keltryn of whom I speak, the younger sister of Dekkeret's Fulkari. Who made application to me the day before yesterday on her sister's behalf. She's said to be quite capable at handling weapons, this Keltryn, and wants now to take advantage of the special training you alone can confer."

"A woman?" Septach Melayn spluttered. "A girl?"

"I'm not asking you to take her as a lover, you know. Only to admit her to your classes."

"But why would a woman want to learn swordsmanship?"

"I have no idea. Perhaps she thinks it's a useful skill. I suggest you ask her that yourself."

"And if she is injured by one of my young men? I have no tyros in my group. The weapons we use have blunted edges, but they can do considerable harm even so."

"No worse than a bruise or two, I hope. She ought to be able to tolerate that. Surely you don't mean to turn the girl away out of hand, Septach Melayn. Who knows? You may learn a thing or two about our sex from her that you had not known before. Take her, Septach Melayn. I make a direct request of it."

"In that case, how can I refuse? Send this Lady Keltryn to me, and I'll turn her into the most fearsome swordsman this world has ever seen. You have my pledge on that, milady. And now—if I have your leave to withdraw—"

Varaile nodded. He grinned down at her, and turned and bounded away like the long-legged boy he had been so many years ago, leaving her to herself in the now-deserted throne-room.

She stood there alone for a time, letting all thought drain from her mind.

Then, slowly, she went from the room, and down to her left, into the maze of passages that led out to the weird old five-peaked structure known as Lord Arioc's Watchtower, from which one had such a wondrous view of the whole Inner Castle—the Pinitor Court and the reflecting pool of Lord Siminave with the rotunda of Lord Haspar beyond it, and the lacy, airy balconies that Lord Vildivar of that same impossibly ancient era had built, and everything else.

How beautiful it all was! How marvelously did that the hodgepodge of curious structures, assembled here across seven thousand years, fit together into this immense, unequalled masterpiece of architecture!

Very well, Varaile thought.

Prestimion is still Coronal, and I still reside here at the Castle, at least for the time being.

At last the hour had arrived when inexorable duty would pull them onward to the Labyrinth: that was the rule, and it had not varied since the time of the founding of the world. Every Coronal had had to go through this, and every Coronal's wife.

May the Divine preserve the Pontifex Confalume, she prayed.

No question, though, that the Pontifex was approaching his end. But let us have a little more time here at the Castle, first. Just a little time more. Some few months. A year. Two, perhaps. Whatever we can have.

7

They were at the beginning of the Plain of Whips, now. Ahead, a red wall rising against the northern horizon, lay the narrow line of flat-topped sandstone bluffs on which the Five Lords had erected their five palaces, with the mighty eastward-flowing torrent of the River Zimr just beyond.

"Look, sir," said Jacomin Halefice, and pointed toward the red hills. "We are almost home, I think."

Almost home, thought Mandralisca, smiling wryly. *Yes.* For him there was only a somber irony in that phrase.

He was at home, more or less, anywhere and everywhere and nowhere in the world. In his overarching indifference, all places were the same in that regard for him. He had looked upon the perilous jungles of the Stoienzar as his home for a while, and before that a cell in the dungeons of Lord Prestimion's Castle, and fine lodgings in the rich sprawling metropolis of Ni-moya before that, and he had lived many another place as well, on and on back to his bitter childhood in a forlorn town amidst the snowy peaks of the Gonghar Mountains, a childhood that he would much prefer to forget. For the past five years this arid and obscure district in central Zimroel was the one that he had chosen to define as "home"; and so, looking up at those sun-baked red bluffs now from the border of the sandy inhospitable plain that stretched before him, he was able with some justice to agree with Halefice that he was almost home, for whatever little value that word might hold.

"There are the lords' palaces now, is that not so, your grace?" said Jacomin Halefice, jabbing a finger toward the high ridge. The aide-de-camp was riding just alongside the Count, astride a fat, placid, pale-lavender mount that was working hard to keep pace with Mandralisca's more fiery steed.

The Count shaded his eyes and stared upward. "Three of them, anyway. I see Gavinius's house, and Gavahaud's, and Gavdat's." The sleek gray domes of ceramic tile gleamed with a reddish glint in the hard midday sunlight. "Too soon to make out the other two, I think. Or are you telling me that you're able to see them already?"

"Actually, I don't quite think I can manage it yet, sir."

"Nor I," said Mandralisca.

The Five Lords, when they had launched their strange and so far quite secretive break with the authority of the central government, had agreed not to make their headquarters in their uncle's old capital of Ni-moya. That would have been wildly imprudent of them. They were, all five, imprudent men by nature; but sometimes they did listen to reason. At Mandralisca's suggestion they had agreed to come all the way out here to the sparsely populated and long neglected province of Gornevon, midway between Ni-moya and Verf on the south bank of the Zimr.

The river, though it was readily navigable for its entire seven thousand miles of length, from the Dulorn Rift in the far west to the coastal city of Piliplok on the Inner Sea, was oddly contrary here. Everywhere else along its path fine anchorages abounded and great prosperous urban centers had sprung up in them, a host of rich inland ports—Khyntor, Mazadone, Verf, and any number more, of which group Ni-moya was the grandest, a sublime queen among the cities of the western continent.

But here in Gornevon a line of steep red sandstone bluffs sprang up vertically right at the shoreline of the river's southern bank. That created an imposing—indeed, impassable—waterfront palisade that stood as an inexorable wall between the river and the lands to the south. Nor was there anything remotely like an anchorage to be found along that stretch of the river, not even a place where small boats could dock.

Which made the Zimr's southern shore altogether inaccessible in this part of the country, and all commerce had forsaken it. On the other bank, directly opposite the site where the palaces of the Five Lords now stood, was the generous crescent harbor that had brought great wealth to the city of Horvenar; on this side, though, there was nothing but the flat-topped red cliffs, with something very much like a desert to the south of them, a parched useless land that no one had ever seen fit to settle, since there was no access from the river and the land approach from the south was extremely difficult. It was here that Mandralisca had persuaded the Five Lords to situate their capital.

It was a cheerless unwelcoming terrain. Gornevon was an arid province. All of it lay in the shadow of the western branch of the mid-continental Gonghar range, and that long and towering chain of snowy-crested precipices prevented the summer rains that blew from the southeast, out of the Shapeshifter lands, from getting here. On the other side of the province stood the mile-high wall that was the Velathys Scarp, which intercepted the winter rains that traveled with the west wind out of the Great Sea; and so Gornevon was a sort of pocket desert in the midst of fertile, prosperous Zimroel, one of the driest places in the entire immense continent.

"If only we were coming into Ni-moya now instead, eh?" said Halefice, with a chuckle.

Mandralisca's response was a thin cool smile. "You love your comforts, don't you, my friend?"

"Who but a madman—or the Five Lords—would prefer this place to Ni-moya, your grace?"

Mandralisca shrugged. "Who but a madman, indeed? But we go where we must go. Our destiny has sent us here: so be it."

The five brothers would not have dared, of course, to use Ni-moya as the base for their insurrection, even though it was their family's ancestral seat, from which their rapacious uncle the Procurator Dantirya Sambail had long ruled Zimroel as a king within the kingdom. Prestimion, having taken Dantirya Sambail prisoner on the battlefield of Thegomar Edge at the conclusion of the Korsibar war, had pardoned him, ultimately, for his perfidious role in the insurrection. The victorious Coronal had left him in possession of his lands and wealth. But he had stripped him of his title of Procurator, and had debarred him from wielding power beyond the boundaries of his own considerable estates. That had been some sixteen years ago. There had been no Procurators in Zimroel ever since.

Dantirya Sambail's second rebellion had brought him to a bloody end at the hand of Septach Melayn in the marshy forests of the Stoienzar. His lands had descended to his coarse, brutal brothers Gaviad and Gaviundar. Eventually, after their deaths, the properties had passed to

Gaviundar's five sons, who yearned to regain the sway over all of Zimroel that their great and terrible uncle once had had; for the central government and its two monarchs, the Pontifex and the Coronal both, were far away on the other and older continent of Alhanroel, where both its capitals were situated.

On populous Zimroel most people felt only the most abstract sort of allegiance to that government. They gave lip service to the Coronal, yes; but it was the power of the Procurator, one of their own, that had always been far more real to them. They had grown accustomed to the reign of their ferocious Procurator. He had been a singularly unlovable man, but under his energetic rule Zimroel had attained much affluence and stability. And therefore it was very likely—so the five sons of Gaviundar told one another—that the people of Zimroel would even after a lapse of a decade and a half choose to accept the Procurator's legitimate heirs, princes of the true Sambailid blood, as their masters.

Naturally it would not have done to begin any such drive toward power in Ni-moya itself. Ni-moya was the administrative center of the western continent, a hive of Pontifical bureaucrats. Let any member of the Sambailid tribe announce that he intended once more to exercise the old family authority over anything other than the family's private lands, and immediately word of it would go forth from Ni-moya to the Labyrinth, and from there to the Castle, and in short order a royal army under the Coronal's command would be setting out for Zimroel to restore matters to their proper order.

Out here in the hinterlands, though, one could do as one wished, even proclaim oneself sovereign over vast domains, and it might be years before word of it filtered back to the Coronal atop Castle Mount or to the Coronal's own overlord, the Pontifex, in his underground lair. Majipoor was so huge that news often traveled slowly even when carried on swift wings.

And thus the five brothers had taken themselves out to this remote outpost and had given themselves resounding new titles: they named themselves the Lords of Zimroel, true successors by right of blood to the Procurators of old. And they had gradually let the word go forth, village by village throughout the adjacent regions of Zimroel on both sides of the river, that they held supremacy here now. They had left the river cities themselves alone, so far, because the river was the main highway across the continent, and any attempt to interfere with commerce on the Zimr would bring quick retribution from the central government.

But they had claimed and won allegiance in the farming communities north and south of the river for some hundreds of miles, reaching to the east as far as Immanala, to the west almost to Dulorn. That provided them with a domain from which they could eventually expand.

It was Mandralisca himself, long the second-in-command to Dantirya Sambail and now the chief adviser to his five nephews, who had suggested their new titles to them.

"You cannot call yourselves Procurators," he said. "It would be like an instant declaration of war."

"But 'lords' — ?" said Gaviral, who was the eldest one, and the quickest-witted of the lot. "Only the Coronal may call himself 'lord' on Majipoor, is that not so, Mandralisca?"

"Only the Coronal can take it as part of his name: Lord Prankipin, Lord Confalume, Lord Prestimion. But any count or prince or duke is a lord of sorts in his own territory, and one can quite properly say, in addressing him, 'my lord.' So we will make a little distinction here. You will be the Five Lords of Zimroel; but you will not try to speak of yourselves as Lord Gaviral, Lord Gavinius, Lord Gavdat, and so on. No: you will be 'the Lord Gaviral,' 'the Lord Gavinius,'" et cetera, et cetera."

"It seems to me a very fine distinction," said Gaviral.

"I like it," said Gavahaud, who of the five was the most vain. He grinned a broad toothy grin. "The Lord Gavahaud! All hail the Lord Gavahaud! It has a fine sound, would you not say, eh, Lord Gavilomarin?"

"Be careful," said Mandralisca. "You have it wrong already. Not Lord Gavilomarin, but the Lord Gavilomarin. When one speaks to him directly one can call him 'milord,' and say, 'Milord Gavilomarin,' but never 'Lord Gavilomarin' alone. Is that clear?"

It took them a while to get it. He was not surprised. In Mandralisca's estimation they were, after all, nothing more than a pack of buffoons.

But they embraced their new titles gladly. In the course of time they made themselves known in this district and several surrounding provinces as the Five Lords of Zimroel. Not everyone accepted the resurgence of Sambailid power gladly: the Vorthinar lord, for one, a petty princeling with lands to the north of the Zimr, had had ideas of his own about establishing authority independent of the Alhanroel regime, and had refused the Sambailid overtures so rudely and categorically that it had been necessary for the brothers to send Mandralisca to deal with him. But there were plenty of men who had loved Dantirya Sambail and resented his overthrow by the outlander Prestimion, and they came from many parts of the western continent to throw in their lot with the Five Lords. Very quietly a shadow Sambailid administration had emerged out here in rural Zimroel.

In their slowly expanding dominion the Five Lords appointed officials and decreed laws. They succeeded in diverting local taxes from the Pontifical tax-collectors to their own. They built five fine palaces for themselves opposite Horvenar atop the red bluffs of Gornevon. The dwellings of Gavdat and Gavinius and Gavahaud were side by side in a single group, with Gaviral's somewhat to the west of the others on a little promontory with a better view of the river than his brothers had, and Gavilomarin's off on the eastern side, separated from the rest by a low lateral ridge; and from those five palaces did they propose very gradually to extend their rule over the continent that their potent uncle once had ruled virtually as a king.

Up to this time the government of the Pontifex Confalume and the Coronal Lord Prestimion in far-off Alhanroel had paid no heed to what had begun to take shape in Zimroel. Perhaps they were still unaware of it.

The Five Lords knew what risks they were running. But Mandralisca had shown them how difficult it would be for the imperial government to take any kind of serious punitive action against them. An army would have to be raised in Alhanroel and transported somehow to the other continent across the great gulf that was the Inner Sea. Then the imperial troops would have to commandeer virtually the entire fleet of Zimr riverboats to carry them upriver to the rebel-held territory, or else march thousands of miles overland, through one probably hostile district after another.

And even if they succeeded in that, and brought the rebellious farmers of the region back under control, it would not be easy to dislodge the Five Lords themselves from their hilltop eyrie high above the Zimr. There was no possibility at all of scaling those red bluffs from the river side. That left only the desert approach from the south—the very district through which Mandralisca and his party were riding now. And that was a hellish road indeed.

8

---

*I*n the evening the Justiciar Corde called for Dekkeret and Dinitak at their hostelry and escorted them to the palace of the Count for a formal banquet, the first of several such events planned for Dekkeret's stay in Normork.

Dekkeret had seen the palace often enough when he was growing up: a blocky building of gray stone, squat and nearly windowless, that clung like some huge limpet to the city wall in a place where the wall made a wide outward curve to get past a jutting spur of Castle Mount. It was a dark, grim-looking place, fortresslike, uninviting. Even the six slim minarets that sprang from its roof, which the architect probably had meant to add a touch of lightness to the palace's appearance, seemed like nothing so much as an array of barbed spears.

The interior was every bit as somber as the outside. The building seemed twice as big inside as without, and perhaps four times as ugly. Dekkeret and Dinitak were conducted down long stretches of shadowy bewildering corridors lit only by smoldering torches and inadequate glowlights, past radiating clusters of spokelike hallways of unadorned stone walls, through rooms with walls of black brick decorated with nothing more than the occasional preposterous statue of some unknown ancient figure or clumsily designed tapestries portraying forgotten lords and ladies of the city engaged in their lordly amusements; and eventually they arrived at the dark, drafty banqueting-hall of Count Considat, where an assortment of Normork's notables awaited them.

It was a dreary evening. Considat spoke first, welcoming Normork's most famous son back to his native city. The Count was young and had succeeded to his title only the year before, and was an amiable and almost diffident man rather more appealing in look and manner than his coarse, ill-bred father had been. But he was a dreadful speaker who droned on and on as though he had no idea of how to bring his speech to an end, unleashing a torrent of fatuous platitudes. At one point Dekkeret dozed off, and only a sharp rap under the table from Dinitak brought him back to the scene.

Then it was Dekkeret's turn to speak, conveying Lord Prestimion's greetings and—since that was the official pretext of his visit—congratulating the Count and Countess on the birth of their son. He extended Lord Prestimion's regret at not being able to be present in person just now. The congratulatory gifts that had been sent by Lord Prestimion were carried in by Dekkeret's men. Justiciar Corde spoke. Several other high officials of the court, obviously eager to make a powerful impression on the future Coronal, spoke also, effusively and to tiresome effect. Then Count Considat spoke again, no more ably than before, but at least with greater brevity. Dekkeret, caught a bit by surprise, improvised a reply. Then, only then, was food at last served, a sorry sequence of overcooked, feebly spiced meats and flaccid vegetables and prematurely opened wines. After-dinner speeches were to follow. Dekkeret made his way through the interminable ceremony by dint of a mighty summoning of patience and discipline.

He realized only too well that many more such evenings were in store for him in the years ahead. Once, when he was much younger, he had imagined that a Coronal's life must be an endlessly glamorous affair of tournaments and feasting and revelry, interrupted now and then by the making of grand, dramatic decisions that would alter the fates of many millions of people. He knew better now.

The next day, with no official functions scheduled before nightfall, Dekkeret took Dinitak on a tour of the city, just the two of them—and a dozen or so bodyguards. It was a clear, warm morning, the air soft and fragrant in the eternal springtime of Castle Mount, the sunlight bright and strong. The soaring jagged crags of the Mount, rising beyond the city wall on all sides of Normork, glinted like ruddy bronze in that brilliant light.

Visitors to Normork often commented on the contrast between the glorious beauty of the city's setting and the dark, hermetic look of the city itself, a tumbled multitude of close-packed gray buildings huddling in the shadow of that colossal black wall. Dekkeret, having been raised here, took the prevailing somberness of Normork for granted without finding anything unusual in it, indeed, without really noticing it at all; but now for the first time he began to see the city through the eyes of its critics. Perhaps, he thought, all the years he had spent dwelling in the airy higher reaches of Castle Mount were starting to alter his outlook toward this place.

The city wall was all but unscalable from without. Everywhere inside the city, though, stone staircases were set flush against its inner face that led to the top. They gave easy access to the broad road, wide enough for ten people to walk abreast on it, that ran along the wall's rim. Dekkeret and Dinitak, accompanied by their inescapable gaggle of security men, ascended by way of the stairs just opposite their hotel.

In silence they set out westward around the city perimeter. After a time Dekkeret beckoned to his companion to follow him to the wall's outer border. Leaning far out over it, he said, "Do you see that highway down there below us? The thing that looks like a white ribbon stretching a long way off into the east? That's the one that comes up from Dundilmir and Stipool and the other cities over yonder on this level of the Mount. That road is the chief route of access to Normork for those cities and everything farther down. But you'll notice that it doesn't actually run *into* Normork anywhere. It can't, because it comes in on the wrong side of town. You've already seen that the only entrance to the city is way around over there, on the side of Normork that faces upslope."

Dinitak looked and nodded. "Yes. It comes straight up to the wall just below where we're standing, but there's no place to enter the city here. So it turns left instead and continues along the outside of the wall, following it all the way around, I suppose, until—until what? Until it reaches that stupid little gate?"

"Exactly. On the other side it joins up with the highway that we came down from the Castle on, and they become a single road that runs into Normork by way of the Eye of Stiamot."

"And they make travelers from downslope go right around the city in order to enter from the upslope side? What an addlepated arrangement!"

"So it is. But changes are coming."

"Oh?"

"I told you I had a plan for this city," said Dekkeret grandly. "We're standing right above the location where one day I intend to cut a second gateway through this wall." He made a broad sweeping gesture, taking in a great swath of the titanic rampart of black stone. "Listen to this, Dinitak! The gate that I have in mind to build will be something truly majestic, nothing remotely like the puny little hole by which we entered yesterday. I'm going to make it fifty feet high and forty feet wide, or even more, so that even a Skandar will feel small when he stands under it. I'll fashion it out of a kind of black wood that I know of from Zimroel, a rare and costly wood that takes a high polish and will shine like a mirror in the morning light, and I'll bind it with big iron bands and the hinges will be of iron too; and by my most sacred decree it's going to stand wide open at all times, except when the city is in peril, if ever it is. What do you say to that, eh?"

Dinitak was silent for a moment, frowning.

"I wonder," he said finally.

"Go on."

"It sounds very impressive, I agree. But do you think they'd genuinely *want* a gate like that here, Dekkeret? I've been here not even a day and a half, but my clear impression already is that what concerns these Normork folk above all else is *safety*. They lust for it beyond all reason. They are the most cautious people in the world. And this enormous impregnable black wall of theirs that they cherish so dearly is the symbol of that obsession. Doubtless that's why the only opening in the wall is such a tiny one, and why they take care to shut that little opening and lock it up tight every evening at sunset. Do you think that the convenience of travelers coming from the downslope cities matters a damn to them, compared with the security of their own precious selves? If you come along and poke a great gaping breach in their wall for them, how likely is it that they're going to love you for it?"

"I'll be Coronal then. The first Coronal ever who was born in Normork."

"Even so—"

"No. They'll accept my gate, I'm sure of it. They'll *love* my gate. Not at first, no, perhaps. I grant you they'll need some time to get used to it. But it'll be an utterly splendid gate, the new symbol of the city, something that people will travel from all over Castle Mount to stare at. And the citizens will point to it and say, 'There it is, there's the gate that Lord Dekkeret built for us, the most magnificent gate that can be found anywhere in the world.' "

"And the fact that it stands open all the time—?"

"Even that. A sign of municipal confidence. What enemies are there for them to fear, anyway? The world is at peace. No invading army is going to come marching up the side of Castle Mount. No, Dinitak— perhaps they'll mutter and mumble at first, but in a very short while they'll all agree that the new gate is the most wondrous thing that's been built here since the wall itself."

"No doubt you are correct," said Dinitak, with just the lightest touch of irony in his tone.

Dekkeret heard it. But he would not let himself be checked. "I know that I am. The gate is going to be my monument. The Dekkeret Gate, is what people will call it in centuries to come. Everyone coming up the Mount from below will pass through it and gape at it in awe, and they'll tell each other that this great gate, the most famous gate in the world, was built long ago by a Coronal Lord named Dekkeret, who was a man of this very city of Normork."

He could not help smiling at his own absurdly pretentious words. His *monument*? Did a Coronal of Majipoor need seriously to worry about whether he would ever be forgotten? All that he had just said began to sound just a bit foolish to him even as the last words of it died away. Dinitak often had that effect on him. The tough little man's hard-won realism frequently was a useful antidote to some of Dekkeret's wilder flights of romanticism.

But not this time, he swore. Regardless of Dinitak's misgivings, the Dekkeret Gate was going to be built. Probably not as his first project after he became Coronal, but he was determined to do it sooner or later. It had been his dream for many years. Nothing Dinitak could say was going to swerve him from it.

They walked onward along the top of the wall.

"That's the Count's palace, isn't it?" Dinitak asked, pointing over the inner parapet. "It looks very different from this angle. But just as hideous."

"Perhaps. Perhaps." Dekkeret felt his mood suddenly darkening. A throbbing began in his temples. He walked toward the parapet for a better view, and found two of Count Considat's black-uniformed security men in his way. He gesticulated at them with such ferocity that they must have thought he meant to fling them over the side. Hastily they moved back.

Dekkeret stared down into the plaza in front of the palace. His face became bleak. His lips were tightly clamped. He pressed the tips of his fingers to the sides of his head and slowly rubbed the area just above his cheekbones.

"What's wrong?" Dinitak asked, when some little while had gone by without a word from him.

"We would have a perfect view of the assassination attempt from up here," said Dekkeret quietly. He sketched out the scene for Dinitak with quick movements of his hand. "Lord Prestimion has just arrived in the plaza. There's his floater, sitting right down there. He steps out of it. Gialaurys walks at his left side. Akbalik is to the right of him. You never knew Akbalik, did you? He died just around the time you were joining us in Stoien city for the final attack on Dantirya Sambail. A wonderful man, Akbalik was. He should be the one about to become Coronal, not me. —And there's Count Meglis on the palace steps, three or four steps from the bottom. The stupid bastard is simply standing there, waiting for Prestimion to go to *him*, when it's supposed to be the other way around. Prestimion isn't expecting that. He waits for Meglis to finish coming down the steps, but he doesn't, and for a couple of moments neither of them moves."

Dekkeret fell silent.

"And where were you standing?" Dinitak asked. "You told me that you were there that day, that you saw the whole thing."

"Yes. Yes. There was a huge crowd, over there on the left, where the plaza runs into that big boulevard. Thousands of people. Guards holding us back. I'm practically at the front, on that side. The second row."

Dekkeret sighed. It was followed by another brooding silence.

Dinitak said, "Then what? The assassin bursts out of the crowd, swinging his sickle? Someone yells to warn the Coronal. The guards move in and cut the man down."

"No. A girl comes out first—"

"A girl?"

"A beautiful girl, very tall, curling reddish-gold hair. Sixteen years old. Sithelle, her name was. My cousin. Standing just in front of me, right against the rope that's holding the crowd back. She adored Lord Prestimion. We got up at dawn to get a good position up in front. She was carrying a bouquet that she had woven herself, hundreds of flowers. Was planning to throw it toward the Coronal, so I assumed. But no.

No." Dekkeret's voice had become a dull low monotone. "She bends down and wriggles under the rope and slips past the guards so that she can *hand* the flowers to Prestimion. A very unwise thing to do. But he's amused. He signals to the guards to let her approach. He takes the flowers from her. Asks her a question or two. And then—"

"The man with the sickle?"

"Yes. Skinny man with a beard. Crazy look in his eye. He comes charging out of nowhere, heading straight for Prestimion. Sithelle doesn't see him coming, but she hears footsteps, I guess, and she turns, and he chops at her with the sickle to get her out of his way." Dekkeret snapped his fingers. "Just like that. Blood everywhere—her throat—"

In a hushed voice Dinitak said, "He kills her, your cousin?"

"She must have died almost instantly."

"And then the guards kill him."

"No," Dekkeret said. "I do."

"*You?*"

"The assassin had been standing five or six places to my left. I came running out of the crowd right after him—I don't know how I got past the restraining rope, don't remember that part of it at all, only that I was out there, and I could see Sithelle with her hand across her throat trying to hold the cut together as she started to fall, and Prestimion standing there frozen with the man with the sickle raising his arm, and Gialaurys and Akbalik starting to move in from the sides but not fast enough. I grabbed the assassin's arm and twisted it until it broke. Then I put my arm around his neck and broke that too. And picked up Sithelle—she was dead by then, that I knew—and walked off into the crowd with her, straight down Spurifon Boulevard into Old Town. No one stopped me. People moved away from me as I approached. Her blood was all over me. I took her to her house and told her parents what had happened. It was the most dreadful hour of my life. It has stayed with me ever since."

"You loved her? You wanted to marry her, did you? You were promised to each other?"

"Oh, no. Nothing of the sort. I loved her, yes, of course, but not in that way. We were cousins, remember. Raised practically like brother and sister. Our families wanted us to marry, but I never had any serious thought of it."

"And she?"

Dekkeret managed a thin smile. "She may have had some fantasy of marrying Lord Prestimion. I know she had pictures of him tacked up all over her room. But nothing could ever have come of that, and she probably realized it. Very possibly she may have been in love with me, I suppose. We were so young then—what did either of us know—?"

He looked down again into the plaza. *Was that her blood still staining the cobbles of the plaza?*

No. No, he told himself, stop being ridiculous!

Dinitak said, "In fact you *were* in love with her, I think."

"No. I'm sure I wasn't, not then. But—the Divine help me, Dinitak!—something has gradually come over me since that time. She won't leave my mind. I look back across the years and I see her, her face, her eyes, her hair, the way she held herself, the way she would run up and down these stairs, the mischief in her glance—and I think, if only she had lived, if only we had had a chance to grow up a little—" Dekkeret shook his head fiercely. "Never mind. She's been dead now longer than she ever was alive. She has no more reality now than someone who comes to you in a dream. Come: let's get ourselves away from this place."

"I'm sorry all this got stirred up for you again, Dekkeret."

"No matter. It's there inside me all the time. Seeing the actual site just made it a little worse for a moment. —That same afternoon, you know, Akbalik found me somehow and took me to see Prestimion, who offered to enroll me as a knight-initiate at the Castle as a reward for saving his life, and everything that's happened to me since has been the direct outcome of what took place down there that terrible day. I remember Prestimion saying to Akbalik, 'Who knows? We may have found the next Coronal here today.' His very words. He was joking then, of course."

"But he was right about that."

"Yes. So it would seem. A direct line, connecting that boy who came running out of the crowd to save Lord Prestimion with the man who'll sit someday where Prestimion sits now on the Confalume Throne." Dekkeret laughed harshly. "Me: Lord Dekkeret! Isn't that astounding, Dinitak?"

"Not to me. But I do sometimes think you have trouble believing you're actually going to be Coronal."

"Wouldn't you, if you were the one?"

"But I'm not the one, and never will be, the Divine be thanked. I'm quite content being who I am."

"As am I, Dinitak. I'm in no hurry to take over Prestimion's job. If he went on being Coronal for the next twenty years, that would be perfectly all right with—"

Dinitak caught at Dekkeret's sleeve. "Hold it a moment. Look— there's something odd going on over there."

He followed the line of Dinitak's pointing arm. Yes: some sort of altercation seemed to be under way about fifty feet farther down the wall, just outside the protective circle of Considat's security force. Half a dozen of the guardsmen were surrounding someone. Arms were waving. There was a lot of angry incoherent shouting.

"It's too improbable that there would be another assassination attempt," Dinitak said.

"Damned right it is. But those halfwits—" Dekkeret raised himself on tiptoe for a better view. A gasp of outrage burst from him. "By the Lady, it's a messenger from the Castle that they're making trouble for! Come on, Dinitak!"

They rushed over. An overwrought-looking guardsman thrust himself in Dekkeret's face and said, "A suspicious stranger, my lord. We attempted to interrogate him, but—"

"Blockhead, don't you recognize the badge of the Coronal's couriers? Step aside!"

The courier was no one Dekkeret recognized, but the golden starburst that was his badge of office was authentic enough. The man, though more than a little worse from wear after the security guards' intervention, pulled himself together stalwartly and held forth to Dekkeret an envelope prominently sealed in scarlet wax with the sigil of the High Counsellor Septach Melayn. "My lord Dekkeret, I bear this message— by order of Prince Teotas, on behalf of the Council, I have ridden from the Castle day and night to give it to you—"

Dekkeret snatched it from him, gave the seal a cursory glance, ripped the envelope open. There was just a single scrawled page within, in Teotas's bold, square, boyish lettering. Dekkeret's eyes traveled quickly over the words, and then over them again, and again.

"Bad news?" Dinitak asked, after a while.

Dekkeret nodded. "Indeed. The Pontifex is ill. He may have had a stroke."

"Dying, is he?"

"That word is not used here. But how can it fail to come to mind, when a man ninety years old is taken ill? I'm summoned immediately back to the Castle." Dekkeret forced a chuckle. "Well, at least we won't have to suffer through another of Count Considat's dreadful banquets tonight: thanks be to the Divine for small mercies. But what might happen after that—" He looked away. He did not know what to think. A dizzying torrent of contradictory feelings rushed through him: sadness, excitement, dismay, euphoria, disbelief, fear.

Confalume ill. Possibly dying. Perhaps already dead.

Did Prestimion know? He was supposed to be off traveling also, just now. As usual. Dekkeret wondered what sort of scene was unfolding back at the Castle in the absence both of the Coronal and the Coronal-designate.

"It may be only nothing," he said. His voice, usually so resonant, was hollow and hoarse. "Old men get ill from time to time. Not everything that *seems* to be a stroke is one. And one doesn't necessarily die of a stroke."

"All this is true," said Dinitak. "But even so—"

Dekkeret held up his hand. "No. Don't say it."

Dinitak would not be halted. "You remarked just a moment ago that you hoped Prestimion went on being Coronal for the next twenty years. And I know you were sincere in hoping that. But you didn't seriously believe that he would, did you?"

9

The first pungatans were coming into view, dotting the wasteland before them.

"These filthy plants!" Jacomin Halefice muttered. "How I loathe them! I would take a torch to the lot of them, if I were allowed!"

"Ah," said Mandralisca. "They are our friends, those plants!"

"Your friends, perhaps, your grace. Not mine."

"They guard our domain," the Count said. "They keep us safe from our enemies, our lovely pungatans."

So they did. This was a wild, cruel desert, and the only traversable road through it was a mere stony track. Venture off it even a dozen yards and you were at the pungatans' mercy—those evil whip-leaved plants that were the only things that flourished here. It would be a major logistical task to guide an army of any size through this land of little water and nothing in the way of wood or edible crops, where what vegetation there was struck out savagely and lethally at all passersby.

But Mandralisca knew the way through this grim plain. "Beware the whips!" he called out, glancing back over his shoulder at his men. "Keep yourselves in line!"

He gave his mount the spurs and rode onward into the pungatan grove.

They were actually quite beautiful, the pungatans, or so it seemed to Mandralisca. Their thick gray stubby trunks, smooth and columnar, rose from the rust-red soil to a height of three or four feet. From the summit of each sprouted a pair of wavy ribbonlike fronds, extending in op-

posite directions for two yards or so with their tips trailing down prettily
along the ground into an intricate coiling tangle of frayed ends. These
fronds seemed delicate and soft; they were so nearly transparent that
they were hard to see except at certain favorable angles. As they fluttered
in the breeze, they might almost seem to be strands of clear seaweed,
surging with the tides.

But one merely had to pass within fifteen or twenty feet of one of the
plants and a deep wash of reddish-purple color came flooding into those
fluttering fronds, and they grew turgid and began to tremble at their tips;
and then—*whack!*—they would uncoil to their full startling length and
strike, a whiplash blow of astonishing swiftness and horrific force. It was
a savage lateral swing that sliced with the power of a sharp sword
through any creature rash enough to have ventured within their range.
That was how they nourished themselves, in this infertile soil: they
killed, and then they fed on the nutrients that leached into the ground
from the decomposing bodies of their victims. One could see fragmentary skeletons scattered all around, the ancient remains of incautious
beasts and, evidently, a good many unwary travelers.

Someone had long ago laid out a safe track through this unappealing wilderness, a narrow zone that passed between the places where the
plants tended to grow. It was marked only by a sparse border of rocks on
either side, and the careless wayfarer could all too readily stray outside
its limits. But Count Mandralisca was not one much given to careless-
ness. He guided his little convoy through the deadly plain without incident and thence up the narrow, interminably switchbacking trail that
took one to the top of the riverfront bluffs and to the compound of
palaces where his masters the Five Lords awaited his return.

What sort of foolishness, Mandralisca wondered, had they managed
to get themselves into in his absence?

He was greeted, as he and his party came riding into the broad colonnaded plaza that fronted the three central buildings, by a sight so very
much in accord with his expectations that he was hard put to choke
back bitter laughter, and to conceal his loathing and disgust.

Gavinius, the brother for whom Mandralisca cared least of all, was
wandering at large in the plaza, drunk—no surprise that! —and reeling
around in a blundering rampage. Flushed and sweaty, clad only in a
loosely flapping linen apron, he was roaming from one stone column to
the next, blowing kisses to them as though they were pretty maidens, all
the while bawling some raucous song. A leather flask of brandy dangled

from one shoulder. A couple of his women —his "wives," Gavinius liked to call them, but there was no evidence that that was so in any formal sense—followed along cautiously behind him as though they hoped somehow to steer him back inside the palace. But they were taking care not to get too close. Gavinius was dangerous when he was drunk.

He came to a lurching, staggering halt as the Count came into view.

"Mandralisca!" he bellowed. "At last! Where have you been, fellow? Been looking for you all day!"

The big man went stumbling forward. Mandralisca swung himself quickly to the ground. It would not be the part of wisdom to remain astride his mount in the presence of the Lord Gavinius.

Of the five brothers, Gavinius was the one who most closely resembled their late father Gaviundar: a huge big-bellied red-faced man with a wide, florid face, unpleasant little blue-green eyes, and great fleshy ears that sprang out at acute angles from the nearly bald dome of his head. Though Mandralisca was a tall man, the Lord Gavinius was even taller, and very much greater in bulk. He took up a stance that was almost nose to nose with Mandralisca and stood rocking alarmingly back and forth on the massive tree trunks that were his legs, squinting at him blearily. "You want a drink, Count? Here. Here. Look at you, you're dusty all over! Where have you been?" Clumsily he unfastened the strap of his brandy flask, nearly dropping it in the process and catching it only by a desperate swipe of his huge paw, and pushed it toward Mandralisca.

"I thank you, milord Gavinius. But I have no thirst just now."

"No thirst? Ah, but you never do. Damn you, why not? What a sorry stick of a man you are, Mandralisca! Have some anyway. You should want to drink. You should love to drink. How can I trust a man who hates to drink? Here. Here. *Drink!*"

Shrugging, Mandralisca took the flask from the bigger man, held it to his lips without quite touching it, pretended to take a swig, and handed it back.

Gavinius corked the flask and flipped it casually over his shoulder. Then, leaning close into Mandralisca's face, he began thickly to say: "I had a dream last night—the most amazing—it was a sending, Mandralisca, a true sending, I tell you! I wanted you to speak it for me, but where were you? Damn you, where were you? It was such a dream—"

"He was away north of the Zimr, you booby, carrying out a punitive mission against the Vorthinar lord," came a dry, hard voice suddenly from one side. "Isn't that so, Mandralisca?"

Gaviral, it was. The only really clever one of the bunch: the future Pontifex of Zimroel, if Mandralisca had his way.

The interruption was a welcome one. Dealing with Gavinius, drunk or sober, was always an irritating business, and it could be perilous besides. Gaviral was capable of being dangerous in his own cunning way, but at any rate there was no risk of his grabbing you up in some bone-crushing demonstration of manly affection, or simply crashing down drunkenly upon you like a toppling tree.

"I have been in the north, yes, milord," said Mandralisca, "and the mission has been accomplished. The Vorthinar lord and all his men went up in flames these five days past."

Gaviral smiled. Alone in this brotherly herd of great uncouth oxen he was a wiry man, small and fidgety, with quick flickering eyes and a narrow, twitchy mouth. He was built on such a different scale from the others that quite possibly he was not his father's son at all, Mandralisca sometimes suspected. But he did have the reddish hair of the whole Sambailid clan, and the distinctive coarseness of feature, and their irrepressible rapacity of spirit. "Dead, are they?" Gaviral said. "Splendid. Splendid! But I had no doubt. You are a good staunch faithful man, Mandralisca. What would we ever do without you? You are a jewel. You are our strong right arm. I commend you with all my heart."

There was profound condescension in Gaviral's effusive tone, an airy insincerity, a lurking disingenuousness, that blared forth in every syllable. He spoke as one might speak to a servant, to a lackey, to a minion — that is, one might speak that way if one were a fool and did not understand the proper ways of addressing those upon whom you are dependent, inferiors though they might be.

But Mandralisca betrayed no sign of taking offense. "Thank you, milord," he said softly, with a grateful little smile and a nod of his head, as though he had been honored with a golden chain, or a knighthood, or the gift of six villages in the fertile north. "I will cherish these words of yours. Your praise means a great deal to me — more, perhaps, than you can realize."

"It is not so much praise, Mandralisca, as a simple statement of the truth," said Gaviral, seeming very pleased with himself.

He was the brightest of the five brothers, yes. But what Mandralisca knew, and Gaviral did not, was that Gaviral was not half so bright as he thought he was. That was his great flaw. He was easy enough to deceive:

merely let him think you were in awe of his superb mind, and he was yours.

Gavinius now broke in abruptly. "I dreamed," he said, returning to his theme as though Mandralisca and Gaviral had not been speaking with each other at all, "such a dream! The Procurator came to me, will you believe it? Walked up and down before me, looked me in the eye, said marvelous things to me. It was a sending, I know it was, but whose was it? Surely not the Lady's. Why would the Lady send the Procurator's spirit to me? Why would the Lady send me a dream in the first place?" Gavinius belched. "You have to explain it to me, Mandralisca. I've been hunting for you all day. Where have you been, anyway?" Then he turned away, scuffing about for his flask in the red sand of the plaza. "And where has my brandy gone? What have you done with my flask?"

"Go inside, Gavinius," Gaviral said in a low but insistent tone. "Lie down. Close your eyes for a while. The Count will speak your dream later for you." The little man gave his hulking brother a sharp thump on the breastbone. Gavinius looked down, blinking in astonishment, at the place where he had been struck. "Go. Go, Gavinius." And Gaviral thumped him again, tapping a little harder this time. Gavinius, still blinking, went lumbering off toward his palace like a befuddled bidlak, with his women tagging along just behind.

The Lords Gavdat and Gavahaud had by this time appeared in the plaza, and Mandralisca saw Gavilomarin coming toward them over the ridge that separated his palace from the others. The brothers clustered around their privy counsellor.

Soft, jowly-faced Gavdat of the cavernous nostrils, as soon as he learned of the successful result of Mandralisca's mission, let it be known that his casting of a thaumaturgic horoscope had made that outcome a certainty. He fancied himself a wizard of sorts, did Gavdat, and dabbled ineptly in magecraft and spells. Vain bull-necked Gavahaud, as ugly as his brothers but convinced to a marvelous degree of his own beauty, offered Mandralisca congratulations with a dainty foppish salute, doubly grotesque in so heavyset a man. Big flabby Gavilomarin, a pallid-souled negligible person who obligingly agreed with anything any of the others might say, clapped his hands in a simpleminded way and giggled happily at the news of the burning of the keep.

"So may they all perish, those who oppose us!" said Gavahaud sententiously.

"There will be many of those, I fear," Mandralisca said.

"The Coronal, you mean?" asked the Lord Gaviral.

"That will be later. I mean others like the Vorthinar lord. Local princes, who see themselves as having a chance to break away from everyone's authority. Once they behold lords like yourself openly defying the Coronal and the Pontifex and succeeding in that defiance, they see no reason to continue to pay taxes to other administrations. Including your own, my lords."

"You will burn them for us, then, as you burned this one," Gavahaud said.

"Yes. Yes. So he will!" cried Gavilomarin, and gleefully clapped his hands again.

Mandralisca threw him a quick baleful smile. Then, tapping his fingertips to the golden paraclet of his office that hung at his breast and glancing swiftly from one brother to the next, he said, "My lords, I have had a long journey this day, and I am very weary. I ask your permission to retire."

As they made their way toward the village a little distance south of Gaviral's palace where the highest-level retainers lived, Jacomin Halefice said hesitantly to Mandralisca, "Sir, may I offer a personal observation?"

"We are friends, are we not, Jacomin?" said Mandralisca.

The statement was so far from the truth that Halefice had difficulty hiding his astonishment. But he recovered after a moment and said, "It seemed to me, sir, that the brothers, when they were speaking with you just now—and I have noticed this before, in truth—you will forgive me for saying so, I hope, but—" There he hesitated. "What I mean to say—"

"Come out with it, will you?"

Halefice said, "Just that they are so very patronizing when they address you. They speak to you as though they are grand and mighty noblemen and you are insignificant, treated like nothing more than a vassal, a mere flunkey."

"I *am* their vassal, Jacomin."

"But not their servant."

"Not precisely, no."

"Why do you abide their insolence, then, sir? For that is what it is, and, forgive me, your grace, but it pains me to see a man of your abilities treated that way. Have they forgotten that you and only you have made them what they are?"

"Oh, no, not so. You give me too much credit, Jacomin. It was the Divine that made them what they are, and also, I suppose, their glorious father Prince Gaviundar, with some help from their lady mother, whoever that may have been." Mandralisca flashed his quick frosty smile again. "All I did was show them how they could make themselves lords of these few unimportant provinces. And, if all goes well, lords of all Zimroel, perhaps, one day."

"And it troubles you not in the least that they treat you with such contempt, sir?"

Mandralisca surveyed his bandy-legged little aide-de-camp with a long, slow, curious look.

He and Jacomin Halefice had been together for more than twenty years, now. They had fought side by side against the forces of Prestimion at Thegomar Edge, when Korsibar had perished at the hands of his own Su-Suheris magus, and the Procurator Dantirya Sambail had been defeated and made a prisoner by Prestimion, and Mandralisca himself, who had fought to the last stages of exhaustion, was wounded and taken prisoner also by Rufiel Kisimir of Muldemar. And the two of them had been near each other again at the time of the second great defeat, among the manganoza thickets of Stoienzar, that time when Dantirya Sambail was slain by Septach Melayn: Halefice had helped Mandralisca slip off into the underbrush and vanish, when Navigorn of Hoikmar was pursuing him and would have put him to death. It was with Halefice's assistance that Mandralisca had been able to make his escape from Alhanroel and find his way into the service of Dantirya Sambail's two brothers.

Halefice's loyalty and devotion were beyond question. He was Mandralisca's right hand, as Mandralisca had been the right hand of the Procurator Dantirya Sambail. And yet, in all their time together, Halefice had never dared to speak so intimately with Mandralisca as he had just done. In its way that was, Mandralisca thought, somewhat moving.

He said carefully, "If they seem to treat me with contempt, Jacomin, it's because their manner is ever a coarse one, as is the style of their whole clan. You remember their elegant father Gaviundar, and his beautiful brother Gaviad. Nor was their uncle Dantirya Sambail known for the gentleness of his tongue. Where you see contempt, my friend, I

see only something of a lack of tact. I take no offense. It is in their nature. They are crude rough men. I forgive them for it, because we are
all players in the same game, do you take my meaning?"

"Sir?" said Halefice blankly.

"Apparently you don't. Let me put it this way: I serve the needs of the
Sambailids, whether they know it or not, and I think they do not, but
also they serve mine. It is the same between you and me, as well. Think
on it, Jacomin. But keep your findings to yourself. Let us not discuss
these things again, shall we?" Mandralisca turned away, toward his own
simple cottage. "Here is the parting of our ways," he said. "I wish you a
good day."

10

*T*he lights remained on and the steward Falco stayed with Prestimion while he calmed himself. Diandolo brought him something cool and soothing to drink. The master of the lodge, virtually beside himself with chagrin that his royal guest had undergone so terrifying a dream under his own roof, produced such an outpouring of solicitousness and fuss that Falco had to order him from the room. Young Prince Taradath, who had accompanied Prestimion to Fa and had a suite of his own across the courtyard, now made a belated appearance, aroused at last from the deep sleep of adolescence by all the furore in the halls. Prestimion sent him away also. His father's nightmares need not be any concern of his.

This was the third day of Prestimion's state visit to Fa. Things had been going predictably thus far, the banquets, the speeches, the conferring of royal honors upon deserving citizens, and all the rest. But for the first two nights running he had had the lost-in-unknown-levels-of-the-Castle dream, although, the Divine be thanked, without the additional anguish of having Thismet entering into it. But this time the thing in all its full ghastliness had descended on him.

"You were shouting something like, '*tizmit, tizmit, tizmit,*' my lord," Falco said. The name of Thismet would mean nothing to him, of course. There were no more than six people in all the world who knew who she had been. "It was so loud I could hear you from two rooms away. '*Tizmit! Tizmit!*'"

"We are likely to say anything in dreams, Falco. It doesn't have to make sense."

"This must have been a very bad one, my lord. You still look pale. —Here, give me that," he said, reaching behind him to take the flask that Diandolo had just brought into the room. "Can't you hear how sore the Coronal's voice is? —Another drink, my lord?"

Prestimion took the flask. It was brandy, this time. He gulped it down like so much water.

Falco said, "Shall I summon a speaker for your dream, lordship?"

"No one speaks the Coronal's dreams except the Lady of the Isle, Falco. You know that. And the Lady is nowhere within reach." Prestimion rose, a little unsteady on his feet, and went to the window. All was dark outside. It was still the middle of a moonless night here in lovely Fa, that gay and ever-charming city of tier upon tier of pink hillside villas with lacy stone balconies. He braced himself on the windowsill and leaned outward, seeking the cool sweet night air.

Twenty years, and Thismet still haunted him.

She and her brother both were long dead, dead and forgotten, so thoroughly forgotten that even their own father had no idea that they had ever lived. Prestimion's team of mages had seen to that, on the battlefield at Thegomar Edge just after the great victory, when by a colossal act of sorcery they had blotted all knowledge of the Korsibar insurrection from the memory of the world.

But Prestimion had not forgotten. And, even after all these years with Varaile, Varaile whom he loved with a fervor that had never ebbed, Thismet persisted in stealing back into his unguarded mind again and again as he slept. He knew he would never rid himself of the hold she had on him. She had been his dedicated enemy; then had come the astounding thunderbolt of their love; and then, when she had been his for scarcely any time at all, that shattering hour on the battlefield at Thegomar Edge in which he had won his crown and lost his bride almost in the same moment.

"I'll leave you now, my lord," Falco said. "You'll want to get back to sleep. It's still three hours to dawn."

"Leave me, yes," said Prestimion.

But he made no attempt to return to his bed. The dream would only be waiting for him there. He took from its bronze case the portfolio of official documents awaiting his signature that went with him everywhere, and set to work. There were always fifty or a hundred things stored up for him to sign, most of them generated by the ever-busy bureaucrats of the Pontificate, some the work of his own governmental departments.

Much of it was trivial stuff, routine proclamations and decrees, trade treaties between one province and another, revisions of the customs code, the sort of workaday business that other Coronals would have sloughed off on aides to read, so that they would merely need to scan a brief appended summary before signing. The papers from the Labyrinth, which had already been approved by the Pontifex or someone acting in his name, did not even require the Coronal's attention, only his countersignature. In theory the Coronal had the right to reject a Pontifical decree and send it back to the Labyrinth for reconsideration, but no one could remember when any Coronal had last availed himself of the privilege. But Prestimion tried to read as much of this material as he could. In part that was due to an overriding sense of duty; but also he found it oddly comforting, on nights such as these, to immerse himself in such meaningless mind-numbing toil.

Dawn was still an hour or two away when he heard sounds from the courtyard: the gate being opened, the whirring hum of an arriving floater, a deep, commanding voice loudly calling for porters. That was strange, Prestimion thought, someone turning up at the royal lodge at an hour like this, and making so much noise about it at that.

He peered out.

The floater was from the Castle. It bore the royal starburst emblem. A big, heavyset man in a belted ankle-length red tunic had emerged from it. His great chest and shoulders led Prestimion to think at first that this might be Gialaurys; but this man was heftier even than the Grand Admiral, with a jutting gut on him that would make Gialaurys seem almost slender by comparison. And he spoke with the pure accent of Castle Mount, not Gialaurys's broad, flat, almost comical Piliplok intonation. Prestimion realized after a moment that it must be Navigorn.

Here? Why? What had happened?

"Falco!" Prestimion called. The steward was at the door almost immediately. He looked as though he, too, had not gone back to sleep. "Falco, the Lord Navigorn has just arrived. He's in the courtyard. See that he's shown up here right away."

The three flights of stairs left Navigorn winded and flushed. He swayed alarmingly in the doorway for a moment, a tall ungainly figure confronting the compactly built Prestimion. With difficulty he said, "Prestimion, I've—just—come—straight from the—Castle. I set out yesterday afternoon, traveled right on through the night." Gingerly Navigorn lowered his bulky form into one of the chairs beside the window, a finely wrought thing of golden kamateros-wood that creaked and groaned beneath his weight, but held firm. "You don't mind if I sit, do you, Prestimion? Sprinting up those stairs—" He grinned. "I'm not exactly in fighting trim these days."

"Sit. Sit. You take up less space this way." Navigorn elaborately settled himself into place. Patiently Prestimion said, "Why are you here, Navigorn? Do you come with bad news?"

The big man's eyes rose to meet his. He seemed to search a moment for the proper way to begin. "The Pontifex may have had a stroke."

"Ah," Prestimion said, exhaling the word almost as though he had been punched in the chest. "A stroke. *May* have had a stroke, you say?"

"There's no confirmation. I apologize, Prestimion, for awakening you with something like this, but—"

"I was awake, as a matter of fact." Prestimion indicated the papers strewn about his desk. "Tell me about this stroke. This *possible* stroke. "

"A message came from the Labyrinth. Numbness in his hand, stiffness in his leg. Mages have been called in."

"Is he going to die?"

"Who can say? You know how tough the old man is, Prestimion. He's made of iron." A pained expression crossed Navigorn's fleshy face. He turned and twisted so restively in his chair that it creaked a protest. He scowled and screwed up his face. "Yes," he said finally. "Yes, this probably is the beginning of the end for him. Just my guess, you understand. Pure intuition. But the man's ninety years old, he's been Pontifex for twenty years and he was Coronal for forty-odd before that—even iron wears out, you know, sooner or later. I'm sorry, Prestimion."

"Sorry?"

"No Coronal ever wants to go to the Labyrinth."

"But every Coronal eventually does, Navigorn. Do you think this catches me unprepared?" And then, almost as if to contradict his own words, Prestimion went over to the sideboard, where a flask of Muldemar wine was sitting, and poured some into a bowl. "Do you want any?" he asked.

"At this hour of the morning? Yes, actually. Yes, I do."

Prestimion handed him the bowl and poured another for himself. They drank in silence. A cascade of troublesome thoughts thundered through Prestimion's brain.

Pacing about the room, he said, "What do you think I ought to do, Navigorn? Return to the Castle right away and await developments? Or set out for the Labyrinth to pay my respects while his majesty is still alive?"

"Phraatakes Rem doesn't seem to think Confalume's death is imminent. I'd go back to the Castle, if I were you. Meet with the Council, discuss things with the Lady Varaile. And *then* take yourself down to the Labyrinth." Navigorn looked up. Suddenly there was a broad incongruous smile on his face. "This is good wine, Prestimion! From your family's vineyards?"

"There's none better, is there? Some more?"

"Please. Yes."

Prestimion filled the bowls again and they sat thoughtfully sipping the rich purple wine for a time, neither of them speaking.

He found it strangely moving that it was Navigorn, rather than Septach Melayn or Gialaurys or his brother Teotas, who had brought him this unsettling news. He and Navigorn had been friends a long while, he supposed, but their friendship had never been the same sort of intimacy that he had with the others. Indeed, they had even been enemies, once, though Navigorn had no recollection of that. That had been in the time of the Korsibar usurpation, when Navigorn had unhesitatingly given his loyalty to the false Coronal, and had fought valiantly on Korsibar's behalf in the civil war.

But of course Navigorn had not regarded Korsibar as a false Coronal. However unlawfully Confalume's ill-advised son had placed himself upon the throne, however much his seizure of power had violated all custom and convention, he had been duly anointed and crowned, and, so far as the people of Majipoor were concerned, he was the proper Coronal. So of course when Prestimion had challenged Korsibar's legitimacy as king and had gone to war to overthrow him, Navigorn had staunchly served the man he recognized as his king. It was only in the hour of Korsibar's defeat, when the world was in chaos and Prestimion's triumph was assured, that Navigorn had urged Korsibar to surrender and abdicate in order to keep the bloodshed from going on any longer.

But stubborn stupid Korsibar had refused to yield, and had died in the battle of Beldak marsh below Thegomar Edge; and Navigorn, kneeling before Prestimion, had admitted his error and begged forgiveness. Which Prestimion had freely given; and more than that besides. For in the great wiping of the world's memory Navigorn had lost all recollection of the civil war and his role in it as Prestimion's enemy, and so he could readily accept Prestimion's invitation to join his Council, of which he had been a valued member all these years since. Time had turned Navigorn old and gouty and fat, but he had served Prestimion as staunchly as ever he had Korsibar. And here he was now, the one who had volunteered to take on the difficult job of carrying to Prestimion the news that his time as Coronal might nearly be over.

"Do you remember, Prestimion, when we all went to the Labyrinth to wait for Prankipin's death, and the old man lingered on and on and on and we thought he'd never die? Ah, there was a time!"

"There was a time indeed," Prestimion said. "How could I forget it?"

His mind leaped back across the decades to that great gathering, that shining array of young lords that had assembled in the underground city in the final days of the long reign of Prankipin Pontifex: the flower of Majipoor's manhood, the princes of the realm, gathering about the dying old man. Among them, thought Prestimion, so many who were destined to die themselves, a year or three later, fighting on behalf of the usurping Korsibar in the needless, foolish war that he had brought upon the world.

Navigorn, lost now in memories, helped himself to more wine without asking. "You came down from the Castle with Serithorn of Samivole, I recall. Septach Melayn was with you, and Gialaurys, and that other friend of yours, that sneaky little man from Suvrael who called himself a duke—what was his name—?"

"Svor."

"Svor, yes. And then there was good old Kanteverel of Bailemoona, and the Grand Admiral Gonivaul, who had never been to sea, and Duke Oljebbin, and Earl Kamba of Mazadone. Nor should I leave out our vile red-faced friend the Procurator Dantirya Sambail, eh, Prestimion?—and Mandrykarn of Stee—ah, there was a man, that Mandrykarn!—Venta of Haplior, also—" Navigorn shook his head. "And so many of them died young. Wasn't that strange? Kamba, Mandrykarn, Iram of Normork, Sibellor of Banglecode, and plenty of others besides—dead, all dead, much too soon. More's the pity, that. Who'd have known, when we were all together at the Labyrinth, that so many of us would be dead so soon afterward?"

It troubled Prestimion that that thought had occurred to Navigorn too. He waited tensely to see if the other man was going to extend the catalog of the dead: to Korsibar, say. Brawny, swaggering Korsibar had been the most conspicuous figure of all at that gathering of lords in the Labyrinth. But Navigorn did not speak Korsibar's name.

And his reflective mood lifted as quickly as it had come. He smiled, sighed, lifted his wine-bowl in salute. "We had ourselves a time, though—didn't we, Prestimion? We had ourselves a time!"

Navigorn began to talk now of the games they had held at the Labyrinth while waiting for Prankipin to die: the Pontifical Games, they had called them, the grandest tournament of modern times. "The wrestling between Gialaurys and that ape Farholt—I thought they'd kill each other, do you know? It seems like just yesterday. And the archery—you were in your prime, then, Prestimion, you did tricks with your bow that day that no one had seen before, or since, for that matter. Septach Melayn winning the fencing over Count Farquanor and making him look such a helpless fool in the bargain. And who was it in the saber? A big man, dark hair, very strong. His face is right at the edge of my mind, but his name is gone. Who was that? Do you remember, Prestimion?"

"I may have been elsewhere for the saber matches that day," Prestimion said, turning away.

"I can still see the rest of the contests so clearly, though. It *does* seem just like yesterday. Twenty years and more, but just like yesterday!"

Just like yesterday, yes, Prestimion thought.

It had been Korsibar who won the saber contests. He was the big dark-haired man who lurked at the edge of Navigorn's mind. But all recollection of Korsibar's identity had long ago been edited from Navigorn's memory, and that of Thismet, Korsibar's sister, as well, and Prestimion was relieved to see that no recollection of them had crept back into Navigorn in the intervening years.

Nor did Navigorn seem to remember the final dramatic event of those famous Pontifical Games, the morning when the ninety contestants in the jousting had come together in full armor in the Court of Thrones, from which they were supposed to be transported to the Arena as a group. Prince Korsibar had burst into the room shouting the news that death had come at last to the aged Pontifex. The long wait was over. The time finally had come for the changing of the reign, and now the Coronal Lord Confalume would become Pontifex, and Confalume would name as the new Coronal young Prince Prestimion of Muldemar.

Or so everyone expected; but that was not what happened. For a dark cloud of sorcery fell upon the minds of the lords assembled in the Court of Thrones, and when it lifted an incredible scene was revealed. Prince

Korsibar, the Coronal's son, had taken the starburst crown from the startled Hjort who held it and placed it on his own brow, and now was sitting in glory in the place where the Coronal was meant to sit, with his father Confalume, appearing bewildered and almost dazed, seated beside him on the Pontifical throne. And the lords who had conspired with Korsibar to do this thing cried out loudly, "All hail the Coronal Lord Korsibar! Korsibar! Korsibar! Lord Korsibar!"

"Thievery!" was the bellowed answer of Gialaurys. "Thievery! Thievery!" And would have rushed forward into the halberds of Korsibar's guard, but that Prestimion reined him in, for he saw that it was certain death to offer any resistance to the takeover. And thus he and his friends withdrew from the room in astonishment and defeat, and the Coronal's throne was Korsibar's, though it had been the tradition on Majipoor since the earliest days that a Coronal's son might never inherit his father's office.

No, Navigorn had no recollection of any of that, or of the great war that had followed and had cost the lives of so many men great and small. Korsibar in time had been overthrown, and Prestimion's sorcerers had sliced his usurpation out of the history of the world. But that day in the Labyrinth blazed as incandescently as ever in Prestimion's mind, that time when the throne that had been promised to him had been snatched from his grasp by treachery, forcing him to launch that bloody war against his own former friends in order to restore the proper order of things.

Navigorn's voice broke him from his reverie: "Will there be a new set of Pontifical Games, Prestimion, when we all go down to the Labyrinth to wait for Confalume to die?"

"We don't know yet that Confalume is dying," Prestimion said curtly. "But even if he is—more games? No. Not this time, I think."

He looked toward the window. Dawn was breaking over Fa.

Navigorn was probably right, he thought: Confalume's stroke was the herald of the old Pontifex's end, and before very long Majipoor would see yet another change of reign. He would go to the Labyrinth to become Pontifex, and Dekkeret would take his seat atop Castle Mount as Coronal.

Was he ready for that? No, of course not. Navigorn had said it truly: no Coronal ever wants to go to the Labyrinth. But to it he would go, all the same, as was his duty.

Prestimion did wonder how so restless a nature as his was going to abide life in the underground capital. Even the Castle had proven too confining to him; throughout his reign he had roamed constantly about the world, seizing every excuse to visit distant cities. He had made no less than three grand processionals, something that few Coronals before him had done. But his whole reign had been like an unending grand processional for him: he had traveled as no Coronal had ever traveled before.

Of course he would not be *required* to hide himself away in the Labyrinth once he became Pontifex. It was merely the custom. The Pontifex, the senior monarch, was supposed to remain secluded; the young and glorious Coronal, it was, who went forth among the populace to see and be seen. He meant to abide by that rule, up to a point. But only up to a point.

How long is it going to be, he asked himself, before everything changes for me?

The Thismet dream, perhaps, had been an omen. The past was reaching out to reclaim him, and soon they would all replay the time of old Prankipin's death once more. But this time he would have the role of the outgoing Coronal that had been Confalume's then, and Dekkeret would be the new prince moving to the center of the stage.

At least there were no new Korsibars waiting in the wings. He had seen to that. Confalume, when he was Coronal, had let it be known that he had chosen Prestimion to succeed him, but had never formally named him as Coronal-designate, feeling that that was an unseemly thing to do while old Prankipin was still alive. Prestimion had not made that mistake. In the interests of an orderly succession he had already named Dekkeret as his heir, and had explained to his own sons why the sons of a Coronal could never hope to inherit their father's throne.

So all was in order. There was no reason for any forebodings. What would be would be, and everything would go well.

Well, then, Prestimion thought, *let the changes begin.*

He was ready for them. As ready as he ever would be.

To Navigorn he said briskly, "I suppose you're right that I'd do best to return to the Castle before heading down to the Labyrinth. I'll want to have a long talk with Varaile first. And I should meet with the Council, of course—prepare them for the succession—"

The only response was a loud snore. Prestimion glanced back at Navigorn. Navigorn was asleep in his chair.

"Falco!" Prestimion called, opening the door. "Diandolo!"

The steward and the page came running.

"Get everything ready for our departure. We'll leave for the Castle right after breakfast. Diandolo, wake up Prince Taradath and tell him that we're leaving, and that it's my intention to leave on time. Oh, and a message has to go to Duke Emelric of Fa, letting him know that my presence at the Castle has suddenly been required and that with great regret I must cancel the rest of my stay here. Before you do that, though, send a courier off to the Lady Varaile at the Castle with word that I'm on my way back, and—well, that should be enough for now." Quietly, so as not to awaken Navigorn, Prestimion began to gather up the scattered papers of state that covered his desk.

11

A pale, tense face appeared in the doorway of Mandralisca's work-chamber. A hesitant tenor voice said, in not much more than a throaty whisper, "Your grace?"

Mandralisca glanced up. A young man; a boy, more accurately. Green eyes, long straw-colored hair. Earnest, starry-eyed look on his face.

He pushed aside the maps that he had been studying. "I know you, I think. You were with me on the Vorthinar mission, weren't you?"

"Yes, your grace." The boy seemed to be trembling. Mandralisca could hardly hear him. "There is a visitor here who says that he has—"

A visitor? This was not a place where visitors came, this isolated ridgetop settlement above that barren, dry, remorseless valley.

"What did you say? A *visitor?*"

"A visitor, yes, sir."

"Speak up, will you? —Are you afraid of me?"

"Yes, sir."

"And why is that?"

"Because—because—"

"Something about my face? The look in my eyes?"

"You simply are a frightening person, sir." The words came out all in a burst. But the boy was gaining courage. His eyes met Mandralisca's squarely.

"Yes. I am. The truth is that I work at it. I find it a helpful thing to be frightening." Mandralisca indicated with an impatient gesture that he should enter the room instead of hovering at the door. The work-chamber, a circular room with an arched roof and burnt-orange mud-plastered walls, was a small one. The entire house was small: the Five Lords might live in palaces, but they had not bothered to provide one for their privy counsellor. "Where do you come from, boy?"

"Sennec, sir. A town not far downriver from Horvenar."

"How old?"

"Sixteen. —Your visitor, sir, says—"

"Let my damned visitor wait. Let him eat manculain turds while he waits. It's you I'm talking to just now. What's your name?"

"Thastain, sir."

"Thastain of Sennec. The rhythm's a little brusque. *Count* Thastain of Sennec: does that sound better? Thastain, Count of Sennec. Count of Sennec and Horvenar. A certain grandeur, that, wouldn't you say?"

The boy did not reply. His expression was a mixture of bewilderment, fear, and, perhaps, irritation or even anger.

Mandralisca smiled. "You think I'm playing some game with you?"

"Who would ever make me a Count, your grace?"

"Who would ever have made *me* one? But I am. Count Mandralisca of Zimroel: there's real poetry for you! I was a country boy just like you, once, a country boy from the Gonghars. It was Dantirya Sambail who put the title on me, the day before he died. 'You have served me well, Mandralisca, and it's high time I gave you a proper reward.' We were in the jungles of the Stoienzar then. We didn't know they were about to catch up with us. I knelt down and he touched my shoulder with his dagger and proclaimed me a Count right there on the spot, Count of Zimroel, a title that no one had ever had before. The next day Prestimion's men found our camp and the Procurator was killed. But I got away, and I took my Countship with me. —We'll make you a Count too, one of these years, maybe. But first we have to turn the Lord Gaviral into a Pontifex. And the Lord Gavahaud, I suppose, into a Coronal."

That brought only a blank-faced stare, and then a puzzled frown.

Perhaps he had said too much. It was time to send the boy away, Mandralisca realized. There was an odd pleasure in all of this, though: Thastain's innocence was a charming novelty, and Mandralisca himself was in a strangely expansive mood this morning. But he had learned long ago to mistrust pleasure, even to fear it. And he was beginning to feel too relaxed with the boy. That was dangerous.

He said, "Do you happen to know the name of this visitor of mine?"

"Barz—Braj—Barjz—"

"*Barjazid?*"

"Barjazid, yes! That's it, sir! Khaymak Barjazid, of Suvrael!"

Yes. Yes. Mandralisca remembered, now: the correspondence, the offer, the invitation to come. It had all slipped from his mind.

"He's traveled a long way, then, this Khaymak Barjazid. Where is he now?"

"In the compound, sir, where everyone is kept who comes up the valley road from the pungatan desert. The guards at the first gatehouse found him and brought him in. He claims that you and he have business to discuss."

Mandralisca felt a stab of excitement. The Barjazid at last! The new one, the brother, the unexpected survivor. He had taken his time about it. He had been dangling the promise of his arrival for most of the past year. And the promise of other things as well. *I can be of great use to you,* Barjazid had written. *Allow me to visit you and show you what I have.* "Thank you, Count Thastain. Tell him to come in."

Thastain moved toward the door. "I'll fetch him, your grace."

"Yes. Do." But—no, Barjazid should have been here months ago. Let the damned slippery bastard fry out there a little while longer. He was no stranger to desert heat, anyway. And it would not do to seem too eager, now that the man—and, Mandralisca assumed, his wares—finally were here. Overeagerness forfeits you the advantage every time. —"Wait, boy!"

"Sir?"

Mandralisca fashioned his long, tapering fingers into a steeple. "One more question, first, before I let you go. Tell me a little more about yourself. Why did you enroll in the service of the Five Lords? What were you hoping to gain by it?"

"To gain, sir? I don't understand. I wasn't looking to gain anything. It was a matter of my duty, your grace. The Five Lords are the rightful rulers of Zimroel, by descent from the Procurator Dantirya Sambail."

"Very prettily spoken, Count Thastain. I admire your devotion to the cause."

Again the boy headed for the door, as though he could not get himself away from Mandralisca's presence too soon.

Mandralisca said, halting him once more, "Do you know, I wonder, what work I performed when I first entered the retinue of the Procurator Dantirya Sambail?"

"How could I know that, sir?"

"How could you, indeed. I was his poison-taster. A very old-fashioned position, that. Something out of the time of myth and fable. Dantirya Sambail felt that he needed one. Or perhaps he just wanted one, as a kind of ornamental decoration, a bit of medieval pageantry. Whatever was put before him to eat or drink, I tasted first. A snip of his meat, a sip of his wine. He never let anything enter his mouth without trying it on me first. I made quite an impression, do you know, standing at his shoulder during banquets at the Castle or the Labyrinth." Mandralisca smiled a second time: close to the quota for the entire morning, he thought. "Go, now. Fetch me my Barjazid."

12

"S hall I go with you?" Varaile asked. "I could, you know."

"Are you that eager to see the Labyrinth again?"

"No more so than you are, Prestimion. But it's been an age since we traveled together. You aren't trying to avoid me, are you?"

He looked at her in genuine surprise. "Avoid you? You have to be joking. But I want this to be a brief, uncomplicated visit, quickly down, quickly back. He apparently isn't as sick as we thought, after all. I'll meet with him for a couple of days, discuss such important business as there happens to be, offer him my wishes for continued long life and good health, and come home. If I go with you, or Dekkeret, or Septach Melayn or Dembitave, or anybody but a Coronal's minimal traveling retinue, the trip is bound to become a much more involved sort of thing, with all manner of formal events suddenly necessary. I don't want to put him under any kind of strain. And I certainly don't want to show up with so many members of the court that Confalume gets the idea that this is some kind of official farewell visit to a dying man."

"I don't remember suggesting that you take the whole court," Varaile said. "I simply offered to accompany you myself."

Prestimion took her hands in his and brought his face very close to hers. They were almost exactly of the same height. Smiling, he touched the tip of his nose to hers. "You know that I love you," he said softly. "I feel that this is a trip I should make alone. If you want to come with me, I'm not going to stop you. But I'd rather just go down there myself and come back as fast as I can. It isn't as though you and I won't have plenty of time to be in the Labyrinth together in the years to come."

"You *will* come right back, then?"

"This time, yes. The next time I go, it'll be for a longer stay, I'm afraid."

He had had much the same kind of conversation with Dekkeret a little while earlier, and not a very different one with Septach Melayn. They were all treating him as though he, and not Confalume, were the invalid. They viewed the probability of the Pontifex's death as an enormous crisis for him, and wanted to gather around him, to protect and comfort him.

They were right to some degree, of course. It *was* a big thing he was facing—not this visit to the Labyrinth, but the inescapable transition that lay somewhere not far ahead in his life. Did they think, though, that he was likely to break down and burst into tears the moment he set foot in the subterranean capital? Did they believe he was so incapable of dealing with the prospect of becoming Pontifex that he must have his nearest and dearest beside him at all times? How could he explain to them that Coronals lived every day of their lives, day and night, in the awareness that they might become Pontifex at any moment? That possibility was inherent in the job; anyone who was unable to handle it was by that very fact unqualified to be Coronal.

In the end, the only member of his household who went with him was Prince Taradath. The boy had been disappointed by the abrupt termination of his long-promised trip to Fa, and had never seen the Labyrinth, besides. Meeting his majesty the Pontifex would be a memorable thing for him.

And it would be useful for Taradath to get a glimpse, however brief, of the administrative machinery of the Pontificate. Taradath, at fifteen, showed signs of ripening into a worthwhile young man, for whom some good role in the government no doubt would be found when Dekkeret was Coronal. The sons of Coronals, aware that they could never be Coronals themselves, often turned out to be frivolous idlers, or, what was much worse, vainglorious empty-headed boobies like Korsibar. Prestimion hoped for better things from his own boys.

They took the customary route to the Labyrinth, down the River Glayge aboard the royal barge through the fertile agricultural lowlands. At another time Prestimion might have made a little processional out of it, stopping at important river cities like Mitripond or Palaghat or Grevvin, but he had promised Varaile that this would be a quick trip. He entered the Labyrinth through the Mouth of Waters, the gate that Coronals used, and descended swiftly through the many levels of the underground city, past the warrens and burrows that were the offices of the bureaucrats and the grand architectural marvels below them—the Hall of Winds, the Court of Columns, the Place of Masks, and the others, those strangely beautiful places that would seem like places of wonder to anyone who loved the Labyrinth, as Prestimion doubted he ever could—and arrived at last at the deepest level, the imperial sector, where the Pontifex had his lair.

Protocol called for the High Spokesman to the Pontifex, the Labyrinth's ranking official, to greet him. That post had been held for the past five years by the venerable Duke Haskelorn of Chorg, a member of a family that traced its descent from the Pontifex Stalvok of ten reigns earlier. Haskelorn was a man nearly as old as Confalume himself, plump and pink-faced, with long drooping cheeks and a thick roll of flesh below his chin. As was the custom here, he wore the tiny mask across his eyes and the bridge of his nose that was a kind of badge of office among the officials of the Pontificate.

"Confalume—" Prestimion began at once.

"—is in fine health, and looks forward to seeing you at once, Lord Prestimion."

Fine health? What was the High Spokesman's idea of fine health? Prestimion had no idea what to expect. But he was confounded, upon entering the vestibule of the maze of rooms, a labyrinth within the Labyrinth, that was the residence of the Pontifex of Majipoor. A smiling Confalume, formally clad in the ornate scarlet-and-black Pontifical robes, was standing—standing!—in the arched doorway at the vestibule's inner end, holding his arms out toward Prestimion in a warm show of welcome.

Prestimion was so thoroughly taken aback that it was a moment before he could speak, and when he found his tongue the best he could do was stammer, "They told me—that you—you were—"

"Dying, Prestimion? Already well on my way back to the Source, eh? Whatever you may have heard, my son, here's the truth: I am risen from my bed of affliction. As you see, the Pontifex stands on his own two legs. The Pontifex walks. A little stiffly, true, but he walks. He speaks, as well. Not yet dead, Prestimion, not even close to it. —You say nothing.

Speechless with joy, are you? Yes, I suppose you are. You are reprieved from the Labyrinth for a little while longer."

"They said you had had a stroke."

"A little swoon, let's say." The Pontifex held up his left hand and clenched it into a fist. The second and fifth fingers would not close; he had to fold them into place with his other hand. "A minor bit of difficulty here, you see? But very minor. And the left leg—" Confalume took a few steps toward him. "A slight drag, you will notice. My dancing days are over. Well, it is not required of me at my age that I move very quickly. —You could call it a stroke, I suppose, but not a very serious one." And then, noticing Taradath standing behind him: "Your son, is he, Prestimion? Grown almost out of all recognition since last I saw him. When was that, boy, five years ago, seven, when I was at the Castle?"

"Eight years ago, your majesty," said Taradath, all too plainly fighting back his awe. "I was seven years old, then."

"And now you're as tall as your father, not that that's such a difficult thing to achieve. And you've got your mother's dark complexion, too. Well, come in, come in, both of you! Don't just stand there!"

There was a quaver in Confalume's voice, Prestimion observed, and he seemed to have acquired an old man's garrulity as well. But he appeared to be in phenomenally fine shape. Confalume had always been a man of more than usual vigor and stamina, of course. Even now, his stocky frame was still muscular-looking and his sweeping thatch of hair, though it had long since turned white, was as thick as ever. Only the soft, papery texture of his cheeks betrayed the Pontifex's great age in any meaningful way. And he did seem to have thrown off all but the most trifling signs of the stroke that had caused such excitement throughout both capitals of the realm.

He led Prestimion and Taradath within. Few visitors ever ventured into the private Pontifical chambers. Confalume's famed collection of treasures decorated every sill and alcove and shelf: figurines of spun glass, carvings of dragon-ivory inlaid with porphyry and onyx, jeweled caskets, a whole forest of strange trees fashioned from strands of woven silver, ancient coins and mounted insects, leather-bound volumes of antique lore, and ever so much more, the hoard of a long acquisitive lifetime surrounding him on all sides. Nor had the Pontifex lost his fascination for the arts of wizardry, either: there were his cherished instruments of magic, still, his ammatepalas and veralistias and his armillary spheres, his rohillas and his protospathifars, his powders and potions and ointments. Perhaps, thought Prestimion, the old man had somehow been able to magic himself up out of his deathbed: certainly if faith in occult matters was sufficient to bring it about, Confalume would live forever.

The Pontifex poured wine for Prestimion and himself, and then for Taradath as well, and showed the boy through some of his rooms of fanciful objects, and engaged them in pleasant superficial conversation about their journey down the Glayge, and current construction projects at the Castle, and the activities of the Lady Varaile, and the like. It was all very charming and not in any way how Prestimion had expected the visit to unfold.

Taradath was no longer awed. He seemed to see the Pontifex as no more than a kindly old grandfather, now.

"Were these men all Pontifexes too?" he asked, pointing to the long row of painted medallions along the upper wall of the room.

"Indeed so," Confalume replied. "This is Prankipin here—you do remember him, of course, don't you, Prestimion?—and Gobryas who was just before him—Avinas—Kelimiphon—Amyntilir—" He could put a name to each portrait. "Dizimaule—Kanaba—Sirruth—Vildivar—"

Listening to Confalume go on and on, reciting the names of his predecessors for thousands of years, Prestimion felt a humbling sense of the immensity of history, that great soaring arch that disappeared at its farther end into the mists of myth, and in which could be found, at the end that was anchored in the present day, none other than his own self.

Most of these men were little more than names to Prestimion. The achievements of the Pontifexes Kanaba and Sirruth and Vildivar were known only to historians now. More recent ones, Gobryas, Avinas, Kelimiphon, yes, he knew something about them, though from all accounts they had been mediocre rulers. The world had come into hard times under the uninspired rule of such men as Gobryas and Avinas. But Prestimion, looking upward at that long array of faces, had a sudden awareness of himself as part of an extraordinary modern dynasty.

Prankipin, up there, Coronal for twenty years or so and Pontifex for forty-three, had inherited a weak and troubled world from his predecessor Gobryas and by wise measures and dynamic leadership had returned it to its former grandeur. If toward the end he had given way to the folly of sorcery and allowed the world to swarm with wizards, well, it was a forgivable flaw for a man who had accomplished so much. Then here was Confalume, not yet a portrait on the wall but an actual breathing man, Pontifex these twenty years past and Coronal forty-three more before that, who had built on Prankipin's glorious foundation and seen to it that prosperity became even more general among Majipoor's fifteen billion people. He, too, needed to be forgiven for his passion for magic, but that was easy enough, Prestimion thought.

And now it was the turn of Prestimion of Muldemar, Lord Prestimion now, Prestimion Pontifex one day to be. Would he be deemed a worthy successor to the great Prankipin and the splendid Confalume? Perhaps so. Majipoor was thriving under his guidance. He had made mistakes, yes, but so had Prankipin, so had Confalume. His own greatest achievement was that he had saved the world from misrule under Korsibar; but no one would ever know that. Had he achieved anything else worthwhile? Certainly he hoped that he had; but he of all people was in no position to know. He was still young, though. He would eventually, so he profoundly hoped and believed, be ranked with those other two as architects of a golden age.

"And is this Stiamot?" Taradath asked.

"He's farther down the row, boy. Of course, the artist had to guess at what he really looked like, but there he is. Here—let me show you—"

Amazingly spry, the damaged left leg dragging only a little, Confalume went shuffling toward the far side of the room. Prestimion watched him going from portrait to portrait with Taradath, calling off the names of the early emperors.

The boy remained down there, peering up solemnly at the faces of Pontifexes who had ruled this world when Stiamot himself was a thousand years unborn. Confalume, returning to where Prestimion still sat, refilled their wine-bowls and said, in a low, confidential tone, "The true reason you came scurrying down here was that you thought I was dying, wasn't it? You wanted to check my condition out with your own eyes."

"I don't know what I thought. But the news out of the Labyrinth about you was very worrisome. It seemed appropriate to pay you a visit. A man of your age, suffering a stroke—"

"I actually thought I was dying myself, as I felt it hit. But only while it was happening. I'm a long way from finished, Prestimion."

"May it truly be so."

"Are you saying that for my sake, or yours?" the Pontifex asked.

"Do you know how unkind that sounds?"

Confalume laughed. "But it's realistic, yes? You don't at all want to be Pontifex yet."

Prestimion cast a wary glance toward Taradath, who was practically at the end of the hall, now, probably beyond earshot. There was a touch of testiness in his voice as he responded, "All of Majipoor wishes you continued good health and long life, your majesty. I am no exception to that. But I do assure you that if the Divine should choose to gather you in tomorrow, I am in every way ready to do what will be asked of me."

"Are you? Well, yes, you say you are, and I must take that at face value, I suppose." The Pontifex closed his eyes. He seemed to be staring into some infinite recess of time. Prestimion studied the tiny fluttering pulses in the old man's veined eyelids, and waited, and continued to wait. Had he fallen asleep? But then, abruptly, Confalume was looking straight at him again, and the keen gray eyes were as penetrating as ever. "I do remember sitting down here with you a long while ago, your first visit here after becoming Coronal, and telling you that after you'd had the job for forty years or so you'd be quite willing to move on to the Labyrinth. Do you recall that?"

"Yes. I do."

"You're halfway to that forty years, now. So you must be at least half sincere when you tell me you're ready to take over. But have no fear, Prestimion. There's still twenty years more to go." Confalume pointed toward the tabletop that bore his collection of astrological devices. "It happens that I cast my horoscope only last week. Unless there was some serious error in my calculations, I'm going to live to the age of a hundred and ten. I'm going to have the longest reign of any Pontifex in the history of Majipoor. What do you say to that, Prestimion? You are relieved, aren't you? Confess it! You are! At least right now, you are. —But I can tell you, my young friend, you'll be utterly sick of being Coronal by the time I make my trip back to the Source. You won't mind leaving the Castle at all. A time will come when you'll be eager to be Pontifex, believe me. You'll be more than ready to retire to the Labyrinth, believe me—more than ready!"

On the way back up the Glayge Prestimion pondered Confalume's words. He had to admit that he had been deceiving himself, if nobody else, in claiming that he was fully ready to let the Pontificate descend upon him. His relief at finding Confalume in this unexpected state of well-being was the unanswerable proof of that. It was a reprieve, unquestionably a reprieve; which meant that he still thought of becoming Pontifex as a grim and inexorable sentence, rather than simply a matter of duty. Though he very much doubted the worth of Confalume's astrological calculations, the evidence seemed to indicate that it still would be a matter of some years before the world had its next change of rulers.

There was no getting around the fact that his mood was very much lighter now. That told him all he needed to know about his insistent professions of readiness for life in the Labyrinth.

Before departing for the Castle, he took Taradath on a brief tour of the city. The boy had seen wonders aplenty already in his short life, but the strangeness of the Labyrinth was like nothing else in the world, these vast echoing halls of curious design that lay so far underground. "The Pool of Dreams, this is called," Prestimion said, gesturing toward the calm greenish water in whose depths mysterious images constantly came and went, some of supernal beauty, some of nightmare repulsiveness, one moment's scene altogether different from another. "No one knows how it works. Or even which Pontifex put it here."

The Place of Masks, where huge bodiless blind-eyed faces rose on marble stalks. The Court of Pyramids, a zone of thousands of close-set white monoliths, purposeless, inexplicable. The Hall of Winds, where cold air emerged in great bursting gusts from stone grids, though they were deep beneath the surface of the world. The Court of Globes—the Cabinet of Floating Swords—the Chamber of Miracles—the Temple of Unknown Gods—

The next day Prestimion and his son took the swift shaft to the surface and returned to the Mouth of Waters, where the royal barge was waiting to carry them upriver to the Castle. But they had only reached Maurix, three days' journey north of the Labyrinth, when they were overtaken by a fast-moving rivercraft that flew the Pontifical flag.

The messenger who came on board had but to speak two words and Prestimion knew what had happened.

"Your majesty—"

It was the phrase one used when addressing a Pontifex. The rest of the story followed only too quickly. Confalume was dead, most suddenly, of a second stroke. Prestimion would have to return to the Labyrinth to preside over his final rites and begin the process of taking over the Pontifical duties.

13

*T*he resemblance was an astonishing one, Mandralisca thought.

Venghenar Barjazid, the dead one, he of the devilish mind-controlling machines, had been an evil-looking little man whose eyes were not quite of the same size or color nor even set on a straight line in his head, and whose lips slid away sideways toward the left side to give him a permanent smirk, and whose skin, dark and leathery and thick from a lifetime of exposure to the ferocious Suvrael sunlight, was as wrinkled and folded as a canavong's hide.

Mandralisca found this new Barjazid just as charmingly repellent as his elder brother had been. A powerful intuition told him, from his very first glimpse of the man, that he had found a significant ally in the contest for world power that lay ahead.

This one was every bit as mean and scrawny of form and disagreeable of visage as his late brother. His eyes too were mismated and misaligned and had the same harsh brightness; his lips too were drawn off into a mocking grimace; he too had the folded, blackened skin of one who has lived too long in barren sun-blasted Suvrael. He looked a shade taller than Venghenar had been, perhaps, and just a touch less self-assured. Mandralisca supposed that he was around fifty: older, now, than Venghenar had been when he had brought his pack of devices to Dantirya Sambail.

And he, too, seemed to have come bearing merchandise. He had brought with him into the room a shapeless, bulging leather-trimmed cloth bag, frayed at the center, which he set down very carefully by his side when he took the seat that Mandralisca offered. Mandralisca gave the bag a quick sidelong glance. The things must be in there, he felt certain: the new collection of useful toys that the Barjazid had brought here to sell to him.

But Mandralisca was never in a hurry to enter into any sort of negotiation. It is essential, he believed, that one must first determine who is going to have the upper hand. And that one will be the one who has the greater willingness to delay getting down to the heart of the matter.

"Your grace," said Barjazid, with a smarmy little bow. "What a pleasure to meet at last. My late brother spoke of you to me with the highest praise."

"We worked well together, yes."

"It's my fervent hope that you'll say the same of me."

"Mine as well. —How did you know where to find me? And why did you think I'd have any reason to want to see you?"

"In truth I thought you had perished long ago, on that same day in the Stoienzar when my brother died. But then word reached me that you had escaped, and were alive and well and living somewhere in this region."

"Word of my whereabouts reached as far as Suvrael?" Mandralisca asked. "I find that surprising."

"Word travels, your grace. Also I have some knowledge of how to make inquiries. I learned that you were here; that you were in the employ of the five sons of one of the Procurator's brothers, and that they perhaps had some thought of regaining the power in Zimroel that their famous uncle once had wielded; and I felt that I might be able to assist you in that enterprise. And so I sent you a message to that effect."

"And took your sweet time getting here," Mandralisca said. "Your letter indicated that you'd be here almost a year ago. What happened?"

"There were delays en route," said Khaymak Barjazid. The quick reply seemed to Mandralisca to be a shade too glib. "You must understand, your grace, that it's a long journey from Suvrael to here."

"Not *that* long. I interpreted your letter to mean that you wanted to meet with me right away. Obviously that was incorrect."

Barjazid looked at him appraisingly. The tip of his tongue slipped into view for an instant, flickering like a serpent's. Softly he said, "I came here by way of Alhanroel, your grace. The shipping schedule favored that route. Besides, I have a nephew, my only living kinsman, in the service of the Coronal at Castle Mount. I wanted to see him again before I headed this way."

"Castle Mount, as I recall it, lies some thousands of miles distant from the nearest seaport."

"The Mount is somewhat out of the way, I admit. But it has been many years since I last had the pleasure of speaking with my brother's son. If I am to give my allegiance to you here in Zimroel, as is my hope, I will probably never have another chance for that."

"I know about that nephew," Mandralisca said. He also had known about Khaymak Barjazid's visit to Castle Mount; but it was a point in Barjazid's favor that the man had volunteered to reveal it himself. Mandralisca steepled his fingers and peered contemplatively at Barjazid over their tips. "Your nephew turned traitor against his own father, is that not so? It was with your nephew's invaluable assistance that Prestimion was able to weaken Dantirya Sambail and leave him vulnerable to the attack that cost the Procurator his life. One might even say that your brother's death in the same battle was also your nephew's direct responsibility. What sort of love can you feel for such a person, kinsman or no? Why would you want to visit him?"

Barjazid shifted about uneasily. "Dinitak was only a boy when he did those things. He came under Prince Dekkeret's influence, and let himself be swept up in a flight of youthful enthusiasm for Lord Prestimion, and that led to consequences that I know he could not have foreseen. I wanted to find out whether over the years he had come to see the error of his ways: whether there could be any reconciliation between us."

"And—?"

"It was asinine of me to think that such a thing was possible. He's still Prestimion's man through and through, and Dekkeret's. They own him completely. I should have known better than to expect to find any trace of family feeling in him. He refused even to see me."

"How sad." Mandralisca did not even try to sound compassionate. "You went all the way to the Castle, and your visit was for nought!"

"Sir, I could get no closer to the Castle than the city of High Morpin. By my nephew's explicit orders, I was denied permission to approach any nearer than that."

A very touching story, Mandralisca thought. But not an entirely convincing one.

It was easy enough to find a more likely explanation for Khaymak Barjazid's lengthy detour to Castle Mount. Quite likely the thought had occurred to him, after he had decided to sell his services to the

Five Lords, that there might be a better price available elsewhere. There was no question that this man was carrying valuable merchandise in that worn bag. Obviously, too, he was looking to peddle it to the highest bidder; and the world's deepest pockets belonged to Lord Prestimion.

If Dinitak Barjazid had been willing to spend just five minutes listening to his uncle's blandishments, this conversation would not now be happening, Mandralisca knew. A lucky thing for us, he told himself, that the younger Barjazid has the good taste to want to have nothing to do with his disreputable uncle.

"An unhappy adventure," he said. "But at least you have it out of your system. And now—perhaps somewhat later than I expected you would—you do at last show up here."

"No one regrets the delay more than I do, your grace. But indeed, I am here." He smiled, revealing a set of nasty snags. "And I have brought with me those certain things to which I alluded in my letter."

Mandralisca glanced once more at the bag. "Which are contained in that?"

"They are."

He took that as his cue. "Very well, my friend. Has the point arrived, do you think, at which we can begin discussing our business?"

"We have already begun our business, your grace," said Khaymak Barjazid calmly, making no movement toward the bag. Mandralisca gave him some points for that. Barjazid also knew the dangers of overeagerness, and was testing his ability to make Mandralisca wait. It was rare that he found himself outplayed like this.

Very well. He would allow Barjazid a small victory here. He waited, saying nothing now.

Again the tongue-tip briefly flickered forth. "You know, I think, that before my lamented brother came into the employ of the Procurator Dantirya Sambail, he operated a guide service in Suvrael, among other enterprises. Prior to that he spent some years at the Castle, serving as an aide to Duke Svor of Tolaghai, a close friend of Prestimion, who was merely Prince of Muldemar then. There was also at the Castle then a certain Vroon, Thalnap Zelifor by name, who—"

Mandralisca felt a burst of irritation. This was overdoing it. Having seized the advantage, Barjazid was all too evidently reveling in his control of the conversation. "Where is this story heading?" Mandralisca demanded. "Back to Lord Stiamot, is it?"

"If I might have your indulgence one moment more, sir."

Again he allowed himself to subside. There had been a wondrously oily way about Barjazid's saying that that Mandralisca was forced to admire. This man was a worthy adversary.

Barjazid continued unruffledly. "If you are aware of these matters already, forgive me. I want only to clarify my own role in my brother's affairs, with which you may not be familiar."

"Go on."

"Permit me to remind you that this Thalnap Zelifor, a wizard by trade as people of his race tend to be, was a maker of devices capable of penetrating the secrets of a person's mind. Prestimion, when he became Coronal, exiled this Vroon for some reason to Suvrael, and placed my brother in charge of escorting him there. Unfortunately the Vroon died en route; but he had been good enough, first, to give my brother some instruction in the art of using his devices, a number of which he had brought with him from the Castle."

"None of this is new to me, so far."

"But you will not have known that I, since I have a certain gift for mechanical matters, assisted my brother in experimenting with these things and gaining knowledge of their operation. Later, I even designed some improved models of them. All this was in Tolaghai city in Suvrael, many years ago. Then came the episode—perhaps you are aware of it, sir—when Prince Dekkeret, then a very young man and not yet a prince, visited Suvrael about that time, had a rather unfortunate encounter with my brother and his son, and took them both as prisoners to Castle Mount, along with much of the mind-reading equipment."

"Your brother told me that, yes."

"Likewise you know that my brother, escaping from the Castle, fled to western Alhanroel and made common cause with Dantirya Sambail."

"Yes," said Mandralisca. "I was there when he arrived. I was there, also, when Prestimion, using one of these devices that had been brought to him by your nephew Dinitak, made it possible for an army under Gialaurys and Septach Melayn to locate our camp and kill both the Procurator and your brother, and very nearly myself as well. The mind-reading devices all fell into Prestimion's hands. I assume he has them locked safely away somewhere at the Castle."

"Very likely he does."

Mandralisca looked yet again, more pointedly this time, at Khaymak Barjazid's battered, bulging bag. Enough of this recitation of ancient history: the sly little man was carrying the game too far. Mandralisca would not be toyed with any longer.

In a brusque, cool tone he said, "This is a sufficient prologue, I think. Many tasks await me today. Show me what you have for me, now."

Barjazid smiled. He drew the bag up on his knees and pressed his fingers to its latch. From within he drew a sheaf of parchment sheets, which he unrolled and spread out over the open lid of the bag. "These are the original plans for Thalnap Zelifor's various instruments of mind control. They have remained in my possession in Suvrael ever since the time when my brother was carried off to the Mount as Dekkeret's prisoner."

"May I see them?" Mandralisca reached forth a hand.

"Of course, your grace. Here are the sketches for three successive models of the device, each one of greater power than the one before. This is the first. This is the one that my nephew stole and delivered to Lord Prestimion for use against my brother. And this is the one that my brother himself was wearing in the climactic battle when Prestimion broke through his defenses."

Mandralisca riffled through the parchment sheets. Barjazid was safe in showing them to him: they made no sense to him whatever.

"And those?" he said, nodding toward several other sheets still in Khaymak Barjazid's hands.

"The designs for later models, still more powerful, of which I spoke a moment ago. In the intervening years I've continued to play with the Vroon's basic concepts. I believe that I have made some important advances in the state of the art."

"You only *believe*?"

"I have not yet had the opportunity to perform tests."

"Out of fear that you'd be detected by Prestimion's people?"

"In part, yes. But also—these are very expensive things to manufacture, sir—you must bear in mind that I am not a wealthy man—"

"I see." They were being invited to finance the Barjazid's research. "So the truth is you have no working models, then."

"I have this," Barjazid said, and drew a flimsy-looking metal helmet from the bag. It was a shimmering lacework of delicate red strands interwoven with gold ones, with a triple row of heavier bronze cords running over its crest. Its design was far simpler than that of the one Mandralisca remembered the other Barjazid wearing in the final struggle in the Stoienzar. That was probably due, to some degree, to a greater refinement of the concept. But the thing seemed *too* simple. It seemed incomplete, unfinished.

"What can it do?" Mandralisca asked.

"In its present form? Nothing. The necessary connections are not yet in place."

"And if they were?"

"If they were, the wearer of the helmet could reach out to anyone in the world and place dreams in his mind. Very powerful dreams, your grace. Frightening dreams. *Painful* dreams, if that were desired. Dreams that could break a person's will. That could beat him to the ground and make him beg for mercy."

"Indeed," Mandralisca said.

He ran his fingers slowly over the lacy meshes, exploring them, fondling them. He draped the helmet over his head, spreading it out, noting how light it was, scarcely noticeable. He took it off and folded it and folded it again, until it was small enough to fit within his closed hand. He weighed it on his outstretched palm. He nodded approvingly, but did not say anything. Perhaps a minute went by. Perhaps more.

Khaymak Barjazid watched the entire performance with what could only be interpreted as mounting anxiety and concern.

Finally he said, "Do you think you would have use for such a device, your grace?"

"Oh, yes. Yes, certainly. But will it work?"

"It can be made to. All of the instruments shown on these plans can be made to work. It merely requires money."

"Yes. Of course." Mandralisca stood up, went to the door, stood staring out into the brightness of the desert morning for a long while. He tossed the Barjazid helmet lightly from hand to hand. What would it be like, he wondered, to be able to send dreams into the mind of one's enemy? Painful dreams, Barjazid had said. Nightmares. Worse than nightmares. A host of terrifying images. Things fluttering by, dangling on fine metal wires. An endless army of big black beetles marching across the floor, making ugly rustling sounds with their feet. Transparent fingers tickling the channels of the mind. Slow spirals of pure fear congealing and twisting in the tortured brain. And—gradually—a sobbing, a whimpering, a begging for mercy—

"Come outside with me," he said to Barjazid over his shoulder, without looking back toward the other man.

They walked up the ridge to a point where several of the domed palaces of the Lords could be seen in the distance. "Do you know what those buildings are?" Mandralisca asked.

"They are the dwellings of the Five Lords. The boy who brought me to you told me that."

"So you know that they call themselves the Five Lords, do you? What else do you know about them?"

"That they are the sons of one of Dantirya Sambail's brothers. That they have lately laid claim to power in certain sectors of central Zimroel. That they have taken upon themselves the title of Lords of Zimroel."

"You knew all those things when you wrote me that letter?"

"All but the part about their calling themselves the Lords of Zimroel."

"Why would news of any of these matters have traveled all the way down to Suvrael?"

"I told you, your grace, I have some skill at making inquiries."

"Apparently you do. The Coronal himself, so far as I know, is ignorant of what's been going on in this part of Zimroel."

"But when he finds out—?"

"Why, there'll be war, I suppose," Mandralisca said. He swung about to face the little man. "I propose to speak very directly, now. These five Lords of Zimroel are stupid and vicious men. I despise everything about them. As you get to know them, so will you. Nevertheless, there are millions of people here in Zimroel who regard them as the rightful heirs of Dantirya Sambail and will follow their banner, once it is openly raised, in a war of independence against the Alhanroel government. Which I believe we can win, with your aid."

"That would please me greatly. It was Prestimion and his people who destroyed my brother."

"You'll have your revenge, then. Dantirya Sambail tried twice to overthrow Prestimion, but because he was already master of Zimroel he attempted both times to carry the insurrection into Alhanroel. That was a mistake. The Coronal and Pontifex can't be beaten in their own territory by invaders from Zimroel. Alhanroel is too big to be conquered from outside, and lines of supply can't be sustained across thousands of miles. But the opposite is also true. No army from the other continent could ever subjugate all of Zimroel."

"You intend to establish Zimroel as a separate nation, then?"

"Why not? *Why* should we be subservient to Alhanroel? What advantage to us is there in being governed by a king and an emperor who live half a world away from us? I will proclaim one of the five brothers, the most intelligent one, as Pontifex of Zimroel. One of the others will be his Coronal. And we will be free of Alhanroel at last."

"There is a third continent," said Barjazid. "Do you have some plan in mind for Suvrael?"

"No," said Mandralisca. The question took him by surprise. He realized that he had given Suvrael no thought at all. "But if it cares to make itself independent too, I suppose that could be managed easily enough. Prestimion's not such a fool as to try to send an army down into your horrifying deserts, and if he did the heat would kill them all in six months, anyway."

An avid glitter appeared in Barjazid's mismatched eyes. "Suvrael would have its own king, then."

"It could. It could indeed." He saw suddenly what Barjazid was driving at, and a broad grin crossed his face. "Bravo, my friend! Bravo! You've named the price for your assistance, haven't you? Khaymak the First of Suvrael! Well, let it be so. I congratulate you, your highness!"

"I thank you, your grace." Barjazid gave him a warm smile of appreciation and fellowship. "A Pontifex of Zimroel . . . a king of Suvrael . . . And what role do you see for yourself, Count Mandralisca, once these brothers are established on their thrones?"

"I? I'll be privy counsellor, as I am now. They'll continue to need someone to tell them what to do. And I'll be the one who tells them."

"Ah. Yes, of course."

"We understand each other, I think."

"I think we do. What's the next move, then?"

"Why, you have to build us your devilish machines. That'll allow us to start making life difficult for Prestimion."

"Very good. I propose to set up a workshop right away in Ni-moya, and—"

"No," Mandralisca said. "Not Ni-moya. *Here* is where you'll do your work, your highness."

"Here? I'll need special equipment—materials—skilled workmen, perhaps. In a remote desert outpost like this, I can't possibly—"

"You can and will. A Suvraelinu like you shouldn't have any problem dealing with desert conditions. We'll bring in whatever you need from Ni-moya. But you have joined us now, my friend. This is your place, now. Here is where you'll stay, and live and do your work, until the war is won."

"You make it seem as though you don't trust me, your grace."

"I trust no one, my friend. Not even myself."

14

*D*ekkeret returned to the Castle by the quickest route, taking the Grand Calintane Highway, which terminated in the broad open space paved with smooth green porcelain cobblestones that was the Dizimaule Plaza. His floater passed over the huge starburst in golden tilework that lay at its center and carried him through the great Dizimaule Arch, the main entrance to the Castle, the gateway to the southern wing. The guards stationed in the guardhouse on the arch's left side waved to him as he passed through, and he acknowledged their salute with a brief, stiff one of his own.

There was an air of barely suppressed tension in the corridors of the Castle as he made his way inward. The faces of those who greeted him at each checkpoint were tightly drawn and solemn; lips were clamped, eyes were hooded.

"From the look of them all," he said to Dinitak, "it would be easy enough to believe that the Pontifex has died in the time it took us to get back here from Normork."

"You would know it already, I think," said Dinitak.

"I suppose I would."

Yes. They would be hailing him as Coronal, would they not, if Confalume had died? People kneeling, making the starburst salute, calling out the traditional cry: "Dekkeret! Lord Dekkeret! All hail Lord Dekkeret! Long life to Lord Dekkeret!" Even though he would not truly become Coronal until the Council had given its assent and Prestimion had formally proclaimed him. But everyone knew who the next Coronal was going to be.

Lord Dekkeret. How strange that sounded to him! How difficult for his mind to encompass!

"It's simply a disquieting time for everyone," Dinitak said. "It must always be this way, when a change of reign is in the air. The old masters leave the Castle; new ones arrive; nothing will be the same again for anyone who lives here." They were at the threshold of the Inner Castle now. The Ninety-Nine Steps rose before them. There they paused. Dinitak's rooms were on this level, far off to the left; Dekkeret lived above, in the suite in the Munnerak Tower that once had been occupied by Prestimion. "I should leave you here," Dinitak said. "You'll need to meet with the Council—with the Lady Varaile, too, I imagine—"

"Thank you for accompanying me to Normork," Dekkeret said. "For sitting through those deadly banquets, and all the rest."

"No need for thanks. I go where you ask me to go."

They embraced quickly, and then Dinitak was gone.

Dekkeret mounted the ancient, well-worn steps two at a time. *Lord Dekkeret,* he thought. *Lord Dekkeret. Lord Dekkeret. Lord Dekkeret.* Astonishing. Unbelievable.

It had not yet happened, though. No new bulletins had come from the Labyrinth since he had received the message summoning him back from Normork. Septach Melayn, the first member of the Council Dekkeret encountered after entering the Inner Castle, was the one who provided him with that news.

The long-shanked swordsman was waiting for him in the little square outside the Prankipin Treasury, just at the top of the Ninety-Nine Steps. "You made a fast journey of it, Dekkeret! We didn't expect you until tomorrow."

"I left as soon as I got the message. Where's Prestimion?"

"Halfway down the Glayge on his way to the Labyrinth, I expect. Came whistling back from Fa the moment we got the news, spent about three minutes with the Lady Varaile, and turned right around and headed south. Wants to pay his respects to old Confalume, you know, while there's still the chance. I'm surprised you didn't pass him on the way up."

"Then Confalume is still—"

"Alive? So far as we know, he is," said Septach Melayn. "Of course, it takes so damned long for us to find anything out up here of what's going on down below. Phraatakes Rem says the stroke isn't a serious one."

"Can we trust him? It's in his interest to maintain as long as he can that his master the Pontifex is still running the show. I know of cases where the death of a Pontifex has been covered up for weeks. Months."

Septach Melayn said, with a shrug, "Of that, my lad, what can I say? For my own part, I'd prefer that Confalume go on being Pontifex for the next fifty years. I understand that you might very well hold a different position about that."

"No," Dekkeret said, catching hold of Septach Melayn's wrist and putting his face very near to the older man's. He was one of a very few Castle princes who came close to matching Septach Melayn in height. "No," he said again, in a low, dark tone. "You are altogether mistaken in that, Septach Melayn. If the Divine means me to be Coronal someday, well, I'll be ready for the task, whenever it comes to me. But I am in no way eager for it to come before its time. Anyone who thinks otherwise is in great error."

Septach Melayn smiled. "Easy, Dekkeret! I meant no offense. None whatever. Come: I'll see you to your rooms, so you can refresh yourself after your journey. The Council will be in session later this afternoon in the Stiamot throne-room. You should attend, if you will."

"I'll be there," said Dekkeret.

But it was a pointless, useless meeting. What was there to say? The highest levels of the government were in a kind of paralysis. The Pontifex had suffered a stroke, perhaps was on the verge of dying, might even already have died. The Coronal had gone off to the Labyrinth, as was appropriate, to attend the bedside of the senior monarch. In both capitals the ordinary functions of the bureaucracy continued as usual, but the ministers who directed those functions found themselves caught in stasis, not knowing from one day to the next how long it would be before they would have to leave office.

Without any real information to work with, the members of the Council could only offer up high-minded statements of hope that the Pontifex would recover his faculties and continue his long and glorious reign. But the uncertainty left its mark on every face. When Confalume died, some of these men would be asked to join the administration of the new Pontifex at the Labyrinth, and others, passed over by the incoming Coronal, would be forced into retirement after many years close to the mainsprings of power. Either alternative carried with it its own problems; and no one could be certain of what would be offered him.

All eyes were on Dekkeret. But Dekkeret had his own destinies to consider. He said little during the meeting. It behooved him to remain quiet during this ambiguous period. A Coronal-designate is a very different thing from a Coronal.

When it was over, he retreated to his private apartments. He had a pleasant suite, by no means the grandest of its kind; but it had been good enough for Prestimion when he was the Coronal-designate, and Dekkeret found it more than satisfactory. The rooms were large and well arranged, and the view, through great curving multi-faceted windows, the work of cunning craftsmen from Stee, was a spectacular one into the abyss called the Morpin Plunge that bordered this wing of the Castle.

He met briefly with his personal staff: Dalip Amrit, the tactful one-time schoolmaster from Normork who was his private secretary, and bustling, hyperefficient Singobinda Mukund, the master of the household, a ruddy-faced Ni-moyan, and Countess Auranga of Bibiroon, who served as his official hostess in the absence of any consort. They brought him up to date on the events of his absence from the Castle. Then he sent them away, and slipped gratefully into the great bathing-tub of black Khyntor marble for a long quiet soak before dinner.

It was his thought to eat alone and get to sleep early. But he had scarcely donned his dressing gown after his bath when Dalip Amrit came to him with word that the Lady Varaile requested his presence at dinner that evening in the royal residence at Lord Thraym's Tower, if he had no other plans.

One did not treat invitations from the Coronal's consort casually. Dekkeret changed into formal costume, a long-waisted golden doublet and close-fitting violet hose trimmed with velvet stripes, and arrived punctually at the royal dining-hall.

He was, it seemed, the only guest. That surprised him just a little; he would have expected Septach Melayn, perhaps, or Prince Teotas and the Lady Fiorinda, or some other members of the inner court. But Varaile alone awaited him, so simply dressed in a long green tunic and a wide-sleeved yellow overblouse that he felt abashed by his own formality.

She presented her cheek for a kiss. They had always been close friends, he and the Lady Varaile. She was no more than a year or two older than he was, and, like him, had been snatched up suddenly out of a commoner's life to make her home among the lords and ladies of the Castle. But she had been born to wealth and privilege, the daughter of the infinitely rich merchant banker Simbilon Khayf of the great city of Stee, whereas he was only the son of a hapless itinerant salesman; and so Dekkeret had always looked up to Varaile as someone who moved easily and comfortably among the aristocracy of the Mount, while he had had to master the knack of it slowly and with great difficulty, as one might learn some advanced kind of mathematics.

Over bowls of golden-brown Sippulgar dates and warm milk laced with the red brandy of Narabal she asked him pleasantly about his visit to Normork. She spoke fondly of his mother, whom she liked greatly; and she told him a few quick bits of Castle gossip that had reached her ears while he was away, lively if insignificant tales of tangled intrigues involving certain men and women of the court old enough to have known better. It was as if nothing in any way unusual had taken place in the world lately.

Then she said, as a course of pale-fleshed quaalfish simmered in sweet wine was set before them, "You know, of course, that Prestimion has gone to the Labyrinth?"

"Septach Melayn told me this afternoon. Will the Coronal be gone long?"

"As long as is necessary, I would think." Varaile turned her huge, dark, glowing eyes on him with sudden unexpected intensity. "*This* time he'll return to the Castle when he's done. But the next time he goes there—"

"Yes. I know, lady."

"You have no reason to look so stricken. For you it will mean the call to greatness, Dekkeret. But for me—for Lord Prestimion—for our children—"

She stared at him reproachfully. That struck him as unwarranted: did she think him so insensitive that he would not understand her predicament? But for love of her he kept his voice gentle. "Yet in truth, Varaile, the death of the Pontifex means the same thing for us all: *change*. Huge and incomprehensible change. You and yours go to the Labyrinth; I don a crown and take my seat on the Confalume Throne. Do you think I'm any less apprehensive than you are about what is to come?"

She softened a little. "We should not quarrel, Dekkeret."

"Are we quarreling, lady?"

She left the question unanswered. "The strain of these anxieties has made us both edgy. I wanted only a friendly visit. We *are* friends, are we not?"

"You know that we are."

He reached for the wine-flask to refresh their glasses. She reached for it at the same moment; their hands collided, the flask toppled. Dekkeret caught it just before it overturned. They both laughed at the clumsiness that this present unrest was creating in them, and their laughter broke, for the moment, the tensions that had sprung up between them.

She was right, Dekkeret knew. She was facing the tremendous sacrifice of giving up her familiar and beautiful surroundings in order to live in a distant and disagreeable place. He, though, would move on to the post that would bring him fame and glory, the one for which he had been preparing himself for ten years or more. What comparison was there, really, in their situations? He told himself to be more gentle with her.

"We should talk of other things," she said. "Have you spoken with the Lady Fulkari since your return to the Castle?"

Dekkeret found it an unfortunate change of subject. Tautly he said, "Not yet. Is there some special reason why I should?"

Varaile seemed flustered. "Why, only that—she is very eager to see you. And I thought that you—having been gone more than a week—"

"Would be just as eager to see her," Dekkeret finished, when it became apparent that Varaile either could not or would not. "Well, yes, I am. Of course I am. But not the first thing. I need a little time to collect myself. If you hadn't summoned me tonight, I'd have spent the evening in solitude, resting from my trip, pondering the future, contemplating the responsibilies to come."

"I beg your pardon for calling you away from your contemplations, then," she said, and there was no mistaking the acidity in her tone. "I was very specific in saying that you were to come to me only if you had no other plans for tonight. I thought perhaps that you might prefer to be with Fulkari. But even an evening of quiet solitary meditation is a plan, Dekkeret. You certainly could have refused."

"I certainly could not," he said. "Not an invitation from you. And so here I am. Fulkari didn't send for me, and you did. Not that I understand why, Varaile. For what purpose, exactly, did you ask me here this evening? Simply to lament the possibility that you'll have to go to the Labyrinth?"

"I think that we're quarreling again," said Varaile lightly.

He would have taken her hand in his, if he dared such familiarities with the Coronal's wife. Taking care to keep his tone temperate and mild, he said, "This is a difficult time for us both, and the stress is taking its toll. Let me ask you a second time: why am I here? Was it only because you wanted someone's company tonight? You could have invited Teotas and Fiorinda, then, or Gialaurys, or Maundigand-Klimd, even. But you sent for me, even though you thought I might be spending the evening with Fulkari."

She said, "I asked for you because I think of you as a friend, someone who understands the emotions I feel as the possibility of a change in the government begins to unfold, someone who—as you yourself pointed out—may be experiencing similar feelings himself. But also it was a way of finding out whether you *were* going to be with Fulkari tonight."

"Ah. How devious, Varaile."

"Do you think so? In that case, I suppose it was."

"Why is that something you would want to know?"

"There are tales around the Castle that you have lost interest in her."

"Untrue."

"Well, then, do you love her, Dekkeret?"

He felt heat surging to his cheeks. This was unfair. "You know that I do."

"And yet, your first night back, you preferred your own company to hers."

Dekkeret toyed with his napkin, twisting it in his hands, crumpling it. "I told you, Varaile: I wanted to be alone. To think about—what is coming for us all. If Fulkari had wanted to see me, she would only have had to say so, and I would have gone to her, just as I've come to you. But no message came from her, only from you."

"Perhaps she was waiting first to see what you would do."

"And now she'll think I'm your lover, is that it?"

Varaile smiled. "I doubt that very much. What she *will* think, though, is that she can't be very important to you. Why else would you be avoiding her like this, on your first night back? That's a mark of indifference, not of passion."

"You heard me say that I love her. She knows that too."

"Does she?"

Dekkeret's eyebrows rose. "Have I left her in doubt of that, do you think?"

"Have you spoken with her of marriage, Dekkeret?"

"Not yet, no. Ah—*now* I see the true purpose of your calling me here!" Dekkeret glanced away. "She asked you to do this, eh?" he said coldly.

Anger flared a moment in Varaile's eyes. "You come very close to the edge with a question like that. But no, no, Dekkeret: this is none of her doing. I am entirely to blame. Will you believe that?"

"I would never challenge your word, milady."

"All right, then, Dekkeret: here is the crux. You will soon become Coronal: that is clear. The custom among us is for the Coronal to have a wife. The king's consort has important functions of her own at the Castle, and if there is no consort who is to perform those functions?"

So *that* was it! Dekkeret did not reply. He cupped his wine bowl and held it without putting it to his lips, and waited for her to continue.

"You're no longer a boy, Dekkeret. Unless I've lost count, and I doubt that I have, you'll be forty soon. You've kept company with the Lady Fulkari for—what is it, three years now?—and not said a word to anyone about marriage. Including, apparently, to her. It's a subject that ought to be on your mind now."

"It is. Believe me, Varaile, it is."

"And will Fulkari be your choice, do you think?"

"You press me too hard here, lady. I ask you to give over this inquisition. You are my queen, and also one of my dearest friends, but these are matters I propose to keep to myself, if I may." Pushing back his chair, he looked at her in a way that set up a wall of silence between them.

Now it was her hand that reached out for his. Affectionately she said, "It was never my intention to cause you any discomfort, Dekkeret. I only wanted to speak my mind about something that causes me great concern."

"I tell you once again: I do love Fulkari. I don't know whether I want to marry her, nor am I sure if she wants me. There are problems between Fulkari and me, Varaile, that I will not discuss even with you. *Especially* with you. —May we once again change the subject, now? What can we talk about? Your children, shall it be? Prince Akbalik: he's been writing an epic poem, isn't that so? And the Princess Tuanelys—is it true that Septach Melayn has promised to begin training her in swordsmanship when she's a year or two older—?"

When he awoke in the morning he found that a note had been slipped under his bedroom door during the night:

Can we go riding tomorrow? Into the southern meadows, perhaps?
                                        —F.

His household people told him that some Vroon had brought it in the small hours. Dekkeret knew who that had to be: little Gurjara Yaso, Fulkari's own magus, an inveterate caster of spells and brewer of potions who was her usual go-between in such matters. Dekkeret suspected the Vroon of having used sorcery even on him from time to time in an attempt to keep Fulkari in the prime place in his heart.

Not that any sorcery was needed: she was constantly in his thoughts. He was not in any way indifferent to Fulkari; and all through his sojourn in Normork he had needed only to let his mind drift briefly away from whatever was happening at the moment and there she was, burning like a beacon in his brain, smiling, beckoning to him, drawing him to her—

Certainly, after a week's separation, the urge to rush to her side upon his return had been a powerful one. But Dekkeret had felt it was important to put some distance between himself and her for the moment, if only to give himself time to begin to comprehend what it was he really wanted from her, and she from him. That resolution shattered in an instant now. He felt a torrent of relief and delight and keen anticipation go through him as he read her note.

"Do I have any official functions this morning?" he asked Singobinda Mukund at breakfast.

"None, sir," replied the master of the household.

"And no news has come from the Labyrinth, I take it?"

"Nothing, sir," said Singobinda Mukund. He gave Dekkeret a horrified look, as though to indicate how astounded he was that Dekkeret should feel there was any need to ask.

"Send word to the Lady Fulkari, then, that I'll meet her in two hours at the Dizimaule Arch."

Fulkari was waiting for him when he arrived, a lovely, willowy sight in a riding habit of soft green leather that clung to her like a second skin. Dekkeret saw that she had already ordered up two high-spirited sporting-mounts from the Castle stables. That was Fulkari's way: she seized the moment, she moved swiftly to do what needed to be done. Her waiting, last night, to see if he would make the first move had not been at all typical of her. And indeed when he had not done so she had made the move herself, by having that note slipped beneath the door.

They had been lovers almost three years now, almost since the first day of Fulkari's residence at the Castle. She was a member of one of the old Pontifical families, a descendant of Makhario of Sipermit, who had ruled five hundred years before. The Castle was full of such nobility, hundreds, even thousands who carried the blood of bygone monarchs.

Though the monarchy could never be hereditary, the offspring of Pontifexes and Coronals were ennobled forever, and had the right to occupy rooms at the Castle for as long as they pleased, whether or not they had any official function in the current government. Some chose to take up permanent residence there and became fixtures at the court. Most, though, preferred to spend much of the year on their family estates, elsewhere on the Mount, visiting the Castle only in the high season.

Sipermit, where Fulkari had grown up, was one of the nine High Cities of Castle Mount that occupied the urban band just downslope from the Castle itself. But she had not actually set foot in the Castle until she was twenty-one, when she and her younger brother Fulkarno were sent by their parents, as young aristocrats usually were, to dwell for some years at court.

Dekkeret had noticed Fulkari almost instantly. How could he not? She looked enough like his long-lost cousin Sithelle, who had fallen before the assassin's blade that terrible day some twenty years before in Normork, to be Sithelle's own ghost walking among them in the halls of the Castle.

She was lean and athletic, as Sithelle had been, a tall girl with arms and legs that were long in proportion to her trunk. Her hair was the same sort of fiery red-gold cascade, her eyes were a similar rich gray-violet, her lips were full, her chin a strong one, also like Sithelle's. Her face was broader than he remembered Sithelle's to have been, and there was a curious tiny cleft in Fulkari's chin that Sithelle's had not had; but in the main the resemblance was extraordinary.

Dekkeret halted in his tracks and gasped when he first saw her. "Who *is* that?" he asked, and on being told that she was the newly arrived niece of the Count of Sipermit, he quickly wangled for her an invitation to a court levee being held the following week by Varaile; and arranged to be there himself, and had her brought up to him for an introduction, and stared at her in such intense fascination that he must have seemed a little mad to her.

"Did any of your ancestors happen to come from Normork?" he asked her, then.

She looked puzzled. "No, excellence. We are Sipermit people, going back thousands of years."

"Strange. You remind me of someone I once knew there. I am of Normork myself, you know. And there was a certain person—the daughter of my father's sister, in truth—"

No, no, there was no way to link her to Sithelle. The resemblance was a mere coincidence, uncanny though it was. But Dekkeret lost little time drawing her into his life. Fulkari was a dozen or so years younger than he, and had had no experience in the ways of the court, but she was quick-witted and lively and eager to learn, and fiercely passionate, and not the least bit shy. It was strange, though, holding her in his arms, and seeing that face, so much like Sithelle's, so close to his own. He and Sithelle had never been lovers, had never even dreamed of such a thing; if anything, he had regarded her more as a sister than a cousin.

Now here he was embracing a woman who seemed almost to be Sithelle reincarnated. At times it felt oddly incestuous. And he wondered: Was he replicating with Fulkari the relationship that he had never had with Sithelle? Was it truly Fulkari that he loved, or was he in love, instead, with the fantasy of his lost Sithelle? That was a considerable problem for him. And it was not the only one she posed for him.

He drew her to him and held her close against him, cheeks touching first, then lips. It made no difference to him that the guardsmen who occupied the post just inside the Dizimaule Arch were watching. Let them watch, he thought.

After a time they stepped back from one another. Her eyes were shining; her breasts rose and fell rapidly beneath the soft, pliant leather.

"Come," she said, nodding toward the mounts. "Let's go down into the meadow."

She vaulted easily into her beast's natural saddle and took off without waiting for him.

Dekkeret's mount was a fine slim-legged one of a deep purple color tinged with blue, of the sort specially bred for swiftness and strength. He settled himself easily in the broad saddle that was an integral part of the creature's back, gripped the pommel that sprouted in the same way just in front of him, and sent the mount speeding forward after her with a quick urgent pressure of his thighs. Cool sweet air streamed past him, lifting and ruffling his unbound hair.

He wondered how many more opportunities he would have to slip away from the Castle like this, a private citizen bound on a journey of private amusement, unattended, unhindered. As Coronal he would rarely if ever be able to go anywhere by himself. His visit to Normork had shown him what was in store for him. There would always be body-guards about, except when he managed somehow to give them the slip.

But now—the wind in his hair, the bright golden-green sun high overhead, the splendid mount thundering along beneath him, Fulkari racing on ahead—

Below the southern wing of the Castle lay a belt of great open mead-ows, through the midst of which ran the Grand Calintane Highway, the one traveled by all wayfarers bound for the Castle. There was no day of the year when these meadows were not in bloom, stunning bursts of blue flanked by bright yellow blossoms, masses of white and red, oceans of gold, crimson, orange, violet. The riding track Fulkari had chosen passed to the left of the highway, into the gently sloping countryside that lay above the nearby pleasure-city of High Morpin, ten miles away.

Dekkeret caught up with her after a time and they rode along side by side. They were far enough down the Mount now that the long shadow of the Castle could be seen reaching out before them, tapering to a slender point. Soon the meadowland gave way to a forest of hakkatinga trees, small and straight-trunked, with reddish-brown bark and dense crowns that grew tightly interlaced with their neighbors to form a thick canopy.

Here the mounts could not go as swiftly, and slowed to a canter without being told.

"I missed you so very much," Fulkari said, as they rode along side by side. "It felt as if you were gone for a month."

"For me also."

"Did you have a lot of important meetings to attend as soon as you came back? You must have been terribly busy all day yesterday."

He hesitated. "I had meetings, yes. I don't know how important they were. But I had to be there."

"About the Pontifex? He's dying, isn't he? That's what everybody's been saying."

"No one knows," Dekkeret said. "Until firm news comes from the High Spokesman, we're all in the dark."

They had reached a part of the forest now where he and she had been more than once before. The treetops were so closely woven to-gether here that even in mid-morning a kind of twilight dusk prevailed. A small stream ran here, which a colony of dam-building granths had blocked with gnawed logs to form a pretty little pond. Along its margin was a thick, soft azure carpet of sturdy, resilient bubblemoss. It was a lovely little secret bower, sheltered, secluded.

Fulkari dismounted and tethered her reins to a low-hanging branch. He did the same. They faced each other uncertainly. Dekkeret knew that the wisest thing to do was to reach for her now, quickly fold her in his arms, draw her down onto that mossy carpet, before anything could be said that would break the magic of the moment. But he could see that she wanted to speak. She held herself apart from him, moistened her lips, paced restlessly about. Words were struggling to burst free within her. She had not brought him here merely for lovemaking.

"What is it, Fulkari?" he asked, finally.

She said, in a tone dark with tension, "The Pontifex *is* going to die soon, isn't he, Dekkeret?"

"It's as I just told you: I don't know. No one at the Castle does."

"But when he does—will you be made Coronal?"

"I don't know that either," he said, hating himself for the cowardly evasion.

She was unrelenting. "There can't be any doubt of it, can there? You've already been named Coronal-designate. The Coronal doesn't ever change his mind and pick someone else, once he does that. —Please, Dekkeret, I want you to be honest with me."

"I expect to be made Coronal when Confalume dies, yes. If Lord Prestimion asks me, that is, and the Council ratifies."

"If you're asked, you'll accept?"

"Yes."

"And what will happen to us, then?" Her voice came to him as though from a great distance.

He had no choice now but to go forward with this. "A Coronal should have a consort. I was discussing that very thing with the Lady Varaile last evening."

"You make it sound so impersonal, Dekkeret. '*A Coronal should have a consort.*'" She seemed frightened at speaking to him so bluntly, he who soon would be king, and yet there was an angry edge to her tone all the same. "Does it happen that there's anyone in particular whom you might select to be your consort, perhaps?"

"You know there is, Fulkari. But—"

"But?"

He said, "You've made it clear in a thousand ways that you don't want to be the consort of a Coronal."

"Have I?"

"Haven't you? A minute ago you asked me if I'd accept the throne if it was offered to me. As though it was a fairly common thing for people to refuse to become Coronal, Fulkari. It was last month, I think, that you wanted to know, out of the blue, whether any Coronal-designate had ever turned it down. And before that, that time when you and I were in Amblemorn—"

"All right. That's enough. You don't need to dredge up any more things of that sort." She appeared close to tears, and yet her voice was still steady. "I asked you to be honest with me. Now I'll be just as honest with you." Fulkari paused a moment. Then she said, regarding him evenly, "Dekkeret, I *don't* want to be the consort of a Coronal."

He nodded. "I know that. But if you don't, why have you let yourself become the lover of the Coronal-designate? For the sake of excitement? Amusement? You knew, when we met, what Prestimion had in mind for me."

"You speak as though these things happen by design. Did I come to the Castle expecting to fall in love with Coronal-designate Dekkeret? Did I pursue you in any way after I arrived? You saw me. You sought me out. We talked. We went riding together. We fell in love. I could just as easily ask you, why did the Coronal-designate choose as his lover a woman who doesn't happen to think it's such a wonderful thing to be the wife of the Coronal?"

"I didn't realize that I had done any such thing. That was something I discovered only gradually, as we got to know each other. It's troubled me tremendously ever since I figured it out."

Her face was flushed with anger. "Because our little emotional entanglement stands in the way of your great ambition?"

"You can't call becoming Coronal my *ambition*, Fulkari. I never asked for it. I never even imagined that it could be possible. It came to me by default, when an earlier logical heir unexpectedly died." How could he make her understand? Why was it such a struggle? "No Coronal ever sets out to win the throne. If it doesn't descend on him out of inevitable logic, he doesn't merit it. For years, now, the logic has pointed to me."

"And must you go along with that logic?"

He looked at her helplessly. "It would be shameful to refuse."

"Shameful! Shameful! That's all you men are concerned with—pride, shame, how things will look! You say you love me. You know how frightened I am of your becoming Coronal. And yet—because your pride won't let you say no to Prestimion—"

Now she *was* weeping. Awkwardly he took her in his arms. She did not resist, but her body was stiff, withdrawn.

Quietly he said, "Explain to me why it is that you don't want to be my consort, Fulkari."

"A Coronal spends all his time reading official documents, signing decrees, going to meetings. Or else he's traveling to some far-off place to attend banquets and make speeches. He has very little time for his wife. How often do you see Prestimion and Varaile together? The Coronal's wife has banquets and functions to go to and speeches to make, too. It seems like a hideous dreary exhausting job. It would devour me. I'm only twenty-four years old, Dekkeret. I don't feel anywhere close to ready to taking on a life like that."

"Hush," he said, as though soothing a child. That was how she seemed to him now, anyway: if not a child, then still adolescent, far from any real maturity. He saw now why Varaile was so troubled over the present state of his relationship with Fulkari. Varaile hoped that Fulkari would be Majipoor's next royal consort, and was afraid that Dekkeret was on the verge of discarding her. But Varaile had no real understanding of the way things really stood.

Did he, though? Fulkari's beauty, her eerie resemblance to Sithelle, had mesmerized him also into thinking that she had in her the material of a royal consort. But evidently she did not. A royal mistress, yes. But not a queen. She had been telling him that, indirectly at first and now quite explicitly, for a long time now. "Hush," he said again, as her sobbing deepened. "It's all right, Fulkari. The Pontifex may not be dying at all. He may go on living for years—years—"

He was saying things now that he did not believe in the slightest. But it seemed more important to comfort her, just then, than to try to address the realities of the situation.

For the realities of the situation were that he *would* become Coronal and that he could not marry Fulkari, who plainly did not want to be a Coronal's wife; and so he had no choice but to break with her forever, here and now. But that was something he did not think he could bring himself to do. Certainly not today; perhaps not ever. It was an impossible situation.

He held her close. He stroked her tenderly. Gradually the sobbing ceased. The stiffness of her stance began to ease.

Then, by an almost imperceptible transition, they found themselves with a single accord passing from anguish and confusion and unreconcilable conflict to the rhythms of desire and need. This was their special place, where they had often come to escape from the bustling intrusiveness of Castle life; and here beside the sweet dark pond the granths had built under the close-woven hakkatingas, a sudden familiar urgency once more overcame them and thrust all other considerations aside.

Fulkari, as ever, took the lead. She kissed him lightly and moved a short way back from him. Touched her hand to the metal clasps of her garment at breast, hip, and thigh. The soft leather gave way as though sliced by an invisible blade. She stepped quickly free of it and stood radiantly bare before him, pale, slender, smiling, irresistible, holding out her hands to him. Her eyes, those gray-violet Sithelle eyes of hers, were shining. They beckoned to him. For Dekkeret there was magic in that bright gleam. Sorcery.

At that moment the issue of who would or would not be the consort of the next Coronal of Majipoor seemed as far away to him, and as unimportant, as the sandy desert wastes of Suvrael. He could not think of such things now. He was helpless against the magic of her beauty. That smile, the sight of her slim naked form, the glow of those marvelous eyes, brought back to blazing life all that had caught him and gripped him again and again these three years past. He reached for her and pulled her lightly toward him, and they sank down together, intertwined, on the carpet of bubblemoss beside the pond.

15

"Today, I think, is our day for the singlestick baton," said Septach Melayn a little doubtfully. "Or is it the basket-hilt saber we do today?"

"Rapier, excellence," said young Polliex, the graceful dark-haired boy from Estotilaup, Earl Thanesar's second son. "Tomorrow's the day for singlesticks, sir."

"Rapier. Ah. Yes, of course, rapier. No wonder you're all wearing your masks." Septach Melayn put the error behind him with a shrug and a smile.

There was a time when he had regarded little errors of memory as sins against the Divine, and did penance for them with extra hours of sword drills. But he had lately made a treaty with himself, and with the Divine as well, concerning such errors. So long as his eye remained keen and his hand was still unfaltering, he would forgive himself for these small slips of his mind. As a man ages he must inevitably resign himself to the sacrifice of one faculty or another; and Septach Melayn was willing to give up some fraction of the excellence of his memory if in return he might keep the unparalleled flawlessness of his coordination for another year or three, or five, or ten.

He selected a rapier from the case of weapons against the wall and turned to face the class. They had already formed themselves in a semicircle, with Polliex at his left and the new one, the girl Keltryn, at the opposite end of the row. Septach Melayn always began the day's work with one end of the row or the other, and Polliex always managed to position himself in a favorable place to be among the first chosen. The girl had very quickly picked up the trick from him.

There were eleven in the class: ten young men and Keltryn. They met with Septach Melayn every morning for an hour in the gymnasium in the Castle's eastern wing that had been his private drilling room since the earliest days of Prestimion's reign. It was a bright, high-ceilinged room whose walls were pierced by eight lofty octagonal windows that admitted copious floods of light until shortly after midday. Some said that the place had been a stable in the days of Lord Guadeloom, but Lord Guadeloom's days had been very long ago indeed, and the room had been used as a gymnasium since time out of mind.

"The rapier," said Septach Melayn, "is an exceedingly versatile weapon, light enough to permit great artistry of handling, yet capable of inflicting significant injury when it is used as an instrument of defense." He scanned the semicircle quickly, decided not to choose Polliex for today's first demonstration, and automatically looked over toward the other side, where Keltryn was waiting. "You, milady. Step forward." He raised his sword and beckoned to her with it.

"Your mask, sir!" came a voice from the middle of the group. Toraman Kanna, it was, the prince's son of Syrinx, he of the dark smooth skin and seductive almond eyes. He was ever one to point out things like that.

"My mask, yes," Septach Melayn said, grinning sourly. He unhooked one from the wall. Septach Melayn always insisted that his pupils wear protective face-masks whenever the sharper weapons were used, for fear that some novice's wild random poke would take out a princely eye and create an inconvenient hullaballoo and outcry among the injured boy's kinsmen.

One day, though, the suggestion had been made to him in class that he too should wear a mask, by way of setting a proper example. It seemed wildly absurd to him that he of all people should be asked to take such a precaution—he whose guard had never been broken by another swordsman, not even once, except only that time at the Stymphinor engagement in the Korsibar war, when he had taken on four men at the same time on the battlefield and some coward had sliced at him from the side, beyond his field of peripheral vision. But for consistency's sake he agreed. Still, it was often necessary for his students to remind him to don the ungainly thing at the outset of each class.

"If you please, milady," he said, and Keltryn moved into the center of the group.

Septach Melayn still had not fully adapted to the concept of a female swordsman. He was, of course, much more comfortable in the company of young men than in that of women or girls: that was simply his nature. There had always been a circle of them in attendance on him. But the fact that his pupils had always been male was not so much a matter of his preference as theirs; Septach Melayn had never so much as heard of a woman's wanting to wield weapons, until this one.

The odd thing was that this Keltryn seemed to have a natural gift for the sport. She was seventeen or so, nimble and swift, with a lean frame that might almost have been a boy's, and the exceptionally long arms and legs that were a mark of advantage in swordsmanship. She had her older sister's coloring and her older sister's sparkling beauty, but Fulkari's every motion was infused with a soft seductiveness that was apparent even to Septach Melayn, though he did not respond to it, whereas this one's movements had an irrepressible coltish angularity that seemed delightfully unfeminine to him. And one could never imagine Fulkari picking up a sword. The weapon seemed not in any way out of place in Keltryn's hand.

She faced him squarely, holding her rapier at rest by her side. The instant Septach Melayn raised his weapon she lifted hers and turned sideways into the fencing position, ready to meet his attack. The profile she presented was a very narrow one: from her first day in the class she had bound her breasts with some tight undergarment so that it appeared she had none at all beneath her white fencing jacket. Just as well, Septach Melayn thought. He was unaccustomed to fencing with someone who had breasts.

This was the first rapier lesson since she had joined the group. Keltryn was holding the weapon oddly, and Septach Melayn shook his head and lightly tapped her sword downward. "Let us begin by considering the placement of the hand, milady. We use the Zimroel style of handle here: the grip is a longer one than you may be familiar with, and we hold it farther back from the guard. You will find it gives greater freedom of action that way."

She made the adjustment. The mask hid any sign of embarrassment or displeasure over the correction. When Septach Melayn lifted his sword again, she raised hers, waggling it as if to indicate that she was impatient to begin the lesson.

Impatience was something he would not tolerate. Deliberately, he made her wait.

"Let us consider certain fundamentals," he said. "Our intention with this weapon, as I believe you know, is to lunge and thrust, and to parry our opponent's counterthrust, and to make our own riposte. The point of the weapon is all we use. The entire body is the target. You should be familiar already with all of that. The special thing I teach you here is the division of the moment. Have you heard the term, milady?"

She shook her head.

"What we say is, a good fencer must seize control of time, rather than being controlled by it. In our daily lives we perceive time as a continuous flow, a river that moves without cease from source to mouth. But in fact a river is made up of tiny units of water, each distinct from every other one. Because they move in the same direction they give the illusion of unity. It is only an illusion, though."

Did she understand? She gave no clue.

Septach Melayn continued, "It is the same with time. Each minute of an hour is a separate entity. The same with each second of a minute. Your task is to isolate the units within each second, and to view your opponent as moving from one unit to the next in a series of discontinuous leaps. It is a difficult discipline; but once you achieve it, it is a simple thing to interpose yourself between one of his leaps and the next. For example—"

He called her on guard, took the offensive immediately, lunged and let her parry, lunged again and this time countered her parry by beating her blade aside, so that he had a clear path to the tip of her left shoulder, which he touched; and withdrew and thrust once more, before she had had time to register that she had been struck, and touched the other shoulder. A third time he slipped within her guard and touched her carefully, very carefully, at the bony middle of her chest, just above the place where he imagined the dividing point between her flattened breasts to lie.

The entire demonstration had taken only a handful of seconds. His movements nowadays seemed slow, terribly slow, to him, but Septach Melayn was judging himself by the standards of twenty years ago. There still was no one who could match his speed.

"Now," he said, shoving his mask back and relaxing his stance, "the purpose of what I've just done was not to show you that I am the superior fencer, which I think we all can take for granted, but to indicate the way the theory of the division of the moment operates. What you experienced just now, I suspect, was a perplexing blur of action in which a taller and more skillful opponent heartlessly came at you from all sides at once and pinked you again and again while you struggled to comprehend the pattern of his moves. Whereas what I experienced was a series of discrete intervals, frozen frames of action: you were here and then you were over there, and I entered the interval between those positions and touched your shoulder. I withdrew and returned and found an opening between the next two intervals and penetrated your guard once again. And so forth. Do you follow?"

"Not in any useful way, excellence."

"No. I didn't suppose you would. But let's replay the sequence, now. I will do everything in precisely the same way. This time, though, try to see me not as a whirlwind of continuous activity, but as a series of still tableaus in which I hold this position and then this one and then the next. That is, you must see me *faster*, so that I appear to be moving more slowly. That may make no sense to you now, but I think that sooner or later it will. —On your guard, milady!"

He ran through it all a second time. This time she was, if anything, even more ineffectual, though she knew the direction his moves would be coming from. There was a desperation to her parrying, a frenzied hurry, that pulled her far off form and forced him to stretch to full extension to touch her as he had before. But she did seem also to be trying to comprehend his enigmatic talk about the division of the moment. She appeared to be attempting somehow to slow the flight of time by waiting until the last possible moment to react to his thrusts. Then, of course, she had to rush her parries. Against a swordsman like Septach Melayn that had to be a recipe for disaster; but at least she was trying to understand the method.

Again he touched shoulder, shoulder, breastbone.

Again he halted and pushed back the mask. She did the same. Her face was flushed, and she had a sullen, glowering look.

"Much better that time, milady."

"How can you say that? I was horrible. Or are you simply trying to mock me . . . your grace?"

"Ah, no, milady. I'm here to teach, not to mock. You handle yourself well, better, perhaps, than you know. The potential is definitely there. But these skills are not mastered in a single day. I wanted to show you, only, the area within which you must work." It was an appealing challenge, he thought, making a great swordsman out of a girl like this.

"Now watch while I run through the same maneuvers with someone to whom my theories are more familiar. Observe, if you will, how calm he remains in the midst of the attack, how he appears to be standing still when actually he is in motion." Septach Melayn glanced toward the middle of the group. "Audhari?"

He was the best of Septach Melayn's pupils, a Stoienzar boy with red freckles all over his face, the great-grandson of the former High Counsellor Duke Oljebbin of Lord Confalume's reign and therefore in some way a distant kinsman of Prestimion's. He was big and strong, with powerful forearms, and the quickest reflexes Septach Melayn had encountered in a long time.

"On your guard," said Septach Melayn, and went at once to the attack. Audhari stood no more chance than anyone else of besting him, but he was able to make the pauses, anyway, to hold back the tumbling of the moments one upon another. And so he was able to anticipate, to parry, to find the opportunity between one instant and the next for a counterthrust or two, in general to hold his own commendably enough, all things considered, as Septach Melayn went methodically about the task of breaking through his guard again and again and again.

Even as he worked, Septach Melayn was able to steal a glance at the watching Keltryn. She was staring intently, in absolute concentration.

She will learn it, he decided. She could never be as strong as a man, she would probably not be as quick as one, but her eye was good, her will to succeed excellent, her stance quite satisfactory in form. He still could not understand why a young woman would want to take up swordsmanship, but he resolved to treat her with as much seriousness as he did any of his other pupils.

"You are not yet able to see," he told the girl, "how Audhari goes about severing one moment from the next. It is done within the mind, a technique that requires long practice. But watch, this time, how he turns to meet each thrust. Pay no attention to me whatever. Watch only him. —Again, Audhari. On your guard!"

"Sir?" The voice was that of Polliex. "A messenger has come, your grace." Septach Melayn became aware that someone had entered the room, one of the Castle pages, evidently. He stepped back from Audhari and cast his mask aside.

The boy was carrying a note, folded in thirds, unsealed. Septach Melayn scanned it hastily from both ends at once, as was his way, taking in the scrawled "V" of the Lady Varaile's signature at the bottom even while he was reading the body of the text. Then he read it more carefully, as though that might somehow alter the content of the message, but it did not.

He looked up.

"The Pontifex Confalume has died," Septach Melayn said. "Lord Prestimion, who was on his way back from the Labyrinth, has turned about and returned to it for his majesty's funeral. As High Counsellor, I am summoned there as well. The class is adjourned. We will, I think, not meet again for some time."

The class dissolved into a buzzing hubbub. Septach Melayn walked through their midst as though they were invisible and went from the room.

So it has happened at last, he thought, and now everything will change.

Confalume gone; Prestimion Pontifex; a new man on the throne at the Castle. A new High Counsellor would have to be named, also. True, Korsibar had kept Oljebbin on in that post after seizing the crown, but surely would soon have replaced him if his reign had lasted long enough for him to think about such things; and Prestimion, after the end of the usurpation, had lost no time putting his own man in the spot. Dekkeret, in all likelihood, would want to do the same. In any case Septach Melayn knew that he belonged with Prestimion in the Labyrinth. That was expected of him, and he would comply. But still—still—they had said that Confalume would recover, that he was in no imminent danger of dying—

All this was a great deal to have to wrap his mind around, so early in the day.

Turning the corridor that connected the east wing with the Inner Castle, Septach Melayn went past the vaulted gray building that was the new Prestimion Archive and the wildly swooping weirdness of Lord Arioc's Watchtower. Entering the Pinitor Court, he caught sight of Dekkeret coming toward him from the other direction, with the Lady Fulkari at his side. They were wearing riding clothes, and had a rumpled, sweaty look about them, as though they had been outside the Castle for a ride in the meadows and were just returning.

Now it begins, Septach Melayn thought.

"My lord!" he called.

Dekkeret looked toward him, openmouthed with surprise. "What was that you said, Septach Melayn?"

"Dekkeret! Dekkeret! All hail Lord Dekkeret!" Septach Melayn cried, hands outstretched to make the starburst sign. "Long life to Lord Dekkeret!" And then, in a quieter tone: "I am the first to utter those words, I think."

They were both staring, Dekkeret and the Lady Fulkari, frozen, astounded. Then Septach Melayn saw them exchange stunned glances. Huskily Dekkeret said, "What is this, Septach Melayn? What are you doing?"

"Offering the proper salutation, my lord. News has come from the Labyrinth, it seems. Prestimion has become Pontifex, and we have a new Coronal to hail. Or will, as soon as the Council can meet. But the thing is as good as done, my lord. You are our king now; and so I salute you. —You seem displeased, my lord. What could I have said to offend you?"

II
The Book of Lords

1

The moist, humid lands beyond the Kinslain Gap were Hjort territory. It was the sort of land where few other people cared to live, but
the Hjorts were native to a steamy world of spongy soil and constant tor-
rid fog, and they found conditions here ideal. Besides, they knew that
they were not well liked by the other races that inhabited Majipoor, who
found their appearance unattractive and their manner abrasive and irritating, and thus they preferred to have a province of their own, where
they could live their lives as they pleased.

Their chief center was the small, densely packed city of Santhiskion.
It contained two million of them, or perhaps even more. Santhiskion
was a breeding-ground for minor bureaucrats, for there was something
in the temperament of urban, well-educated Hjorts that inclined them
favorably toward becoming customs collectors and census-takers and
building-inspectors and the like. Hjorts of a different sort lived in the valley of the Kulit that lay to the west of the city—people who were simpler folk in the main, villagers, farmers, who kept to themselves and
patiently went about the business of raising such crops as grayven and
ciderberries and garryn that they shipped to the populous cities of western Alhanroel.

Just as the Hjorts of Santhiskion city were given by nature to
painstaking list-making and record-keeping and report-writing, the rural
Hjorts of the valley were lovers of ritual and ceremony. Their lives re-
volved around their farms and their produce; everywhere about them
lurked invisible gods and demons and witches, who might be threats to

the ripening fields; it was necessary constantly to propitiate the benevolent beings and to ward off the depredations of unfriendly ones by acting out the rites appropriate to the day of the year. In each village there
was a certain official who kept the calendar of rites, and every morning
announced the proper propitiations for the week ahead. Knowing how
to keep the calendar was no easy matter; lengthy training was involved,
and the calendar-keeper was revered for his skills the way a priest would
be, or a surgeon.

In the village of Abon Airair the calendar-keeper was named Erb
Skonarij, a man so old that his pebbly-textured skin, once ashen-
colored, had faded to a pale blue, and whose eyes, once splendidly huge
and gleaming, now were dull and sunken into his forehead. But his
mind was as alert as ever and he performed his immensely involuted cal-
endrical tasks with undiminished accuracy.

"This is the tenth day of Mapadik and the fourth day of Iyap and the
ninth of Tjatur," Erb Skonarij announced, when the elders of the village
came to him in the morning to hear the day's computations. "The
demon Rangda Geyak is loose among us. Thus it is incumbent on us to
perform the play of the contending geyaks this evening." And the storyteller whose responsibility it was to narrate the play of the contending
geyaks began at once to make ready for the show, for among the Hjorts
of the Kulit Valley no distinction was made between ritual and drama.

They had brought with them from their home world a complex calendar, or series of calendars, that bore no relation to the journey of Majipoor around its sun or to the movements of any other heavenly body:
their year was 240 days long, divided into eight months of thirty days by
the reckoning of one calendar, but also into twelve months of twenty
days by a different reckoning, and likewise six months of forty days,
twenty-four months of ten days, and 120 months of two days.

Thus any given day of the year had five different dates in the five different calendars; and on certain special conjunctions of days, especially
involving the months named Tjatur in the twelve-month calendar, Iyap
in the eight-month calendar, and Mapadik in the twenty-four-month
calendar, particularly important holy rites had to be celebrated. And this
night the conjunction of dates was such that the rite of *Ktut*, the war between the demons, must be enacted.

The people of Abon Airar began to gather by the storytellers' mound
at dusk, and by the time the sun had dropped behind Prezmyr Mountain the entire village was assembled, the musicians and actors were in

place, the storyteller was perched atop his high seat. A great bonfire blazed in the fire pit. All eyes were on Erb Skonarij; and precisely at the moment when the hour known as Pasang Gjond arrived, he gave the signal to begin.

"For many months now," the storyteller sang, "the two factions of the geyaks have been at war. . . ."

The old, old story. Everyone knew it by heart.

The musicians lifted their kempinongs and heftii and tjimpins and sounded the familiar melodies, and choristers with greatly distended throat-sacs brought forth the familiar repetitive bass drone that would continue unbroken throughout the performance, and the dancers, elaborately costumed, came forth to act out the dramatic events of the tale.

"Great has been the sorrow of the village as the demons make war against each other," sang the storyteller. "We have seen green flames darting by night among the gerribong trees. Blue flames have danced atop gravestones in the cemetery. White flames move along our roof-beams. The harm to us has been great. Many of us have fallen ill, and children have died. The garryn we have gathered has been ruined. The fields of grayven are devastated. Harvest time is almost upon us and there will be no grayven to harvest. And all of this has befallen us because there is sin in the village, and the sinners have not given themselves over to be purified. The demon Rangda Geyak moves among us—"

Rangda Geyak moved among them even as the storyteller spoke: a huge hideous figure costumed to look like an ancient female of the human kind, with a coarse mop of white hair and long, dangling breasts and great yellow crooked teeth that jutted like fangs. Red flames darted from her hair; yellow flames sprang from her fingertips. Back and forth she strode along the edge of the mound, menacing those who sat in the front rows.

"But now, the sorcerer Tjal Goring Geyak comes, and does battle with her—"

A second demon, this one a giant equipped with the four arms of a Skandar, pranced forward out of the shadows and confronted the first. Together now they danced in a circle, face to face, taunting each other and jeering, while the storyteller recited the details of their combat, telling how they hurled fiery trees at each other, and caused immense pits to open in the village square, and made the waters of the placid River Kulit surge above their banks and flood the town.

The essence of the tale was that the contest of the geyaks brought great grief and woe to the village as it raged, for the demons were unconcerned by the incidental damage they were inflicting as they struggled up and down the town and the surrounding fields. Only when the sinners who had brought this calamity upon the townsfolk came forth to confess their crimes would the demons cease their warfare and turn against the evildoers, taking up flails and wielding them as weapons to drive them out of the village.

The three dancers who were to play the guilty sinners sat to one side, watching the spectacle with everyone else. Their time to take the stage was still hours away; the storyteller must first relate in full detail the arrival of other demons, the one-winged bird and the one-legged dragon and the creature that eats its own entrails, and many more. He must speak of demonic orgies, and the drinking of blood. He must tell of transformations, the beasts that interchanged shapes. He must tell of the beautiful young women who wordlessly make obscene overtures to young men on lonely roads late at night. He must—

As the old tale unfolded Erb Skonarij, watching from the seat of privilege that was his by virtue of his decades as the village's keeper of the calendars, felt a sudden searing pain within his skull, as though a band of hot iron had been clamped around his brain.

It was a fearful sensation. He had never known such pain.

He began to think that the hour of his death had come at last. But then, as it went on and on without surcease, the thought came to him that perhaps he would *not* die, that he would simply be forced to suffer like this forever.

And it was, he realized after a time, an agony not of the body, but of the spirit.

Something was striking a knife into his soul. Something was whipping his innermost self with a whip of fire. Something was hammering at the substance of his being with a massive jagged boulder.

He was the sinner. *He* had brought the fury of the demons down upon the village. *He, he, he,* the keeper of the calendars, the guardian of the ceremonies: he had failed in his task, he had violated his trust, he had betrayed those who depended on him, and unless he confessed his guilt right here and now the entire village would suffer for his iniquities.

Rising from his place of honor, he came tottering forward into the center of the stage.

"Stop!" he cried. "I am the one! I must be punished! For me, the flails! For me, the whips! Drive me out! Cast me from your midst!"

The music died away in a confusion of discordance. The humming of the choristers ceased. The storyteller's cadenced voice cut off in mid-phrase. They were all staring at him. Erb Skonarij looked out into the audience and saw the wide bewildered eyes too, the open mouths.

The throbbing in his skull was unrelenting. It was splitting him apart.

Someone's hand was around his arm. A voice close by his right ear-membrane said, "You must sit down, old man. The ceremony will be spoiled. You of all people—"

"No!" Erb Skonarij pulled himself free. "I am the one! I bring the demons!" He pointed toward the storyteller, who was gaping at him in amazement and fright. "Tell it! Tell it! The treason of the calendar-keeper, tell it! Set me free, will you? Set us all free! I can no longer bear the pain!"

Why would they not listen to him?

A desperate lurch brought him up before the two demons, the Rangda Geyak, the Tjal Goring Geyak. They had halted now in their dance. Erb Skonarij scooped up the flails that they were meant to use at the climax of the ceremony and thrust them into their hands.

"Beat me! Whip me! Drive me out!"

The two masked figures still stood motionless. Erb Skonarij pressed his hands to his pounding forehead. The pain, the pain! Did no one understand? They were in the presence of real sin: they must expel it from the village, and all would suffer, he most of all, until it was done. But no one would move. No one.

He uttered a muffled cry of despair and rushed toward the roaring bonfire. This was wrong, he knew. The sinner must not punish himself. He must be forced from their midst by the united effort of all the villagers, or the exorcism would have no value to the village. But they would not do it; and he could no longer bear the pain, let alone the shame or the grief.

He was amazed at how soothing the warmth of those flames was. Hands clutched at him, but he knocked them aside. The fire . . . the fire . . . it sang to him of forgiveness and peace.

He cast himself in.

2

Mandralisca lifted the helmet from his head. Khaymak Barjazid sat facing him, watching him avidly. Jacomin Halefice stood near the door of Mandralisca's chamber, with the Lord Gaviral beside him. Mandralisca shook his head, blinked a couple of times, rubbed the center of his brow with his fingertips. There was a ringing in his ears, a tightness in his chest.

For a time no one spoke, until at last Barjazid said, "Well, your grace? What was it like?"

"A powerful experience. How long did I have the thing on?"

"Fifteen seconds or so. Perhaps half a minute at most."

"That's all," Mandralisca said, idly fondling the smooth metal mesh. "Strange. It seemed like a much, much longer time." The sensations that had just gone coursing through him still reverberated in his spirit. He realized that he had not yet entirely returned from his journey.

In the immediate aftermath of the experiment an odd jangling restlessness gripped him. Every nerve was sensitized. He felt the beating of the hot sun against the walls of the building, heard the whistling of the desert wind across the plain of pungatans far below, had an oppressive sense of the thick musky atmosphere of the air about him in here.

Rising, he roved the perimeter of the circular room, cruising it like some caged beast. Halefice and even Gaviral stepped to the side, scuttling out of his way as he strode past the place where they were standing. Mandralisca barely noticed them. To his mind in its currently elevated state they seemed like nothing more than little scurrying animals to him, droles, mintuns, hiktigans, unimportant creatures of the forest. Insects, even. Mere insects.

He had *gone down into* that little metal helmet, somehow. His entire mind had entered it; and then, in a way he could not begin to comprehend, he had been able to hurl himself outward, like a burning spear soaring through the sky—

Barjazid said, "Do you have any idea how far you went, or where?"

"No. Not at all." How curious to be holding a conversation with an insect. But he forced himself to pay attention to Barjazid's query. "I perceived it as a considerable distance, but for all I know it was no farther than the city on the other side of the river."

"It was probably much farther, your grace. The reach is infinite, you know: there's no more effort involved in reaching Alaisor or Tolaghai or Piliplok than there is in going next door. It's the directionality that we can't control. Not yet, anyway."

"Could it reach the Castle, do you think?" asked the Lord Gaviral.

"As I have just told his grace the Count Mandralisca," Barjazid said, "the reach is infinite." Mandralisca noticed that Barjazid had already learned to be extremely patient with Gaviral. That was a very good idea, when dealing with someone who is very stupid but who has a great deal of power over you.

"So we could reach out with it and hit Prestimion, then?" asked Gaviral avidly. "Or Dekkeret?"

"We might, in time," Barjazid replied. "As I have also just observed, we do not yet have real directionality. We can only strike randomly thus far."

"But eventually," Gaviral said. "Oh, yes, eventually—!"

It was all that Mandralisca could do to keep himself from cutting Gaviral down with some contemptuous remark. Reach out and hit Prestimion? The *fool*. The *fool*. That was the last thing they wanted to do. The boy Thastain had a shrewder grip of political strategy than any of these five brainless brothers. But this was not the moment to foment a breach with one of the men who were, at least in theory, his masters.

He considered what Barjazid's helmet had just allowed him to accomplish. That was more interesting to him than anything these people might have to say.

He had cast forth his mind and hurt someone with the helmet. Of that he was certain. He had no idea clear idea of whom, or where; but he had no doubt that he had encountered another mind someplace far away, a priest of some kind, perhaps, at any rate someone who was officiating at a ritual, and had penetrated it, and had damaged it. Extinguished it, perhaps. Certainly done great harm. He knew what it was like to injure someone: a very distinctive feeling of pleasure, almost sexual in nature, which he had experienced many times in his life. He had felt it just now, with a new and astounding intensity. Some distant stranger, recoiling in pain and shock at his thrust—

—he had flown like a spear, a burning spear soaring halfway across the world—

Like a god.

"Your brother would never let me try the helmet," Mandralisca said to Khaymak Barjazid. Returning to his desk, he tossed the device down in the middle of it. "I asked him more than once, while we were camped there in the Stoienzar. Just to find out what it was like, you know. The kind of sensation it was. 'No,' he said. 'I would not dare risk it, Mandralisca. The power is too great.' He meant that I might injure myself, I assumed. But as I thought about it afterward I saw a different meaning in the phrase. 'The power is too great for me to trust you with it,' is what he was really saying. I think he feared I might go poking around in *his* mind."

"He was constantly afraid of something like that—that the helmet might be used against him."

"Was I not his ally?"

"No. My brother never saw anyone as an ally. Everyone was dangerous. Remember, his own son turned against him during Dantirya Sambail's rebellion, and brought one of the helmets to Prestimion and Dekkeret. No one could ever have persuaded Venghenar to let anyone else get near a helmet after that."

"I watched Prestimion destroy him with the helmet that Dinitak brought him," Mandralisca said.

His voice sounded strange in his own ears. He understood that he must still not have fully shaken off the effect of having donned that helmet. These three men still seemed like insects to him. They had no significance whatsoever.

"Your brother," he said to Barjazid, speaking as though the other two were not in the room, "was standing right next to me, with his own helmet on. He and Prestimion were having a duel of some sort with their helmets, hundreds of miles apart, thousands, maybe. I saw your brother collecting himself for one final thrust; but before he could unleash it, Prestimion hit him with the helmet-force and knocked him to his knees. 'Prestimion,' your brother said, and started to moan, and Prestimion struck him once or twice more, and I could see then that his mind was altogether burned out. An hour or two later Septach Melayn and Gialaurys burst upon us. One of them came upon him and slew him."

"As we will slay Prestimion," said the Lord Gaviral grandly.

Mandralisca acted as though Gaviral had not said anything. Slay Prestimion? That was no answer to the problem of attaining freedom for the western continent. *Constrain* Prestimion, yes. *Control* him. *Use* him. That was what this helmet would achieve, in the fullness of time. But why kill him? That would only put Dekkeret into the high seat of power at the Labyrinth and bring some other Coronal to the summit of Castle Mount, and they would have to start the process of extricating Zimroel from the grip of Alhanroel all over again. It was hopeless, though, to expect any of the Five Lords to understand such things before they were explained to them.

"The helmet will give us our revenge, yes," said Khaymak Barjazid.

Mandralisca ignored that too. It was such a commonplace thing to say. And it was not even sincere, Mandralisca thought. Barjazid had no interest in revenge. His brother's death at Prestimion's hand did not seem to matter greatly to him. He would just as readily have sold himself to his brother's killers as to his brother's killers' enemies, if the price had been right. The selling was all that mattered. What interested this Barjazid most was money, security, comfort: petty unimportant things, all three. There was a bright spark of malevolence in Barjazid that Mandralisca appreciated, a chilly malign intelligence, but the man was fundamentally trivial, a little bundle of unusual marketable skills and very ordinary hungers.

Mandralisca's restlessness had returned. The stink of other human flesh in the room was becoming unendurable now. The heat. The pressure of other consciousnesses too close against his own.

He gathered up the flimsy little helmet and tucked it like so much pocket-change into a pouch at his hip. "Going outside," he said. "Too warm in here. Some fresh air."

The long shadows of afternoon were beginning to creep westward across the ridge. The palaces of the Five Lords, up there on the summit of the hill overlooking the village, were bathed in ruddy light. Mandralisca walked through the village in long strides, no particular destination in mind. The other three men followed along behind, struggling to keep up with him.

Such small men, he thought. Gaviral. Halefice. Barjazid. Small of stature, small of soul as well. Halefice, for one, knew it: he wanted only to serve. Gaviral dreamed of reigning as a king here in Zimroel, and was no more fitted for it than a rock-monkey would be. And ugly little Barjazid—well, he had his merits, he was tough and smart, at least. Mandralisca did not entirely despise him. But essentially he was nothing. *Nothing*.

"Your grace?" Halefice had caught up with him. The aide-de-camp said, "Begging your pardon, your grace, but perhaps your use of that device has tired you more than you realize, and you should rest for a time, instead of—"

"Thank you, Jacomin. I'll be all right." Mandralisca kept on moving, not even facing toward Halefice as he spoke. They were in the thick of the village, now, among the smiths and the pot-sellers, with the wine-shops just beyond, and then the market of breads and meats.

It had not been an easy matter, building a self-sufficient village out here in this dry desolate land, where crops had to be coaxed from the unwilling red earth with the aid of water pumped drop by drop from the maddeningly unreachable river just over the hill, but they had done it. *He* had done it. He knew nothing about farming, nothing about raising livestock, nothing about creating villages out of thin air, but he had done it, he had drawn the plans and given the orders and made it happen, even to the lavish palaces of the Five Lords at the top of the ridge, and now, striding through it this strange afternoon, he felt—what?

A sense of anticipation. A sense of standing at the threshold of a new place, a strange and wonderful place.

Already he held the Five Lords of Zimroel in his hands, whether they knew it or not. Soon he would hold Prestimion and Dekkeret as well. He would be the master of all Majipoor. Was that not a fine thing, for a country boy of the snowy Gonghar land who had started out in life with no assets other than a quick mind and lightning-swift reflexes?

He passed the wine-shops, shaking off flasks that the merchants there eagerly implored him to take, and went on through the bread-market. One of the bread-sellers put a biscuit into his hand with a reverent bow and a murmured prayer. There was awe in his eyes, as though he and not Gaviral were a Lord of Zimroel. The wine-merchants and bread-sellers understand, Mandralisca thought, where the real power resides in this place. He bit into the biscuit—it was one of the little round ones called a lorica, with a topknot on the upper side to make it seem something like a crown. A good choice, thought Mandralisca. He devoured it in three bites.

On the far side of the bread-market the ridge rose sharply to a point where one could see the river far below, boiling and churning against the foot of the cliff. He strode toward it. Halefice still walked along beside him on the left, a step or two to the rear. Barjazid was on the other side. The Lord Gaviral did not seem to have followed them up the hill from the marketplace.

Mandralisca stood staring at the river for a long while without speaking. Then he drew the helmet from his pouch. It rested in the palm of his open hand, a bunched-up little mass of metal mesh. Barjazid gave him a worried look, as though wondering if Mandralisca might have it in mind to hurl it into the water below.

To the Suvraelinu he said suddenly, "Barjazid, did you ever want to kill your father?"

That drew a startled glance. "My father was a kindly man, your grace. A merchant who dealt in hides and dried beef, in Tolaghai city. It would never have entered my mind—"

"It entered mine, a thousand times a day. If *my* father were still alive now I'd put this helmet on and try to kill him with it right now."

Barjazid was too astounded to answer. He and Halefice were both peering at him strangely.

Mandralisca had never spoken of these things with anyone. But those few seconds of using the Barjazid helmet had opened something in his soul, apparently.

"He was a merchant too," he said. He looked straight out into the river gorge, and the hated past swam before his eyes. "In Ibykos, which is a muddy trifling little town in the scarp country of the Gonghars, a hundred miles west of Velathys. It rains there all summer and snows all winter. He dealt in wines and brandies, and was his own best customer, and when he was drunk, as almost always he was, he would hit you just as readily as look at you. That was how he talked to you, with his hands. It was in my boyhood that I learned to move as quickly as I do. To jump back fast—out of his reach."

Even after nearly forty years Mandralisca could see that grim face, so much now like his own, in the eye of his mind. The long lean jaw, the clamped lips, the black scowl, the gathering brow; and the mer-

ciless hand flashing out, swift as a pungatan-whip, to split your lip or
swell your cheek or blacken your eye. Sometimes the beatings had
gone on and on and on, for the slightest of reasons, or for no reason
at all. Mandralisca barely could summon up a recollection of his pallid, timid mother, but the monstrous brutal irascible father still rose
like a mountain in his memory. Year after year of that, the curses, the
backhand slaps, the sudden pokes and jabs and smacks, not only from
him but from the other three too, his older brothers, who imitated
their father by hitting anyone smaller than themselves. There had
never been a day without its bruise, without its little ration of pain
and humiliation.

He shut his fist on the helmet, squeezing it tight.

"Each night I sent myself to sleep by imagining I had murdered him
that day. A knife in the gut, or poisoned wine, or a trip-wire in the dark
and a hidden noose, I slew him fifty different ways. Until the day I told
him out loud that I would do it if I got the chance, and I thought he was
going to kill *me* there on the spot. But I was too fast for him, and when
he had chased me from one end of the town to the other he gave up,
warning me that he'd break me in half the next time he got his hands
on me. But there never was a next time. A carter came by who was setting forth to Velathys, and he gave me a ride, and I have not seen the
Gonghars since. I learned many years later that my father died in a
brawl with a drunken patron in his shop. My brothers too are dead, I believe. Or so do I profoundly hope."

"Did you go straight into the service of Dantirya Sambail, then?"
Halefice asked him.

"Not then, no." His tongue was loose, now. His face felt strangely
flushed. "I went first to the western lands, to Narabal in the south, on
the coast—I wanted to be warm, I wanted never to see snow again—
and then to Til-omon, and Dulorn of the Ghayrogs, and many another place, until I found myself in Ni-moya and the Procurator
chose me to be his cupbearer. I was in his bodyguard then, and he
saw me at a demonstration of the batons—I am quick with the singlesticks, you know, quick with any sort of duelling weapon—and he
called me out to talk with me after I had beaten six of his guardsmen
in a row. And said to me, 'I need a cupbearer, Mandralisca. Will you
have the job?'"

"One did not refuse a man like Dantirya Sambail," said Halefice
piously.

"Why would I have refused? Did I think the task was beneath me? I was a country boy, Jacomin. He was the master of Zimroel; and I would stand at his side and hand him his wine, which meant I would be in his presence constantly. When he met with the great ones of the world, the dukes and counts and mayors, or even the Coronals and Pontifexes, I would be there."

"And did you become his poison-taster then, also?"

"That came later. There was a whispered tale, that season, that the Procurator would be done to death by one of the sons of his cousin, who had been regent in Zimroel when Dantira Sambail was young, and had been put aside by him. It would be by poison, they said, poison in his wine. This talk came to the Procurator's own ear; and when I handed him his wine-bowl the next time, he looked into it and then at me, and I knew he mistrusted it. So I said, by my own free will, because I mattered not at all to myself and he mattered a great deal, 'Let me taste it first, milord Procurator, for safety's sake.' I have no liking for wine, on account of my father, you understand. But I tasted it, while Dantira Sambail watched, and we waited, and I did not fall down dead. And after that I tasted his wine with every bowl, to the end of his days. It was our custom, even though there were never any threats against him ever again. It was a bond between us, that I would sip a bit of his wine before I gave him the bowl. That is the only wine I have ever had, the wine I tasted on behalf of Dantirya Sambail."

"You weren't afraid?" asked Khaymak Barjazid.

Mandralisca turned to him with a scornful grin. "If I had died, what would that have mattered to me? It was a chance worth the taking. Was the life I was leading so precious to me that I would not risk it for the sake of becoming Dantirya Sambail's companion? Is being alive such a sweet wondrous thing, that we should cling to it like misers clutching their bags of royals? I have never found it so. —In any case there was no poison in the wine, then or ever, obviously. And I was at his side forever after."

If he had ever loved anyone, Mandralisca thought, that person was Dantirya Sambail. It was as if they shared a single spirit divided into two bodies. Though the Procurator had already managed to bring the entirety of Zimroel into his power before Mandralisca entered his service, it was Mandralisca who had spurred him on to the far greater enterprise of encouraging Confalume's son Korsibar to seize the throne of Majipoor. With Korsibar as Coronal, and indebted to Dantirya Sambail for his crown, Dantirya Sambail would have been the most powerful figure in the world.

Well, it had not worked out, and both Korsibar and the Procurator were long gone. Dantirya Sambail had played and lost, and that was that. But for Mandralisca there were other games yet to play. He gently stroked the helmet in his hand.

Other games to play, yes. That was all existence was, really: a game. He alone had seen the truth of that, the thing that others failed to realize. You lived for a time, you played the game of life, ultimately you lost, and then there was nothing. But while you played, you played to win. Great wealth, fine possessions, grand palaces, feasting and the pleasures of the flesh and all of that, those things meant nothing to him, and less than nothing. They were only tokens of how well you had played; they had no merit in and of themselves. Even the wielding of power itself was a secondary thing, a means rather than an end.

All that mattered was *winning*, he thought, for as long as you could manage it. To play and to win, until the time came when, inevitably, you lost. And if it had meant risking the chance of drinking poison that was meant for the Procurator, if that was the price of entering the game, why, surely the risk was worth the reward! Let other men wear the crowns and hoard up great stockpiles of treasure. Let other men surround themselves with simpering women and drink themselves blind with tingling wine. Those were not things that he needed. When he was a boy, everything that had been of any importance to him was denied to him, and he had learned to live with nothing whatsoever. Now there was very little that he wanted, except to see to it that no one could ever again place himself in a position to deny him anything.

Barjazid was staring at him again as though reading his mind. Mandralisca saw that he had, once again, revealed too much of himself. Anger rose in him. This was a weakness he had never indulged in before. He had said enough, and more than enough.

Swinging abruptly around, he said, "Let's go back to my chamber."

If I ever catch him using his helmet on me, Mandralisca told himself, *I will take him out into the desert and stake him down between two pungatans.*

"I will try this toy of yours again, I think," he said to Barjazid, and quickly slipped the helmet over his brow, and felt its force seize hold of him; and he sent his mind soaring forth until it made contact with another, not troubling to determine whether it belonged to a human or a Ghayrog, a Skandar or a Liiman. Probed it for a point of entry. Entered it, then, piercing it like a sword.

Slashed it.

Left it in ruins.

Mastery. Ecstasy.

3

---

*D*ekkeret said, "So this is the imperial throne-chamber! I've always wondered what it was like."

Prestimion made a flamboyantly grandiose gesture. "Take a good look. It'll be yours someday."

With a rueful smile Dekkeret said, "Have mercy, my lord! I'm barely accustomed to wearing a Coronal's robes and here you are already opening the doors of the Labyrinth for me!"

"I see you still call me 'my lord.' That title is yours now, my lord. I am 'your majesty.'"

"Yes, your majesty."

"Thank you, my lord."

Neither man made any attempt to smother his laughter. This was their first formal meeting as Pontifex and Coronal, and neither of them could deal with the magnitude of that fact without a certain leavening of amusement.

They were in the uttermost level of the Labyrinth, the site of the Pontifex's private residence and of the great public chambers of the imperial branch of the monarchy, the throne-chamber and the Great Hall of the Pontifex and the Court of Thrones and the rest. Dekkeret had arrived at the subterranean capital late the previous evening. He had never had reason to go to the Labyrinth before, though he had heard tales of it all his life: the grimness of it, the airlessness, the sense that it gave you of being cut off from all life and nature, condemned to live down deep, out of sight of the world, in a realm of eternal night lit by harsh, glittering lamps.

At first view, though, the place struck him as far less forbidding than he had anticipated. The upper rings had the rich, bustling vitality of a mighty metropolis, which was, after all, what the Labyrinth in fact was: the capital of the world. And then there were the architectural wonders deeper down, the myriad strangenesses with which ten thousand years of Pontifexes had bedecked their city. Finally, there was the grandeur and richness of the imperial sector itself, where such magnificence had been lavished that even the opulence of the Castle was put in the shade.

Dekkeret had spent the night in the chambers reserved for Coronals during their visits to the court of the senior monarch. It was the first time he had occupied any of the Coronal's residences anywhere. He had halted a moment, struck by awe at the sight of the great door to the suite that now was his, with its intricate carvings and the swirling starburst symbols done in gold and the royal monogram repeated again and again, LPC, LPC, LPC, *Lord Prestimion Coronal*, which soon would be replaced by the LDC of his own ascension. Only one step remained for that. He had been proclaimed by Prestimion, and he had been confirmed by the Council; now he needed only to return to the Castle for his coronation ceremony. But the funeral of Confalume and the coronation of the new Pontifex must take precedence over that.

The new Pontifex had already gone through the ancient rite of taking possession of his new home. Since Prestimion had already been traveling on the Glayge when the news had come to him of Confalume's death, he had returned to the Labyrinth by the river route; but instead of entering the capital by way of the Mouth of Waters, the customary entrance from the Glayge, he was required by tradition this time to go entirely around the city to the far side, the one that faced the southern desert, and come in via the much less congenial Mouth of Blades.

That was simply a stark gaping hole in the desert floor, walled about with bare timbers to keep the drifting sands from filling it in. Across the front of it was a row of antique rusted swords, said to be thousands of years old, set tip-upward in a matrix of concrete. Behind that unwelcoming entrance waited the seven masked guardians of the Labyrinth — by custom, two Hjorts, a Ghayrog, a Skandar, and even a Liiman were included among them — who soberly went through the ritual of inquiring after Prestimion's business in this place, ostentatiously conferred

among themselves to decide whether to let him in, and then demanded
from him the traditional entry-offering, which had to be something of
his own choice. Prestimion had brought with him the cloak that the
people of Gamarkaim had sent to him as a coronation gift when he became Coronal, woven of the cobalt-blue feathers of giant fire-beetles
and said to give its wearer protection against harm from flame. By surrendering it here, to be housed forever in the museum where such gifts
were kept, he was declaring that in the Labyrinth he would always be
safe from every external menace.

Then he entered; and custom now obliged him to descend through
each of the levels of the spiraling city on foot. That was no small journey. Varaile walked beside him all the way, and his three sons and his
daughter, though the Lady Tuanelys, too young to keep pace, was borne
on a Skandar guard's back for much of the distance. At each stage great
crowds gathered around him, tracing the Labyrinth symbol in the air
with their fingertips and crying out his new name: "Prestimion Pontifex!
Prestimion Pontifex!" He was Lord Prestimion no longer.

Meanwhile his succession to the senior throne had been proclaimed
at each of the levels below, first at the Court of Columns, then in the
Place of Masks, and then the Hall of Winds, the Court of Pyramids, and
upward as far as the Mouth of Blades. So when he reached each of these
places it was already consecrated to his reign. And at last Prestimion
came to the imperial sector, where he knelt first beside the embalmed
body of his predecessor Confalume where it lay in state on the dais of
the Court of Thrones, and then went to his own new dwelling-place,
and there received from the High Spokesman of the Pontificate the spiral emblem of his office and the scarlet-and-black robes. The rest could
not be done until Dekkeret arrived.

And now Dekkeret had come. The age-old custom called for Prestimion to receive the new Coronal in the imperial throne-chamber.
And so the High Spokesman Haskelorn called on Dekkeret at the
Coronal's suite the morning after his arrival, and they rode together in
a small floater through the long and winding passages of the imperial
sector down an ever-narrowing tunnel to a point where not even the little vehicle could enter. Walking side by side, now, they advanced
through a passageway that was sealed every fifty feet by bronze doors,
until they came to the final door, emblazoned with the Labyrinth sign
and the newly inscribed monogram of Prestimion Pontifex where Confalume's had been only hours before. Old Haskelorn touched his palm

to the monogram and the door swung open and there stood Prestimion, smiling.

"Leave us," he said to Haskelorn. "This meeting involves just the two of us."

Prestimion showed Dekkeret the throne-chamber itself, first.

It was a great globe of a room, its curving sides covered from floor to ceiling with smooth, gleaming yellow-brown tiles that seemed to burn with an inner light of their own. But the throne-chamber's only illumination came from a single massive glowfloat that hovered in midair and emitted a steady ruby luminosity. Directly below it stood the Pontifical throne, on a platform reached by three broad steps: an enormous high-backed chair with long, slender legs that were tipped with fierce claws, so that they seemed like those of some giant bird. It was entirely covered over with sheets of gold, or, perhaps, for all Dekkeret could tell, made of one solid mass of the priceless metal. Amid the simplicity of the huge room the throne itself blazed with a dreadful power.

One might easily think Confalume had designed this chamber, since it was the Labyrinth's counterpart of the resplendent throne-room that Confalume had built for himself at the Castle when he was Coronal. But this room was not Confalume's work. It bore no sign of the late monarch's taste for baroque extravagance of style. The throne-chamber of the Labyrinth was a room so ancient that no one quite knew who had built it: the common belief was that it went back to a time even before the reign of Stiamot.

The effect was awe-inspiring and somehow preposterous at one and the same time.

"What do you think?" Prestimion asked.

Dekkeret had to fight back more giggles. "It's extremely—majestic, I'd say. Majestic, that's the word. Confalume must have loved it. You aren't really going to use it, are you?"

"I have to," Prestimion said. "For certain high functions and sacred ceremonies. Haskelorn's going to draw up a guidebook for me. We have to take these things seriously, Dekkeret."

"Yes. I suppose we do. I noticed long ago how seriously you take the Confalume Throne. How many times have I seen you sitting in it, over the years—five? Eight?"

Prestimion looked a bit ruffled. "I took the Confalume Throne very seriously indeed. It is the symbol of the Coronal's grandeur and power. A little *too* grand for my own private tastes, which is why I preferred to use the old Stiamot throne-room most of the time. I would never have built a thing like the Confalume Throne, Dekkeret. But that doesn't mean I underestimate its importance in sustaining the power and majesty of the government. Neither should you."

"I didn't mean to imply that I would. Only that when I think of you sitting here on this great golden chair, and me up there at the Castle atop old Confalume's big block of opal—" He shook his head. "By the Divine, Prestimion, we're just *men*, men whose bladders ache when we go too long without pissing and whose stomachs growl when we don't get fed on time."

Quietly Prestimion said, "Yes, we are that. But also we are Powers of the Realm, two of the three. I am this world's emperor, and you are its king, and to the fifteen billion people over whom we rule we are the embodiment of all that is sacred here. And so they put us up on these gaudy thrones and bow down to us, and who are we to say no to that, if it makes our job of running this immense planet any easier? Think of them, Dekkeret, whenever you find yourself performing some absurd ritual or clambering up onto some overdecorated seat. We are not provincial justices of the peace, you know. We are the essential mainsprings of the world." Then, as if realizing that his tone had grown too sharp, Prestimion grinned broadly. "We, and the fifty million unimportant public officials who actually have the job of doing all the things that we in our grandeur command them to do. —Come, let me show you the rest of this place."

It was an extensive tour. Prestimion led him along quickly. Though Dekkeret's legs were considerably longer than Prestimion's, he was hard-pressed to keep up with the older man, who set a pace that was in keeping with the lifelong restlessness and impulsiveness of his nature.

They went first through a concealed door at the rear of the throne-chamber, and then down a long hallway into the vast dark space known as the Court of Thrones, where somber walls of black stone swept together high overhead to meet in pointed arches. The only light within the Court of Thrones was provided by half a dozen wax tapers along the walls, set far apart in sconces shaped like upstretched hands. The two large thrones of red gamba-wood that gave the room its name, not so numbingly grand as the one in the throne-chamber but imposing enough in their own way, rose side by side on stepped platforms at the rear of the room. One bore the starburst symbol of the Coronal, and the other, the greater one, the spiraling maze that was the Pontifical sign.

Shuddering, Dekkeret said, "It appears more fit to be a torture-chamber than a throne-room, if you ask me."

"In truth I do agree. I have no good memories of this room: it is the place where Korsibar's sorcerers bamboozled us all, and as we stood stunned by their magic he seized the crown and put it on his own head. I wince even now, whenever I come in here."

"It never happened, Prestimion. Ask anyone, and that's what they'll tell you. The whole episode is gone from everyone's mind. You should thrust it out of yours."

"Would that I could. But I find that some painful memories don't want to fade. For me it's still quite real." Prestimion ran his hand uneasily through his thin, soft golden hair. His expression was bleak. He seemed to be wrenching himself by sheer force of will away from that moment of the past. — "Well, there is where we will sit, the two of us, a couple of days from now, and I'll put the crown on you myself."

"I should take this opportunity to tell you," said Dekkeret, "that once I am on the throne I plan to ask your brother Teotas to be my High Counsellor."

"You say it as if you're asking my permission. The Coronal chooses whomever he wishes for that post, Dekkeret." There was a certain brusqueness in Prestimion's tone.

"You know him better than anyone in the world. If you think there's some flaw in him that I've overlooked—"

"He has a very short temper," Prestimion said. "But that's not a flaw anyone who spends five minutes in his company could possibly overlook. Other than that, he's perfect. A wise choice, Dekkeret. I approve. He'll serve you well. That is what you wanted me to say, isn't it?" It was clear from his impatience with this discussion that Prestimion had other things on his mind. Or perhaps merely wanted to conceal the pleasure he felt at having so great an honor descend on his brother. — "Look here, now. There's something else in here for you to see."

Dekkeret followed Prestimion through the shadows to an alcove on the left, in which he perceived a sort of altar covered with white damask, and then, as he went closer, a figure lying atop it, facing upward, hands clasped across his breast.

"Confalume," said Prestimion in the lowest of tones. "Lying in the place where I'll lie myself, twenty or forty years from now, and you yourself will be, twenty or forty years after that. They've embalmed him to last a hundred centuries or more. There's a secret vault in the Labyrinth where the last fifty Pontifexes are buried—did you know that, Dekkeret? No. Neither did I. A long, long line of imperial tombs, each with its own little marker. Tomorrow we put Confalume in his."

Prestimion knelt and pressed his forehead reverently against the side of the altar. Dekkeret, after a moment, did the same.

"I met him once when I was a boy: did I ever tell you that?" Dekkeret said, when they had risen. "I was nine. It was in Bombifale. We were there because my father was showing samples of his goods—agricultural machinery, I think, is what he was dealing in then—to the manager of Admiral Gonivaul's estate, and Lord Confalume was Gonivaul's guest at the same time. I saw them go out riding together in Gonivaul's big floater. They went right past me in the road, and I waved, and Confalume smiled and waved back. Just the sight of him made me tremble. He seemed so strong, Prestimion, so radiant—practically godlike. That smile of his: the warmth, the power of it. It's a moment I'll never forget. And then, that afternoon, I went with my father to Bombifale Palace, and the Coronal was holding court, and once again he smiled at me—"

He broke off his story and looked toward the still, shrouded figure lying there atop the altar. It was not easy to accept the fact that a monarch of so much force and grandeur could have vanished from the world between one moment and the next, leaving only this husk behind.

Prestimion said, "He may have been the greatest of them all. Flawed, yes. His vanity, his love of luxury, his weakness for wizards and sooth-sayers. But what trifling faults those were, and how wonderful his accomplishments! Guiding the world for sixty years—the heroic power of him—as you say, almost godlike. History will be very kind to him. Let's hope we're remembered half as warmly as he will be, Dekkeret."

"Yes. I pray that we are."

Prestimion began to move toward the exit of the great hall. But as he reached the door he halted and once more indicated the two thrones, the entire length of the room away, with a quick taut nod, and then looked back at the alcove where the dead Pontifex lay. "The single worst moment of his reign took place over there, right in front of those thrones, when Korsibar grabbed the starburst crown." Dekkeret followed

Prestimion's pointing arm. "I was looking straight at Confalume, just then. He seemed numb. Staggered by it—broken, shattered. They had to take him by the elbows and lead him up the steps and seat him on the Pontifical throne, with his son sitting up there beside him. There. Those very thrones."

All so long ago, Dekkeret thought. Ancient history, buried and forgotten by all the world. Except Prestimion, it seemed.

Who was caught up now in the grip of his own tale. "I had an audience with Confalume a day or two later, and he still appeared to be dazed by the thing that Korsibar had done. He seemed old—weak—beaten. I was furious at having been done out of the throne, and that he had acquiesced in the theft; yet, seeing him in that state, I could only feel compassion for him. I asked him to call out the troops against the usurper, and I thought he was going to weep, because I was asking him to launch a war against his own son. He would not do it, of course. He told me that he agreed that I was the one who should have been Coronal, but that now he had no other path but to accept Korsibar's coup. He begged me for mercy! Mercy, Dekkeret! And out of pity for him I went away without pressing him further." There was a sudden startling look of torment in Prestimion's eyes. "To see that great man in ruins, like that, Dekkeret—that this was mighty *Confalume* with whom I was speaking, now only the pathetic shadow of a king—"

So he will not let go of it, Dekkeret thought: the usurpation and all its consequences still resonated in Prestimion's spirit down to this very moment.

"What an awful thing that must have been to witness," he said, since he felt he must say something, as they emerged into the vestibule.

"It was an agony for me. And for Confalume also, I would think. —Well, eventually my sorcerers carved all memory of Korsibar's little bit of mischief from his mind, and from everyone else's as well, and he returned to being his old self and lived on happily for many years thereafter. But I still carry the memory of it in my soul. If only I could have forgotten it too!"

"There are certain painful memories that don't want to fade, is what you told me only a minute ago."

"True enough."

Dekkeret realized in dismay that a painful memory of his own had unexpectedly begun to stir in him. He tried to push it back down into the place from which it had come. But it would not be pushed.

Prestimion, seeming more cheerful now, opened another door. A giant Skandar guard stood just within. Prestimion waved him aside. "Beyond here," he said, in an easier tone, "the private dwelling of the Pontifex begins. It goes on and on: dozens of rooms, three score of them, at least. I still haven't been all the way through the whole place. Confalume's collections are here, do you see?—all his toys of magic, his paintings and statues, the prehistoric artifacts, the ancient coins, the stuffed birds and mounted bugs. The man scooped up every manner of thing with both hands throughout his life, and here it all is. He's left everything to the nation. We'll give him an entire wing in the new Archive building at the Castle. Look—here, do you see this, Dekkeret—?"

Dekkeret, who was barely paying attention, said, "I also have an unpleasant memory that refuses to fade."

"And what is that?" Prestimion asked. He seemed disconcerted by the interruption.

"You were there when it happened. That day in Normork when the madman tried to assassinate you, and my cousin Sithelle was killed instead—?"

"Ah. Yes," said Prestimion, sounding a little vague, as though he had not given the incident a moment's thought in twenty years. "That lovely girl. Yes. Of course."

It all came rushing back yet again. "I carried her through the streets, bleeding all over me, dead in my arms. The worst moment of my life, bar none. The blood. That pale face, those staring eyes. And later in the day they brought me before you, because I had saved your life, and you rewarded me with a knight-initiate's post, and everything began for me in that moment. I was just eighteen. But I've never fully been able to break free of the pain of Sithelle's death. Not really. It was only after she was dead that I realized how much I loved her." Dekkeret hesitated. He was not sure, even after having gone this far, that he wanted to share this with Prestimion, for all that the older man had been his guide and mentor these nearly twenty years. But then the words came surging forth as if by their own volition: "Do you know, Prestimion, I think that it's on account of Sithelle that I took up with Fulkari? I think I was drawn to her at the outset, and am held by her still, because when I look at her I see Sithelle."

Prestimion still did not appear to comprehend the depth of his feelings. To him this was just so much conversation. "You think so, do you? How interesting, that the resemblance should be so strong." He did not sound interested in the slightest. "But of course I'm in no position to know. I saw your cousin only that once, and for just an instant. It was a long time ago—everything was happening so quickly—"

"Yes. How could you possibly remember? But if there were some way of standing them next to each other, I know you'd think that they must be sisters. To me, Fulkari looks more like Sithelle than she does her own actual sister. And so—the root of my obsession with her—"

"Obsession?" Prestimion blinked in surprise. "Wait, there! I thought you were in love with her, Dekkeret. Obsession is something else again, something not quite as pretty and pure. Or are you telling me that you think the two terms are synonymous?"

"They can be, yes. Yes. And in this case I know that they are." There was no turning back from this, now. "I swear it, Prestimion, the thing that drew me to Fulkari was her resemblance to Sithelle, and nothing else. I knew nothing about her. I had never spoken a word with her. But I saw her, and I thought, *There she is, restored to me,* and it was like a trap closing on me. A trap that I had set for myself."

"Then you don't love her? You've simply been using her as a surrogate for someone you lost long ago?"

Dekkeret shook his head. "I don't want to think that's true. I do love her, yes. But it's very clear that she's the wrong woman for me. Yet I stay with her even so, because being with her seems to call Sithelle back into life. Which is no reason at all. I've got to get free of this, Prestimion!"

Prestimion seemed puzzled. "The wrong woman for you? Wrong in what way?"

"She doesn't want to be a Coronal's consort. The whole idea of it terrifies her—the duties, the demands on my time and hers—"

"She told you this?"

"In just so many words. I asked her to marry me, and she said she would, but only if I didn't let myself be made Coronal."

"This is astounding, Dekkeret. Not only do you love her for the wrong reasons, you say, but she's not suited to be your queen in any case—and yet you refuse to break with her? You have to, man."

"I know. But I can't find the strength."

"Because of your memories of your lost Sithelle."

"Yes."

"These confusions of yours add up to a very unhealthy business, Dekkeret. They are two different people, Sithelle and Fulkari." Prestimion's voice was stern, and as close to fatherly as Dekkeret had ever heard it sound. "Sithelle's gone forever. There's no way that Fulkari can be Sithelle for you. Put that out of your mind. And she's not even a good choice for a wife on her own terms, it seems."

"What am I supposed to do, though?"

"Part with her. A complete break." Prestimion's words fell upon him like boulders. "There are plenty of other women at this court who'll be glad to keep company with you until you decide you want to marry. But this relationship is one that has to be severed. You should thank the Divine that Fulkari refused you. She's obviously not right for you. And it makes no sense to marry a woman simply because she reminds you of someone else. "

"Don't you think I know that? I do. I do. And yet—"

"Yet you can't free yourself of this obsession with her."

Dekkeret looked away. This was becoming shameful, now. He had diminished himself woefully in Prestimion's eyes, he knew. In a small and very unkingly voice he said, "No. I can't. And you can't possibly comprehend it, can you, Prestimion?"

"On the contrary. I think I can."

There was an uncomfortable silence for a moment or two. All this while they had continued to walk between the rows of Confalume's showcases of treasures, but neither of them was looking at anything.

In a different, more intimate tone, Prestimion said, "I can understand how the line between love and obsession can become blurred. There was a woman in my life once also, whom I loved and who was taken from me by violence—Confalume's daughter, she was, the twin sister of Korsibar—it's a long story, a very long story—" Prestimion seemed to be having trouble finding the words. "She was killed in the last hour of the civil war, slain right on the battlefield by Korsibar's treacherous magus. I mourned her for years, and then, more or less, I put her behind me. Or thought I did. In time I found Varaile, who is right for me in every respect, and all was well. Except that Thismet— that was her name, Thismet—haunts me still. Hardly a month goes by when I don't dream of her. And wake up in a cold sweat, bellowing in pain. I have never told Varaile why that is. No one has any knowledge of this. No one except you, now."

Dekkeret had not expected any such confession. It was an astonishing thing. "We all have our ghosts, I see. Who will not quit their hold on our souls, no matter how many years may go by."

"Yes. I thank you for sharing these private things with me, Dekkeret."

"You don't think the less of me for all that I've said?"

"Why would I? You're human, aren't you? We don't expect our Coronals to be perfect in every regard. We'd put marble statues on the throne instead, if we did. And this suffering of yours can be healed, perhaps. I could have Maundigand-Klimd try to cleanse your mind of all memory of your dead cousin."

"The same way he's cleansed yours of Thismet?" responded Dekkeret sharply, without a moment's pause.

Prestimion gave him a startled look. Dekkeret realized that in the depths of his shame he had suddenly felt impelled to strike back at the very man who was striving to ease his pain, and his hasty words had been hurtful ones.

"Forgive me. It was a wicked thing to say."

"No, Dekkeret. It was a truthful thing to say. You were well within your rights to say it." Prestimion made as if to slip his arm around Dekkeret's shoulders, but the younger man was too tall for that. He took Dekkeret lightly by the wrist instead. "This has been a valuable conversation: one of the most important you and I have ever had. I know you much better now than ever I did before, in all these years."

"And do you think that a man who carries a burden of this sort is worthy of being Coronal?"

"I'll pretend you didn't say that, I think."

"Thank you, Prestimion."

"And my remark a moment ago, about Maundigand-Klimd—obviously it upset you. I'm sorry for that. As you say, we all have our ghosts. And perhaps it is true that we're condemned to carry them around with us to the end of our days. But I meant only that your memories of your dead cousin seem to be causing you great pain, and you have a world to govern, and a consort to choose, and much else facing you now, for which you'll need the full powers of your spirit, without distraction. I think that perhaps Maundigand-Klimd *could* heal you of your loss. But you may very well not want to surrender your memories of Sithelle despite all the pain they cause you—just as I, I suppose, want to cling to what remains to me of Thismet. So let's say no more of this, eh? I'm confident that you'll heal yourself in your own way. And will deal properly with this matter of Fulkari, too."

"I hope so."

"You will. You're a king now. Indecision is a luxury allowed only to the common folk."

"I was one of those, once," said Dekkeret. "It's not something one ever fully escapes." Then he smiled. "But you're right: now I must learn to be a king. That's a subject I fear I'll spend the rest of my life studying."

"So you will, and you'll never feel you've mastered it all. Don't let that worry you. I felt the same way, and Confalume before me, and Prankipin, very likely, as well, and so on and so on back to Stiamot and the kings who came before him. It's a thing that goes with the job. We are *all* common folk, Dekkeret, under our crowns and robes. The test for us is how well we rise above that. But you'll have me to call on, when doubts arise."

"I know that, Prestimion. I give thanks daily for that."

"And also I've arranged that you'll have my chamberlain Zeldor Luudwid for your own, when you get back to the Castle. He knows more about how to behave like a Coronal than I do myself. If there's a problem, simply ask him. He's yours as my gift."

"Thank you—your majesty."

"Say nothing of it—my lord."

4

"*E*ven a self-maintaining garden needs a certain degree of mainte-nance," Dumafice Moal told his visiting nephew, as they set out together into the uppermost terrace of the magnificent park that Lord Havilbove had laid out three thousand years before. "Hence my contin-uing employment, dear nephew. If the park were as really perfect as peo-ple commonly believed, I'd be selling sausages in the streets of Dundilmir this day."

The garden sprawled for forty miles along the lower slopes of Castle Mount. It began at Bibiroon Sweep, below the city of Bibiroon in the Free Cities ring, and angled down the Mount in a broad eastward-reaching curve toward the uppermost cities of the Slope Cities group, approaching at its downslope end the cities of Kazkas, Stipool, and Dundilmir. The site that the garden occupied was known as Tolingar Barrier, though nowadays it was a barrier no longer. Once it had been an almost impenetrable zone of black sharp-edged spiky hillocks, the outcropping remnants of a million-year-old flow of lava from some vol-canic vein deep within the Mount. But the Coronal Lord Havilbove, who had devoted much of his reign to the construction of this garden, had had the lava hills of Tolingar Barrier ground down to fine black sand, which proved a fertile soil for the great garden that would be planted there.

Lord Havilbove, a native of the lowland city of Palaghat in the Glayge Valley, was a fastidious and orderly man who loved plants of all kinds but disliked the ease with which even the finest of gardens quickly became unruly and departed from its plan if not given constant finicky care. Therefore, while his platoons of brawny laborers were toiling to pulverize the lava beds of Tolingar Barrier, craftsmen in the workshops of the Castle were striving, through experiments in controlled breeding, to create plants and shrubs and trees that needed no touch of a gardener's shears to maintain their graceful forms.

It was a time when the science of such biological miracles was still understood on Majipoor. The efforts of Lord Havilbove's technicians met with gratifying success. The plants intended for his garden achieved a perfect symmetry as they grew, and when they reached a size that was appropriate in relationship to the plants about them, they held that size ever after.

Superfluous leaves and even whole unnecessary boughs dropped away automatically, and quickly crumbled into a compost that enhanced the fertility of the lava soil. Enzymes in their roots suppressed the growth of weeds. Every plant bore flowers, but the seeds that those flowers produced were sterile; only when a plant reached the natural end of its life cycle did it bring forth fertile ones, so that it could replace itself with another that soon would have the same size and form. Thus the garden remained in unchanging balance.

Whenever he learned of a beautiful tree or shrub anywhere in the world, Lord Havilbove sent for specimens of it, with roots and soil attached, and gave them to the genetic surgeons of the Castle so that they could be modified for self-maintenance. Truckloads of bright-hued ornamental minerals came to the garden also—the yellowish-green stone known as chrysocolla, and the blue one called heart-of-azure, and red cinnabar, and golden crusca, and dozens more. Each of these was used as a ground cover in a different level of the garden, the differing colors being deployed by Havilbove with a painter's eye, so that as one stood upon the peak at Bibiroon Sweep and looked down over the entirety of the garden one saw a great splash of pale crimson here, and one of vivid yellow there, and zones of scarlet, and blue, and green, all of them with plantings complementary to the color of the ground.

Lord Havilbove's successor, Lord Kanaba, was equally devoted to the garden, and Lord Sirruth, who came after him, was sympathetic enough to it to keep its staff in place and even expand its budget. Then came the Coronal Lord Thraym, who was at first preoccupied with ambitious building projects of his own at the Castle, but who was smitten with love for Lord Havilbove's garden upon his first visit there. He saw to it that funds were provided to carry it to its final state of perfection. Thus it took a century or more to bring the great garden into being; but then it remained ever after as one of the treasures of the Mount, a famed sight that every inhabitant of Majipoor yearned to have the privilege of beholding at least once.

Dumafice Moal had been born in Dundilmir, just downslope from the garden's lower tip, and from boyhood on he visited it at every opportunity he had. He never doubted that it was his destiny to be part of the garden's staff; and now, at the age of sixty, he had more than forty years of devoted service behind him.

Self-maintaining though the garden was, it nevertheless required a staff of considerable size. Millions of people visited the garden every year; a certain amount of damage was unavoidable; paths and fountains had to be repaired, ornamental plazas tidied, stolen plants replaced. Nor was the garden safe from marauding animals that came in from outside. There was plenty of open space on Castle Mount in the districts between the Fifty Cities, where wild creatures still thrived. The forested slopes of the Mount teemed with beasts of many kinds, from hryssa-wolves and jakkaboles and slinking long-fanged noomanossi to such lesser creatures as sigimoins and mintuns and beady-eyed droles. Jakkaboles and hryssa-wolves, dangerous things that they were, posed no threat to the elegant plantings. But a pack of little burrowing droles, poking their long toothy snouts into the ground in search of grubs, could uproot an entire bed of eldirons or tanigales between midnight and dawn. An infestation of tentworms could spread ugly canopies of coarse silk over half a mile of blooming thwales and swiftly reduce the plants to naked stubs. A flock of hungry vulgises settling in the treetops to build their nests—or a swarm of ganganels—spotted cujus—

So it was Dumafice Moal's daily task to patrol the garden from sunrise onward, searching out the enemies of the plants. It was constant warfare. For a weapon he carried a long-handled energy-thrower, tuned to its lowest power; and when he came upon some work of destruction in progress, he would apply just enough heat to drive out the forces of destruction without damaging the plantings themselves.

"Often it starts very inconspicuously," he told his nephew. "A trace of upturned soil leads you to a tiny parade of little red insects, and if you follow along it you discover a small mound, something that a visitor wouldn't give a second look to—but those of us who know what to look for understand that these are the hatchlings of the harpilan beetle, which, if left to its own devices for long, will—ah—see here, boy—"

He poked at the border of a row of Bailemoona khemibors with the tip of his energy-thrower. "Do you see it, Theriax—right there—?"

The boy shook his head. The boy, Dumafice Moal was beginning to believe, was not particularly observant.

He was his youngest sister's child, from Canzilaine, virtually at the foot of the Mount. Dumafice Moal himself had never married—his devotion was to the garden—but he came from a large family, brothers and sisters and cousins scattered from Bibiroon and Sikkal down the Mount to Amblemorn, Dundilmir, and several other of the Slope Cities. From time to time some relative of his would come to see the garden. Dumafice Moal liked to take them on private tours, early in the day before the gates were open to the public, while he was making his morning rounds.

The khemibors were a southern species with bright blue flowers and glossy leaves of the same color, and they had been planted in beds of vivid orange rock, to wondrous visual effect. Dumafice Moal's practiced eye had noted a certain dulling of the gleaming surfaces of the leaves of the plants closest to the path: a sure sign that himmis-bugs had taken up residence on their undersides. He slipped his energy-thrower under the nearest row, checking its adjustment slide carefully to make certain that the power was switched to the lowest level.

"Himmis-bugs," he said, pointing. "We used to spray for them, but it never did much good. So we cook them instead. Watch how I proceed to make things hot for the little vermin."

Just as he began to move the long rod about, a curious sensation at the back of his skull started to afflict him.

It was a very odd thing. It was somewhat like an itch, though not quite. He felt a mild warmth back there, and then something not so mild. A sharp stinging pain, then, as if some disagreeable insect were attacking him. But when he brushed the back of his head with his free hand he detected nothing.

He continued to prod the soil beneath the khemibors with his energy-thrower. The stinging sensation grew more intense. It became a fierce burning feeling now, highly localized—like a hot beam of light focused on a single point of his head, drilling, trying to cut its way through—

"Theriax?" he said, lurching, nearly falling.

"Uncle? Are you all right?"

The boy reached out to steady him. Dumafice Moal shrugged him away. He was beginning to feel a different sort of pain: an inward one, a bewildering distress that he could only describe to himself as a pain of the soul. A sense of his own inadequacy, of having performed his life-long tasks poorly, of having failed the garden.

How odd, he thought. *I always worked so hard.*

But there was no hiding from the feeling of shame that now was pervading every corner of his spirit. It engulfed him entirely; he was sinking into it as into a dark deep pit, an abyss of guilt.

"Uncle?" the boy said, from very far away. "Uncle, I think you may be burning the—"

"Hush. Let me be."

He saw only too clearly how poorly he had done his work. The garden was hopelessly infested with ravenous enemies. Pests of all sorts lurked everywhere: blights, molds, rusts, murrains, chewing creatures, sucking creatures, chafing creatures, burrowing creatures, biting creatures. Swarms of flies, clouds of gnats, armies of beetles, legions of worms. The thunderous sound of a billion tiny jaws chomping at once roared in his ears. Wherever he looked he saw more of them, and even more on the way: eggs, cocoons, nests, preparing to release new predators by the millions. And all of it his fault—his—his—

They all must burn.

"Uncle?"

Burn! Burn!

Dumafice Moal turned the energy-thrower to a higher level, and a higher one still. A dull rosy glow sprang up in the bed of khemibors. *Burn!* Let the himmis-bugs cope with that! He went quickly from row to row, from bed to bed, from terrace to terrace. Spirals of greasy blue smoke began to rise from newly created heaps of ash. The trunks of trees were turning black with the scars of combustion. Vines hung in angular, disheveled loops.

There was much to do. It was his duty to purify the garden, all of it, here and now. He would work at it all day, and far into the night if necessary, and onward to the following dawn. How else could he cope with the unbearable burden of guilt that roiled the deepest recesses of his soul?

He moved on and on, torching this, blasting that. Clouds of ash now leaped up with every step he took. Black haze veiled the morning sun. An acrid carbonized taste invaded his nostrils. The boy followed along behind him, astounded, dumbstruck.

Someone was calling down to him from a higher terrace: "Dumafice Moal, have you gone insane? Stop it! Stop!"

"I must," he called back. "The garden is shameful to me. I have failed in my duties."

Sparks were flying all around, now. Trees blossomed into bright flame. Here and there, huge blazing limbs broke free and toppled, shrouded in red, into the plantings below. He was aware that he was doing some damage to the gardens, but not nearly so much as these insects and animals and fungoid pests had achieved. And it was necessary damage, purgative damage. Only through fire could the garden be purified—could he be absolved of his shame—

He went on, beyond the alluailes and the flask-trees, deep into the navindombe bushes now. Behind him rose a dark, red-flecked mist of smoking embers. He aimed the energy-thrower here, here, here. Trees crashed in the distance. Enormous boughs landed with the soft sighing impact of wood that has burned from the inside out: dream-branches, dream-light. Cinders crunched underfoot. The ash was a thick, soft black powder that rose in choking puffs. The sky was turning red. A savage gloom prevailed everywhere. He no longer felt the pain at the top of his skull, no longer felt the guilt, even, of his failure—only the joy of what he was achieving now, the triumph of having restored purity to what had become impure, of having negated negation.

Angry voices cried out behind him.

He turned. He saw stunned faces, goggling eyes.

"Do you see?" he asked them proudly. "How much better it all is, now?"

"What have you done, Dumafice Moal?"

They came rushing through the cinder-beds toward him. Seized him by the arms. Threw him down, bound him hand and foot, while all the while he protested that his work was still unfinished, that much remained yet to be done, that he could not rest until he had saved the entire garden from its foes.

5

Word was beginning to spread up and down Castle Mount and outward into the lands beyond: the old Pontifex Confalume was dead, Lord Prestimion had gone to the Labyrinth to take the senior throne, Prince Dekkeret of Normork was to become the new Coronal. Already the portraits of the late Pontifex were being brought out of storage and put on display, bedecked now with the yellow streamers of mourning: Confalume as a vigorous young lord with bright keen eyes and a thick sweep of chestnut hair, Confalume the beloved gray-haired Coronal, Confalume the regal old Pontifex of the past two decades, whatever people could lay their hands on. Soon portraits of the new Lord Dekkeret would be generally available, and they would go up too on every wall and in every window, and, alongside them, pictures of the former Lord Prestimion, now Prestimion Pontifex, wearing the scarlet-and-black robes of his newly assumed high office.

Everywhere, preparations for great celebrations were getting under way: festivals, parades, pyrotechnic displays, tournaments, a worldwide holiday of joy. The arrival of a new Coronal on the scene was something of a novelty for modern-day Majipoor.

Over the thirteen thousand years of Majipoor's history it normally happened only two or three times in a person's life that a Pontifex died and new rulers came to the two capitals. But in the past century a change of monarchs had been even more of a rarity than that. Confalume had been Pontifex for the past twenty years, and Coronal for the forty-three before that. So more than sixty years had gone by since the

Pontifex Gobryas had died and was succeeded by the dashing young Lord Prankipin, who had chosen Prince Confalume to be his Coronal; and very few were still alive who remembered that day. Prankipin himself, dead some twenty years now, was only a name to the billions of younger folk who had come into the world during the Pontificate of Confalume.

The new Lord Dekkeret was not widely known outside the confines of the Castle—new Coronals rarely were—but everyone knew that he was a close and trusted associate of Lord Prestimion, and that was good enough. Lord Prestimion, like Lord Confalume before him, had been a greatly beloved Coronal, and there was general faith that he would choose a successor wisely and well.

Most people were aware that Dekkeret was of common birth, a young man of Normork who had first come to the attention of Lord Prestimion by thwarting an attempt on the Coronal's life, back at the beginning of Prestimion's reign. That was a most unusual thing, a commoner chosen to be Coronal, but it did happen every few hundred years. They knew that Dekkeret was a man of imposing stature and lordly mien, sturdy and handsome. Those who had had any contact with him in his travels through the world in his years as Prestimion's designated heir had discovered that he was good-natured and easy of spirit, a man of open heart and generous soul. More than that, what sort of Coronal he would be, they would learn soon enough. Prestimion, throughout his years as king, had often left the Mount to visit cities far and wide. Very likely Dekkeret would do the same.

In the city of Ertsud Grand, midway up Castle Mount, the custodians of the Summer Palace began to make plans for an early visit by the new Coronal to the auxiliary residence that was maintained there for his use.

At this point such talk was, they knew, mainly wishful thinking. Ertsud Grand, a city of nine million people in the circle of the Mount known as the Guardian Cities, had been a favorite secondary residence of Coronals for centuries; but Lord Gobryas, who had come to the throne almost ninety years ago, had been the last one to make any regular use of the beautiful dwelling that was set aside for him there. Lord Prankipin had visited the Summer Palace no more than half a dozen times in his twenty years on the Mount. Lord Confalume, though, had gone there only twice in a reign two times as long. As for Lord Prestimion, he had never been to Ertsud Grand at all, and seemed altogether unaware that the Summer Palace existed.

Yet it was a beautiful palace in a beautiful city. Ertsud Grand was known as the City of Eight Thousand Bridges, though its citizens would always tell wondering visitors, "Of course, that's an exaggeration. Probably there are no more than seven or eight hundred." Streams from three sides of the Mount met and mingled there, providing the city with a watery underbedding before draining downward to create the Huyn River, one of the six that descended the slopes of Castle Mount.

A network of canals connected the various sectors of Ertsud Grand, so that it was possible to go all about the city by boat. All the main canals flowed toward the Central Market—which in fact was in the eastern half of the city, rather than being truly central—where, in a gigantic cobble-stoned plaza bordered by tall warehouses of white stone, luxury goods from every part of Majipoor were bought and sold. Here were dealers in unusual meats and fishes, in exotic spices, in voluptuous furs from the cold northern marches of Zimroel, in the green pearls of the tropical Rodamaunt Archipelago and the transparent topaz that was mined by night at Zeberged, in the wines of a hundred regions, in the small animals and strange insects that the people of Ertsud Grand favored as pets, and much more besides.

To provide the western sector of the city with a focal point that would be as important an attraction in its way as the Central Market was on the eastern side, the ancient planners of Ertsud Grand had dammed up half a dozen of the larger streams, creating the body of water known as the Great Lake. It was perfectly circular and a rich sapphire blue in color, ten miles in circumference and glinting like a giant mirror in the midday sun. All around its shores were the palaces and mansions of wealthy merchants and the city's nobility, and a host of pleasure-pavilions and sporting parlors. Boats and flat-bottomed barges of the most elaborate sort, painted in bright colors, went back and forth among these buildings all day long.

The Summer Palace, the masterwork of the long-ago and otherwise forgotten Lord Kassarn, was situated on a large artificial island in the Great Lake's precise center. It was, in fact, two palaces, one within another: an outer one made of pink marble and an inner one fashioned entirely of bamboo canes.

The marble palace was a kind of habitable continuous wall: a joined series of pavilions, their roofs supported by columns inlaid with gold and lapis lazuli, with a multitude of apartments and colonnaded cloisters and banquet-halls and courtyards. The guest rooms—there were scores of them, spacious and airy—were decorated with fanciful murals of the lives of the early Coronal Lords. Here, once upon a time, Coronals seeking respite from the routines of the daily business of the Castle would come in summer to hold court and give lavish feasts for their chief lords, the nobility of the cities of the Mount, and visiting dignitaries.

Within this ringlike marble building, which occupied the entire perimeter of the island, was an extensive park where wild animals of many sorts were allowed to roam—gibizongs, plaars, semboks and dimilions, shy and dainty bilantoons, prancing spiral-horned gambulons, small furry krefts that ran around like animated balls of fluff with stiff upraised tails, and a herd of fifty white kibrils whose red eyes blazed in their broad foreheads like huge rubies. And at the very heart of the park was the Summer Palace proper, intended as the Coronal's private refuge.

It was most elegantly designed, made of the sturdy black bamboo of Sippulgar, which has canes nearly as hard as iron. The canes were six inches in diameter, cut to twenty-foot lengths, gilded, and bound by silken cords. Not a single nail had been used anywhere. The roof also was made of bound lengths of Sippulgar cane, varnished annually with the red sap of the grifafa tree, which preserved it against all decay. Interior columns, these likewise of bamboo canes tied three together, formed its supports. Sea-dragon emblems in red surmounted each column.

The Summer Palace stood on a little hillock that lifted it above the rest of the island, affording the Coronal a vista of the distant shores of the Great Lake. So artfully had the building been constructed that it would be only the work of a single day, supposedly, to dismantle it and shift it to face in a different direction, in case the Coronal should tire of the view from his bedroom and request another. Those who had been allowed to tour the palace in modern times—visiting dukes and counts, members of the families of former Coronals, important captains of industry who had come to Ertsud Grand leading trade missions—were inevitably told of this special feature of its design. In Lord Kassarn's day, so the story went, the palace was taken down and repositioned every year just before the Coronal came to Ertsud Grand for his summer retreat. Sometimes, at the Coronal's request, it had been done more frequently than that. But no one actually could remember the last such occasion.

Though visits by Coronals to the Summer Palace had become uncommon events in modern times, and no Coronal at all had gone there during the past thirty-five years, the municipality of Ertsud Grand kept both structures, the marble pavilion and the one of bamboo, constantly in readiness for his lordship's imminent arrival. Maintenance of the buildings was entrusted to a curator with the title of Major-Domo of the Palaces, and he had a staff of twenty full-time employees who swept the hallways, dusted the paintings and statues, trimmed the shrubbery, fed the beasts of the park, repaired what needed to be repaired, and each week put fresh linens on the beds in all the innumerable rooms.

The position of major-domo was hereditary. For the past five hundred years it had been a perquisite of the family of Eruvni Semivinvor, who had been a kinsman of a famous ancient mayor of Ertsud Grand. The current major-domo—Gopak Semivinvor, the fourth of that name—had held the post for almost half a century, and so it had fallen to him to greet Lord Confalume on the occasion of the second of his two visits to the Summer Palace.

That visit, which had lasted four days, was the high point of Gopak Semivinvor's life. Again and again he relived it in the years that followed: hailing the Coronal and his wife the Lady Roxivail as they disembarked from the royal barge, conducting them through the marble outer palace and the game park to the bamboo palace, opening their wine for them and personally serving them their first meal, then leaving them together in splendid regal privacy. Public rumor had it that the Coronal's marriage was a troubled one; Gopak Semivinvor was convinced that Lord Confalume and Lady Roxivail had come to Ertsud Grand in an attempt at reconciliation, and he never ceased to believe that such a reconciliation had indeed taken place during those four days, despite all the subsequent evidence to the contrary.

During the remaining years of Lord Confalume's reign and the whole of Lord Prestimion's, Gopak Semivinvor had lived eternally in expectation of the next royal visit. He arose each dawn—the major-domo lived in a cottage in a quiet corner of the game park—and conducted a full inspection of the outer palace and then the inner one, compiling a long list of work for his staff to do before the visiting Coronal's party arrived. It was a source of great disappointment to him that that visit never came. But still the inspections went on; still the bamboo roofs received their yearly coat of varnish; still the stone-floored halls of the outer palace were swept and the marble building-blocks repointed. Gopak Semivinvor was eighty years old, now. He did not intend to die until he had once more played host to a Coronal in the Summer Palace of Ertsud Grand.

When news of the impending ascension of Prince Dekkeret to the royal throne reached the ears of Gopak Semivinvor, his first response was to consult his magus for a prognostication of the likelihood that the new Coronal would visit the Summer Palace.

Like many people of the era of the Pontifex Prankipin and the Coronal Lord Confalume, Gopak Semivinvor had developed a profound faith in the ability of soothsayers to foretell the future. The particular school of shamans to which he subscribed was based in Triggoin, the capital city of Majipoori sorcery, in northern Alhanroel beyond the desolate Valmambra desert. It was known as the Advocacy of the Four Names; in recent years it had won a wide following in Ertsud Grand and several neighboring cities of the Mount. Gopak Semivinvor patronized a tall, preternaturally pale Four Names sorcerer named Dobranda Thelk, who was very young for a practitioner of his trade, but had a cold intensity in his gaze that carried a sense of absolute conviction.

Would the Coronal, Gopak Semivinvor asked, soon come calling at the Summer Palace?

Dobranda Thelk closed his glittering eyes for a moment. When he reopened them he seemed to be peering deep into Gopak Semivinvor's soul.

"It is quite clear that he will come," said the magus. "But only if the palace is in in good order, and all is in full accordance with expectation."

Gopak Semivinvor knew that it could never be otherwise so long as he was in charge of the palace. And such a wild throb of joy ran through him that he feared that his breast would burst.

"Tell me," he said, laying a royal on the sorcerer's tray and then, after a moment's consideration, putting a five-crown piece beside it, "what particular things must I do to ensure the complete comfort of Lord Dekkeret when he is at the Summer Palace?"

Dobranda Thelk mixed the colored powders that he used in divination. He closed his eyes again and murmured the Names. He spoke the Five Words. He sifted the powders through his hands, and said the Names a second time, and then the Three Words that could never be written down. When he looked up at Gopak Semivinvor those potent eyes of his were as hard as auger-bits.

"There is one thing above all else: you must see to it that the Coronal sleeps in proper relationship to the powerful stars Thorius and Xavial. You are able to locate those stars in the sky, are you not?"

"Of course. But how am I to know which position of the palace is the one that provides the proper relationship?"

"That will be revealed to you in dreams," replied Dobranda Thelk.

"By a sending, do you mean?"

"It could be in that form, yes," said the magus, and from the coolness of his tone Gopak Semivinvor knew that the consultation was at an end.

Three times in his long life Gopak Semivinvor had experienced sendings of the Lady of the Isle, or so he believed: dreams in which the kindly Lady had come to him and offered him reassurance that his life's journey followed the correct path. There had been no specific information for him to use in any of those three dreams, only a general feeling of warmth and ease. But that night, as he made ready for bed, he knelt briefly and asked the Lady to grace him with a fourth sending, one that would guide him in his desire to serve the new Coronal in the best possible way.

And indeed, not long after he had given himself over to sleep, Gopak Semivinvor felt the sensation of warmth in his scalp that he regarded as the portent of a sending. He lay perfectly still, suspended in that condition of observant receptivity that everyone learned as a child, in which the sleeper's mind was simultaneously lost in slumber and vigilantly aware of whatever guidance the dream might bring.

This seemed different from his previous sendings, though. The sensations were not particularly benign. He felt a touch, definitely a touch, from outside, but not a kindly one. The pressure against his scalp was greater than it had been those other times, was even painful, in a way; the air seemed to grow chill around his sleeping body; and there was no trace of that feeling of well-being that one always expected to have from contact with the mind of the Lady of the Isle of Sleep. Yet he maintained his receptivity to what was to come, holding his mind open and allowing it to be flooded with an awareness of—

Of what?

Discontinuity. Disparity. Incongruity. *Wrongness.*

Wrongness, yes. A powerful sense that the hinges of the world were coming undone, that the joints of the cosmos were loosening, that the gate of terror stood open and a black tide of chaos was pouring through.

He awakened then, sitting up, holding himself tightly in his own arms. Gopak Semivinvor was sweating and trembling so distemperately that he wondered if his last moments might be upon him. But gradually he grew calm. There was still a strange pressure in his brain, that feel-

ing as of something pushing from without—a disturbing feeling, a
frightening one, even.

Some moments passed, and then clarity of mind began to return,
and a certain degree of ease of soul; and with that came the conviction
that he understood the meaning of the oracle's words.

You must see to it that the Coronal sleeps in proper relationship to the
powerful stars Thorius and Xavial. Plainly the present configuration of
the bamboo palace was an improper one, unluckily aligned, out of tune
with the movements of the cosmos. Very well. The building was designed to be dismantled and reconstructed along a different axis. That
was what must be done. The palace needed to be turned on its foundation.

That the palace had not been dismantled and moved in hundreds of
years—maybe as much as a thousand—did not trouble the major-domo
for more than an instant. Some small prudent voice within him suggested that the project might be more difficult than he suspected, but
against that tiny objection came the insistent clamor of his desire to get
on with the work. Desperate haste impelled him: the magus had spoken, the troubling dream had somehow provided reinforcement, and
now he must make the palace ready, in accordance with the com-
mandment that had been laid upon him, and lose no time about it. Of
that he had no doubt. Doubt did not seem an option in this enterprise.

Nor did it concern him that he did not, at the moment, know which
orientation of the building would be more desirable than the present
one. It had to be moved, that was clear. The Coronal would not come
unless it was. And he had every reason to think that the appropriate po-
sitioning would be revealed to him as he set about the task. He was the
Major-Domo of the Palaces, and had been for nearly fifty years; it had
been given into his hands to care for this wonderful building and keep
it ready at all times for the use of the anointed Coronal; one might even
say that destiny had chosen him to perform that special task. He was
confident that he would perform it correctly.

Gopak Semivinvor rushed out into the night—a mild one and warm,
Ertsud Grand's climate being one of almost unending summer—made
his way through the game park to the bamboo palace's front gate, scattering nocturnal mibberils and thassips as he ran, and sending big-eyed
black menagungs fluttering up into the treetops. Panting, dizzy with ex-
ertion, he leaned against the gatepost of the building and stared upward
until he located the brilliant red star Xavial, which marked the midpoint

of the sky, the great axis of the universe. Its mighty counterpoise, bright Thorius, lay not far to the left of it.

Now—how to determine the right position for the building, the one that represented the proper relationship to Thorius and Xavial—?

He turned, and turned, and, unsure, turned again, and yet again. His mind began to reel and swirl. It seemed to Gopak Semivinvor after a time that he was standing still, and the whole vault of the sky was whirling furiously about him. East, west, north, south—which direction was the right one? This way, and the Coronal's bedroom would face the row of great mansions along the eastern shore of the lake; this, and he would be looking toward the pleasure-houses of the western shore; turn like this, and his rooms would yield the sight of the dense forest of furry-leaved kokapas trees that rimmed the lake's southern edge. Whereas to the north—

To the north, equidistant between the stars Xavial and Thorius, was the blazing white star Trinatha, the sorcerers' star, the star that rested in the heavens above the city of wizards, Triggoin.

Into the soul of Gopak Semivinvor came flooding the ineluctable certainty that Trinatha was the key to what the magus Dobranda Thelk had meant by the "proper relationship." He must swing the building around until the Coronal's bedroom pointed along the line that ran between Thorius and red Xavial to holy Trinatha, the white star of wizardry, Dobranda Thelk's own guiding star.

Yes. Yes. It was precisely the midnight hour, the Hour of the Coronal. What could be more auspicious? He caught up a sharp stick and began scratching deep gouges in the soft velvet of the lawn that ringed the bamboo palace, ugly brown lines that indicated the precise configuration to which the building must be shifted. He worked with frantic urgency, trying to finish the task of sketching his plan before the stars, as they journeyed through the night sky, had moved on into some other pattern of relationship.

In the morning Gopak Semivinvor summoned his entire crew, the twenty men and women who had worked under his supervision for so long, some of them nearly as long as he himself had been major-domo. "We will dismantle the building at once, and reposition it by ninety degrees, a little more or a little less, so that it faces in this direction," he said, holding his hands out in parallel along the lines gouged in the lawn to indicate how he meant the palace to be turned.

They were obviously dismayed. They looked at one another as

though to say, "Is he serious?" and "Can the old man have lost his mind?"

"Come," Gopak Semivinvor said, clapping his hands impatiently. "You see the patterns in the grass. These two long lines: they mark the place where the Coronal's bedroom window must face when the re-building is complete." To his foreman he said, "Kijel Busiak, you will have a row of stakes driven immediately into the ground along the lines I've drawn, so that there'll be no chance of confusion later on. Gorvin Dihal, you will arrange at once for the weaving of a complete set of new binding-cords for the canes, since I fear the ones that exist will not survive the dismantling. And you, Voyne Bethafar—"

"Sir?" said Kijel Busiak timidly.

Gopak Semivinvor stared toward the foreman in annoyance. "Is there some question?"

"Sir, is it not true that the story that the building was designed to be taken apart and quickly reassembled is nothing but a myth, a legend, something that we tell to visitors but don't ourselves believe?"

"It is not," Gopak Semivinvor said. "I have studied the history of the Summer Palace deeply for many decades, and I have no doubt not only that it can be done, but that it *has* been done, over and over again in the course of the centuries. It simply has not been done recently, that is all."

"Then you have some manual, sir, which would explain the best way of carrying out the work? For of a certainty no one alive has any memory of how the thing is done."

"There is no manual. Why would such a thing be necessary? What we have here is a simple structure of bamboo canes joined by silken cords and covered with a roof of the same sort. We unfasten the cords; we part the roof-beams, remove them, and set them aside; we take down the outer walls cane by cane. Then we draw a careful plan of the interior and remove the interior walls also, and restore them in the same relative positions, but facing the new way. After which, we reinsert the canes of the walls in their foundation-slots and reconstruct the roof. It is simplicity itself, Kijel Busiak. I want the work to commence at once. There is no telling when Lord Dekkeret will choose to appear in our midst, and I will not have a half-finished palace sitting here when he does."

It did seem to him, as he contemplated the task, that the old tales of taking the building down and putting it back together in a single day must be just that: old tales. The job appeared rather more complicated than that. More likely it would take a week, ten days, perhaps. But he foresaw no difficulties. In the heat of the excitement that suffused his spirit at the thought that a royal visit was at last imminent, he could not doubt that it would be child's play to dismantle the palace, shift every orientation by ninety degrees, and re-erect it. Any provincial architect should be capable of handling the job.

There were some other mild protests, but Gopak Semivinvor was short with them. In the end his will prevailed, as he knew it must. The work began the next day.

Almost at once, unanticipated problems cropped up. The roof-beams turned out to be slotted together most intricately at the building's peak, and the jointures by which they were fastened to the supporting columns and the upper tips of the canes that formed the building's walls were similarly unusual in design. Not only was the style of them antiquated but the technique of fitting the tenons into the mortises was oddly and needlessly baffling, as if they had been designed by a builder determined to win praise for his originality. Gopak Semivinvor heard little about this from his workmen, for they feared the old man's wrath and suffered under the lash of his impatience. But the work of disassembling the building went on into a second week, and a third. Gopak Semivinvor now was heard to say that it might be best to dismiss the whole batch of them and bring in younger workers who might be more cunning practitioners.

The ends of many of the beams broke as they were pulled apart. The unusual slots cracked and could not be repaired. An entire interior wall crashed down unexpectedly and the canes were shattered. Word went forth to Sippulgar for replacements.

Eventually, though—the whole process took a month and a half—the Summer Palace had been transformed into a heap of dismembered canes, many of them too badly damaged to be re-used. The foundation, laid bare now, proved to be also of cane, badly disfigured by dry rot. A number of the slots into which the canes of the wall had been inserted swelled through an uptake of humid air as soon as the canes they had held were removed, and it did not appear as if the old canes could be inserted in them again.

"What do we do now?" Kijel Busiak asked, as he and Gopak Semivinvor surveyed the site of the devastation. "How do we reassemble it, sir? We await your instructions."

But Gopak Semivinvor had no idea of what to do. It was clear now that the Summer Palace of Lord Kassarn was by no means as simple in

form as everyone had thought; that it was, rather, a complex and marvelous thing, a little miracle of construction, the eccentric masterpiece
of some great forgotten architect. Taking it apart had inevitably caused
great damage. Few of the original components of the palace could be
employed in the reconstruction. They would have to construct a new
palace, a flawless imitation of the first one, from the beginning. Who,
though, had the skill to do that?

He understood now that he had, driven by that strange and irresistible pressure at the back of his skull, that eerie sending which had
not been a sending of the benevolent Lady, destroyed the Summer
Palace in the process of dismantling it. It would not, could not, now be
shifted to a more auspicious orientation. There was no Summer Palace
at all, any more. Gopak Semivinvor sank down disconsolate against one
of the piles of roof-beams, buried his face in his hands, and began to sob.
Kijel Busiak, who could not find any words to speak, left him there
alone.

After a time he rose. Walking away from the ruined building without
looking back, the major-domo took himself to the rim of the island, and
stood for a long while at the edge of the Great Lake with his mind utterly empty of thought, and then, very slowly, he stepped out into the
lake and continued to walk forward until the water was over his head.

6

Septach Melayn said, "Again, milady. Up with your stick! Parry! Parry! Parry!"

Keltryn met each thrust of the tall man's wooden baton with a quick, darting response, successfully anticipating every time the direction from which he would be coming at her, and getting the baton where it needed to be. She had no illusions about her ability to hold her own in any sort of contest with the great swordsman. But that was not expected of her, or of anyone. What was important was the development of her skills; and those skills were developing with remarkable speed. She could tell that by the way Septach Melayn smiled at her now. He saw real promise in her. More than that: he seemed to have taken a liking to her, he who was reputed to have no more interest in women than a stone would. And so, since his return from the Labyrinth, he had begun affording her the rare privilege of private tutoring in the art.

She had done as much as she could without him throughout the weeks of his absence at the Labyrinth for the funeral of the old Pontifex and the ceremonies that marked Prestimion's succession to the imperial throne. During that time Keltryn had sought out members of Septach Melayn's class in swordsmanship and made them drill with her, one on one.

Some, who had never reconciled themselves to the anomalous presence of a woman in the class, simply laughed her off. But a few, perhaps for no other reason than that they saw it as an opportunity to spend some time in the company of an attractive young woman, were willing enough to humor her in that request. Polliex, the Earl of Estotilaup's handsome son, was one of that group. He was tremendously good-looking—indeed, the handsomest boy Keltryn had ever known—and only too aware of that fact himself. He interpreted Keltryn's invitation to practice at rapier and singlesticks with him as a portent of conquest.

But Keltryn, at the moment, was not looking to become anybody's conquest, and Polliex's flawlessly contoured face was irrelevant anyway when hidden behind a fencer's mask. After several sessions with him at which he insisted on asking her, more than once in the face of her polite refusal, to join him for a weekend in riding the mirror-slides and enjoying other amusements at the pleasure-city of High Morpin, just downslope from the Castle, she canceled further drills with Polliex and turned instead to Toraman Kanna, of Syrinx, the prince's son.

He was a striking-looking young man too, slim and sinuous, with olive-hued skin and long dark hair. In fact he had an almost feminine beauty about him, so much so that it was generally assumed he was one of Septach Melayn's playmates. Perhaps he was; but Keltryn quickly found out that he found women attractive too, or, at at any rate found her to be. "You should hold your weapon like this," Toraman Kanna said, standing behind her and lifting her arm. And then, after he had corrected her position, he let his hand slide up the side of her fencing jacket and rest lightly on her right breast. Just as easily, she pushed it aside. Possibly he thought it was his princely prerogative to touch her like that. They did not drill together a second time.

Audhari of Stoienzar provided her with no such complications. The big freckle-faced boy seemed hearty and normal enough, but what concerned him when he was with her in the gymnasium was fencing, not flirtation. Keltryn had already discovered that he was the most proficient fencer in the class. Now, meeting with him day after day, she concentrated on learning from him how to master Septach Melayn's trick of dividing each moment into its component parts and then subdividing those, until time itself was slowed and one could step *between* the partitions that kept each moment from the next, thus making oneself easily capable of matching and often of anticipating the actions of one's opponent. It was not an easy science to master. But Audhari, because he was not the awesomely perfect swordsman that Septach Melayn was, was able by the very flaws in his technique to give Keltryn access to his considerable knowledge of the method.

By the time Septach Melayn returned from the Labyrinth, she was nearly as good as Audhari, and superior to all the rest in the class. Septach Melayn noticed that at once, the first time the group met; and when she approached him, somewhat timidly, to ask for private instruction, he agreed without hesitation.

They met for an hour, every third day. He was patient with her, kindly, tolerant of the mistakes that she inevitably made. "Here," he said. "This way. Look high and thrust low, or vice versa. I can read your intentions. You signal too much with your eyes." Their blades met. His slipped easily past hers and touched her lightly on the clavicle. If this were in earnest she would have been slain five times a minute. Never once did she break through his own guard. But she did not expect to. He was the complete master. No one would ever touch him. "Here!" he cried. "Watch! Watch! Watch! *Hup!*"

She worked at stopping time, tried to turn his smooth movements into a series of discontinuous leaps so that she could enter the interval between one segment of time and its successor and finally touch the tip of her blade to him, and almost managed to do it. But even so he always eluded her, and then he had that wonderful knack of seeming to come back at her from two sides at once in the counterthrust, and she had no way of defending against that.

She loved drilling with him. She loved *him*, in a way that had nothing to do with sex. She was seventeen and he was—what? Fifty? Fifty-five? Old, anyway, very old, though still dashing and elegant and extremely handsome. But he was not at all interested in women, so everyone said. Not in *that* way, anyhow, though he seemed to like women as friends, and was often seen in the company of them. That was fine with Keltryn. All she wanted from men, at this point in her life, was friendship, nothing more. And Septach Melayn was a wonderful friend to have.

He was charming and funny, a playful, buoyant man. He was wise: had not Lord Prestimion chosen him to be High Counsellor of the Realm? He was said to be a connoisseur of wines, he knew much about music and poetry and painting, and no one at the Castle, not even the Coronal, had a finer wardrobe. And of course he was the best swordsman in the world. Even those to whom swordsmanship was a meaningless pastime admired him for that: you had to admire someone who was better than everyone else at something, regardless of what the something was.

Also Septach Melayn was kind and good, liked by all, as modest as his great attainments permitted him to be, famously devoted to his friend the Coronal. He was altogether a paragon, the happiest and most enviable of men. But as she got to know him better, Keltryn began to wonder whether there might not be a core of sadness somewhere within him that he worked hard to keep concealed. Doubtless he hated growing old, he who was such a masterly athlete and so beautiful to behold. Perhaps he was secretly lonely. And maybe he wished that there was someone, somewhere among the fifteen billion people of this giant planet, who could give him an even match on the dueling-grounds.

In the third week of their private lessons Septach Melayn removed his mask suddenly, after she had carried out an especially well handled series of interchanges, and said, peering down at her from his great height, "That was quite fine, milady. I've never seen anyone come along quite as fast as you have. A pity that we'll have to bring these lessons to a halt very soon."

He could not have hurt her more if he had slashed her across the throat with the edge of his rapier.

"We will?" she said, horrified.

"The Pontifex will be arriving at the Castle shortly for Lord Dekkeret's coronation ceremony, and after that the real changes of the new regime will begin. Lord Dekkeret will want his own High Counsellor. I think he plans to appoint Prestimion's brother Teotas. As for me, I've been asked to continue in Prestimion's service, this time as High Spokesman to the Pontifex. Which means, of course, that I'll be leaving the Castle and taking up residence at the Labyrinth."

Keltryn gasped. "The Labyrinth—oh, how terrible, Septach Melayn!"

With a graceful shrug he said, "Ah, not so bad as it's credited with being, I think. There are decent tailors there, and some estimable restaurants. And Prestimion doesn't plan to be one of those reclusive Pontifexes who hides himself away at the bottom of the whole thing and doesn't come out into daylight for the rest of his life. The court will do a good deal of traveling, he tells me. I imagine he'll be shuttling up and down the Glayge as often as any Pontifex ever has, and going farther afield, too. But if I'm down there with him, and you're up here, milady—"

"Yes. I see."

He paused ever so slightly. "It would not occur to you, I suppose, to move to the Labyrinth yourself? We could continue our studies, of course, in that case."

Keltryn's eyes widened. What was he saying?

"My parents sent me to the Castle to get a broader education, excellence," she replied, almost whispering it. "I don't think they ever imagined—that I would go—that I would go *there*—"

"No. The Castle is all light and gaiety; and the Labyrinth, well, it is otherwise. This is the place for young lords and ladies. I know that." Septach Melayn seemed oddly uncomfortable. She had never seen him other than perfectly poised. But now he was fidgeting; he was tugging nervously at his carefully trimmed little beard; his pale blue eyes were having trouble meeting hers.

It could not be that he felt bodily desire for her. She knew that. But all the same he plainly did not want to leave her behind when he followed Prestimion to the underground capital. He wanted the lessons to continue. Was it because she was such a responsive pupil? Or was it their unexpected friendship that he cherished? He is a lonely man, she thought. He's afraid that he'll miss me. She was astounded by the idea that the High Counsellor Septach Melayn might feel that way about her.

But she could not go with him to the Labyrinth. Would not, could not, should not. Her life was here at the Castle, for the time being, and then, she supposed, she would return to her family at Sipermit, and marry someone, and then—well, that was as far as she could carry the thought. But the Labyrinth fit nowhere into the expected course of her future.

"Perhaps I could visit you there now and then," she said. "For refresher courses, you know."

"Perhaps you could," said Septach Melayn, and they let the subject drop.

Her sister Fulkari was waiting for her in the recreation-hall of the sector of the Castle's western wing known as the Setiphon Arcade, where they both had their apartments, and their brother Fulkarno as well. Fulkari used the swimming pool there almost every day. Keltryn usually joined her there after her fencing lesson.

It was a splendid pool, a huge oval tank of pink porphyry with an inlay of bright malachite in starburst patterns running completely around it just beneath the surface of the water. The water itself, which came warm and cinnamon-scented from a spring somewhere far below the surface of the Mount, was of a pale rosy hue and seemed almost like wine. Supposedly this sector of the Castle had been a guesthouse for visiting princes from distant worlds in the reign of some long-forgotten Coronal at a time when commerce between the stars was more common than it had later become, and this was part of their recreational facilities. Now it served the needs of royal guests from closer at hand.

No one was at the pool but Fulkari when Keltryn arrived. She was moving back and forth with swift, steady strokes, tirelessly swimming from one end of the pool to the other, turning, starting on the next lap. Keltryn stood at the pool's edge, watching her for a time, admiring the suppleness of her sister's body, the perfection of her strokes. Even now, at seventeen, Keltryn still looked upon Fulkari as a woman and saw herself as a mere gawky girl. The seven years' difference in their ages seemed an immense gulf. Keltryn coveted the ripeness of Fulkari's hips, the greater fullness of Fulkari's breasts, all those tokens of what she regarded as her sister's superior femininity.

"Aren't you coming in?" Fulkari called.

Keltryn stripped off her fencing costume, threw it casually aside, and slipped into the water beside Fulkari. The water was silky and soothing. They swam side by side for some minutes, saying little.

When they wearied of swimming laps, they bobbed up together and floated, paddling gently about. "What's bothering you?" Fulkari asked. "You're very quiet today. Did badly in your fencing lesson, did you?"

"Quite the contrary."

"What is it, then?"

Keltryn said in a stricken tone, "Septach Melayn told me that he's going to be moving to the Labyrinth. They're going to hold the coronation ceremony soon, and then he'll become Prestimion's High Spokesman down there."

"I suppose that ends your career as a swordsman, then," said Fulkari, with no particular show of sympathy.

"If I stay here, yes. But he's asked me to move to the Labyrinth so we can continue our lessons."

"Really!" Fulkari exclaimed, and chortled. "To move to the Labyrinth! You! — He didn't ask you to marry him, too, did he?"

"Don't be silly, Fulkari."

"He won't, you know."

Keltryn felt anger rising in her. There was no reason for Fulkari to be so cruel. "Don't you think I know that?"

"I just wanted to make sure you weren't getting any funny ideas about him."

"Becoming Septach Melayn's wife is something that has never entered my mind, I assure you. And I'm quite certain it's never entered his. —No, Fulkari, I just want him to go on training me. But of course I'm not going to move to the Labyrinth."

"That's a relief." Fulkari clambered from the pool. Keltryn, after a moment, followed her. Putting her hands behind her, Fulkari leaned back and stretched voluptuously, like a big cat. Languidly she said, "I never understood this thing of yours with swords, anyway. What good is being a swordsman? Especially a female one."

"What good is being a lady of the court?" Keltryn retorted. "At least a swordsman has some skill with something other than her tongue."

"Perhaps so. But it's a skill that can't be put to any purpose. Well, you'll grow out of it, I suspect. Let some prince catch your fancy and that's the last we'll all hear of your rapiers and your singlesticks."

"I'm sure you're right," said Keltryn tartly, and made a face. She leaped nimbly to her feet, ran down the margin of the pool to the far end, and dived in again, making such a shallow jump that the sting of hitting the water ran painfully through her breasts and belly. Swimming with short, choppy, angry strokes, she swam back to where Fulkari was sitting and popped her head up into view.

"Is that Coronal of yours going to get us good seats at the coronation?" she asked, flashing a malicious toothy smile.

"*My* Coronal? In what way is he *my* Coronal?"

"Don't be cute with me, Fulkari."

Primly Fulkari said, "Prince Dekkeret—*Lord* Dekkeret, I should say—and I are simply friends. Just as you and Septach Melayn are friends, Keltryn."

Keltryn scrambled up over the side of the pool and stood above her sister, dripping on her. "We're not exactly friends in the same way as you and Dekkeret, though."

"What ever could you mean by that?"

"You're *doing* it with him, aren't you?"

Flashes of color appeared in Fulkari's cheeks. But there was only a moment's delay before she replied, almost defiantly, "Well, yes. Of course."

"And therefore you and he—"

"Are friends. Nothing more than friends."

"You aren't going to marry him, Fulkari?"

"This is really none of your business, you know."

"But are you? Are you? The Coronal's wife? Queen of the world? Of course you are! You'd be a fool to say no! And you won't, because you're not a fool. You aren't a fool, are you?"

"Please, Keltryn—"

"I'm your sister. I have a right. I just want to know—"

"Stop it! Stop!"

Abruptly Fulkari stood up, searched about her for a towel, slung it around her shoulders as though she felt the need for a garment of some sort, however useless, and began to pace stormily about. She was obviously very annoyed, and flustered as well. Keltryn could not remember the last time her sister had seemed flustered.

"I didn't mean to upset you," she said, making an attempt to sound conciliatory. "You're the best friend I have in the world, Fulkari. It doesn't strike me as being out of line for me to ask you if you're going to marry a man you're obviously in love with. But if it bothers you so much to talk about these things, I'll stop. All right?" Fulkari cast the towel aside and walked back toward her. She sat down once more beside her. The storm seemed to have passed. After a little bit Keltryn said, eyes bright with fresh curiosity, "What is it like, Fulkari?"

"With him, you mean?"

"With anyone. I don't have any real idea, you know. I haven't ever—"

"No!" said Fulkari, genuinely amazed. "Are you serious? Never? Not at *all*?"

"No. Never."

Fulkari appeared to be having trouble believing that. It had seemed harmless enough a thing to admit, but Keltryn found herself wishing that she could call back her own words. She felt herself blushing all over. Ashamed of her innocence, ashamed to be naked like this now with her own sister, ashamed of the thinness of her thighs, the boyish flatness of her buttocks, the meagerness of her small, high breasts. Fulkari, sitting here face to face with her, looked by comparison like some goddess of womanhood.

But Fulkari's tone was gentle, loving, tender as she said, "I have to tell you that this is a real surprise. Someone as outgoing and lively as you—taking a fencing class with a bunch of boys, no less—I thought, certainly she's been with two or three by now, maybe even more—"

Keltryn shook her head. "Not so. Not one. Nobody at all."

With a twinkle Fulkari said, "Don't you think it's time, then?"

"I'm only seventeen, Fulkari."

"I was sixteen, the first time. And I thought I was getting a slow start."

"Sixteen. Well!" Keltryn tossed her head, shaking water from the moist red-gold curls. "But we've always been different, you and me. I'm much more of a tomboy than you ever were, I bet." She leaned close to Fulkari and said in a low voice, "Who was it?"

"Madjegau."

"*Madjegau?*" The name emerged in such a derisive shriek that she clapped her hand over her own mouth. "But he was such a—nincompoop, Fulkari!"

"Of course he was. But they can be nincompoops and still be attractive, you know. Especially when you're sixteen."

"I've never felt much attraction for nincompoops, I have to confess."

"You wouldn't understand. It's a matter of hormones. I was sixteen and ripe for it, and Madjegau was tall and handsome and in the right place at the right time, and—well—"

"I suppose. I confess I can't see the attraction. —Does it hurt, the first time, when they go inside you?"

"A little. It's not important. You're concentrating on other things, Keltryn. You'll see. One of these days, not too far in the future—"

They were both giggling now, all animosities gone, sisters and friends.

"After Madjegau, were there many others? Before Dekkeret, I mean?"

"There were—some." Fulkari glanced over doubtfully at Keltryn. "I don't really think I ought to be talking about this."

"You can tell me. I'm your sister. Why should we have secrets? —Come on. Who else, Fulkari?"

"Kandrigo. You remember him, I think. And Jengan Biru."

"That's three men, then! Plus Dekkeret."

"I didn't mention Velimir yet."

"Four! Oh, you're shameless, Fulkari! Of course I knew there had to be some. But four—!" She threw Fulkari a flashing inquisitorial look. "There aren't any more, are there?"

"I can't believe I'm telling you all this. But no, no others, Keltryn. Four lovers. That's not really a lot, over the course of five years, you know."

"And then Dekkeret."

"And then Dekkeret, yes."

Keltryn leaned toward Fulkari again, staring raptly into her eyes. "He's the best one, isn't he? Better than all the others put together. I know he is. I mean, I don't *know*, but I think—I'm quite sure—"

"Enough, Keltryn. This is absolutely not something I'm going to discuss."

"You don't need to. I see the answer on your face. He's wonderful: I'm certain of that. And now he's Coronal. And you're going to be queen of the world. Oh, Fulkari—Fulkari, I'm so happy for you! I can hardly tell you how much I—"

"Stop it, Keltryn." Fulkari rose in one quick, brusque motion and began to gather up her clothing. Crisply, irritably, she said, "I think it's about time for us to go."

Keltryn saw that she had struck a nerve. Something was wrong, definitely wrong. But she couldn't let matters drop here.

"You *aren't* going to marry him, Fulkari?"

A chilly silence. Then: "No. I'm not."

"He hasn't asked? He has someone else in mind?"

"No. To both questions."

"He's asked, and you've turned him down?" said Keltryn incredulously. "Why, Fulkari? Why? You don't love him? Is he too old for you? Do *you* have someone else in mind? —I can't help it, Fulkari. I know all this is bothering you. But I just can't understand how you can—"

To Keltryn's amazement, Fulkari suddenly seemed close to tears. She tried to hide it, turning quickly away, standing with her face toward the wall and fumbling furiously with her clothes. But Keltryn could see the quivering movements of Fulkari's shoulders, as of sobs barely being repressed.

In a dark, hollow voice Fulkari said, with her back still turned, "Keltryn, I do love Dekkeret. I do want to marry him. It's *Lord* Dekkeret I don't want to marry."

Keltryn found that mystifying. "But—what—"

Fulkari turned to face her. "Do you have any idea what it involves, being the Coronal's wife? The endless work, the responsibilities, the official dinners, the speeches? You ought to take a look at the schedule they post for the Lady Varaile. It's a nightmare. I don't want any part of it. Maybe I'm foolish, Keltryn, maybe I'm shallow and silly, but I can't do anything about what I'm like. Marrying the Coronal seems to me very much like volunteering to go to prison."

Keltryn stared. There was real torment in Fulkari's voice, and Keltryn had no doubt of her pain. She felt a rush of compassion for her;
but then, almost immediately after, came annoyance, anger, even
outrage.

She had always thought of herself as the child, and Fulkari as the
woman, but all of a sudden everything was reversed. At twenty-four,
Fulkari seemed to think that she was still a girl. But did she believe she
was going to be a girl all the rest of her life? Did she want nothing more
for herself than going riding in the meadows, and flirting with handsome men, and sometimes making love with them?

Keltryn knew that it was best not to continue pressing her sister on
any of this. But words came pouring out of her despite herself.

"Forgive me for saying this, Fulkari. But I'm amazed by what you've
just told me. You're in love with the most desirable and important man
in the world, and he loves you and wants to marry you. But he's about
to become Coronal, and you say it's just too much trouble to be the
Coronal's wife? Then I have to tell you you *are* a fool, Fulkari, the
biggest fool that ever was. I'm sorry if that hurts you, but it's true. A fool.
And I'll tell you something else: if you don't want to marry Dekkeret, I
will. If I can ever get him to notice me, that is. If I could put on ten or
fifteen pounds, I'd look just like you, and I'll learn to do whatever it is
that men and women do with each other, and then—"

Coldly Fulkari said, "You're talking nonsense, Keltryn."

"Yes. I know I am."

"Then stop it! Stop! Stop!" Fulkari *was* crying now. "Oh, Keltryn—
Keltryn—"

"Fulkari—"

Keltryn rushed toward her. Held her tight. Felt her own tears coursing down her cheeks.

7

Jacomin Halifice said, "The Lord Gaviral respectfully requests your presence at his palace, Count Mandralisca."

Mandralisca looked up. "Is that how he said it, Jacomin? 'Respectfully requests'?"

Halefice smiled for perhaps half a second. "The phrase was my own, your grace. I thought it sounded more courtly to say it so."

"Yes. I dare say you did. It didn't seem like Gaviral's style at all. —Well, tell him I'll be there in five minutes. No, let's make it ten, I think."

Let Gaviral respectfully wait. Mandralisca glanced down at the Barjazid helmet, lying before him on his desk in a little glittering heap. He had been playing with it all afternoon, donning it and sending his mind out into the world, testing the powers of the thing, trying to coax from it more knowledge of what it could do, and he wanted a little time to review what he had achieved.

He had so little control over it, so far. He could not direct it toward any particular region of the world, nor could he choose to make contact with any specific individual. Barjazid had assured him several times that they would eventually solve the directionality problem. Aiming the power of the helmet at any one person was a more difficult challenge, but Barjazid seemed to think that in time that could be achieved also. Certainly both things had been possible with earlier models, such as the one that Prestimion had used to strike down Barjazid's brother Venghenar. This newer one had greater range and delicacy of effect—it was a rapier, not a saber, capable not simply of inflicting massive injury but of inducing light deflections in the minds it touched—but certain other qualities of precision had been lost.

Meanwhile, Barjazid said, it would be a good idea for Mandralisca to practice using the helmet daily, to accustom himself to its operation, to build up in himself the mental resilience needed to withstand the strains it imposed on the operator. And so he had. Day after day, he had visited citizens of Majipoor at random, sliding into their minds, tickling their souls with little unpleasant suggestions. It was interesting to see what kind of impact it was possible to have, even on a well guarded mind.

He had found that he was able to enter almost anyone he chose, though sleeping minds were much more vulnerable than waking ones. He could break down the defenses of the soul with a few deftly placed jabs, just as he had been able to do so splendidly in his baton-dueling days, when his agility of movement and his superior reflexes had brought him championship after championship in the tournaments, and, what was even more valuable, the great approbation of Dantirya Sambail. Using the helmet was very similar. In the tournaments, one did not wield the baton as a bludgeon; one baffled and bewildered one's opponent with it, besieging him so with lightning-swift flicks of the pliant nightflower-wood stick that he left himself open for the climactic attack. Here, too, Mandralisca had discovered, it was best to undermine the victim's own sense of purpose and security with a few light prods and nudges, and let him continue the process of destruction on his own. The gardener in Lord Havilbove's park, the custodian of the bamboo palace at Ertsud Grand, the hapless calendar-keeper at that Hjort village, and all the rest of them—how easy it had been, really, and how pleasing!

Why, just today—

But the Lord Gaviral had respectfully requested his presence at his palace, Mandralisca reminded himself. One must not keep the Lords of Zimroel waiting unduly long, or they grow petulant. He slipped the helmet into the pouch at his hip where it resided whenever it was not in use, and set out up the path to Gaviral's hilltop palace.

The palaces of the Five Lords appeared impressive from the outside, but their interiors reflected not only the haste with which the entire outpost had been constructed but the general tastelessness of the brothers. The architect—a Ghayrog from Dulorn, Hesmaan Thrax by name—had designed them to inspire awe in viewers approaching them from below: each of the five buildings was a huge dome of smooth and perfectly set tile, gray with a red undercast, rising to a great height and topped with the red crescent moon that was emblematic of the Sambailid clan. Within, though, they were bare echoing halls with rough unfinished walls and oddly mismatched furnishings badly placed.

Gaviral's home was the best of the sorry lot. Its main hall was a vast soaring space that a great man like Confalume would have expanded easily into, and further enhanced with his own grandeur—he had never seemed out of place amidst the immensity of the throne-room he had built for himself at the Castle—but a petty creature like Gaviral was diminished by it. He seemed an irrelevance, an afterthought, in his own high hall.

As the eldest son of Dantirya Sambail's brother Gaviundar, he had been entitled to first choice of the rich possessions that once had adorned the Procurator's superb palace in Ni-moya. To him had fallen the most admirable of the statuary and hangings, the floor-coverings woven from the pelts of haiguses and steetmoy, the strange sculptures fashioned of animal bone that Dantirya Sambail had brought back from some expedition into the chilly Khyntor Marches of northern Zimroel. But all these treasures had suffered some abuse over the years, especially during the time following the death of Dantirya Sambail when mountainous drunken Gaviundar had inhabited the procuratorial palace. Many of the finest things were battered and chipped and stained, mountings had come unsprung, cracks had developed in delicate and irreplaceable objects. And now that they had descended to Gaviral's custody they were negligently, almost randomly, displayed, strewn here and there about the echoing oversized chambers of the building like the neglected toys of some indifferent child.

Gaviral himself lounged in the midst of this shabby disheveled array in a broad thronelike chair that looked as though it had been designed for one of his four brothers, all of whom were much larger men than he was. A couple of his women crouched at his feet. All five of the Sambailids had furnished themselves with harems, in defiance of all custom and propriety. A flask of wine was clutched in his hand. Compared with his brothers, Gaviral was a model of sobriety and polite deportment; but he was a heavy drinker, nonetheless, like all his tribe.

Behind Gaviral's left shoulder stood a second of the brothers. The Lord Gavdat, this one was, the plump, heavy-jowled, ineffably stupid one who liked to play with sorcery and prognostication. He was garbed today, absurdly, in the manner of a geomancer of the High City of Tidias, far away on Castle Mount: the tall brass helmet, the richly brocaded robe, the elaborately figured cloak. Mandralisca could not recall when he had last seen anything so ludicrous.

He made a formal gesture of obeisance. "Milord Gaviral. And milord Gavdat."

Gaviral held out his flask. "Will you have some wine, Mandralisca?"

After all this time they had still not succeeded in learning that he detested wine. But he declined politely, with thanks. There was no use trying to explain such things to these people. Gaviral himself drank deeply, and, with a courteousness of which Mandralisca would have thought him incapable, handed the flask to his shambling uncouth brother. Gavdat tipped his head so far back that Mandralisca marveled that his brass helmet did not fall off, drained the flask almost to the bottom, and indolently tossed it to the side, where it spilled its last dregs on what once had been a dazzlingly white steetmoy rug.

"Well, then," Gaviral said finally. His quick little eyes flickered from side to side in that characteristic manner of his that was so like a small rodent's. He brandished some papers that he held crumpled in one hand. "You've heard the news from the Labyrinth, Mandralisca?"

"That the Pontifex is seriously ill following a stroke, milord?"

"That the Pontifex is dead," Gaviral said. "The first stroke was not fatal, but there was a second one. He died instantly, so say these reports, which have been some time in reaching us. Prestimion has already been installed as his successor."

"And Dekkeret as the new Coronal?"

"His coronation will soon take place," said Gavdat, intoning the words as though he were transmitting messages from some invisible spirit. "I have cast his auspices. He will have a short and unhappy reign."

Mandralisca waited. These remarks did not seem to call for comment.

"Perhaps," said the Lord Gaviral, running his fingers through his thinning reddish hair, "this would be an auspicious moment for us to proclaim the independence of Zimroel under our rule. The formidable Confalume gone from the scene, Prestimion preoccupied with establishing his administration at the Labyrinth, an untried new man taking command at the Castle—what do you say, Mandralisca? We pack up and return to Ni-moya, and let it be known that the western continent has lived long enough under the thumb of Alhanroel, eh? We present them with an accomplished fact, *poof!* and defy them to object."

Before Mandralisca could reply there came a loud clattering and crashing in the outside hall, and some hoarse shouts. Mandralisca assumed that these noises were harbingers of the arrival of the blustering bestial Lord Gavinius, but to his mild surprise the newcomer was bulky thickset Gavahaud, he who fancied himself a paragon of elegance and grace. The interruption was a welcome one: it gave him a moment to find the most diplomatic way of framing his response. Gavahaud came in muttering about encountering an unexpected obstacle in the sculpture-hall outside. Then, seeing Mandralisca, he glanced toward Gaviral and said, "Well? Does he agree?"

No question that they were seething with the yearning to unleash their war against Prestimion and Dekkeret. They wanted only for him to pat them on their heads and praise them for their high ambitions and warlike souls.

All three brothers had their attention focused intently on him now: gimlet-eyed Gaviral, bloodshot Gavahaud, moist-eyed foolish Gavdat. It was almost poignant, Mandralisca thought, how dependent they were on him, how terribly eager they were to have him confirm whatever pitiful shreds of strategy they had contrived to work out for themselves.

He said, "If you mean, milord, do I agree that this is the proper time to announce ourselves independent of the imperial government, my answer is that I do not believe it is."

Each of the three reacted in his own way to Mandralisca's calm declaration. Mandralisca observed all three reactions in a single glance, and found them instructive.

Gavdat seemed to recoil almost in shock, his head snapping back so sharply that his soft cheeks jiggled like puddings. Very likely he had made use of his instruments of prognostication to arrive at a very different expectation. Haughty Gavahaud, obviously also startled and disappointed, glared at Mandralisca in astonishment, as though Mandralisca had spat in his face. Only Gaviral took Mandralisca's reply calmly, looking first to one brother and then the other in a smug self-congratulatory way that could mean only one thing: *There! Did I not tell you so? It's important to wait and check things out with Mandralisca.* It was the mark of Gaviral's intellectual preeminence, in this mob of loutish thick-brained brothers, that he alone had some glimmering of self-awareness, some knowledge, perhaps, of how stupid they all really were, how badly they needed their privy counsellor's guidance in any matter of significance.

"May I ask," Gaviral said carefully, "just why you feel as you do?"

"Several reasons, milord." He enumerated them on his fingers. "The first: this is a time of general mourning throughout Majipoor, if I recall correctly the reaction to the Pontifex Prankipin's death twenty years ago. Even in Zimroel the Pontifex is a revered and cherished figure, and in this case the Pontifex was Confalume, the most highly regarded monarch in centuries. I believe it would seem tasteless and offensive to undertake a revolutionary break with the imperial goverment in the very hour when people everywhere are expressing, as I have no doubt they are, their grief at the death of Confalume. It would forfeit us a great deal of sympathy among our own citizens, and would stir an unprofitable degree of anger among the people of Alhanroel."

"Perhaps so," Gaviral conceded. "Go on."

"Second: a proclamation of independence needs to be accompanied by a demonstration that we are capable of making good on our words. I mean by that that we are only in the most preliminary stages of organizing our army, if indeed we have come as far even as the preliminary stages. Therefore—"

"You foresee a war with Alhanroel, do you?" the Lord Gavahaud asked, in a lofty tone. "Is it possible that they would dare to attack us?"

"Oh, yes, milord. I very much think they would attack us. The much-beloved Prestimion is in fact a man of strong passions and no little fury when he is crossed: I have ample evidence of that out of the experience of your famous uncle Dantirya Sambail. And Lord Dekkeret, from what I know of him, will not want to begin his reign by having half his kingdom secede. You can be quite certain that the imperials will send a military force our way as soon as they've digested our proclamation and can levy a body of troops."

Gavdat said, "But the distances are so great—they'd have to sail for many weeks just to reach Piliplok—and then, to march across hostile territory all the way to Ni-moya—"

It was a reasonable point. Perhaps Gavdat was not quite so much of a fool as he seemed, Mandralisca thought.

"You're right, milord, that operating a line of supply that stretches all the way across the Inner Sea from Castle Mount to Ni-moya will be a very challenging task. That is why I think we'll ultimately be successful in our revolt. But they will have no choice, I think, but to try to regain their grasp of us. We must be fully prepared. We must have troops waiting at Piliplok and all the other major ports of our eastern coast, possibly as far south as Gihorna."

"But there's no harbor good enough for a major landing in Gihorna!" Gavahaud objected.

"Exactly so. That's why they might attempt it: to take us by surprise. There's no big harbor there, but there are minor ones all up and down the province. They might make several landings at once in places so obscure they don't expect us to think of them. We must fortify the whole coast. We must have a second line of defense inland, and a third at Nimoya itself. And we'll need to assemble a fleet to meet them at sea in the hope of preventing them from reaching our shores in the first place. All this will take time. We should be well along in the task before we tip our hand."

"You should know," Gavdat said, "that I have cast the runes very carefully, and they predict success in all our endeavors."

"We expect no other outcome," said Mandralisca serenely. "But the runes alone won't ensure our victory. Proper planning is needed also."

"Yes," said Gaviral. "Yes. You see that, brothers, do you not?"

The other two looked at him uncomfortably. Perhaps they sensed in some dim way that quick little Gaviral was somehow outflanking them, allying himself suddenly with the voice of caution now that he realized that caution might be required.

"There is a third point to be considered," Mandralisca said.

He made them wait. He had no desire to overload their brains by piling too many arguments together too quickly.

Then he said, "It happens that I am testing a new weapon, one that is vital to our hopes of victory. It is the helmet that the little man Khaymak Barjazid brought to me, a version of the one that was used—unsuccessfully, alas—by Dantirya Sambail in his struggle against Prestimion long ago. We are making improvements in the weapon. I am extending my mastery over it day by day. It will do terrible destruction, once I'm ready to unleash it. But I am not quite ready, my lords. Therefore I ask you for more time. I ask you for time enough to make the great victory that milord Gavdat so accurately predicts a certainty."

8

As though in a dream Dekkeret roamed the myriad halls of the Castle that would from now on bear his name, examining everything as though seeing it for the first time.

He was alone. He had not made a special point of asking to be left alone, but his manner, his expression, had left no doubt of his need for solitude. This was the fourth day since Dekkeret's return from the festivities at the Labyrinth that had confirmed Prestimion's ascent to the imperial throne, and every moment up till now had been taken up in planning for his own coronation. Only this morning had an opening developed in the press of business, and he had taken the opportunity to wander out into the Pinitor Court and go drifting off by himself through some few of the many levels of the Castle's topmost zone.

He had lived at the Castle more than half his life. He had been eighteen when his thwarting of the attempt on Prestimion's life had earned him the award of knight-initiatehood, and now he was thirty-eight. Though he still signed his name, when official duties required it of him, "Dekkeret of Normork," it would be more accurate to call himself "Dekkeret of the Castle," for Normork was only a boyhood memory and the Castle was his home. The eerie tower of Lord Arioc, the harsh black mass of the Prankipin Treasury, the delicate beauty of the Guadeloom Cascade, the pink granite blocks of Vildivar Close, the spectacular sweep of the Ninety-Nine Steps—he passed through these things every day.

He passed through them now. Down one hall and up the next. He turned a bend in a corridor and found himself staring through a giant crystal window, a window so clear as to be essentially invisible, providing a sudden stunning view of open air—an abyss that descended mile after mile until it was sealed at its lower end by a thick layer of white cloud. It was a vivid reminder that they were thirty miles high, up here at the Castle, sitting at the tip of the biggest mountain in the universe, provided with light and air and water and all other necessities by ingenious mechanisms thousands of years old. You tended to forget that, when you spent enough time at the Castle. You tended to begin to think that this was the primary level of the world, and all the rest of Majipoor was mysteriously sunken far below the surface. But that was wrong. There was the world, and then there was the Castle; and the Castle loomed far above all.

The gateway before him led back into the Inner Castle. On his left lay Prestimion's archival building, rising behind the Arioc Tower; to his right was the white-tiled hall where the Lady of the Isle resided when she came to the Castle to visit her son, and just beyond that Lord Confalume's garden-house, with its bewildering collection of tender plants from tropical regions. He went through the gate that lay beside the Lady's hall and found himself in the maze of hallways and galleries, so bewildering to newcomers, that led to the core of the Castle.

He avoided going near the halls of the court. They were all very busy in there, officials both of the outgoing regime and his own still only partly formed administration—discussing matters of protocol at the coronation ceremony, making lists of guests according to rank and precedence, et cetera, et cetera. Dekkeret had had enough of that, and more than enough, for the moment. Left to his own devices, the coronation rite would have at best an audience of seven or ten people, and would take no longer than the time necessary for Prestimion to take the starburst crown from its bearer and place it on the brow of his successor, and cry, "Dekkeret! Dekkeret! All hail Lord Dekkeret!"

But he knew better than to think it could be as simple as that. There had to be feasting, and rituals, and poetry readings, and the salutations of the high lords, and the ceremonial showing of the Coronal's shield, and the crowning of his mother the Lady Taliesme as the new Lady of the Isle of Sleep, and whatever else was required to invest the incoming Coronal with the proper majesty and awesomeness. Dekkeret did not intend to interfere with any of that. Whatever innovations his reign would bring, and he certainly intended that there would be some, he was not going to expend his authority this early over trivial matters of ceremony. On the other hand, he took care now to keep away from the rooms where the planning was taking place. He turned instead toward the very center of the royal sector, deserted now in this time of transition from one reign to another.

A pair of great metal doors, fifteen feet high, confronted him now. These were Prestimion's doing, a project that had been in progress for a decade or more and was still a long way from completion. The left-hand door was covered, every square inch of it, with scenes from the events of Lord Confalume's reign. The door opposite it still presented only a smooth blank surface.

I will have that door engraved with the deeds of Prestimion, done in a matching style by the same artisans, Dekkeret told himself. And then I will have both doors gilded, so that they will shine forever down the ages.

He touched one of the heavy bronze handles and the door, precisely and delicately calibrated, swung back to admit him to the Castle's heart.

The simple little throne-room of Lord Stiamot was the first thing he came to. He moved on past it, still wandering without a plan, into yet another hodgepodge of little corridors and passageways that he could not remember ever having ventured into before; he was just beginning to conclude that he was lost when he turned to his left and discovered that he was staring into the grand vaulted chamber that was Lord Prestimion's judgment-hall, with the numbing extravagance of the Confalume throne-room just beyond it.

It is wrong, Dekkeret thought, to have to approach these great rooms through such a maze of chaos. Prestimion had carved his judgment-hall out of a dozen or so ancient little rooms; Dekkeret resolved now to do the same with the hallways he had just come through, clearing them all away to create some new formal room, a Chapel of the Divine, perhaps, in which the Coronal might ask for the gift of wisdom before going into the judgment-hall to dispense the law. The Dekkeret Chapel, yes. He smiled. Already he saw it in the eye of his mind, a stone archway over there, and the passage connecting it to the judgment-hall emblazoned with brilliant mosaics in green and gold—

Bravo! he thought. Not even crowned yet, and already launched on your building program!

It surprised him, how easily he was taking to this business of becoming the Coronal Lord of Majipoor. There still remained concealed within him, somewhere, Dekkeret the boy, only child of the struggling merchant Orvan Pettir and his good wife Taliesme, the boy who had roamed the hilly streets of walled Normork with his lively young cousin Sithelle and dreamed of becoming something more than his father had managed to be—a Castle knight, perhaps, who one day would hold some high place in the government: how could that boy not be flabbergasted to find his older self about to accede to the very highest place of all?

He denied none of that. But his older self was less easily awed by such things. A Coronal, he knew by now, is only a man who wears a green robe trimmed with ermine, and on certain formal occasions is permitted to don a crown and occupy a throne. He is still a man, for all that. *Someone* must be Coronal, and, through an unlikely chain of accidents, the choice had fallen upon him. That chain had passed through Prestimion's long-ago visit to Normork and Sithelle's death; through his own unhappy hunting trip in the Khyntor Marches and the impulsive journey of penance to Suvrael that had followed it, leading to his discovery of the Barjazids and their mind-controlling helmets; and through the war against Dantirya Sambail and Akbalik's death, which had removed the expected heir to the crown. Thus it had come down to him. So be it, then. He will be Coronal. He will nevertheless remain a man, who must eat and sleep and void his bowels and one day die. But for the time being he will be Lord Dekkeret of Lord Dekkeret's Castle, and he will build the Dekkeret Chapel over there, and in Normork he will, as he had told Dinitak Barjazid what was beginning to seem like a hundred years ago, eventually build the Dekkeret Gate, and perhaps also—

"My lord?"

The voice, breaking into his ruminations this way, startled him more than a little.

Nor did Dekkeret believe at first that he was the one being addressed. He was still not used to that title, "my lord." He looked around, thinking to find Prestimion somewhere in the vicinity; but then he realized that the words had been intended for him. The speaker was the Su-Suheris Maundigand-Klimd, High Magus to the court of Prestimion.

"I know I intrude on your privacy, my lord. I ask your forgiveness for that."

"You do nothing without good reason, Maundigant-Klimd. Forgiveness is hardly necessary."

"I thank you, sir. As it happens, I have something of importance to bring to your attention. May we confer in some place less public than this?"

Dekkeret signalled the two-headed being to lead the way.

He had never quite understood how Prestimion, a man of the most dogged and ingrained skepticism when it came to all matters mystical and occult, happened to maintain a magus among his circle of intimates. Confalume had been a man much given over to sorcery, yes, and Dekkeret understood that Prankipin before him had had the same irrational leanings; but Prestimion had always seemed to him to be someone who relied on the evidence of his reason and his senses, rather than on the conjurings and prognostications of seers. His High Counsellor, Septach Melayn, was if anything of a more realistic cast of mind yet.

Dekkeret did know that Prestimion, for all his skepticism, had spent some time at the wizards' capital of Triggoin in the north, an episode in his life of which he was most unwilling to speak; and that he had made use of the services of certain master wizards of Triggoin in his war against the usurping Korsibar, and from time to time on other occasions during his reign. So his attitudes toward the magical arts were more complex than it appeared at first glance.

And Maundigand-Klimd seemed never to be far from the center of things at court. Dekkeret did not get the impression that Prestimion kept the Su-Suheris around simply as a sop to the credulity of all those billions of common folk in the world who swore by soothsayers and necromancers, nor was he just a mere decoration. No, Prestimion actually *consulted* Maundigand-Klimd on matters of the highest importance. That was something that Dekkeret meant to discuss with him before the handover of power was complete. Dekkeret himself had only the most casual interest in the persistence of the mantic arts as a phenomenon of modern culture, and no belief whatever in their predictive value. But if Prestimion thought it was useful to keep someone like Maundigand-Klimd close at hand—

And keep him close at hand is what he had done. The Su-Suheris led him now to the private apartments that he had occupied since the earliest days of Prestimion's reign: just across the Pinitor Court from the Coronal's own residence, indeed. Dekkeret had heard that these rooms had belonged to Lord Confalume's forgotten son Prince Korsibar before his usurpation of the throne, that dark deed that had been wiped from the memories of almost everyone in the world. So they were important chambers.

Dekkeret had never had reason to enter them before. He was surprised at how starkly they were furnished. None of the claptrap gadgetry of professional sorcery here, the ambivials and hexaphores, the alembics and armillary spheres, with which the charlatans in the marketplaces awed the populace; nor any of the thick leather-bound volumes of arcane lore, printed in black letter, that stirred such fear among those who feared such things. Dekkeret saw only a few small devices that might have been the calculating machines of a bookkeeper, and quite probably were, and a small library of books that had nothing whatever mystical about their outer appearance. Otherwise Maundigand-Klimd's rooms were virtually empty. Of beds, chairs, Dekkeret saw nothing. Did the Su-Suheris sleep standing up? Evidently so.

And carried on conversations the same way. It was going to be an awkward business, Dekkeret saw. It always was, with a Su-Suheris. Not only were they so inordinately tall—their foot-long necks and elongated spindle-shaped heads brought them to rival Skandars in height, if not in overall bulk—but there was the *weirdness* of them, the inescapable *alienness* of them, to contend with. The two heads, primarily: each with its own identity, independent of the other, its own set of facial expressions, its own tone of voice, its own intensely penetrating pair of emerald-hued eyes. Was there another two-headed race anywhere in the galaxy? And their pale skins, hairless and white as marble, their perpetually somber miens, the hard-edged lipless slits that were their unsmiling mouths—it was all too easy to perceive them as terrifying icy-souled monsters.

Yet this one—this two-headed *sorcerer*—was Lord Prestimion's counsellor and friend. That required explanation. Dekkeret wished he had sought it long before this moment.

Maundigand-Klimd said, "I've long been aware of your distaste for the so-called occult sciences, my lord. Permit me to begin by telling you that I share your attitude."

Dekkeret frowned. "That seems a very strange position for you to take."

"How so?"

"Because of the paradox it contains. The professional magus claims to be a skeptic? He speaks of the occult sciences as the '*so-called*' occult sciences?"

"A skeptic is what I am, yes, though not quite in the sense that you are, lordship. If I read you correctly, you take the position that all prediction is mere guesswork, hardly more reliable than the flipping of a coin, whereas—"

"Oh, not all prediction, Maundigand-Klimd." It was unnerving, looking from one head to the other, attempting to maintain eye contact with only one pair at a time, trying to anticipate which head would speak next. "I concede that Vroons, for example, have a curious knack for choosing the proper fork in the road to take, even in completely unfamiliar territory. And your own long affiliation with Lord Prestimion leads me to conclude that much of the advice you've given him has been valuable. Even so—"

"These are valid examples, yes," said the Su-Suheris—it was the left head, the one with the deeper voice, that spoke. "And others could be provided, things difficult to explain except by calling them magical. Undeniably they are effectual, however mystifying that is. What I refer to, when I say we share a certain outlook toward sorcery, involves the multitude of bizarre and, if you will, barbaric cults that have infested the world for the past fifty years. The folk who flagellate one another and douse themselves in the blood of bidlaks butchered alive. The worshippers of idols. The ones who put their faith in mechanical devices or fanciful amulets. You and I both know how worthless these things are. Lord Prestimion, throughout his reign, has quietly and subtly attempted to let such practices go out of vogue. I'm confident, my lord—" somewhere along the way, Dekkeret realized, the right head had taken over the conversation "—that you will follow the same course."

"You can be sure that I will."

"May I ask if it is your plan to appoint a High Magus when your reign officially begins? Not that I am applying for the job. You should know, if you are not already aware of the fact, that the new Pontifex has asked me to accompany him to the Labyrinth once the ceremonies of your coronation are behind us."

Dekkeret nodded. "I expected as much. As for a new High Magus, I have to tell you, Maundigand-Klimd, that I haven't given the matter a bit of thought. My present feeling is that I don't have any need of one."

"Because you would regard whatever he told you as essentially useless?"

"Essentially, yes."

"It is your choice to make," said Maundigand-Klimd, and from his tone it was clear that the matter was one of utter indifference to him. "However, for the time being there still *is* a High Magus in the Coronal's service, and I feel obliged to inform the new Coronal that I have had a perplexing revelation that might have some bearing on his reign. The former Lord Prestimion advises me that it woud be appropriate for me to bring this revelation to your attention."

"Ah," said Dekkeret. "I see."

"Of course, if your lordship prefers not to—"

"No," Dekkeret said. "If Prestimion thinks I should hear it, by all means share it with me."

"Very well. What I have done is cast an oracle for the outset of your reign. The omens, I regret to say, were somewhat dark and inauspicious."

Dekkeret met that with a smile. "I'm grateful, then, for my lack of belief in the mantic arts. It's easier to handle bad news when you don't have much faith in its substance."

"Precisely so, my lord."

"Can you be more specific about these dark omens, though?"

"Unfortunately, no. I know my own limitations. Everything was shrouded in a haze of ambiguities. Nothing had real clarity. I picked up only a sense of strife ahead, of refusals to offer allegiance, of civil disobedience."

"You saw no faces? You heard no names named?"

"These visions do not function on such a literal level."

"I confess I can't see much value in a prediction so murky that it doesn't actually predict anything," said Dekkeret. He was growing impatient with this now.

"Agreed, my lord. My visions are highly subjective: intuitions, impressions, sensations of the most subtle kind, glimpses of probability, rather than concrete details. But you would do well to be on guard, all the same, against unexpected reversals of circumstance."

"My historical studies tell me that a wise Coronal should always do just that, with or without the advice of mages to guide him. But I thank you for your counsel." Dekkeret moved toward the door.

"There was," said Maundigand-Klimd, before Dekkeret had quite managed to take his leave, "just one aspect of my vision that was clear enough for me to be able to describe it to you in any meaningful way. It involved the Powers of the Realm, who had gathered at the Castle for a certain ceremony of high ritual importance. I sensed their auras, all clustered around the Confalume Throne."

"Yes," Dekkeret said. "We do have all three Powers at the Castle just now: my mother, and Prestimion, and I. And what exactly were we doing in this dream of yours, the three of us?"

"There were four auras, my lord."

Dekkeret looked puzzledly at the magus. "Your dream misleads you, then. I know of only three Powers of the Realm." He counted off on his fingers: "The Pontifex, the Coronal, the Lady of the Isle. It's a division of authority that goes back thousands of years."

"Unmistakably I felt a fourth aura, and it was the aura of a Power. A fourth Power, my lord."

"Are you saying that a new usurper is about to proclaim himself? That we're going to play out the Korsibar business all over again?"

From the Su-Suheris came the Su-Suheris equivalent of a shrug: a partial retraction of the forked column of his neck, a curling inward of his long-clawed six-fingered hands. "There was no evidence in my vision that favors such a possibility. Or that denies it, either."

"Then how—"

"I have one other detail to add. The person who carried the aura of the fourth Power of the Realm carried also the imprint of a member of the Barjazid family."

"What?"

"It was unmistakable, sir. I have not forgotten that you brought the man Venghenar Barjazid, and of course his son Dinitak, to the Castle as prisoners, though it was twenty years ago. The pattern of a Barjazid soul is extraordinarily distinctive."

"So Dinitak's going to be a Power!" cried Dekkeret, laughing. "How he'll love to hear that!" The nonsensical revelation, coming at the climax of this lengthy and baffling conversation, struck him as wonderfully laughable. "Will he push me aside and make himself Coronal, do you think? Or is it the post of Lady of the Isle that he's got his eye on?"

Nothing disturbed Maundigand-Klimd's impenetrable gravity. "You give insufficient credence, lordship, to my statement that my visions are subjective. I would not say that the Barjazid who was cloaked in a Power's majesty was your friend Dinitak, nor could I say that he was not. I can only tell you that I felt the Barjazid pattern. I caution you against too literal an interpretation of what I tell you."

"There are other Barjazids, I suppose. Suvrael may still teem with them."

"Yes. I remind you of the man Khaymak Barjazid, who not long ago attempted to enter Lord Prestimion's service, but was turned away at the advice of his own nephew Dinitak."

"Right. Venghenar's brother—of course. *He's* the one who's going to be a Power, then, you think? It still makes no sense, Maundigand-Klimd!"

"Again I caution you, lordship, against seeking so literal an explanation. Obviously it's absurd that there can be a fourth Power of the Realm, or that a member of the Barjazid clan could so much as aspire to that distinction. But my vision cannot be dismissed out of hand. It has symbolic meanings that at this point not even I can interpret. But one thing is clear: there will be trouble in the early part of your reign, my lord; and a Barjazid will be involved in it. More than that, I cannot say."

9

"Are you still awake?" Fiorinda asked.

Teotas, beside her, muttered an affirmative. "What hour is it, anyway?"

"I don't know. A very late one. What keeps you up?"

"Too much wine, I suppose," he said. The pre-coronation banquet that evening had gone on and on, everybody carrying on like drunken roaring fools, Prestimion and Dekkeret side by side at the high table, Septach Melayn, Gialaurys, Dembitave, Navigorn, and half a dozen other members of the Council, everyone in a rare good humor. Abrigant had come up from Muldemar for the occasion, bringing with him ten cases of wine of a glorious vintage dating far back into the time of Lord Confalume, and doubtless all ten cases contained nothing but empty bottles now.

But it was an evasive answer. Teotas knew that the wine was not to blame for his wakefulness. He had had as much to drink as anybody, he supposed. The irony was that wine was wasted on him—and he a prince of Muldemar, a member of the family that made the finest wines in the world! He might just as well be drinking water. His intense, churning soul burned the alcohol as fast as it could enter him: it had no effect on him at all. He had never really been drunk in his life, never even pleasantly tipsy, and that was a heavy price to pay for being spared from hangovers as well.

What was bothering him, he knew, had nothing to do with last night's debauchery. It was, in good part, uneasiness over the vastness of

the changes that were about to come over his existence, now that Prestimion's time as Coronal was over and his brother's new life in the
Labyrinth was about to commence.

In theory, Teotas thought, he himself would feel no great impact
from any of that. He was the youngest of the four princely Muldemar
brothers, with no hereditary obligations, free to live out his life as he
pleased. Prestimion, the eldest, had always been destiny's darling, rising
swiftly and inevitably to the throne of the world. Taradath, the brilliant
second brother, had perished in the Korsibar war. To sturdy Abrigant,
the third, the family fief at Muldemar had descended, and he lived
there now at Muldemar House, as princes of Muldemar had for centuries, presiding over the winemakers and dispensing justice to his ador-
ing citizens.

Teotas, though, had lived the life of a private citizen until Prestimion
had chosen him for the Council. He had taken to himself a wife, the excellent Lady Fiorinda of Stee, a childhood friend of Prestimion's wife
Varaile, and together they had reared three admirable children; and
when Prestimion named him to the Council, he made himself one of
its most useful members. All in all, he had created a satisfying life for
himself, though there was that unhappy quirk in his character that prevented him from taking full pleasure even in the utter fulfillment of all
ambition and desire.

And now—now—

The to-ing and fro-ing of these coronation ceremonies was finally
coming to an end. Soon everyone would have settled down in his proper
place. For Prestimion and Varaile, that place would be the Labyrinth.
And Varaile wanted Fiorinda—her sister-in-law and chief lady-in-
waiting—to live there with her.

Did Varaile understand that that would mean, for Fiorinda, the up-
rooting of her entire family? Of course she did. But the two women were
inseparable friends. It must seem to Fiorinda and to Varaile as well that
it was better for Fiorinda and her family to move to the subterranean
capital in the south than for them to be parted from one another.

Teotas, though, had lived at the Castle since he was a boy. He knew
no other home, except only the family estate at Muldemar House, and
that was Abrigant's property now. The Castle's thousands of rooms were
like extensions of his own skin. He roved far and wide through the
meadowlands outside, he hunted in the forest preserves of Halanx, he
enjoyed the giddy pleasures of the juggernauts and mirror-slides of High

Morpin, he wandered now and again down to Muldemar to reminisce about old times with Abrigant. As his sons grew toward manhood he took them with him in his wanderings among the cities of the Mount, bringing them to see the stone birds of Furible in their mating flight, and the lovely burnt-orange towers of Bombifale, and the festival of the flaming canals of Hoikmar. Castle Mount was his life. The Labyrinth held no appeal for him. That was no secret to anyone.

He had always indulged Fiorinda in every whim. This was more than a whim; but he would, if he could, indulge her in this too. But this one was very hard.

There was a final twist in the situation that made his yielding well-nigh impossible. Dekkeret, upon returning from Prestimion's coronation, had asked him to serve him as High Counsellor of the Realm. "It will provide continuity," Dekkeret had said. "Prestimion's own brother, taking the second highest post at the Castle, and who else is better qualified than you, a key member of Prestimion's own Council—?"

Yes, it made sense. Teotas was honored and flattered.

But was Dekkeret aware that Varaile had already summoned Fiorinda to be her companion at the Labyrinth? Apparently he was not. And the two appointments were irreconcilable.

How could he be Lord Dekkeret's High Counsellor at the Castle while Fiorinda was the Lady Varaile's chief lady-in-waiting at the Labyrinth? Were Dekkeret and Varaile expecting them simply to rip their marriage apart? Or were they supposed to divide their time, half the year at one capital and half at the other? That was plainly unworkable. The Coronal needed his High Counsellor at his side all the time, not off for months communing with the Pontifex in the Labyrinth. Varaile would not want to be parted that long from Fiorinda, either.

One of them would have to make a great sacrifice. But which one?

Thus far Teotas had shied away from discussing the matter with Fiorinda, hoping forlornly that some easy miraculous solution would present itself. He knew how unlikely that was. It was ever his inclination to yield to her wishes, yes. But to decline the post of High Counsellor— it would be almost treasonous; Dekkeret needed and wanted him; there was no other obvious choice. Varaile could surely find other ladies-in-waiting. It was not as if—but then, on the other hand—

He saw no answer, and it was tearing him asunder.

That was one part of Teotas's anguish. But also there were the dreams.

Night after night, dreams so terrible that he had come by now to fear falling asleep, because once he plunged into that dark land beyond his pillow he became prey to the most monstrous horrors. It helped not at all to tell himself after he had awakened that it had merely been a dream. There was nothing *mere* about dreams. Teotas knew that dreams hold powerful significance: that they are the harbingers of the invisible world, tapping for admission at the boundaries of our souls. And dark dreams like his could only be the tappings of demons, of lurking forces beyond the clouds, the ancient beings that once ruled this world and might one day seize it from those who had come to possess it.

Sleep now terrified him. Awake, he could defend himself against anything. Sleeping, he was as helpless as a child. That was infuriating, that he should have no defense. But he could not fight off sleep forever, try as he might.

It was coming for him now, despite everything.

"Yes, Teotas, yes, sleep. . . ." Fiorinda was stroking his forehead, his cheeks, his throat. "Relax. Let go, Teotas, let go of everything."

What could he say? *I dare not sleep. I fear demons, Fiorinda? I am unwilling to put myself at their mercy?*

Her embrace was sweet and soothing. He rested his head against her soft warm breasts. What was the use of fighting? Sleep was necessary. Sleep was inevitable. Sleep was . . .

A tumbling downward, a free descent, a willy-nilly plummeting.

And then he is crossing a bare blackened plateau, a place of clinkers and ash, of gaping crevasses, of gaunt dead trees, and he is growing older, much older, with every step he takes. He is inhaling old age like some poisonous fume. His skin puckers and becomes cracked and wrinkled. He sprouts a coat of coarse white hair on his chest and belly and loins. His veins bulge. His ankles complain. His eyes grow bleary. His knees are bent. His heart races and slows. His nostrils wheeze.

He struggles forward, fighting the transformation and always losing, losing, losing. The pallid sun begins to slip below the horizon. The path he is following, he knows not why, is ascending, now. Every step is torment. His throat is dry and his swollen tongue is like a lump of old cloth in his mouth. Gummy rheum drips from the rims of his eyes and trickles across his chest. There is a drumming in his temples and a coldness in his gut.

Creatures that are little more than filmy vapors dance through the air about him. They point; they laugh; they jeer. *Coward,* they call him. *Fool. Insect. Pitiful creeping thing.*

Feebly he shakes his fist at them. Their laughter grows more raucous. Their insults become more vicious. They lay bare his utter worthlessness in fifty different ways, and he lacks the strength to contradict them, and after a time he knows that no contradiction is possible, because they are speaking the simple truth.

Then, as though they are no longer able to sustain interest in any entity as trivial and contemptible as he, they melt away and are gone, leaving only a trailing cloud of tinkling merriment behind them.

He staggers on. Twice he falls, and twice he claws his way to his feet, feeling the harsh scratch of bone on bone, the thick rustle of dark blood pushing through narrowed arteries. He would not have believed that being old could be such agony. Darkness comes swiftly. He finds himself deep in starless moonless night and is grateful that he no longer has to look upon his own body. "Fiorinda?" he croaks, but there is no response. He is alone. He has never been anything but alone.

A light, now, blinks into being in the distance, and rapidly intensifies to become a cone of luminous green, widening to fill the heavens, a geyser of pale radiance spurting aloft. As the wind sweeps through it, it stirs swirls of a grayer color, whirlpools of light within light. Accompanying this outburst of brightness is a rushing, whispering sound, like the murmur of distant water. He also hears what sounds like subterranean laughter, resonant, slippery. He goes forward, entering a sort of green cloud that seeps from the ground. The air is electric. His pores tingle. A sour smell drifts upward in his nostrils. His bent and aching body sweats and steams. There is what seems to be a mountain ahead, but as he moves on through the cloud Teotas realizes that what he sees is a giant living thing, squat and enormous and incomprehensible, sitting upright on a kind of throne.

A god? A demon? An idol? Its brown, leathery skin is thick and glossy, and ridged like a reptile's hide. Its massive body is low and long, blunt-snouted, goggle-eyed, with a high vaulting back, fat sides, bulging belly, pedestal-like underparts. Teotas has never seen a creature so huge. That mouth alone—

That mouth—

That gaping mouth—

Teotas is unable to halt himself. The mouth yawns like the entrance to the cavern of caverns, and he marches onward, no longer moving with difficulty: gliding, rather, speeding toward that mouth, rushing toward it—

Wider and wider. That great cavern fills the sky. A terrible bellowing comes from it, loud enough to shake the ground. Landslides begin; rocks fall in thundering avalanches; there is no place to take refuge except within the mouth itself, that waiting mouth, that eternally gaping mouth—

Teotas rushes forward into the blackness.

"It's all right," someone is saying. "A dream, only a dream! Teotas— please, Teotas—"

He was bathed in sweat, shivering, a huddled heap. Fiorinda cradled him in her arms, murmuring an unending flow of soothing words. Gradually he could feel himself coming back from the nightmare, though its residue, like an oily slick, still laps at the edges of his mind.

"Only a dream, Teotas! It wasn't real!"

He nodded. What could he say, how to explain? "Yes. Only a dream."

10

*P*restimion said, "So now it's finally over and done with, all the jolly festivals and amusements. Now the real work begins, eh, Dekkeret?"

It had taken him back to earlier days, these weeks of formal ceremonies that marked the end of the old reign and the beginning of the new. He had been through all this once before, only that time *he* was the one whose ascent to the throne was being celebrated. The influx of coronation gifts from all over the world—had he ever actually unpacked more than a fraction of those myriad boxes and crates?—the rite of the passing of the crown, the coronation banquet, the recitals from *The Book of Changes*, the chanting of *The Book of Powers*, the passing and repassing of the wine-bowls, the gathered lords of the realm rising to make the starburst salute and cry out the greeting to the new Coronal—

"Prestimion!" they had cried. "Lord Prestimion! Hail, Lord Prestimion! Long life to Lord Prestimion!" So long ago! It seemed to him now that his entire reign as Coronal had gone by in the twinkling of an eye, and now here he was mysteriously transformed into a man of middle years, no longer as buoyant and impulsive as he once had been, nor as good-humored, either—a little testy at times, indeed, he would admit—and now they had done it all once again, the immemorial rituals played out anew, but this time the name they called was that of Dekkeret, Dekkeret, Lord Dekkeret, while he himself looked on from one side, smiling, willingly surrendering his share of glory to the new monarch.

But some part of him would always be Coronal, he knew.

His boyish younger self stood before him in the mirror of his memory like some other person, that youthful, agile Prestimion of two decades ago: that endlessly resilient young man who had survived the humiliation of the Korsibar usurpation and the ghastly bloodlettings of the civil war, to make himself Coronal despite all. How he had fought for it! It had cost him a brother, and a lover, and much bodily suffering besides, nights camped on muddy shores, days spent trekking through the deadliest desert this side of Suvrael, mounts shot out from beneath him on the battlefield, wounds whose scars he still carried. Dekkeret was fortunate to have been spared any of that, let alone anything like a repetition of it. His rise to the throne had been orderly and normal. It was a much simpler way to become king.

Everything should have been simple for me, too, Prestimion thought. But that was not the fate that the Divine had in mind for me.

He stood with Dekkeret—*Lord* Dekkeret—in the Confalume throne-chamber, just the two of them, amid the echoes. As they looked far across the floor of brilliant yellow gurnawood to the throne itself, that massive block of ruby-streaked black opal rising on its stepped pedestal of dark mahogany, Dekkeret said, "You'll miss it, I know. Go on, Prestimion: climb up there one last time, if you like. I'll never tell."

Prestimion smiled. "I never cared to sit on it when I was Coronal. It would feel even wronger for me to sit on it now."

"But you took your place on that throne often enough when you were king, and you put a good face on it then."

"It was my job to put a good face on it, Dekkeret. But now the job's yours. I have no business up there, even for sentiment's sake."

He continued to ponder the great throne, though, for a time. He could not help, even now, but be amused by the pretentiousness of the astoundingly costly throne-room Confalume had so grandly thrust into the heart of the Castle, and the throne itself that was its jewel. But at the same time he honored it for the symbol of rightful power that it was, and for the way it summoned up in his mind the memory of Confalume himself, who in some senses had been more of a father to him than his own.

At length he said, "You know, Dekkeret, we have to take the old

man's gaudy throne very seriously while we're seated upon it. We need
to believe with every fiber of our souls in its majesty. Because what we
really are are performers, you know, and there's our stage. And for the
little time we strut that stage, we need to believe that the play is real and
important: for if *we* don't seem to believe it, who else will want to?"

"Yes. Yes, I do comprehend that, Prestimion."

"But now I have a different stage for myself, and no one will see me
moving back and forth upon it. —Let's get ourselves out of this place,
shall we?" Prestimion gave the great throne a final, almost fond, glance.

They crossed from the throne-room into to the judgment-hall, a
room of his own making. It was of no trifling degree of splendor itself.
Would they think, someday, that the ancient Lord Prestimion had been
a man as much given to ostentatiousness and grand display as his predecessor Lord Confalume? Well, let them think it, then. That was nothing for him to concern himself over. History would invent its own
Prestimion, as it had invented its own Stiamot, its own Arioc, its own
Guadeloom. It was a process with which no man could interfere. He
was probably well on his way toward becoming mythical already.

Dekkeret said, "These rooms beyond here—I'm going to clear them
away, and build a chapel for the Coronal, I think. I feel it's needed
here."

"A good idea."

"A chapel right here, you mean?"

"The general idea of building things. I like it that you already have
that in mind. If you want a chapel here, build one. Put your mark on
the Castle, Dekkeret. Take it in your hands. Shape it as you will. This
place is the sum of all the kings who have lived in it. We'll never be finished building it. So long as the world lasts, there'll be new construction
up here."

"Yes. Majipoor expects it of us."

It pleased Prestimion to be making this last tour of these sacred
rooms with the sturdy, strong-willed man whom he had picked to succeed
him. Dekkeret would be a splendid Coronal, of that he was sure. It was
a necessary thing for him to know that he had bestowed such a successor upon the world. However great his own accomplishments had been,
history would not forgive him if he provided Majipoor with a weakling
or a fool as the next king.

Great Coronals had made such mistakes in the past. But Prestimion
was confident that no one would ever lay that charge against him.

Dekkeret would live up to all expectations. He would be a different sort of king from his predecessor, yes, earnest and straightforward where Prestimion had often relied on craftiness and manipulation. And Dekkeret cut a grand and heroic figure, who commanded respect merely by walking into a room, whereas Prestimion, built by the Divine on a much smaller scale, felt that he had had to achieve kingliness by sheer force of personality.

Well, these differences would make it easier for the people of future years to tell one of them from the other, anyway. "In the time of Prestimion and Dekkeret," they would say, hearkening back as if to a golden age, the way sometimes people spoke of the times of Thraym and Vildivar, or Signor and Melikand, or Agis and Klain. But those kings existed only as interchangeable paired names, not as individuals in their own right. Prestimion hoped for a kinder fate. So different was he from Dekkeret that those who lived in time to come would of necessity always see in the eyes of their minds the image of the quick, supple little Prestimion, the master archer, the great planner, and the broad-shouldered big-bodied form of Dekkeret beside him, and they would know, forever, which one was which. Or so Prestimion hoped.

"Shall we stroll out to the Morvendil Parapet?" he asked, gesturing toward the northwestern gate. "The view from there by night is one I've often enjoyed."

"And will again, many times," said Dekkeret. "You *will* come visiting often?"

"As often as is appropriate for a Pontifex to show his nose at the Castle, I suppose. But that's not often at all, is it? And you won't want me here, anyway. However you may feel right now, you'll not want me snooping around the premises once you start believing that the place is really yours."

Dekkeret chuckled, but made no other response.

They went quickly through the halls, out into the dusk. Distant guards saluted them. Others, shadowy figures who might have been princes of the realm, peered at them from afar also, but no one dared approach: who would interrupt the private conference of the Pontifex and the Coronal? A covered walkway that carried an inscription from Lord Dulcinon's time took them into the Gaznivin Court, which had

a balcony at its lower end that gave access to Lord Morvendil's
Parapet.

What sort of ruler Lord Morvendil had been, or even when he had
lived, were matters of which Prestimion had no knowledge, but the
parapet itself, a long and narrow breastwork of black Velathyntu stone,
had long been one of Prestimion's private places of refuge from the
cares of the crown. Here the Mount tapered to a narrow point, falling
away below the Castle wall in a steep declivity that gave a spectacular
view of several of the High Cities and part of the band of Inner Cities
just below. Darkness was coming on quickly down there, and islands of
light were springing up against the giant mountain's flank. It was always
instructive to consider that this small spot of light off to the left was actually a city of six million people, and that dot there the home of seven
million more. And that one down there, pressed up snugly against the
side of the mountain and surrounded by a semicircle of inky blackness,
was Prestimion's own lovely Muldemar.

Memories stirred in him of his youth in that beautiful city, his happy
family life, the warm and loving mother and the strong noble father,
taken so early by death, who had seemed as kingly as any Coronal. What
a warm community, what a satisfying existence! He had never known a
moment of sadness or despair. If the Castle had not called to him, he
would be Prince of Muldemar now, busy and content among the grapes
and wine-cellars.

But it had seemed a natural and normal thing for him to move outward from the bosom of his family and the princely responsibilities of
the city of his birth to the service of mankind. So the yearning had come
over him to be Coronal, and thus to hold all of Majipoor in warm fa-
milial embrace, he the focus of everyone's dreams, he the benign leader,
he the father of the world.

Was that how he had seen it then, or was it simple power-hunger that
had impelled him to the throne? He could not say. There had, of
course, been some component of the desire for mastery in his rise
through the Castle hierarchy. But that had been far from his dominant
motive, he was certain — very far. Prestimion had learned that in the Korsibar war.

He had fought then for the throne, yes, fought desperately, but not so
much because he simply *wanted* it, as Korsibar had, but because he was
sure he deserved it, that he was needed for it, that he was the necessary
and unique man of his era. No doubt many a dread tyrant and monstrous

villain had felt the same way precisely about himself, in the long course of human history going back to the all but forgotten times of Old Earth. Well, so be it; Prestimion had faith in his own understanding of his own motives. And so, he knew, did all of Majipoor. He was beloved by all, and that was the confirmation of everything. He had served ably as Coronal; so would he serve now, now that he was Pontifex.

He looked toward Dekkeret, who was standing a little apart, plainly unwilling to intrude on his reflections. "Have you given thought yet to how you will begin?"

"New decrees and laws, you mean? Overturning ancient precedents, repealing existing protocols, standing the world on its head? I thought I might wait some little while before setting out on that course."

Prestimion laughed. "A wise position, I think. The Coronal who governs wisest is the one who governs least. Lord Prankipin put the world back on its course by lessening the grip of government; Confalume followed that course, and so have I. The benefits can be seen on every side. —But no, no, I wasn't speaking of legislative matters, only symbolic ones. Is it your intention to sequester yourself here at the Castle until you've fully settled into your tasks, or will you show yourself to the people?"

"If I hide here until I feel I've fully settled into my tasks, I may grow old and die before the world sees my face. But surely it's too soon for a grand processional, Prestimion!"

"I would say that it is. Save the processional for the traditional fifth year, unless circumstances force it sooner. But once I became Coronal I lost little time in visiting the nearby cities, if nothing farther. Of course, I was ever a restless man: you are more content to see the same set of doors and windows several weeks running, I think. Still, there's something to be said for a Coronal's getting himself away from the Castle as often as is seemly. One gets a damned narrow view of the world from thirty miles up."

"So I would think," said Dekkeret. "Where did you go, in your first months?"

"In the very beginning, I simply slipped away with Septach Melayn and Gialaurys, saying nothing about it to anyone, going in the night to places like Banglecode or Greel or Bibiroon. We wore wigs and false whiskers, even, and kept our ears open, and learned much about the world that had been given us to govern. The Night Market of Bombi-fale—ah, now that was a time! We tasted foods no Coronal may ever have eaten before. We visited the dealers in sorcery-goods. It was there that I met Maundigand-Klimd, who had no difficulty seeing through my disguise. —Not that I recommend such subterfuges to you."

"No. Such things as wigs and false whiskers are not my style, I suspect."

"A little later I journeyed in a more formal way. I would take Teotas or Abrigant with me, Gialaurys, Navigorn, various members of my Council. And visit the cities of the Mount—Peritole, Strave, Minimool, down the Mount even to Gimkandale—never imposing myself on any one place for long, because of the expense it would involve for them, merely arriving and making a speech or two, listening to complaints, promising miracles, and moving along. It was in this phase of my reign that I came to Normork, you may recall."

"How could I ever forget it?" said Dekkeret gravely.

"Finding Maundigand-Klimd on one trip, and you on another; and there was a third journey, a visit to Stee, where I met the Lady Varaile. Fortuitous meetings, all three, the merest of accidents, and yet how they transformed my reign, and my life! Whereas if you remain sequestered at the Castle—"

Dekkeret nodded. "Yes. I do take the point."

"One more question, and then we should go in," Prestimion said. "Maundigand-Klimd came to you, did he not, with his tale of perceiving a Barjazid as a Power of the Realm? What did you make of that story?"

"Why, very little, if anything." Dekkeret indicated surprise that Prestimion would so much as mention anything so fantastic. "The three positions are filled, and let us hope no vacancies develop for many years to come."

"You take his words very literally, I see."

"The Su-Suheris made the very same comment. But how else am I to look upon words, other than as things with meanings? You seem to find it diverting to listen now and then to the murmurings of sorcerers, but to me they are all worthless idlers and parasites, even your cherished Maundigand-Klimd, and their prognostications are mere vapor to me. If a magus comes to me and says that in his dreams he has seen a Barjazid wearing the aura of a Power of the Realm, why should I search for hidden meanings and buried subtleties? I look first at the message itself. That particular message strikes me as foolishness. So I put it out of mind."

"You do yourself an injustice by ignoring Maundigand-Klimd's warning."

A certain note of exasperation came into Dekkeret's voice now. "We should not quarrel on this happy day, Prestimion. But—forgive me—what sense can there be in his prophecy? The Barjazids are all loathsome scoundrels, my friend Dinitak aside. The world would never embrace them as kings."

"But Dinitak might, you think?"

"It would be very far-fetched. I grant you I could choose to name him as my successor, which would indeed make him a Power of the Realm, and if I did, I think he'd be a capable ruler, if perhaps somewhat stern. But I assure you most assuredly, Prestimion, that it'll be many years before I begin fretting about finding a replacement for myself, and when I do I doubt very much that my choice would ever land on Dinitak. Two commoners in a row may be more than the system can stand. Dinitak has many virtues and is, I suppose, my closest friend, but he's not, I think, generous enough of soul to be considered even in jest as a potential Coronal. He is a hard man, without much charity in him. Therefore—"

Prestimion held up one hand. "Enough! I beg you, Dekkeret, put aside the Power of the Realm part of this prophecy entirely. You've just ruled Dinitak out, and as for Khaymak Barjazid, I have as much trouble imagining him as Coronal as you would. Focus instead on Maundigand-Klimd's warning that there will be difficulties in the early days of your reign, and that some Barjazid will be involved in them."

"I'm prepared to deal with whatever arises. First let it arise, though."

"You will remain alert, though?"

"Of course I will. It should go without saying. But I will not take up arms against phantoms, for all that you tell me about the wisdom of your magus. And I tell you, Prestimion, I will be reluctant to take up arms at all, no matter what troubles may arise, if there's a peaceful solution available to me. —Shall we drop this discussion now, Prestimion? We have our farewell dinner to prepare ourselves for."

"Yes. So we do."

In any case, Prestimion saw, there was no point in continuing this. It was clear to him that what he was trying to do was about as fruitful as butting his head against the great wall of Normork. Butt all you pleased; the wall would never yield. Neither would Dekkeret.

Perhaps I am too sensitive on this, Prestimion thought, having had two doses of insurrection one upon another in the early years of my own reign. I am conditioned by my own unhappy experiences always to expect trouble; when it is absent, as it has been these many years since the death of Dantirya Sambail, I mistrust its absence. Dekkeret has a sunnier spirit: let him deal with Maundigand-Klimd's gloomy prophecy as he pleases. Perhaps the Divine will indeed grant him a happy start to his reign despite everything. And dinner is waiting.

11

*K*haymak Barjazid said, "I have a thought, your grace. —You mentioned, some time back, your difficult relationship with your father and your brothers."

Mandralisca shot him a startled, angry look. For the moment he had forgotten altogether that he had ever spoken of his painful childhood to Barjazid, or anyone else. And he was not at all accustomed to being addressed in a way that ventured to breach the walls he had erected around his inner life.

"And if I did?" he said, in a voice tipped with blades.

Barjazid squirmed. Terror came into the little man's mismatched eyes. "I mean no offense, sir! No offense at all! Only that I see a way of intensifying the power of the helmet you hold in your hands, a way which would make use of—certain of your—experiences."

Mandralisca leaned forward. The sting of the sudden intrusion into his soul still reverberated in him, but he was interested all the same. "How so?"

"Let me see how to put this," said Barjazid carefully. He held himself like a man setting out to have a philosophical dialogue with a snarling, infuriated khulpoin, all yellow fangs and blazing eyes, that he has unexpectedly encountered on a quiet country road. "When one uses the helmet, one generates the power from within oneself," said Barjazid. "It is my belief that one would be able to increase the device's power if one were to draw on some reservoir of pain, of fury, of—I could almost say 'hatred.' "

"Well, say it, then. *Hatred*. It's a word I understand."

"Hatred, yes. And so certain things occurred to me, sir, remembering what you had told me that day concerning your boyhood —your father. Your—early unhappiness—" Barjazid chose his words painstakingly, obviously aware that he was treading on dangerous ground here. He understood that Mandralisca might well not want to be reminded of the things that he had blurted out, so very much to his own surprise, that day that he and Barjazid and Jacomin Halefice were walking through the marketplace. But Mandralisca, controlling himself, signalled to him to go on. And Barjazid most artfully did: he hinted, he alluded, he talked in euphemisms, all the while painting the portrait of the boy Mandralisca eternally in fear of his savage drunken father and his blustering bullying brothers, suffering daily at their hands and storing up a full measure of loathing for them that would, one day, overflow upon the world. Loathing that could be turned into an asset, that could be harnessed, that could become a source of great power. And offered some suggestions concerning how that might be achieved.

This was all very valuable. Mandralisca was grateful to Barjazid for sharing it with him. But he regretted, all the same, having parted even for a moment the veil that shrouded his early life. He had always found it useful to have the world perceive him as a monster carved out of ice; there were great risks in giving someone a glimpse of the vulnerable boy of long ago who lay hidden somewhere behind that chilly facade. He would gladly call back, if he could, all that he had told this little man that strange afternoon.

"Enough," Mandralisca said, finally. "You've made your point clear. Now go, and let me get down to work." He reached for the helmet.

Late autumn in the Gonghars, shading into early winter. The light but unending rain of the warm season has begun to give way to the cold and equally endless rain of autumn, heavy with sleet, that will yield in another few weeks to winter's first snows. This is the cabin, the squalid shack, the tumbledown ill-favored house, where the wine-seller Kekkidis and his family live, here in the sad little mountain town of Ibykos. The hour is far along in the afternoon, dark, cold. Rain drums on the rotting lichen-encrusted roof and drips through the usual leaky places, landing in the usual buckets with a steady *pong pong pong*. Mandralisca does not dare to light a fire. Fuel is not wasted in this household, and any fuel not consumed on behalf of his father is deemed a waste of fuel; no one matters here but his father, and fires are lit when his father returns from his day's toil, not before.

Today that may be hours from now. Or, perhaps—the Divine willing—never.

For three days now Kekkidis and his oldest son Malchio have been in the city of Velathys, a hundred miles away, arranging to buy up the stock of some fellow wine-merchant who has died in an avalanche, leaving half a dozen hungry babes. They are due back today; indeed, are already more than a little overdue, because the floater that runs between Velathys and Ibykos leaves at dawn and reaches Ibykos by midafternoon. It is almost dark, now, but the floater has not arrived. No one knows why. Another of Mandralisca's brothers has been waiting at the station since noon with the wagon. The third is at the wine-shop, helping their mother. Mandralisca is alone at home. He diverts himself with luxurious fantasies of cataclysms befalling his father. Perhaps—perhaps, perhaps, perhaps!—something bad has happened on the road. Perhaps. Perhaps.

His other way of passing the time, and keeping warm, is by practicing with the singlestick baton that he has carved from a piece of nightflower wood. That is the finest kind of baton, a nightflower-wood baton, and Mandralisca saved all last year, one square copper at a time, to buy himself a decent-sized stave, which he has whittled and whittled until it is of the perfect length and weight, and fits his hand so well that one might think a master craftsman had designed the hand grip. Now, holding the baton so that it rests lightly in his palm, he moves deftly back and forth through the room, feinting at shadows, jabbing, parrying. He is quick; he is good; his wrist is strong, his eye is keen; he hopes to be a champion some day. But right now he is mainly interested in keeping warm.

He imagines that his opponent is his father. He dances round and round the older man, mockingly prodding at him, tapping him at the point of each shoulder, beneath the chin, along his cheek, playing with him, outmaneuvering him, humiliating him. Kekkidis has begun to growl with fury; he lashes out with his own baton with a two-handed grip, as though swinging an axe; but the boy is ten times as fast as he, and touches him again and again and again, while Kekkidis is unable to land a single blow.

Perhaps Kekkidis will never come home at all. Perhaps he'll die somewhere on the road. Let it be, Mandralisca prays, that he is already dead.

Let him have had an avalanche too.

The hills above Ibykos are snow-covered already, the wet heavy snow typical of the cusp of the season. Mandralisca, closing his eyes, pictures the rain pounding down, imagines it striking the black granite bedrock, slicing at an angle into the accumulated snowdrifts, working like little knives to cut them loose and send them gliding in billowy clouds down the side of the hill toward the highway below, just as the Velathys floater goes by—hiding it altogether from sight until spring—Kekkedis and Malchio buried beneath a thousand tons of snow—

Or let a sudden sinkhole open in the highway. Let the floater be swallowed up in it.

Let the floater swerve wildly off the road. Let it plunge into the river.

Let the engine die halfway between Velathys and here. Let them be caught in a blizzard and freeze to death.

Mandralisca punctuates each of these hopeful thoughts with furious thrusts of his baton. Jab—jab—jab. He whirls, dances, turns lightly on the tips of his toes, strikes while his body is facing more than halfway away from his foe. Comes in overhead, a descending angle, impossible to defend against, bolt of lightning. Take *that! That! That!*

The sound of the wagon pulling up, suddenly. Mandralisca wants to weep. No avalanche, no sinkhole, no fatal blizzard. Kekkedis is home again.

Voices. Footsteps outside, now. Coughing sounds. Someone stamping his feet, two someones, Kekkidis and Malchio knocking snow off their boots.

"Boy! Where are you, boy? Let us in! Do you have any idea how cold it is out here?"

Mandralisca leans his baton against the wall. Rushes to the door, fumbles with the latch. Two tall men on the threshold, one older than the other, two bleak scowling lantern-jawed faces, long greasy black hair, angry eyes shining through. Mandralisca can smell the brandy on their breath. There is the smell of fury about them, too: a sharp, musky stink, boiling out from beneath their fur robes. Something must have gone wrong. They stomp past him, brushing him aside. "Where's the fire?" Kekkidis asks. "Why is it so damnably cold in here? You should have had a fire ready for us, boy!"

No way to deal with that. Denounced if he prepares a fire, denounced if he doesn't. The old story.

Mandralisca hurries to bring in some kindling from the pile on the back porch. His father and his brother, still in their coats, stand in the middle of the room, rubbing their hands to warm them. They are talking about their journey. Their voices are harsh and bitter. Evidently the venture has been a failure; the agents for the other wine-merchant's estate have been too sharp for Kekkidis, the cheap and easy purchase of distress-sale merchandise has fallen through, the whole trip has been a waste of time and money. Mandralisca keeps his head down and goes about his business, asking no questions. He knows better than to call attention to himself when his father is in a mood like this. Best to stay out of his way, cling to the shadows, let him vent his rage on pots and pans and stools, not on his youngest son.

But it happens anyway. Mandralisca is half a step too slow performing some task. Kekkidis is displeased. He snarls, curses, abruptly sees Mandralisca's baton leaning against the wall not far from where he stands, grabs it up, prods the boy sharply in the gut with its tip.

That is unbearable. Not so much the pain of being prodded by the baton, although it nearly takes his breath away, but that his father should be handling his baton at all. Kekkedis has no business touching it, let alone using it against him. The baton is *his*. His only possession. Bought with his own money, carved into shape with his own hands.

Without stopping to think, Mandralisca reaches out for it as Kekkedis is drawing it back for a second thrust. Lightning-fast, he steps forward, seizes the baton by the tip, pulls it toward him, trying to yank it from his father's hand.

It is a terrible mistake. He knows that even as he is committing it, but for all his quickness he is unable to stop himself. Kekkidis stares at him, wild-eyed, sputtering with astonishment at so flagrant an act of defiance. He rips the baton from Mandralisca's grasp, twisting laterally with vicious force that Mandralisca's slender wrist cannot resist. Grabs the baton by each end, grinning, snaps it easily over his knee, grins again, holds the broken pieces up to display them for him, and casually tosses them into the fire. All of it takes only a moment or two to accomplish.

"No," Mandralisca murmurs, not yet believing it has happened. "Don't—no—please—"

A year's savings. His beautiful baton.

Thirty-five years later and a thousand miles or so to the north and east, the man who calls himself Count Mandralisca of Zimroel sits in a small circular room with an arched roof and burnt-orange mud-plastered walls on a ridge overlooking the desert wastes of the Plain of Whips. He wears a helmet of metal mesh on his brow; his hands are clenched beside him as though each one grips one of the sundered halves of the broken baton.

He sees his father's face before him. The triumphant vindictive grin. The pieces of the baton held aloft—tossed into the flames—

Mandralisca's searching mind soars upward—outward —remembering—hating—

Don't—no—please—

Teotas, defeated by sleep yet again, sleeps. He can do nothing else. His spirit fears sleep but his body demands it. Each night he fights, loses, succumbs. And so now, despite the nightly struggle, once more he lies sleeping. Dreaming.

A desert, somewhere, nowhere real. Hallucinations rise like heat waves from the rocks. He hears groans and occasional sobs and something that could be a chorus of large black beetles, a dry rustling sound. The wind is hot and dusty. The dawn has a blinding brilliance. The rocks are bright nodes of pure energy whose rich-textured red surfaces vibrate in patterns that continually change. On one face of every stony mass he sees golden lights circling gracefully. On the opposite face pale bluish spheres are unceasingly born and go bubbling into the air. Everything shimmers. Everything shines with an inner light. It would all be marvelously beautiful, if it were not so frightening.

He himself has been transformed into something hideous. His hands have become hammers. His toes are hooked claws. His knees have eyes but no eyebrows. His tongue is satin. His saliva is glass. His blood is bile and his bile is blood. A brooding sense of imminent punishment assails him. Creatures made of vertical ribs of gray cartilage make dull booming noises at him. Somehow he understands their meaning: they are expressing their scorn, they are mocking him for his innumerable inadequacies. He wants to cry out, but no sound will leave his throat. Nor can he flee the scene. He is paralyzed.

"Fi—o—rin—da—"

With a supreme effort he manages to utter her name. Can she hear him? Will she save him?

"Fi—o—rin—da—"

He plucks at the twisted and disheveled coverlet. Fiorinda lies beside him like someone's discarded life-size doll, cut off from him behind the wall of sleep—he knows she's there, can't reach out to her, can't make any sort of contact. One of them is on some other world. He has no way of telling which of them it is. Probably me, he decides. Yes. He is on another world, asleep, dreaming, dreaming that he lies in his bed in the Castle, asleep, next to the sleeping Fiorinda, who is beyond his reach. And he is dreaming.

"Fiorinda?"

Silence. Solitude.

He realizes now that he must be dreaming that he is awake. He sits up, reaches for the night-light. By its faint green glow he sees that he is alone in the bed. He remembers, now: Fiorinda has gone to the Labyrinth with Varaile, not a permanent separation, only a postponement of the decision, a short visit to help Varaile get herself established in her new home. And then they will decide which one of them is to take the position that has been offered, whether Fiorinda is to be lady-in-waiting to the wife of the new Pontifex or he to be High Counsellor to Lord Dekkeret. But how can he be High Counsellor, when he is nothing more than the most loathsome of insects?

Meanwhile he is alone at the Castle. Assailed by merciless dreams.

Night after night . . . terror. Madness. Where can he hide? Nowhere. There is no place to hide. Nowhere. Nowhere.

"Do you hear something?" Varaile asked. "One of the children crying, perhaps?"

"What? What?"

"Wake up, Prestimion! One of the children—"

He made a further interrogative noise, but showed no sign of being willing to awaken. After a moment Varaile realized that there was no reason why he should. The hour was very late. He was exhausted; since their arrival at the Labyrinth his days, and many of his nights as well, had been taken up in meetings, conferences, discussions. The officials of the departed Confalume's Pontificate had to be interviewed and assessed, the new people that Prestimion had brought with him from the Castle had to be integrated into the system here, there were applications for favor to study, petitions to grant—

Let him sleep, Varaile thought. This was something she could handle by herself.

And there it came again: a weird throttled sound that seemed to be trying to be a shriek, but was emerging instead as a moan. From its pitch, she thought she recognized the voice as that of Simbilon, who although he was nearly eleven still had a clear, pure contralto. So it was to his room that she went first, making her way uncertainly through the bewildering complex of rooms that was the imperial residence. A bobbing globe of orange slave-light drifted just overhead, illuminating her path.

But Simbilon lay sleeping peacefully amidst his clutter of books, a dozen or more scattered all around him on the bed and one still open, the pages flattened across his chest where the book had fallen when sleep overtook him. Varaile lifted it from him and set it beside his pillow, and went from the room.

The strange sound came to her again, more urgent, now. It frightened her to think that one of her children might be making a sound like that. Hastily she crossed the hall and entered the room where Tuanelys slept in a tumbled heap of stuffed animals, her bed mounded high with furry blaves and sigimoins and bilantoons and canavongs and ghalvars, and even a long-nosed manculain, her current favorite, transformed by the maker's hand into something cuddly and charming, though the real manculains of the jungles of Stoienzar, covered all over by poisonous yellow spines, were as far from cuddly as animals could be.

But no stuffed animals surrounded her now. Tuanelys apparently had flung them pell-mell in all directions, as if they were nasty vermin that had invaded her bed. Even the beloved manculain had been discarded: Varaile saw it across the room, lying upside down on the little girl's dresser, where, as it landed, it had jostled aside a dozen or so of the pretty little glass vessels that Tuanelys liked to collect. Several seemed to be broken. As for Tuanelys herself, she had kicked off her coverlet and lay in a tight little huddled heap, knees drawn up almost to her chin, her whole form rigid, her nightgown pulled up and bunched under her arms so that her small slim body was bare. She was glossy as though with fever. A pool of sweat had stained the sheet about her.

"Tuanelys, love—"

Another moan that wanted to be a shriek. A ripple of convulsive force ran through the girl: she grimaced, shuddered and shivered, kicked out with one leg and then the other, clenched her fists, pulled her head down into her shoulders. Varaile lightly touched her shoulder. Her skin was cool, normal: no fever. But Tuanelys shrank away at the touch. She began to moan again, a moan that turned swiftly into a racking sob. Her features were distorted into a hideous mask, eyes tight shut, nostrils flaring, lips pulled back, teeth bared.

"It's only me, sweetheart. Shhh. Shhh. Nothing's wrong. Mother's here. Shhh, Tuanelys. Shhh."

She tugged at the girl's nightgown, drew it down over her waist and thighs, turned her so that she lay on her back, and gently stroked her forehead, all the while continuing to murmur gently to her. Gradually the tension that had gripped Tuanelys seemed to ease a little. Now and again a ripple of response to some horrendous inner vision still went through her, but such things were beginning to come farther apart, and the terrible mask that her face had become relaxed into her normal visage.

Varaile became aware of someone standing over her shoulder. Prestimion? No: Fiorinda, Varaile realized. She had awakened and come down the hall from her own lodgings to see what was the matter. "A nightmare," Varaile said, without looking around. "Fetch a bowl of milk for her, will you?"

Tuanelys's eyes fluttered open. She seemed dazed, disoriented, more bewildered even than one might expect a child to be who had been awakened in the middle of the night. This was only her second week of living in the Labyrinth. They had tried to arrange her room here to be as much as possible like the one she had had at the Castle, but, even so—the disruption of her life, the magnitude of the upheaval—

"Mommy—"

Her voice was hoarse. The word was one that she hadn't used in two years or more.

"It's all right, Tuanelys. Everything's all right."

"They had no faces—only eyes—"

"They weren't real. You were dreaming, love."

"Hundreds and hundreds of them. No faces. Just—eyes. Oh, mommy—mommy—"

She was quivering with fear. Whatever vision had impinged upon her sleeping mind was still alive within her now. Bit by bit she began to describe to Varaile what she had seen, or tried to, but the descriptions were fragmentary, her words largely incoherent. She had seen something awful, that was clear. But she lacked the ability to make the nightmare real for Varaile. White creatures—mysterious pallid *things*—a marching horde of faceless men—or were they giant worms of some sort?—thousands of staring eyes—

The details scarcely mattered. A little girl's nightmares would have no significant meaning; the thing that was significant was that she was having nightmares at all. Here in the safety of the Labyrinth, in these coiling chambers at the very bottom of the imperial sector, something dark and fearful had succeeded in reaching down to touch the mind of the daughter of the Pontifex of Majipoor. It was not right.

"They were so cold," Tuanelys was saying. "They hate everything that has warm blood in its veins. Dead men with eyes. Sitting on white mounts. Cold—so cold—you touched them and you froze—"

Fiorinda reappeared, bearing a bowl of milk. "I warmed it a little. The poor child! I wonder if we should put a drop of brandy in it."

"Not this time, I think. Here, Tuanelys, let me pull the covers up over you. Drink this, sweetheart. It's milk. Just sip it—slowly, a little at a time—"

Tuanelys sipped from the bowl. The strange fit seemed to be passing from her. She was looking around for her stuffed animals. Varaile and Fiorinda gathered them up and arranged them beside her on the bed. She found the manculain and thrust it under the coverlet, up close against herself.

Fiorinda said, "Teotas also, all last month, the most horrible nightmares. I wouldn't be surprised if he's having one of them right now. —Do you want me to stay with her, Varaile?"

"Go back to sleep. I'll look after her."

She took the emptied milk bowl from Tuanelys's hand and lightly eased the little girl's head down against her pillow, holding her there, stroking her to guide her onward, back into sleep. For a moment or two Tuanelys seemed completely calm. Then a fresh shudder went through her, as though the dream were returning. "Eyes," she murmured. "No faces." That was where it ended. Within minutes she was peacefully sleeping. Light little-girl snores came from her. Varaile stood watch over her for a time, waiting to be completely sure that all was well. It seemed to be. She tiptoed out and went back to her own bedroom, where she found Prestimion still sound asleep, and lay by his side, awake, until the Labyrinth's sunless dawn arrived.

Standing before the Lord Gaviral in the great hall of Gaviral's palace, Mandralisca idly tossed the Barjazid helmet from one hand to the other, a gesture that had virtually become a tic for him in recent weeks.

"A progress report, my lord Gaviral," he said. "The secret weapon of which I've spoken, this little helmet here? I've gone far in mastering its use."

Gaviral smiled. His smile was not a heartwarming thing: a quick twitch of his meager little lips, baring a ragged facade of largely triangular teeth, and a chilly glow flashing for an instant in his small deep-set eyes. He ran his hand through his coarse and thinning covering of dull-red hair and said, "Are there any specific results to report?"

"I've penetrated the Castle with it, milord."

"Ah."

"And the Labyrinth."

"Ah. *Ah!*"

That had been a favorite locution of Dantirya Sambail, that double "ah," with a moment's pause between them and a whiplash emphasis on the second one. Gaviral could not have been very old when Dantirya Sambail died, but he had managed to copy the Procurator's intonation perfectly. It was odd and not in any way amusing to hear that double "ah" coming from Gaviral's lips, as though by some act of ventriloquy beyond the grave. The Lord Gaviral had more than a touch of his famed uncle's ugliness, but scarcely any at all of his dark wit and black devious shrewdness, and it did not sit well with Mandralisca to be treated to so accurate an imitation of the Procurator's manner. Those were feelings that he kept to himself, though, as he did so many others.

"I am ready now," Mandralisca said, "to propose an alteration of our strategy."

"And that would be—?"

"To move ourselves somewhat more aggressively into a position of visibility, milord. I suggest that we quit this place out here in the desert and transfer our center of operations to the city of Ni-moya."

"You perplex me, Count. This is a step you have warned us against since the beginning of our campaign. It would, you said, send an immediate signal to the Pontifical officials that swarm everywhere in Ni-moya that a revolt had broken out in Zimroel against the authority of the central government. Only last month you warned us against tipping our hand prematurely. Why, now, do you contradict your own advice?"

"Because I have less fear of the central government now than I did last year, or even last month."

"Ah. Ah!"

"I still believe we should proceed with immense caution toward our goal. You will not hear me counselling any declarations of war against the government of Prestimion and Dekkeret: not yet, at any rate. But I see now that we can afford to take greater risks, because the weapons at our disposal"—and he hefted the helmet—"are more substantial than I had earlier imagined. If Prestimion and Company attempt to harm us, we can fight back."

"Ah!"

Mandralisca waited for the second one, glaring fiercely at Gaviral in expectation. But it failed to come.

After a moment he said, "We will go to Ni-moya then. You will reoccupy the procuratorial palace, although you will not, at any time, attempt to reclaim the title of Procurator. Your brothers will take possession of dwellings nearly as grand. For the present you will live there purely as private citizens, however, claiming authority only over your family's own estates. Is that understood, milord Gaviral?"

"Does that mean we're not to be regarded as lords any more?" said Gaviral. It was evident from his expression that that possibility was distressing to him.

"In the inwardness of your own households, you will still be the Lords of Zimroel. In your intercourse with the people of Ni-moya you will be the five princes of the House of Sambail, and nothing more—for the time being. Later on, milord, I have a finer title even than 'Lord' for you, but that will have to wait some while longer."

An excited gleam came into Gaviral's ugly face. He leaned forward eagerly. "And what would that finer title be?" he asked, though he already knew the answer.

"Pontifex," said Mandralisca.

12

"**M**y lord," Dekkeret's chamberlain said, "Prince Dinitak is here."

"Thank you, Zeldor Luudwid. Ask him to come in."

It amused him to hear the chamberlain promoting Dinitak to the principate. No such title had ever been conferred on him, and Dekkeret had no particular plan for doing so, nor had Dinitak shown the slightest desire to be raised to the nobility. He was still Venghenar Barjazid's son, after all, a child of the Suvrael desert who once had collaborated with his disreputable father in swindling and exploiting travelers who had hired them as guides through that forbidding land. The Castle Mount aristocracy had accepted Dinitak as Dekkeret's friend, because Dekkeret gave them no choice in that. But they would never abide Dekkeret's thrusting him in among them as a member of their own exalted caste.

"Dinitak," Dekkeret said, rising to embrace him.

In recent weeks Dekkeret had adopted as his headquarters one of the segments of the Methirasp Long Hall, which was not a hall at all, but rather a series of octagonal chambers within Lord Stiamot's Library. The library itself was a continuous serpentine passageway that wound back and forth around the summit of Castle Mount to a total length of many miles, and, according to legend, contained every book that had ever been published in any world of the universe. At one point directly beneath the greensward of Vildivar Close it opened out into the twelve chambers of the Methirasp Hall. They were set aside for the use of scholars; but it was a rare day when more than one or two of them were occupied.

Dekkeret, coming upon the rooms in one of his explorations of the Castle, had taken an immediate fancy to them. They were lofty chambers two stories high, their walls covered with mural paintings of sea-dragons and fanciful beasts of the land, knights in tournament, natural wonders, and much else, all rendered in a delightful medieval style. Far overhead, brightly colored ceilings, done in vermilion and yellow and green and blue and covered with a fine, clear varnish that made them gleam like crystal, provided warm reflected light. Connecting corridors lined on both sides with rows of books led to the library proper. Dekkeret found himself coming back again and again to this pleasing sanctuary within the Castle, and eventually had chosen to have the segment of it known as Lord Spurifon's Study closed off and made into an auxiliary office for himself. It was here that he received Dinitak Barjazid this day.

They talked quietly of idle things for a time—a visit Dinitak had lately made to the great city of Stee, and Dekkeret's plans for a journey to that city and some of its neighbors on the Mount, and the like. It was not hard for Dekkeret to see that some suppressed inner tension was at work within his friend's soul, but he let Dinitak set the pace for the conversation; and gradually he came around to the matter that had led him to seek this private audience with the Coronal.

"Have you seen much of Prince Teotas of late, your lordship?" Dinitak asked, with a new sort of intensity entering into his tone.

Dekkeret was jarred by the unexpected mention of Teotas's name. The problem of Teotas had become a touchy one for him.

"I see him now and again, but not very often," Dekkeret replied. "With the business of who is to be High Counsellor still up in the air, he seems to be avoiding me. Doesn't want to refuse the post, but can't bring himself to accept it, either. I blame Fiorinda for that."

Dinitak's cool penetrating eyes registered surprise. "Fiorinda? How is Fiorinda involved in your choice of a High Counsellor?"

"She's married to the man I've chosen, isn't she, Dinitak? Which gives us a layer of complication that I never took into account. I suppose you're aware that she's gone off to the Labyrinth to be with the Lady Varaile, leaving Teotas behind." Dekkeret riffled irritatedly through the piles of papers on his desk. It bothered him to be discussing the increasingly troublesome Teotas problem, even with Dinitak. "I would never have supposed that she'd ask Teotas to decide between being High Counsellor and parting with his wife."

"Is it as serious as that, do you think?"

Angrily Dekkeret swept the papers into a stack. "How do I know? Teotas barely speaks to me at all nowadays. But why else is he hesitating to accept the appointment? If Fiorinda has given him some sort of ultimatum about her living at the Labyrinth, he can't very well stay here and become High Counsellor, not if he wants to keep his marriage together. Women!"

Dinitak smiled. "They are difficult creatures, are they not, my lord?"

"It never for an instant occurred to me that she'd place remaining as lady-in-waiting to Varaile above her husband's chance to hold a position at the Castle that's second only to my own. Meanwhile Septach Melayn has already taken himself off to the Labyrinth to be Prestimion's High Spokesman and the post of High Counsellor goes unfilled here. —Teotas looks like a wreck, besides. All of this must be pulling him apart."

"He looks very bad, yes," Dinitak agreed. "But it's my belief that his problem with Fiorinda is not the only thing that's at work on him."

"What are you saying? What else is going on?"

Dinitak's gaze rested squarely on Dekkeret. "Teotas has sought my company more than once, recently. I think you know that he and I have never had much to do with each other. But now he is in pain and crying out for help, and he dares not go to you because of this High Counsellor business, for which he sees no resolution. So he has come to me instead. Hoping, perhaps, that I will speak to you about him."

"As you are now doing. But what kind of help can I provide? You say he's in pain. But if a man can't make up his own mind about something as important as the High Counsellorship—"

"This has nothing to do with the High Counsellorship, my lord. Not in any direct way."

Dekkeret, mystified and growing impatient now, said sharply, "Then what else can it be?"

"He is receiving sendings, Dekkeret. Night after night, the most terrible dreams, the most agonizing nightmares. It has reached the point where he's afraid to allow himself to sleep."

"Sendings? Sendings are benevolent things, Dinitak."

"Sendings of the Lady, yes. But these are not from her. The Lady does not send dreams of monsters and demons who chase people across a blasted landscape. Nor does the Lady send you dreams that convince you of your own total worthlessness and make you believe that every act of your life has been fraudulent and contemptible. He says that some nights he awakens actually despising himself. *Despising.*"

Dekkeret began to toy fretfully with his papers again. "Teotas should see a dream-speaker, then, and get his head cleared around. By the Divine, Dinitak, this is maddening! I offer the most important post in my government to a man who seems to me to be eminently qualified for it, and now I discover that he can't accept it because his wife won't let him, and that he's all in a fluster over a few bad dreams besides—! Well, it's simple enough. I'll retract my offer and Teotas can go scuttling down to the Labyrinth to be with Fiorinda. Maybe old Dembitave wants to be High Counsellor. Or perhaps I can drag Abrigant up here from Muldemar to take the job. Or else I suppose I can ask one of the younger princes, Vandimain, perhaps—"

"My lord," said Dinitak, cutting in brusquely, "I remind you that I said Teotas was receiving sendings."

"Which is a statement that makes no sense to me."

"What I mean is that someone is thrusting these terrible dreams into the mind of Teotas from afar. You continue to think that the Lady of the Isle is the only person in the world with the capacity to enter someone's sleeping mind. "

"Well? Isn't that so?"

"Do you remember a certain helmet, Dekkeret, a little thing of metal mesh, that my late father used on you long ago when you were trekking with us through the Desert of Stolen Dreams in Suvrael? Do you recall a later version of the same device that I myself used in your presence, and Lord Prestimion used also, when we were fighting against the rebel Dantirya Sambail? That helmet gives one the capacity to enter minds at a great distance. Prestimion himself could confirm that, if you were to ask him."

"But those helmets and all the documents associated with their construction and operation are kept under lock and key in the Treasury of the Castle. No one's been near those things in years. Are you trying to tell me that they've been stolen?"

"Not at all, my lord."

"Then why are we discussing them?"

"Because of the dreams Teotas is having."

"All right. So Teotas is having very bad dreams. That's not a trivial thing. But dreams, in the end, are just dreams. We generate them out of the darkness of our own souls, unless they're put into us from outside, and the only one who's able to do that is the Lady of the Isle. Who certainly would never send anyone dreams of the sort that you say Teotas is getting. And you yourself have just agreed that we control the only other machine that can do such a thing, which is the helmet that your father used to use."

"How sure can you be," Dinitak asked, "that the devices you keep locked in the Treasury are the only ones in existence? I am familiar with the workings of the helmet, lordship. I know what it can do. What is happening to Teotas is the sort of thing it can do."

For the first time Dekkeret began to see where Dinitak had been trying this whole while to lead him. "And just who is it, do you think, who owns this other helmet and is bedeviling poor Teotas with it?"

A gleam came into Dinitak's eyes. "My father's younger brother Khaymak was the mechanic who constructed my father's mind-controlling helmets for him. Khaymak has remained in Suvrael all these years, going about whatever slippery business it is that he goes about. But you may recall that he turned up on Castle Mount only last year—"

"Of course," said Dekkeret. "Of course!" It was all starting to fall into place now.

"Turned up on Castle Mount," Dinitak continued, "seeking to enroll himself in the service of Lord Prestimion. I myself saw to it—disliking the embarrassment, I will admit, of having such an unsavory kinsman around the place—that he was denied permission to come anywhere near the Castle. I see now that this was a huge mistake."

"You think that he's built another helmet?"

"Either that, or he's designed one and was searching for a patron who would finance the construction of a working model. I was fairly sure that that was why he was coming to Prestimion; and I saw nothing good coming from any of that, and so the gates of the Castle were closed to him. But I think he's found a patron somewhere else, and has fashioned a new helmet by now, and is using it on Teotas. And, it could be, on many others as well."

Dekkeret felt a chill.

"Just before my coronation," he said slowly, "Prestimion's Su-Suheris magus came to me and told me that he had had some sort of vision in which some member of the Barjazid clan somehow made himself a Power of the Realm. The whole thing seemed nonsensical to me, and I put it out of my mind. I never said anything to you about it because to me it carried treasonous implications, that you might be thinking of overthrowing me and making yourself Coronal in my place, which seemed too absurd even to think about."

"I am not the only Barjazid in this world, my lord."

"Indeed. And Maundigand-Klimd cautioned me against interpreting his vision too literally. But what if it meant, not that this Barjazid was going to become a Power—and what other Power could he become, if not Coronal?—but that he was going to *attain* power, power in the general sense of the word?"

"Or that he was going to sell his helmet and his services to some other person who would wield that power," Dinitak said.

"But who would that be? The world's at peace. Prestimion dealt with all our enemies years ago."

"The poison-taster of Dantirya Sambail still lives, my lord."

"Mandralisca? I haven't so much as thought of him in years! Why, he must be an old man now—if he's still alive at all."

"Not so old, I think. Perhaps fifty, at most. And still quite dangerous, I suspect. I touched his mind with mine, you know, when I wore the helmet the day of that final battle in the Stoienzar. Only briefly, but it was enough. I will never forget it. The hatred coiled within that mind like a giant serpent—the anger aimed at all the world, the lust to injure, to destroy—"

"Mandralisca!" murmured Dekkeret, shaking his head. He was lost in the wonder and horror of the recollection.

Dinitak said, "He was, I think, a greater monster than his master Dantirya Sambail. The Procurator knew when to rein in his ambitions. There was always a certain point that he was unwilling to go beyond, and when he reached that point, he would find someone else to undertake the task on his behalf."

Dekkeret nodded. "Korsibar, for example. Dantirya Sambail, though always hungry for more power, didn't try to make *himself* Coronal. He found a proxy, a puppet."

"Exactly. The Procurator preferred ever to remain safely behind the scenes, avoiding the worst risks, letting others do his dirty work for him. Mandralisca was of a different sort. He was always willing to risk everything on a single throw of the dice."

"Serving as a poison-taster, for instance. What sane man would take a job like that? But he seemed heedless of the risk to his own life."

"I think he must have been. Or perhaps he felt it was a risk worth taking. By letting his master know that he was willing to put his life on the line for him, he would worm his way into Dantirya Sambail's heart. That must have seemed a reasonable gamble to him. And once he found himself at the Procurator's elbow, I think he led Dantirya Sambail on, from one monstrous deed to the next, possibly just for the sheer amusement of it."

"Such a person is beyond my understanding," said Dekkeret.

"Not mine, alas. I've had closer acquaintance with monsters than you. But you're the one who will have to stop him."

"Ah, but wait! We are moving very quickly here, Dinitak, and these conjectures carry us a great distance." Dekkeret jabbed a forefinger at the smaller man. "What are you telling me, in fact? You've conjured up that old demon Mandralisca; you've put your father's thought-control weapon in his hands again; you've suggested that Mandralisca is gearing up to launch yet another war against the world. But where's the proof that any of this is real? To me it seems that it's all built out of nothing more than Teotas's bad dreams and Maundigand-Klimd's ambiguous vision!"

Dinitak smiled. "The original helmet is still in our possession. Let me get it out of the Treasury and explore the world with it. If Mandralisca still lives, I'll find out where he is. And for whom he's working. What do you say, my lord?"

"What can I say?" Dekkeret's head was throbbing. He had been on the throne barely more than a month, Prestimion was far away and ignorant of all this, and he had no High Counsellor to turn to. He was entirely on his own, save for Dinitak Barjazid. And now the possibility of an ancient enemy stirring somewhere far away suddenly lay before him. In a voice grim with apprehension and frustration Dekkeret said, "What I say is this: find him for me, Dinitak. Discover his intentions. Render him harmless, in whatever way you can. Destroy him, if necessary. You understand me. Do whatever must be done."

13

*F*ulkari was crossing the Vildivar Balconies, heading in the direction of the Pinitor Court, when the moment she had been dreading for weeks finally arrived. Through the gateway from the Inner Castle and onto the Balconies at the far end came the Coronal Lord Dekkeret, magnificent in his robes of office and surrounded, as he always was these days, by a little group of important-looking men, the inner circle of his court. Her only path led her straight toward him. There was no avoiding it, now: they must inevitably confront each other here.

She and Dekkeret had not spoken at all in the weeks that had gone by since his ascent to the throne. Indeed she had seen him just a handful of times, and then only at a great distance, at court functions of the kind that highborn young ladies of Fulkari's sort, descendants of former royal families of centuries gone by, were expected to attend. There had been no contact between them. He had scarcely looked toward her. He behaved as if she were invisible. And she had sidestepped any possibility of contact as well. One time at a royal levee when it seemed that his path across the great throne-room would certainly bring them face to face, she had taken care to slip away into the crowd before he came anywhere near her. She feared what he might say to her.

It was obvious to everyone that whatever relationship once had existed between them was over. Perhaps he was unwilling to say so to her in so many words, but Fulkari had no doubt that it was at an end. Only the fact that he had not yet brought himself to make a formal break with her kept it alive in her heart. Yet she knew how foolish that was.

They had kept company for three years, and now they did not speak at all. Could anything be more clear than that? Dekkeret had asked her to marry him and she had refused him. That had ended it. Was it really necessary, she wondered, for him to acknowledge formally something that was plain to all?

Yet there he was, no more than a hundred yards away and coming straight toward her.

Would he continue to pretend she was invisible when they encountered each other on this narrow balcony? That would be agony, Fulkari thought. To be humiliated like that in front of Dinitak and Prince Teotas and the Council ministers Dembitave and Vandimain and the rest of those men. An agony of her own making—she had no doubts about that—but an agony all the same, marking her as nothing more than a discarded royal mistress. And not even that, actually. Dekkeret had not yet become Coronal the last time they had made love. So all she was was someone who had been the lover of the new Coronal when he was still only a private individual, one of the many women who had passed through his bed over the years.

She resolved to address the situation squarely. I am no mere discarded concubine, she thought. I am Lady Fulkari of Sipermit, in whose veins flows the blood of the Coronal Lord Makhario, who was king in this Castle five centuries ago. What had Lord Dekkeret's ancestors been doing five centuries ago? Did he even know their names?

She and Dekkeret were no more than fifty feet apart now. Fulkari looked straight toward him. Their eyes met, and it was only with great effort that she kept herself from glancing aside; but she held her gaze.

Dekkeret appeared tense and weary. And wary, as well: gone now was the cheerful open countenance of the lighthearted man who had been her lover these three years past. He seemed under great strain now. His lips were closely clamped, his forehead was furrowed, there was a visible throbbing of some sort in his left cheek. Was it the cares of his high office that had done this to him, or was he simply reacting to the embarrassment of this accidental encounter in front of all his companions?

"Fulkari," he said, when they were closer. He spoke softly and his voice seemed as rigid and tightly controlled as was the expression of his face.

"My lord." Fulkari bowed her head and offered him the starburst salute.

He halted before her. She was close enough to him, here in the tight confines of the little balcony promenade, that she was able to observe a thin line of perspiration along his upper lip. The two men who had been walking closest to the Coronal, Dinitak and Vandimain, stepped back from him and seemed to fade into the background. Prince Teotas, who looked terribly weary and tense himself, bloodshot and haggard, was staring at her as though she were some sort of phantom.

Then Teotas and Dinitak and Vandimain faded back even farther, so that they appeared to vanish altogether, and Fulkari could see only Dekkeret, occupying an immense space at the center of her consciousness. She faced him steadily. Tall woman though she was, she came barely breast-high to him.

There was a silence between them that went on and on and on. If only he would reach out his hand to her, she told herself, she would hurl herself into his embrace in front of all these others, these great men of the realm, these princes and counts and dukes. But he did not reach out.

Instead he said in that same tight tone, after what felt like years but more likely had been only five or six seconds, "I've been meaning to send for you, Fulkari. We need to speak, you know."

Fatal words. The words she had hoped not to hear.

We need to speak? Of what, my lord? What is there left for us to say?

That was what she wished she could say. And then move past him and walk swiftly on. But she kept her gaze level and maintained a cool tone of high formality in her reply: "Yes, my lord. Whenever you wish, my lord."

Dekkeret's forehead was glistening now with sweat. This must be as hard for him as it was for her, Fulkari realized.

He turned to his chamberlain. "You will arrange a private audience for the Lady Fulkari for tomorrow afternoon, Zeldor Luudwid. We will meet in the Methirasp Hall."

"Very good, sir," the chamberlain said.

"He wants to see me, Keltryn!" Fulkari said. They were in Keltryn's modest, cluttered apartment in the Setiphon Arcade, two flights down from the more imposing suite that Fulkari herself occupied. She had gone straight to Keltryn's place after her encounter with Dekkeret. "I was passing through one of the Vildivar Balconies, and he was coming the other way with Vandimain and Dinitak and a lot of other people, and we had no choice but to walk right up to each other." Quickly she described the brief meeting, Dekkeret's uneasiness, her own conflicting emotions, the arm's-length nature of the quick conversation, the appointment for her to see him the following day.

"Well, why shouldn't he want to see you?" Keltryn asked. "You aren't any uglier than you were last month, and even a busy man like the Coronal likes to have someone next to him in bed now and then, I'd imagine. So he saw you there in front of him, and he thought, 'Oh, yes, Fulkari—I remember Fulkari—'"

"What a child you are, Keltryn."

Keltryn grinned. "You don't think I'm right?"

"Of course not. The whole notion is contemptible. Obviously you must think that both he and I are completely trivial people—that he sees nothing more in me than a handy plaything for lonely nights, and that all it would take for me to go running to him is a quick snap of his fingers—"

"But you're going to go to see him, aren't you?"

"Of course. Am I supposed to tell the Coronal of Majipoor that I can't be bothered to accept his invitation?"

"Well, then, you'll find out fast enough whether I'm right or not," Keltryn said. Her eyes were sparkling triumphantly. She was enjoying this. "Go to him. Listen to what he has to say. I predict that within five minutes he'll be sliding his hands all over you. And you'll turn to jelly when he does."

Fulkari stared at her sister in mingled fury and amusement. She *was* such a child, after all. What did she know about men, she who had never given herself to one? And yet—yet—standing as she did outside the whole sweaty business of men and women, Keltryn just might have a certain perspective that Fulkari herself, caught in the thick of all this intrigue, did not.

After all, Keltryn at seventeen wasn't all that callow and raw. There was a no-nonsense wisdom about her that Fulkari was beginning to come to respect. It was a mistake to go on regarding her as a little girl forever. Changes were taking place. You could see it in her face: Fulkari was startled to see that she looked less boyish, suddenly, as though she were finally making the transition from coltish girl to real womanhood.

Fulkari roamed around the room, restlessly picking up and putting down one and another of the cut-glass bottles that Keltryn liked to collect. A flood of contradictory thoughts roared through her.

At length she turned and said, the words coming out in a high-voiced fluty tone that gave her that odd feeling once more that Keltryn was the older sister and she the younger one, "How *can* he seriously want to start it all over again, Keltryn? After what I said to him when he asked me to marry him? No. No, it just isn't possible. He knows there's no point in stirring everything up a second time. And if he's merely interested in a bedmate, with no complications involved, the Castle is full of other women, much more suitable than I am, who'd be happy to oblige. He and I have too much history to allow anything of that sort to happen now."

Keltryn gave her a wide-eyed, serious stare. "And if he *does* still want you, anyway? Isn't that what you want also?"

"I don't know what I want. You know I love him."

"Yes."

"But he's looking for a wife, and I've already said I don't want to marry a Coronal." Fulkari shook her head. She felt some measure of clarity returning to her troubled mind. "No, Keltryn, you're wrong. The last thing Dekkeret wants is to get entangled with me again. I think that the reason he's asked for me to come to him is because he's realized that he never did get around to telling me formally that it's over, and he feels a little guilty about it, because he owes me that much at a minimum. He's been so busy being Coronal that he's left me dangling, essentially, and it's time for him to do the right thing. And when we ran into each other like that on that balcony he must have thought, 'Oh, well, I really can't let things drift on like this any longer.' "

"Maybe so. And how do you feel about that? That he's summoned you just to finish everything off? Truthfully."

"Truthfully?" Fulkari hesitated only an instant. "I hate it. I don't want it to be over. I told you: I still love him, Keltryn."

"Yet you told him you wouldn't marry him. What do you expect him to do? He has to get on with his life. He doesn't need mistresses now: he needs a wife."

"I didn't refuse to marry him. I refused to marry the *Coronal*."

"Yes. Yes. You keep saying that. But it's the same thing, isn't it, Fulkari?"

"It wasn't, when I said it. He hadn't been officially proclaimed, yet. I suppose I hoped he'd give it all up for me. But of course he didn't."

"It was a crazy thing to ask, you know."

"I realize that. He's been preparing himself for the past fifteen years to succeed Lord Prestimion, and when the moment comes I say, 'No, no, I'm much more important than all that, aren't I, Dekkeret?' How could I have been so stupid?" Fulkari turned away. This was giving her a headache. She had come running to Keltryn, she saw, in some kind of frenzy of muddled girlish excitement—"He wants to see me!"—and Keltryn had methodically exposed the full extent of her confusions. That was valuable, but also very painful. She wanted no more of this discussion.

"Fulkari?" Keltryn said, when some time had passed in silence. "Are you all right?"

"More or less, yes. —What about going for a swim?"

"I was just going to suggest the same thing."

"Fine," Fulkari said. "Let's go." And then, to change the subject: "Are you still keeping up with your fencing, now that Septach Melayn's gone to the Labyrinth?"

"Somewhat," Keltryn said. "I meet twice a week in the gymnasium with one of the boys from Septach Melayn's class."

"Audhari, is it? The one from Stoienzar that you told me about?"

"Audhari, yes."

That was interesting. Fulkari waited for Keltryn to say something more about Audhari, but nothing was forthcoming. She scrutinized Keltryn's face with care, wondering if some telltale sign of embarrassment or discomfort would show through, something that would reveal that her little virgin sister had finally taken herself a lover. But none of that was visible. Either Keltryn was a more accomplished actress than Fulkari had given her credit for being, or there was nothing more than innocent fencing-practice going on between her and this Audhari.

Too bad, she thought. It was time for a little romance in Keltryn's life.

Then abruptly Keltryn said, as they reached the pool, "Tell me, Fulkari. Do you know Dinitak Barjazid at all well?"

Fulkari frowned. "Dinitak? What makes you ask about him?"

"I'm asking because I'm asking." And now, to her immense surprise, Fulkari saw the signs of tension that had been absent when Audhari's name had come up. "Is he a friend of yours?" Keltryn said.

"In a very casual way, yes. You can't spend much time around Dekkeret without getting to know Dinitak too. He's usually to be found not very far from Dekkeret, you know. But he and I have never been particularly close. Acquaintances, really, rather than friends. —Will you tell me what this is about, Keltryn? Or is it something I'm not supposed to know?"

Keltryn now wore an expression of elaborate indifference. "He interests me, that's all. I happened to run into him yesterday over by Lord Haspar's Rotunda, when I was on my way to fencing practice, and we talked for a couple of minutes. That's all there is. Don't get any ideas, Fulkari! All we did was talk."

"Ideas? What ideas would you mean?"

"He's very—unusual, I thought," Keltryn said. She seemed to be measuring her words very carefully. "There's something fierce about him—something mysterious and stern. I suppose it's because he's from Suvrael originally. Every Suvraelinu I've ever met has been a little strange. The hot sun must do that to them. But he's strange in an interesting way, if you know what I mean."

"I think I do," Fulkari said, calibrating the gleam that had come into her sister's eyes just then. She knew as well as anyone did what a gleam like that in the eyes of a seventeen-year-old girl meant.

Dinitak? How odd. How interesting. How unexpected.

Dekkeret said, "I owe you an apology, Fulkari."

Fulkari, out of breath after a long frantic sprint through the interminable coils and twists of Lord Stiamot's Library, was slow to reply. She had arrived twenty minutes late for her audience with the Coronal, having taken one wrong turn after another in the endless miles of the collection. She had never seen so many books in her life as she had just now while running through those corridors. She had no idea that there were that many books in existence. Had anyone ever read any of them? Would there be no end to these thousands of shelves? Finally an ancient, fossilized-looking librarian had taken pity on her and guided her through the maze to Lord Dekkeret's secluded little study in the Methirasp Long Hall.

"An apology?" she said at last, if only to be saying something at all.

Dekkeret's desk was a barrier between them. It was piled high with official documents, long parchment sheets formidably festooned in ribbons and seals. They seemed to be marching across the brightly polished surface of the desk toward him, an encroaching army demanding his attention.

Dekkeret looked tired and ill at ease. Today he wore no fine regal robes, only a simple gray tunic loosely belted at the waist.

"An apology, yes, Fulkari." He appeared to be forcing the words out. "For having drawn you into such an unhappy, impossible relationship."

She found his statement baffling. "Impossible? Perhaps. But I was the one that made it that way. Why should you feel that you have to apologize for anything? —And why call it 'unhappy,' Dekkeret? Was it really such an unhappy relationship? Is that how it seemed to you?"

"Not for a long while. But you have to agree that it ended unhappily."

The phrase went reverberating through her soul. *It ended. It ended. It ended.*

Yes. Of course it had ended. But she was unwilling to hear the words themselves. Those few crisp syllables, spoken aloud, had the finality of a descending blade.

Fulkari waited a moment for the impact to lessen. "Even so," she said. "I still don't understand what it is that you feel you need to apologize for."

"You couldn't possibly know. But that's why I asked you to come here today. I can't conceal the truth from you any longer."

Restlessly she said, "What are you talking about, Dekkeret?"

She could see him groping for words, struggling to organize his reply.

He seemed to have aged five years since they had last been together. His face was pale and drawn, and there were shadows under his eyes, and his broad shoulders were hunched as though sitting up straight was too much of an effort for him today. This was a Dekkeret she had never seen before, this tired, suddenly indecisive man. She wanted to reach out to him, to stroke his brow, to give him whatever comfort she could.

Hesitantly he said, "When I first met you, Fulkari, I was instantly attracted to you. Do you remember? I must have looked like a man who had been struck by a bolt of lightning."

Fulkari smiled. "I remember, yes. You stared and stared and stared. You were staring so hard that I began to wonder if there was something wrong with the way I was dressed."

"Nothing was wrong. I simply couldn't stop staring, that was all. Then you moved along, and I asked someone who you were, and I arranged to have you invited to a levee that the Lady Varaile was holding the following week. Where I had you brought forward to be introduced to me."

"And you stared some more."

"Yes. Surely I did. Do you remember what I said, then?"

She had no clear memory of that. Whatever he had told her then, it was lost to her now, swept away in the confusion and excitement of that first moment. Uncertainly she replied, "You asked if you could see me again, I suppose."

"That was later. What did I say *first?*"

"Do you really suppose that I can remember everything in such detail? It was so long ago, Dekkeret!"

"Well, I remember," he said. "I asked you if you were of Normork blood. No, you replied: Sipermit. I told you then that you reminded me very much of someone I had known in Normork long ago—my cousin Sithelle, in fact. Do you recall any of that? An extraordinary resemblance, your eyes, your hair, your mouth and chin, your long arms and legs—so much like Sithelle that I thought I was seeing her ghost."

"Sithelle is dead, then?"

"These twenty years. Slain in the streets of Normork by an assassin who was trying to reach Prestimion. I was there. She died in my arms. I never realized until many years later how much I had loved her. And then, when I saw you that day at court—looking at you, knowing nothing whatever about you, thinking only, *Here is Sithelle restored to me—*"

He broke off. He glanced away, abashed.

Fulkari felt her cheeks flaming. This was worse than humiliating: it was infuriating. "You weren't attracted to me for myself?" she asked. There was heat in her voice, too, that she could not suppress. "You were drawn to me only because I looked like somebody else you once had known? Oh, Dekkeret—Dekkeret—!"

In a barely audible tone he said, "I told you that I owed you an apology, Fulkari."

Tears crowded into her eyes—tears of rage. "So I was never anything to you but a kind of flesh-and-blood replica of someone else you weren't able to have? When you looked at me you saw Sithelle, and when you kissed me you were kissing Sithelle, and when you went to bed with me you were—"

"No, Fulkari. That's not how it was at all." Dekkeret was speaking more forcefully now. "When I told you I loved you, it was *you* I was telling it to—Fulkari of Sipermit. When I held you in my arms, it was Fulkari of Sipermit that I was holding. Sithelle and I never were lovers. We probably never would have been, even if she had lived. When I asked you to marry me, it was you I was asking, not Sithelle's ghost."

"Then why all this talk of apologies?"

"Because the thing I can't deny is that I was drawn to you originally for the wrong reason, no matter what happened later. That instant attraction I felt, before we had ever spoken a word to each other—it was because some foolish part of me was whispering that you were Sithelle reborn, that a second chance was being given to me. I knew even then that it was idiotic. But I was caught—trapped by my own ridiculous fantasy. So I pursued you. Not because you were you, not at first, but because you looked so much like Sithelle. The woman I fell in love with, though, was you. The woman I asked to marry me: you. *You*, Fulkari."

"And when Fulkari refused you, was that like losing Sithelle a second time?" she asked. Her tone was one of mere curiosity, only. It surprised her how quickly the anger was beginning to fade.

"No. No. It wasn't like that at all," said Dekkeret. "Sithelle was like a sister to me: I never would have married her. When you refused me—and I knew you would; you had already given me a million indications that you would—it tore me apart, because I knew I was losing *you*. And I saw how my original crazy notion of using you as a replacement for Sithelle had led me step by step into falling in love with a real living woman who didn't happen to want to be my wife. I wasted three years of our lives, Fulkari. That's what I'm sorry about. The thing that drew me to you in the first place was a fantasy, a will-o'-the-wisp, but I was caught by it as though by a metal trap; and it held me long enough for me to fall in love with the true Fulkari, who wasn't able to return my love, and so—a waste, Fulkari, all a waste—"

"That isn't so, Dekkeret." She spoke firmly, and met his gaze evenly, calmly. Every trace of anger was gone from her now. A new assurance had come over her.

"You don't think so?"

"Maybe it was a waste for you. But not for me. What I felt for you was real. It still is." Fulkari paused only a moment, then plunged boldly onward. What was there to lose? "I love you, Dekkeret. And not because you remind me of anyone else."

He seemed astonished. "You love me still?"

"When did I ever tell you I had stopped?"

"You seemed furious, just a moment or two back, when I was telling you that what first led me to pursue you was the image of Sithelle that I still carried in my mind."

"What woman would be pleased to hear such a thing? But why

should I allow it to continue to matter? Sithelle's long gone. And so is the boy who may or may not have been in love with her—even he wasn't sure—a long time ago. But you and I are still here."

"For whatever that might be worth," said Dekkeret.

"Perhaps it could be worth a great deal indeed," said Fulkari. —"Tell me something, Dekkeret: just how difficult would it really be, do you think, to be the Coronal's wife?"

14

"My lord?" Teotas said, peering through the open doorway.

He stood at the threshold of the threshold of the Coronal's official suite, that great room whose giant curving window revealed the breathtaking abyss of open space that abutted this side of the Castle.

Dekkeret, when Teotas had asked him for this meeting, had proposed that Teotas come to him in the chamber in the Methirasp Long Hall that he seemed to be using as his main office these days. But Teotas had felt uncomfortable with that. It was irregular. This was the room that he associated with the grandeur and might of the Coronal Lord. Again and again during the reign of his brother Prestimion had he met here with the Coronal in some time of crisis. What he wanted to discuss with Lord Dekkeret now was a matter of the highest concern, and it was in this room, only in this room, that he wanted to discuss it. One did not ordinarily make demands upon Coronals. But Dekkeret had yielded gracefully to his request.

"Come in, Teotas," Dekkeret said. "Sit down."

"My lord," Teotas said a second time, and offered the starburst salute.

The Coronal was seated behind the splendid ancient desk, a single polished slab of red palisander wood with a natural grain resembling the starburst emblem that Coronals since Lord Dizimaule's day had used— a span of five hundred years or more. For Teotas there was something of a shock in seeing Lord Dekkeret actually sitting at that desk that Lord Prestimion had occupied for so many years. But he needed that shock.

It was important for him to remind himself at every opportunity that presented itself that the great imperial shift had occurred once more, that Prestimion had gone off to the Labyrinth to become Pontifex, that this beautiful desk, which had been Lord Confalume's before it was Prestimion's, and Lord Prankipin's before it was Confalume's, was Lord Dekkeret's now.

Dekkeret fitted it well: better, in truth, than Prestimion had. The desk had always seemed too huge for the small-framed Prestimion, but the much bigger Dekkeret was a more appropriate match for the desk's majestic dimensions. He was dressed in the traditional royal way, robes of green and gold with ermine trim, and he radiated such strength and confidence now that Teotas, weary unto exhaustion and close to the limits of his strength, felt suddenly aged and feeble in the presence of this man who was only a few years younger than he was himself.

"So," Dekkeret said. "Here we are."

"Here we are, yes."

"You look tired, Teotas. Dinitak tells me that you've been sleeping badly of late."

"I'd rather have it that I wasn't sleeping at all. When I give myself over to sleep it brings me the most terrible dreams—dreams so frightful I can barely believe that my mind is capable of inventing such things."

"Give me an example."

Teotas shook his head. "No point in trying. I'd have difficulty describing it. Not much remains in my mind after I awaken except a sense that I've been through a terrifying experience. I see strange hideous landscapes, monsters, demons. But I won't try to portray them. What seems so terrifying to the dreamer himself has no power over anyone else. —And in any event I haven't come here to talk about my dreams, my lord. There's the matter of my pending appointment as High Counsellor."

"What about it?" Dekkeret asked, in so cool and casual a way that Teotas could see that he had been anticipating some discussion of that very topic. "I remind you, Teotas, I've had no formal acceptance of the post from you."

"Nor will you," Teotas said. "I've come to you to ask you to withdraw my name from consideration."

Quite clearly Dekkeret had anticipated that. The Coronal's voice was still very calm as he said, "I would not have chosen you, Teotas, if I didn't think that you were the man most suited for the post."

"I'm cognizant of that. It's a matter of the deepest regret to me that I can't accept this great honor. But I can't."

"May I have a reason?"

"Must I provide one, my lord?"

"Not 'must,' no. But I do think some explanation would be appropriate."

"My lord—"

Teotas could not go on, for fear of what he might say. He felt a stirring, deep within himself, of the famous temper that once had been so widely feared. Why would Dekkeret not simply release him from the offer and let him be? But the heat of his fury had been much diminished by time and the weariness that comes with despair. He was able now to find nothing more within himself than a crackle of annoyance, and that quickly passed, leaving him drained and desolate and numb.

He covered his face with his outspread hands. After a little while he said again, "My lord—" in a faint, indistinct way. Dekkeret waited, saying nothing. "My lord, do you see how I look? How I conduct myself? Is this the Teotas you remember from earlier times? From six months ago, even? Do I seem to you like a man fit to undertake the duties of the High Counsellor of the Realm? Can't you see that I'm half out of my mind? More than half. Only a fool would choose an unstable person like me for such an important post. And you are anything but a fool."

"I do see that you seem ill, Teotas. But illnesses can be cured. —Have you discussed this matter of refusing the post with his majesty your brother?"

"Not at all. I don't see any need to burden Prestimion with my troubles."

"If the Divine had granted me a brother," Dekkeret said, "I think I would be ready and willing to hear of any troubles of his, at any hour of the day or night. And I think it would be the same for Prestimion."

"Nevertheless, I will not go to him." This was becoming a torment, now. "In the name of the Divine, Dekkeret! Find yourself some other High Counsellor, and let me be done with it! Surely I'm not indispensable."

It seemed to occur to the Coronal, finally, that Teotas was in agony. Gently he said, "No one is indispensable, including the Pontifex and the Coronal. And I'll withdraw the appointment, if you give me no choice about it."

"Thank you, my lord." Teotas rose as if to go.

But Dekkeret was not done with him. "I should tell you, though, that Dinitak believes that these dreams of yours, which must truly be appalling, are not the work of your own brain at all. He thinks they're being sent in by an enemy from outside—a kinsman of his, a Barjazid, he suspects, who is using some version of the thought-control helmet that we once employed against Dantirya Sambail."

Teotas gasped. "Can that be so?"

"At this moment Dinitak is searching for proof of his theory. And will take the necessary action, if he finds that what he suspects is true."

"I find myself perplexed at this, my lord. Why would anyone want to be sending me bad dreams? Your friend Dinitak wastes his time, I think."

"Be that as it may, I've authorized him to look into it."

Teotas felt that he was coming to the limits of his reserve of strength. He had to make an end of this. "Whatever he finds will make no difference to our discussion here," he said. "The real issue is what has become of my marriage. —You know, I think, that Fiorinda is at the Labyrinth with Varaile?"

"Yes."

"She is as important to Varaile as you claim that I am to you. But I will not live apart from her indefinitely, my lord. There is no solution, then, other than for one of us to give up the royal appointment, and it has been my rule always to place Fiorinda's needs and desires above my own. Therefore I will not serve you as High Counsellor."

"You may think differently about this," said Dekkeret, "once we have freed you from these dreams. Giving up the High Counsellorship is no light matter. I promise you, I'll release you if you feel, even after the dreams are gone, that you don't want the job. But can we hold the decision in abeyance until then?"

"You are inexorable, my lord. But I am adamant. Dreams or no dreams, I want to be with my wife, and she wants to be with Varaile at the Labyrinth."

He moved again toward the door.

"Give it one more week," Dekkeret said. "We'll meet again a week from now, and if you feel the same way, I'll name someone else to the post. Can we agree on that? One more week?"

Dekkeret's tenacity was maddening. Teotas could bear it no longer. "Whatever you say, my lord," he muttered. "One week more, yes. Whatever you say." He made a hasty starburst salute and rushed from the room before the Coronal could utter another word.

*   *   *

That night Teotas lies awake for hours, too tired even to sleep, and he begins to hope that just this once he will be spared, that he will go through the night from midnight to dawn without descending even for a moment into the realm of dreams. Better not to sleep at all, he thinks, than to endure the torture that his dreams have become.

But somehow he passes without knowing it, once again, from wakefulness to sleep. There is no sudden transition, no sense of crossing a boundary. Somehow, though, he has entered yet another strange place, where he knows he will suffer. As he moves forward into it, the power of the place only gradually makes itself known to him, gathering slowly, mounting with each step he takes, oppressing him only a little at first, then more, then much more.

And now Teotas finds himself under the full stress of this place. He is in a region of thick-stemmed gray shrubs, broad-leaved and low. A thick mist hovers. The general tone here is a colorless one: hue has bled away. And there is the awful pull coming from the ground, that clamp of gravity clinging with inexorable force to every part of him. His eyelids are leaden. His cheeks sag. His gut droops. His throat is a loosely hanging sac. His bones bend under the strain. He walks with bent knees. What does he weigh here? Eight hundred pounds? Eight thousand? Eight million? He is unthinkably heavy. Heavy. Heavy.

His weight nails his feet flat to the ground. Each time he pulls one upward to take another step, he hears a reverberating sound as the planet recoils against the separation. He is aware of the blood lying dark and sleepy along the enfeebled arteries of his chest. He feels a monstrous iron hump riding on his shoulders. Yet he walks on. There must be an end to this place somewhere.

But there is no end.

Halting, Teotas kneels, just to regain his breath. Tears of relief burst forth as some of the stress is lifted from his body's bony framework. Like drops of quicksilver the slow tears roll down his cheek and thump into the ground.

When he feels that he is ready to go on, he attempts to rise.

It takes him five tries. Then he succeeds, rocking himself, levering himself up on his knuckles, rump in air, intestines yanked groundward, spine popping, neck creaking. Up. Up. Another push. He stands. He gasps. He walks. He finds the path he had been following a little while ago: there are his footprints, nearly an inch deep on the sandy soil. He fits his feet into the imprints and moves onward.

The gravitational drag continues to increase. Breathing has become a battle. His rib cage will not lift except under duress; his lungs are stretched like elastic bands. His cheeks hang toward his shoulders. There is a boulder in his chest. And it all keeps getting worse. He knows that if he remains here much longer he will be squeezed flat. He will be squeezed until he is nothing more than a film of dust coating the ground.

The effect continues to worsen. He can no longer remain upright. He has become top-heavy, and the mass of his skull turns his back into a curved bow; his vertebrae slide about, grinding and cracking. He yearns to lie down flat, surrendering to the awful force, but he knows that if he does, he will never be able to rise again.

The sky is being pulled down on top of him. A gray shield presses against his back. His knees are taking root. He crawls. He crawls. He crawls. He crawls.

"Help me!" he cries. "Fiorinda! Prestimion! Abrigant!"

His words are like pellets of lead. They spill from his mouth and plummet into the ground.

He crawls.

There is a ghastly pain in his side. He fears that his intestines are breaking through his skin. His bones are separating at the elbows and knees. He crawls. He crawls.

He crawls.

"Pres—tim—i—on!"

The name emerges as an incoherent gargle. His gullet is stone. His earlobes are stone. His lips are stone. He crawls. His hands sink into the ground. He wrenches them free. He is at the end of his resources. He will perish. This is the finish: he is about to die a slow and hideous death. The gray mantle of the sky is crushing him. He is caught between earth and air. Everything is impossibly heavy. Heavy. Heavy. Heavy. He crawls. He sees only the rough bare soil eight inches from his nose.

Then, miraculously, a gateway appears before him, a shimmering golden oval in the air just ahead of him.

Teotas knows that if he can reach it, he will free himself from this realm of unendurable pressure. But reaching it is a challenge almost beyond his means. Every inch that he gains represents a triumph over implacable forces.

He reaches it. Inch by inch by inch he pulls himself forward, clawing at the ground, digging his nails in and hauling his impossibly heavy body toward that golden gateway, and then it hovers just in front of him, and he puts his hands to its rim and drags himself to his feet, and thrusts one shoulder through, and his head and neck just afterward, and somehow manages to raise one leg and move it across the threshold. And he is through. He feels himself falling, but the drop is only a couple of feet, and he lands all asprawl on a platform of brick and lies there gasping for breath.

His weight is normal, here on the other side. This is the real world out here. He is still asleep, but he senses that he has left his bedroom and is wandering around on some outer parapet of the Castle.

Nothing looks familiar. He sees spires, embrasures, distant towers. He is on a narrow winding path that appears to be going up and up, spiraling around a tall upjutting outbuilding of the Castle that he cannot even begin to identify. The black sky is speckled with a dazzle of stars, and the cold light of two or three of the moons shines along the horizon. He continues to climb. He imagines that he can hear a dire shrieking wind whipping past the summit of the Mount, though he knows he should not hear any such thing in these privileged altitudes.

The brick pathway that he is following grows ever steeper, ever narrower. The steps are cracked and broken beneath his feet, as though no one has bothered to come up here in centuries and the brickwork has simply been left to erode. It seems to him that he is climbing up the external face of one of the watchtowers along the Castle's periphery, ascending a terrifying precarious track with an infinitely long drop on either side of him. He grows a little uneasy.

But there is no going back. Following this track is like climbing the spine of some gigantic monster. The path is too narrow here to allow him to turn, and to try to descend it walking backward is inconceivable, so no retreat is possible. Icy sweat begins to trickle down his sides.

He turns a bend in the path and the Great Moon suddenly fills the sky. It is crescent tonight, dazzlingly brilliant, a gigantic bright pair of white horns hanging in front of him. By its frosty blaze he sees that he has clambered out onto a solitary spire of the colossal Castle and has reached a point close to its tip. Far away to his right he sees what he thinks are the rooftops of the Inner Castle. To his left is only a black abyss.

There is no going higher from this position. Nor is there any turning back. He can only stand here shivering on this dizzying upthrust point, whipped by the howling wind, waiting to awaken. Or else he can choose to step out into the emptiness and float downward to whatever awaits him below.

Yes. That is what he will do.

Teotas turns to his left and looks out toward the darkness, and then he puts one foot over the course of bricks that marks the edge of the path, and steps across.

But this is no dream. He is really falling.

Teotas does not care. It is like flying. The cool air from below brushes his hair like a caress. He will fall and fall and fall, a thousand feet, ten thousand, perhaps all the way to the foot of Castle Mount; and when he reaches the bottom, he knows, he will be at peace. At last. Peace.

III

The Book of Powers

1

*T*he Pontifex Prestimion had not been expecting to return to Castle Mount so soon, nor had he anticipated any such sad occasion as the funeral of a brother. Yet here he was once more hastening upriver from the Labyrinth, choking with grief, for Teotas's burial rites. The ceremony would not be held at the Castle itself, but rather at Muldemar House, the family estate, the place where Teotas had been born and where he would rest now forever beside a long line of his princely ancestors.

It was years since Prestimion had been to Muldemar. There was no real reason for him to visit it. He had often gone there during his days as a prince of the Castle to visit his mother the Lady Therissa, but his accession to the Coronal's throne had automatically brought her the title and duties of Lady of the Isle of Sleep, and she had been a resident of that island ever since. And likewise Prestimion's coming to the throne had made Muldemar House his brother Abrigant's domain, and Prestimion was not eager to overshadow his brother's authority in his own house.

But then had come the bewildering, agonizing news of Teotas's death; and Prestimion had come hurrying back to the ancestral home. Abrigant himself, an imposing figure in a dark blue doublet and a cloak striped with black and white, with a yellow mourning badge pinned to his shoulder, greeted him when the Pontifical party arrived at the gateway to Muldemar city. His eyes looked red and raw from sorrow. He was a tall man, the tallest by a head and shoulders of the four brothers who had grown up here together decades ago, and when he wrapped the Pontifex in a close and long embrace it was a well-nigh smothering one.

He released Prestimion and stepped back. "I bid you welcome to Muldemar, brother. Think of this place as being as much your home now as ever it was."

"You know how grateful I am for those words, Abrigant."

"And now that you've come, we can proceed with our burying."

Prestimion nodded grimly. "Has there been word from our mother?"

"She sends a warm message of love, and tells us that she joins with us in our grief. But she will not be with us here."

That news came as no surprise. There had never been any likelihood that the Lady Therissa would attend the ceremony. She was too old now for the arduous journey by sea and land from the Isle of Sleep to Castle Mount, and in any case the distance was so great that she could not have arrived here quickly enough. Abrigant had delayed the rite considerably as it was, in order to make it possible for Prestimion to be there. The Lady Therissa would mourn her youngest son from afar.

Prestimion was startled at how much older Abrigant seemed than when they last had met. That had been at the crowning of Dekkeret, not very long ago. Just as Teotas had, Abrigant had begun very quickly to show his years. He stood a little stoopingly, now. The luster of Abrigant's glistening golden hair appeared to have dimmed greatly in just the past few months, and the vertical lines of age that had just been beginning to emerge on either side of his nose now seemed very deeply etched. Obviously the death of Teotas had fallen heavily upon him. Abrigant and Teotas, the third son and the fourth, had been extremely close, especially in these recent years when Prestimion's royal responsibilities had kept him apart from the others.

"We are the only two left now," Abrigant said, with a kind of wonder in his words, as though he could not believe his own statements. The tone of his voice was dark and sepulchral, like the gusting of a distant wind. "And so strange, so wrong, that our brothers should be dead this young! How old was Taradath when he fell in the Korsibar war? Twenty-four? Twenty-five? And now Teotas, who was younger even than myself, and is gone so much before his time—!"

The haunted look in Abrigant's eyes was an awful thing to behold.

"Do you have any idea what could have driven him to it?" Prestimion asked. He had barely begun to come to terms with the whole thing himself.

In a guarded voice Abrigant replied, "It was a fit of madness, of a kind that had been coming upon him more and more often. That is all I would care to say, brother. Dekkeret will speak with you about it in more detail later. But come: here are the floaters that will take us to Muldemar House." He gestured toward Varaile and Fiorinda, who had taken up a place just to Prestimion's left throughout the conversation, and were standing silently while Prestimion and Abrigant spoke. "Here, my sisters—"

The two women had rarely left each other's side during the journey from the Labyrinth. Both of them were swathed in the yellow robes of mourning, and both seemed so grief-stricken still that there was no way a stranger could have told which one was the widow of the late prince, and which merely the sister-in-law. Fiorinda's three small children, two girls and a boy of five, huddled behind their mother, peeping out shyly, showing little comprehension of the tragedy that had overtaken their family. "This floater is yours," Abrigant told them. He ushered them toward it. The Lady Tuanelys and young Prince Simbilon would travel with their mother and aunt and cousins also. "And I will ride with the Pontifex in this one," he said, indicating his own floater. Prestimion entered it, and his two older sons climbed in beside him, and Abrigrant gave the vehicle the command to proceed.

Abrigant seemed to unwind and expand during the course of the journey from Muldemar city to the estate itself. Perhaps he was relieved, at this dark time, to have his elder brother arrive to assume some of his burdens.

He complimented Prestimion on how much his children had grown and how well they looked. Young Taradath was indeed beginning to look quite princely, and Prince Akbalik also, though Simbilon still seemed far from getting his growth. And it did not seem to Prestimion that the Lady Tuanelys, who had been suffering lately from nightmares that had a troublesome resemblance to the dreams of the sort Teotas had supposedly been having, looked at all well. Disturbing dreams had begun to afflict Varaile also, lately. But Prestimion said nothing about that to Abrigant.

"And this year's wines!" Abrigant was saying. He sounded almost exuberant now. "Wait until you sample them, Prestimion! A year of years, a year for the ages! The red in particular, as I was saying to Teotas only— last—month—"

His voice slowed and then halted in mid-sentence. All exuberance vanished and the haunted look abruptly returned to his eyes.

Prestimion said quickly, "Ah, look there, Abrigant: Muldemar House! How beautiful it is! How much I've missed being here!" It was as though he felt it was his task, not only as Pontifex but as the eldest of the family, to keep Abrigant from sinking into despondency.

To his two sons he said: "I was born here, you know. This evening I'll show you the rooms where I used to live." As if they had never seen the place before; but his concern now was merely to distract Abrigant from his sorrow.

Prestimion himself, laboring under his own sharp sense of great loss, felt lifted from his dark mood by the sight of his boyhood home.

Who could fail to respond to the extraordinary beauty of the vale of Muldemar? Amidst all the varied splendors of Castle Mount it stood out as a place of grace and calm. It was bordered on one side by the broad face of the Mount itself, and on the other by Kudarmar Ridge, a secondary peak of the Mount that would, anywhere else in the world, have been regarded as a mountain of majesty and grandeur in its own right. Lying as it did in the sheltered pocket between those two lofty peaks, Muldemar vale was favored all the year round by soft breezes and gentle mists, and its soil ran rich and deep.

Prestimion's ancestors had settled here even before the Castle itself existed. They were farmers, then, who had come up from the lowlands with cuttings of the grapevines they grew down there. Over the centuries their wines had established a reputation for themselves as the foremost ones of Majipoor, and grateful Coronals, over the centuries, had ennobled the vintners of Muldemar, bringing them upward eventually to be dukes and then princes. Prestimion was the first of his line who had gone on to hold the Coronal's throne, and after it the Pontifical seat.

The family lands ran for many miles through the choicest zone of the vale, a broad green realm stretching from the Zemulikkaz River to the Kudarmar Ridge. Deep within the estate lay the white walls and soaring black towers of Muldemar House itself, a domain of two hundred rooms laid out in three sprawling wings.

Abrigant had been thoughtful enough to provide Prestimion with the rooms that once had been his, a second-level apartment that looked out through gleaming windows of faceted quartz to the great vista of Sambattinola Hill. Little had changed here since he last had occupied it, more than twenty years before: the walls still bore the same subtle murals in quiet shades of amethyst and azure and topaz pink, and the window seat in which the young Prestimion had spent so many pleasant hours was furnished with some of the same books that he had read there long ago.

Household servants whom Prestimion did not recognize, no doubt the sons and daughters of the ones he had known, were on hand to help the Pontifex and his family settle in. This caused a minor clash with Prestimion's own staff, for custom required that the Pontifex bring his own servants with him wherever he traveled, and they guarded that prerogative jealously. "You may not enter," said sturdy strapping Falco, who had the title of First Imperial Steward now, and took his promotion very seriously. "These rooms belong to the Pontifex, and you may not look upon him." It saddened Prestimion to see these good people of Muldemar staring timidly at him over Falco's shoulder in awe and wonder, as though he were not a man of Muldemar himself but had descended into their midst from some other planet; and he instructed Falco that it was his intention, in this house, to waive the usual Pontifical prerogatives and allow ordinary common citizens to have access to his presence. Falco did not like that at all.

Varaile and Prestimion would share the master bedroom; Varaile put Tuanelys, who awakened often now crying in the night, in the room just adjacent. Taradath, Akbalik, and Simbilon were left to shift for themselves beyond. It was a suite of many rooms.

"I wish I could have Fiorinda nearby me as well," Varaile said.

Prestimion smiled. "I know you're accustomed to her presence close at hand. But this apartment was not designed to provide space for a lady-in-waiting when I lived in it. Would that it had been, but that was not how things were done."

"It's not for myself that I want Fiorinda near," said Varaile, with a bit of snap in her voice. "She's the one in need of comfort, and I wish that I could give it."

"They'll have put her in the rooms she and Teotas usually had when they were here. No doubt she'll have a maid of her own to look after her there."

But Varaile could not put Fiorinda from her mind. "How she suffers, Prestimion. And I as well. Teotas would never have undertaken that walk in the night if she had been beside him. But Fiorinda and Teotas were apart all those weeks before he—died, and the fault was mine. I should never have taken her with me from the Castle."

"The separation was meant to be only temporary. And who could guess that Teotas had it in him to destroy himself?"

Varaile threw a strange look his way. "Is *that* what he did?"

"Why would a man climb out onto a dangerous and almost inaccessible tower in the middle of the night, if not to destroy himself?"

"The Teotas I knew was not a suicidal man, Prestimion."

"I agree. But what was he doing out there, then? Sleepwalking? No one sleepwalks like that. Drunk? Teotas was never known as a heavy drinker. Under a spell, perhaps?"

"Perhaps," Varaile said.

His eyes widened. "You sound almost serious."

"Why not? Is it such an impossible idea?"

"Let's assume that it isn't, then. I'll grant you that there are some magics that actually work. But who would lay a spell of self-destruction on the Pontifex's brother, Varaile?"

"Who, indeed?" she replied sharply. "Isn't that what you need to find out?"

Prestimion nodded absently. The mystery had to be unraveled, yes. But how? How? Who could look into dead Teotas's mind and produce the needed answers? They were roaming into very mysterious territory now. "I need to discuss all this with Dekkeret," he said. "Dekkeret was the last person to see Teotas alive, only a few hours before his death. Abrigant says he knows something about what happened."

"You should speak to him, then. By all means, Prestimion."

From Abrigant, Prestimion learned that Dekkeret was still at the Castle, but would be traveling down to Muldemar House later that day, now that he knew Prestimion had arrived. And in mid-afternoon came hubbub and hullaballoo from without, as a procession of royal floaters bearing the starburst emblem drew up outside. Prestimion looked out to see the towering figure of the Coronal, in full formal robes, entering the building. He noted with more than a little interest that the Lady Fulkari walked at his side.

Dekkeret seemed grim and determined, and very much in charge of things. It was evident that he had begun already to take on the intangible qualities of kingliness, here in the early months of his reign. Prestimion was pleased by that. He had never had any doubt of the wisdom of his choice of Dekkeret to succeed him, but that look of grandeur that Dekkeret wore now was a welcome confirmation all the same.

There was no chance before dinner for a conference with him, nor during the meal either. Coronals had not been uncommon visitors at Muldemar House over the centuries, and the princes of Muldemar maintained guest quarters for them in the east wing, as far from Prestimion's present suite as was possible to be. Their first opportunity for a meeting was at the dinner table, but dinner was a somber, formal event at which private conversations were impossible. Prestimion and Dekkeret embraced, as it behooved the Pontifex and Coronal to do whenever they were present at the same event, and then they took their seats at opposite ends of the long table. Fulkari sat beside Dekkeret, Varaile adjacent to Prestimion, with Fiorinda next to her.

The rest of the gathering that was assembled in the great banquet hall was few in number. Abrigant and his wife Cirophan were accompanied by their two adolescent boys. Prestimion's two older sons were there also. The only other guests were Septach Melayn and Gialaurys, who had come with the Pontifex to Muldemar. Abrigant spoke briefly of the solemn occasion that had brought them together this night, and they lifted their glasses in Teotas's memory. Then dinner was served, a fine one; but it was an oddly assorted group, the prevailing mood was a subdued one, and there was little conversation.

Afterward Dekkeret came to Prestimion and said, "You and I should talk after dinner, your majesty."

"We should, yes. Shall I bring Septach Melayn?"

"I think it should just be the two of us," said Dekkeret. "You can share what I have to say with the High Spokesman later, if you wish. But Abrigant feels that you and I ought to discuss these things just between ourselves at first."

"Abrigant knows what you're going to tell me?" Prestimion asked.

"Some. Not all."

Prestimion chose for the site of their meeting the tasting-room of Muldemar House, a place that had always exerted a strange charm over him, though there were those who said that they found the place gloomy. It lay at the mouth of a deep cool cavern of green basalt on the lowest level of the building, extending far underground into the bedrock of the Mount itself. Along both sides the entire passage was lined from floor to ceiling with a royal ransom in Muldemar wines, vintages stretching over hundreds of years, back through the mists of time. An ancient iron door sealed the room off from the rest of the building. There was no part of Muldemar House where he and Dekkeret could find greater seclusion.

He had requested that Abrigant's cellarmaster leave a bottle of brandy for them on the tasting-room table. It was amusing to see that the bottle that the man had chosen, a big-bellied hand-blown globelet, was an outrageously precious one with what was surely more than a century of dust on it and a faded label dating it to the reign of Lord Gobryas, predecessor of Prankipin as Coronal. Prestimion poured two generous bowlfuls and they sipped for a time in silence, savoring the brandy reflectively.

At length Dekkeret said, "I feel great sadness at your loss, Prestimion. I loved Teotas greatly. How sorry I am that this wondrous liquor, if I'm ever fortunate enough to taste it again, will always summon the memory of his death for me."

Prestimion nodded gravely. "I never thought that I'd outlive him. Even though he was aging quickly, and looked so much older than he was, there were many years between us. And then to have something like this happen—this—"

"Yes," said Dekkeret. "But perhaps he was never meant to live a long life. As you say, he was aging quickly. There was always a fire burning within him. As though he had a furnace inside his breast, and was consuming himself for fuel. That temper of his—his impatience—"

"I have some of those qualities myself, you know," Prestimion said. "But only a tincture. He had the full dose." He applied himself thoughtfully to his brandy for a time. Its texture was marvelously smooth, but its long-pent-up flavor erupted within one's mouth like an exploding galaxy. Then he said, when he judged the silence to have gone on long enough, "He killed himself, didn't he, Dekkeret? What else could it have been, but suicide? But why? Why? He was under great stress, yes, but what kind of stress is there that could possibly drive a man like Teotas to take his own life?"

Quietly Dekkeret said, "I think he was murdered, Prestimion."

"*Murdered?*"

Prestimion could not have been more astounded if Dekkeret had slapped him in the face.

"Or, let us say, he was forced by something outside himself into a frame of mind in which dying seemed more attractive to him than living; and then he was maneuvered into a place where death was a very easy thing to find."

Prestimion hunched forward, staring intently. Dekkeret's words went through him like a whirlwind. This was not anything that he wanted to believe. But the world does not let one believe only the things one chooses to believe.

"Go on," he said. "Let me hear it all."

"He came to me in my office," said Dekkeret, "on the last afternoon of his life. As you know, I had invited him to serve as my High Counsellor—that was how much regard I had for him, Prestimion—but he would neither say me yea or nay about taking the post, and finally I sent for him to press him on it."

"Why was he so hesitant? Was it on Fiorinda's account?"

"That was the reason he gave, yes. That the Lady Varaile had requested the Lady Fiorinda to be her companion at the Labyrinth, and Teotas would not let his own ambitions stand in the way of that. But also there were the dreams he was having. Every night, apparently, a siege of nightmares beyond all describing."

"Yes. Varaile heard about that from Fiorinda. —There are a lot of bad dreams going around these days, you know. My own daughter Tuanelys has been troubled by them. And Varaile as well, lately."

"Even she?" Dekkeret said. He seemed to register the news with the deepest interest. "Nothing so savage as the ones that afflicted Teotas, I do sincerely hope. The man was in ruinous condition when I met with him. Pale, bloodshot, trembling. He told me straight out that he dreaded going to sleep each night, for fear of the dreams. Whatever resolution of the Fiorinda problem we might have tried to work out became impossible to discuss, because those dreams of his had wrecked him so. He said that he had become convinced, through his dreams, that he was unworthy of being High Counsellor. He begged me to release him from the appointment. Which I suppose I simply should have done, considering the shape he was in. But I wanted him, Prestimion, I wanted him badly. I asked him finally to put the whole matter aside for one more week, and it seemed to me as he was leaving that he had agreed to that."

"But instead, feeling terrible shame and guilt over having told you he wanted to decline the appointment, and not wanting to go through the whole thing again with you the following week, he headed straight from your office to some remote spire of the Castle, clambered out to the edge, and jumped off."

"No."

"That was what I was told that he did."

"He jumped, yes. But not right after his meeting with me. It was in the afternoon that I saw him. It was in the middle of the night when he fell to his death."

"Yes. I did know that, actually. There was talk that he'd been sleep-walking. Which would make it an accident, rather than suicide."

"It was neither, Prestimion."

"You really believe that he was murdered?"

"There is a device—a little metal helmet: do you remember it?—that allows one to reach across great distances and interfere with the workings of someone else's mind. With my own eyes I beheld you using such a helmet fifteen years ago."

"Of course. The one that your friend Dinitak stole from his father and brought to us to use against Dantirya Sambail."

"Which was a copy of an earlier one, you recall, that Dinitak's father Venghenar had stolen from the Vroon who invented it, and which he employed in the Procurator's service."

"All these deadly helmets have been kept under seal in the Treasury ever since those days. Is it your notion that someone's made off with one of them and was using it against Teotas?"

"The Barjazid helmets are still at the Castle, where they belong, and all of them remain under our control," Dekkeret replied. "But there are other Barjazids beside Dinitak in this world, Prestimion. And other helmets."

"You know this to be a fact?"

"Dinitak is my source. His father's younger brother, Khaymak Barjazid by name, still lives, and still understands the making of the helmets. It was this Khaymak who used to construct the things for Venghenar when they all lived in Suvrael long ago. He continues to possess the plans and sketches he used. While you were still Coronal, he came to the Castle to offer some new and improved model to you, but Dinitak found out about it first and turned him away, not wanting anyone of his sort sniffing around at court. So Khaymak took himself off to Zimroel and sold the helmet plans to a certain Mandralisca, whose name you will, I think, remember."

Dekkeret's words fell upon Prestimion with devastating impact. "The poison-taster? He's still alive?"

"Evidently so. And in the service of five extraordinarily loathsome brothers who happen to be the the nephews of our old friend Dantirya Sambail. And they, as I have only just begun to discover, have launched some sort of local insurrection against our rule in a desert district of central Zimroel."

"This is beginning to move too quickly for me," Prestimion said. He poured fresh bowls of brandy for them both, and took a long, slow sip. "—Let us go back a little. This Khaymak Barjazid has put a mind-controlling helmet in the hands of Mandralisca the poison-taster?"

"Yes."

"And—surely this is where you have been heading with all of this—Mandralisca has used the helmet to reach into Teotas's mind and drive him to the edge of insanity. *Over* the edge, indeed, to the point where he would take his own life."

"Yes, Prestimion. Precisely so."

"What's your proof of this?"

"I authorized Dinitak to withdraw one of the old helmets from the Treasury and conduct a little investigation with it. He reports that mental broadcasts are emanating from somewhere in the vicinity of Nimoya. He believes the operator is none other than Mandralisca, who appears to have been striking randomly all over the world. And not always randomly, since one of his broadcasts was aimed at Teotas, with the results that we all have seen."

"You believe that what Dinitak says is true?"

"I do."

"And how long have you known all this?"

"About three days."

Once again Prestimion felt the whirlwinds of chaos roaring through his mind. "You heard me say that my little daughter Tuanelys has been having bad dreams. Varaile, occasionally, too. My brother, my daughter, my wife: can it be that this Mandralisca has found a way of making the Pontifex's own family his target?"

"That could be so."

"And the Pontifex next? Or the Coronal?"

"No one is safe, Prestimion. No one."

My brother. My daughter. My wife.

Prestimion closed his eyes and pressed the tips of his fingers to the lids. A tumultuous welter of emotions surged through him: fury, foremost, but sadness, also, and a bleak sense of exhaustion of the spirit, and

even fear. Had the Divine, he wondered, placed some curse on his entire reign? First the Korsibar usurpation, and then the plague of madness that had been the consequence of his high-handed act in wiping
out the entire world's memories of the civil war, and then the attempt
by Dantirya Sambail to unseat him. Now these new vermin, these five
brothers, spurred to yet another rebellion by this devilish Mandralisca,
who seemed to have a dozen lives—and, worst of all, an invisible threat
reaching even into his family itself—

When he looked at Dekkeret again he saw that the younger man was
regarding him worriedly, even tenderly. In haste Prestimion strove to restore his mantle of regal poise.

"I am reminded," he said, slowly, calmly, "of Maundigand-Klimd's
prophecy that a Barjazid would somehow make himself a Power of the
Realm. I told you of that, did I not? Yes. You thought he might have been
speaking of Dinitak, and scoffed at that, and I warned you not to take the
prophecy too literally. Well, we will have no Barjazids as literal Powers of
the Realm, I think, but here is one who is certainly wielding power, in the
abstract sense. We will locate him before he does further harm, and take his
helmets from him, and see to it that he is able to build no more of them.
And we'll deal at last with that serpent Mandralisca, too, and pull his fangs."

"That we will."

"You will report to me daily, Dekkeret, concerning any further dis-
coveries Dinitak may make."

"Absolutely." Dekkeret finished the last of his brandy. "The uprising,
or whatever it is, in Zimroel needs handling also. I may go there in person to deal with it."

Prestimion lifted an eyebrow. "Under the pretext of a grand processional, you think? So early in your reign? And so far?"

"I should do whatever seems appropriate, Prestimion. I've only just
begun to consider what that will be. Let's discuss this further, shall we,
after the funeral. —Do you plan to remain here at Muldemar for any
length of time?"

"A few days, only. At most a week."

"And then back to the Labyrinth, is it?"

"No. To the Isle of Sleep," Prestimion replied. "My mother remains
in residence there. For the second time she has lost a son. It'll do her
good to have a visit from me in such a dark hour." Rising, he said, "We
should rejoin the company above, I think. Send for your Dinitak, and
let's meet with him here somewhere in the next few days."

"I will, Prestimion."

As they ascended the stairs Prestimion said, "I note that you come here with the Lady Fulkari. I found that somewhat surprising, after the conversation that you and I had had about her."

"We are betrothed," said Dekkeret, with a tiny smile.

"Even more of a surprise. It was my impression that Fulkari had rejected the idea of becoming the consort of the Coronal, and you were searching for some way to break with her. Am I wrong about that?"

"Not at all. But we held further discussions. We explained ourselves more clearly to each other. —Of course, there'll be no announcement of any plans for a royal marriage until the pain of this business with Teotas has had a chance to fade."

"Naturally not. But I hope you'll give me proper notice when the time comes. I would have liked Confalume to officiate at my wedding, if events had permitted." Prestimion paused and caught Dekkeret for a moment by the hand. "It would give me great pleasure to officiate at yours."

"Let it be the Divine's will that you do," said Dekkeret. "It would be a good thing, anyway, that the next time the Pontifex travels to Castle Mount from the Labyrinth it's for a happier occasion than the present one."

2

"**M**y lord, may I come in?" Abrigant said to Dekkeret, who had gone to the door to answer his knock.

Teotas's funeral was three days in the past, now. Dinitak had come down from the Castle at Prestimion's request. He and Prestimion and Dekkeret had been meeting for more than an hour. Things had not gone entirely smoothly. Something was amiss, though Dekkeret had no idea what it was. Prestimion seemed to be in a dark, cold, brooding mood, saying little, sometimes putting a curious bit of overemphasis on some otherwise innocuous statement. It was as if some change had come over him the other day, once Dekkeret had raised the likelihood that it was the Barjazid helmet that was to blame for what had befallen Teotas.

Abrigant's knock offered a welcome break in the tension. Dekkeret went quickly to the door of Prestimion's suite to see who it was, leaving Prestimion and Dinitak huddled over the helmet that Dinitak had brought down to Muldemar House with him. Prestimion was examining the helmet closely, poking at it with a fingertip and muttering under his breath, staring at it with open hatred as though it were some malevolent living thing that gave off poisonous exhalations. The Pontifex was radiating such an intensity of feeling that Dekkeret was glad to have an excuse to get away from him for a moment.

"It's your brother you're looking for, I suppose," said Dekkeret. He gestured rearward with his thumb. "Prestimion's back there."

Abrigant seemed surprised and perhaps dismayed to discover

Dekkeret answering at Prestimion's door. "Am I interrupting official business, my lord?"

"There's a fairly important meeting going on, yes. But I think we can take a break for a little while." Dekkeret heard footsteps behind him. Prestimion, frowning, emerged from within. "The Pontifex evidently feels the same way."

Abrigant looked toward his brother and said, with some chagrin, "I had no idea, Prestimion, that you and the Coronal were having a conference, or I certainly would never have presumed—"

"A little intermission in the proceedings was in order, anyway," Prestimion said. His tone was affable enough. But the tight set of his mouth and jaws showed exactly how displeased he was by the interruption. "Is there some urgent news that I need to know about, Abrigant?"

"News? No news, no. Only a little bit of family business. A matter of a minute or two." Abrigant seemed off-balance. He shot a swift glance at Dekkeret, and then one at Dinitak, who now had come out from within also. "This really can wait, you know. It was hardly my intention to—"

Prestimion cut him off. "No matter. If we can take care of it as quickly as you say—"

"Shall Dinitak and I go back inside, and leave this sitting-room to the two of you?" asked Dekkeret.

"No, stay," said Abrigant. "This isn't really anything that requires privacy, I suppose. With your permission, my lords: I will need only a moment." To Prestimion he said, "Brother, I've just been speaking with Varaile. She tells me that you and she will be leaving here in a day or two: not for the Labyrinth, though, but for the Isle of Sleep. Is this so?"

"It is."

"It was my thought to go to the Isle myself, actually, as soon as I've dealt with all current business here. Our mother should not be alone at a time like this."

Prestimion appeared irritated and confused. "Are you saying that you'd like to accompany me there, Abrigant?"

Abrigant's face now mirrored Prestimion's puzzlement. "That isn't exactly what I had in mind. One of us must surely go to her; and I simply assumed that the responsibility for undertaking the trip would fall to me. The Pontifex, I felt, is likely to have important official duties at the Labyrinth that would prevent him from making such a long journey." And, with increasing discomfort: "It's certainly not customary for Pontifexes to visit the Isle, as I understand it. Or Coronals either, for that matter."

"A great many things that aren't customary have been happening in recent years," Prestimion returned smoothly. "And I can do my Pontifexing wherever I happen to be." His face darkened. "I am the eldest of her sons, Abrigant. I think this task is one for me to handle."

"On the contrary, Prestimion—"

Dekkeret was beginning to find it more than a little embarrassing to be listening to this conversation between the brothers. He had been an unwilling witness to it in the first place; but now that it had turned into a tense dispute, it was something that he very much did not want to be overhearing. Something was going on here that only a member of the family could fully understand, and that no outsider should see.

If Abrigant, who had relinquished all public duties upon Dekkeret's ascent to the throne and had more leisure for family matters these days than his royal brother, believed that he should be the one to comfort their mother in this difficult hour—well, Dekkeret conceded, he did have good reason for thinking that. But Prestimion was the older brother. Should he not be the one who decided which one of them was to go to the Isle?

And Prestimion was Pontifex as well. No one, Dekkeret thought, not even the Pontifex's brother, should say something like "On the contrary" to a Pontifex.

In the end that was the conclusive point. Prestimion listened for a few moments more, confronting Abrigant with folded arms and containing himself with an only too apparent show of elaborate patience as Abrigant argued his case; and then he said simply, "I understand your feelings, brother. But I have other reasons, reasons of state, for needing to be abroad at this present moment. The Isle will be merely the first stop on my journey." He was staring unwaveringly at Abrigant now. "What I must deal with," Prestimion said, "is the matter that was under discussion here when you knocked at the door just now. Since it would be convenient as well as desirable for me to go to the Isle, there's no need for you to make the trip as well."

Abrigant greeted that with an instant or two of silence and a baffled stare. It seemed to be gradually sinking in upon him that Prestimion's words amounted to a command.

Dekkeret had no doubt that the Pontifex's brother was still displeased. But there could be no pursuing the issue beyond this point. Abrigant forced a smile that showed only a wintry warmth. "Well, then, Prestimion, in that case I have to yield to you, don't I? Very well, I yield. Carry my love to our mother, if you will, and tell her that my thoughts have been with her from the first moment of this tragedy."

"That I will do. And your task now will be to comfort the Lady Fiorinda. I leave her in your care."

Abrigant did not seem to be prepared for that either. He was already upset by his capitulation to Prestimion on the journey to the Isle, and further bewilderment appeared on his face at this latest statement of Prestimion's. "What? Fiorinda's going to stay here, then? She won't be accompanying Varaile on these travels of yours?"

"That would not be a good idea, I think. Varaile will send for her when we have returned to the Labyrinth. Until that time, I prefer to let her remain at Muldemar." Then—in a gesture that seemed to Dekkeret to be rather more of a display of imperial strength than of fraternal affection—Prestimion held out his arms stiffly toward Abrigant and said, "Come, brother, give me an embrace, and then I must get on with this meeting."

When Abrigant had gone from the room and they had gone back within, Dekkeret turned to Prestimion and said, by way of breaking the vacuum of uneasy silence that lingered in Abrigant's wake, "What exactly are these travels of which you were speaking a moment ago, majesty? If I may know."

"I've made no final decision yet." The sharpness remained in Prestimion's voice. "But there's no question but that you and I will be in motion in the months ahead." He gathered up the helmet, which he had left lying on the table, and poured the soft metal meshes from his right hand to the left one like a hoard of golden coins. "Foh! I never thought I'd be handling this filthy thing again. It was almost the killing of me, once. You remember that, do you?"

"We can never forget it, your majesty," Dinitak said. "We saw you brought to your knees from the effort of using it, that time when you were sending your spirit all through the world to heal people of the madness."

Prestimion smiled a pale smile. "So I was. And you said to Dekkeret,

'Get it off his head,' as I recall it, and Dekkeret answered that it was forbidden to handle a Coronal in such fashion, and you told him to remove it anyway, or the world would need a new Coronal in a very short
while. And so Dekkeret removed it from my head. —I wonder, Dinitak,
would you have taken it from me yourself if Dekkeret hadn't finally
been willing to do it?"

Quickly Dekkeret said, not bothering to conceal the annoyance in
his voice, "The question's unfair, Prestimion. Why ask him such a
thing? I *did* take the helmet off you when I saw what it was doing to
you."

But Dinitak turned to Dekkeret and said coolly, "I have no objection
to replying to the Pontifex's question." And, to Prestimion: "I would have
removed it, yes, your majesty. One holds the person of a Coronal sacred,
up to a point. But one doesn't stand idly by while the Coronal's life is in
danger. I understood the power of that helmet better than either of you.
You were pouring all your strength into it, majesty, and you had used it
long enough. It was placing you in great peril." Dinitak's dark face had
grown very flushed. "I would not have hesitated to pull it from your
brow if Dekkeret found himself unable to do so. And if Dekkeret had
tried to prevent me, I would have pushed him aside."

"Well spoken," Prestimion said, with a little gesture of applause. "I
like the way you said that: '*I would have pushed him aside.*' You've never
gone in very much for diplomacy or tact, have you, Dinitak? But you're
certainly an honest man."

"The only one his family has managed to produce in ten thousand
years," said Dekkeret, and laughed. Dinitak, after a moment, broke into
laughter also, with unfeigned heartiness.

Only Prestimion maintained a sober mien. The strange tension that
had been settling about him since the first moments of this afternoon's
meeting had heightened after Abrigant's departure. Now there was a
powerful undercurrent of edginess about him, as though he were contending with some explosive inner force that he could barely hold in
check.

But his voice was calm enough as he threw the helmet back down
on the table and said, "Well, may the Divine preserve me from ever having to don that thing again! I remember its powers only too vividly. A
man my age has no business going near it. When we need it again, it'll
be you, Dinitak, who'll do the work, eh? Not me." He looked then
toward his Coronal. —"And not you either, Dekkeret!"

"The thought had not occurred to me, I assure you," Dekkeret replied. He wanted very much to return to the theme that Prestimion had so casually brushed aside. —"You said a minute ago, Prestimion, that the two of us would be in motion. Where will you be going, do you think?"

"What I intend to do is something Pontifexes rarely have done. Which is to travel hither and yon about the land, according to no fixed plan. This for the sake of guarding my family against the reach of our friend Mandralisca's malice."

Dekkeret nodded. "That seems wise."

"I'll go to the Isle first, of course, probably by way of the northern route out of Alaisor: they tell me that the prevailing winds will be better this time of year, going that way. Once I've seen to my mother I'll return to the mainland by way of the southern path, via Stoien or Treymone. Stoien, I think: that would be best. If I choose to go back then to the Labyrinth, that'll provide the most direct route. But where I go once I reach Alhanroel will depend on the doings of Mandralisca and his five brutish masters, how much trouble they intend to create, how much jeopardy I find myself in."

"You will find yourself in none, I pray," said Dekkeret fervently. He studied Prestimion with care. The Pontifex still had that strange look about him. Something was ticking within Prestimion, ticking, ticking. —"And what journeys do you have in mind for me, may I ask?"

"You said yourself, just before the funeral, that you were thinking of going to Zimroel and investigating the situation there yourself," said Prestimion. "Only time will tell whether a step like that will be necessary. I hope that it won't: a new Coronal has too much to do at the Castle to be going jaunting off to the other continent. But under the present circumstances you surely should put yourself into a position that will allow you to get yourself out there as swiftly as possible, if need be."

"The western coast, you mean."

"Exactly. While I'm sailing to the Isle, you should be following in my tracks, zigzagging across the western lands to Alaisor also."

"You want me to take the land route, then?"

"Yes. Go by land. Show yourself to the people. It always stirs up good feelings when the Coronal comes to town. Your overt pretext will be that you're making a kind of processional—not the full thing with all the banqueting and circuses, but only a preliminary sort, the new Coronal making a quick tour of the most important cities of central and western Alhanroel.

Take Dinitak with you, I think. You'll want to monitor events on the other continent very closely, and that helmet of his will allow you to do that. Once you've reached Alaisor, start down the coast, finishing up at Stoien, say, where you'll wait for me to return from visiting my mother. When I'm done at the Isle, I'll meet you at Stoien or thereabouts, and we'll confer and evaluate the situation as we see it then. It may be necessary for you to go to Zimroel and bring matters under control there. Or perhaps not. How does this sound to you?"

"In perfect conformity with my own ideas."

"Good. Good." Prestimion seized Dekkeret's hand and wrung it with startling force.

Then, at last, his icy self-control broke. He turned quickly away and went striding briskly around the room in quick furious steps, fists clenched, shoulders rigid. Dekkeret suddenly understood the aura of tension that had surrounded Prestimion this day: the man had been overflowing all this while with barely contained rage. That was only too plain now. That his own family should be under attack—his wife and his daughter, and of course Teotas—that was something he could not and would not abide. The Pontifex's face looked gray with fatigue, but there was a bright spark of anger in his eyes.

A hot stream of words that had been withheld too long came boiling out of him now.

"By the Divine, Dekkeret, can you imagine anything more intolerable! Yet another rebellion? Are we never to be spared such things? But this time we'll put a finish to the rebels and their rebellion both. We'll hunt down this Mandralisca and make an end to him once and for all, and these five brothers as well, and all who swear allegiance to them."

Prestimion was moving agitatedly about the room all the while, barely pausing to look in Dekkeret's direction. "I tell you, Dekkeret, whatever was left of my patience is worn away. I've spent the twenty years of my reign, Coronal and Pontifex both, struggling with enemies such as no ruler of Majipoor since Stiamot's time has had to cope with. Drive my brother to madness, will they? Enter the dreams of my little girl, even? No. *No!* I've had enough and more than enough. We'll cut them down. We'll abolish them root and branch. Root and branch, Dekkeret!"

Dekkeret had never seen Prestimion in such rage. But then the Pontifex seemed to regain some measure of poise. He halted his frenzied pacing and took up a stance in the middle of the room, letting his arms dangle, breathing slowly in and out. Then he waved Dekkeret and Dinitak unceremoniously to the door. His voice was calmer, now, but it was chilly, even harsh. "Go, now, the two of you. Go! I need to speak with Varaile, to let her know what's ahead for us."

Dekkeret was more than happy to be excused from the Pontifex's presence. This was a new Prestimion, and a frightening one. He was aware that Prestimion had ever been an impulsive and passionate man, his intrinsic shrewdness and caution constantly at war with surging temper and impatience. But there had always been a leavening quality of good humor and playful wit about him that gave him the ability to find sources of fresh strength even in times of the most arduous crisis.

Moderation in the face of adversity had been Prestimion's defining characteristic throughout his long and challenging reign. Dekkeret had already noticed that in his middle years he seemed to have grown crusty and conservative, as men will often do, and had lost a good deal of that resilience. Prestimion appeared to be taking this Mandralisca business as a personal affront, rather than as the attack on the sanctity of the commonwealth that it actually was.

Perhaps it is for this reason, Dekkeret thought, that we have a system of double monarchy here. As the Coronal grows older and more rigid, he moves on to the higher throne and is replaced at the Castle by a younger man, and thereby the wisdom and experience of age is yoked to the flexibility and vigor of buoyant youth.

Fulkari greeted Dekkeret with a warm embrace when he returned to their quarters after parting from Dinitak. She had just been bathing, it seemed, and wore only a thick furry robe and a bright golden strand at her throat. A sweet aroma of bathing-spices rose from her breasts and shoulders. He felt some of the stress of his meeting with Prestimion beginning to ebb from him.

But clearly she was able to tell, just at a single glance, that things were not right. "You look very strange," she said. "Did things go badly between you and Prestimion?"

"Our meeting covered a lot of difficult ground." Dekkeret flung himself down carelessly on a velvet-covered divan. It creaked in protest as his big form landed on it. "Prestimion himself is becoming rather difficult."

"In what way?" said Fulkari, seating herself at the divan's foot.

"In a dozen ways. The long weariness of holding high office has had its effect on him. He laughs much less than he did when he was younger. Things that once might have seemed funny to him no longer amuse him. He gets angry very easily. He and Abrigant had a peculiar little argument that never should have taken place in front of me. Or at all, for that matter." Dekkeret shook his head. "I don't mean to speak harshly of him. He's still an extraordinary man. And we mustn't forget that his youngest brother has just met a horrifying death."

"Small wonder that he's behaving like this, then."

"But it's painful to see. I feel for him, Fulkari."

She grinned mischievously. Taking one of his feet in her hands, she began to knead and massage it. "And will you also grow cranky and ill-tempered when you're Pontifex, Dekkeret?"

He winked at her. "Of course. I'd think something was wrong with me if I didn't."

For an instant she appeared, despite the wink, to have taken him seriously. But then she laughed and said, "Good. I find cranky, ill-tempered men very attractive. Almost irresistible, as a matter of fact. Just the thought of it excites me."

She slithered up the divan toward him until she was nestling in the crook of his arm. Dekkeret pressed his face against her copper-bright hair, inhaled its fragrance, kissed her lightly on the nape of her neck. Slipping his one hand into the front of her robe, he lightly traced the line of her collarbone with his fingers, then let the hand slide lower to cup one of her breasts. They remained like that for a time, neither of them in a hurry to move onward to the next stage.

He said, after a while, "We'll be returning tomorrow to the Castle."

"Will we, now?" said Fulkari dreamily. "That's nice. Although it's very nice here too. I wouldn't mind staying another week or two." She wriggled against him, fitting her body more snugly into place against his.

"There's plenty of work waiting for me at home," Dekkeret persisted, wondering why he was so perversely bound on shattering the developing mood. "And once I've caught up with that there'll be a little traveling for us to do."

"A trip? Ooh, that's nice too." She sounded almost on the edge of sleep. She was coiled against him in a state of utter relaxation, warm and soft, like a drowsy kitten. "Where will we be going, Dekkeret? Stee? High Morpin."

"Farther. Much farther. —Alaisor, in fact."

That woke her up quickly. She drew back her head and stared at him in amazement. "Alaisor?" she said, blinking at him. "But that's thousands of miles away! I've never been that far from the Mount in my life! Why Alaisor, Dekkeret?"

"Because," he said, wishing most profoundly that he had saved all this for later.

"Just *because*? Clear to the other side of Alhanroel, just *because*?"

"It's at the Pontifex's request, actually. Official business."

"The matter that you and he were just discussing, you mean?"

"More or less."

"And what matter exactly was that?" Fulkari had extricated herself from his embrace, now, and had swung around to face him, sitting cross-legged at the foot of the divan.

Dekkeret realized that caution was in order here. He was hardly in a position to share much of the real story with her—the rebellion that was supposedly starting up in Zimroel, the reappearance of Mandralisca, the possibility that the Barjazid helmet had been used to drive Teotas to his death. Those were not affairs that he was able to speak of with her. Fulkari was still a private citizen. A Coronal might share such things with his wife, but Fulkari was not his wife.

Picking his words judiciously, Dekkeret said, "A few odd things have been going on lately across the sea. What sort of things isn't particularly important right now. But Prestimion wants me to head west and station myself somewhere along the coast, so that if it turns out to be necessary for me to go to Zimroel in the near future, I'll already be well on the way there."

"Zimroel!" She said it as though he were talking about a voyage to the Great Moon.

"To Zimroel, yes. Perhaps. None of this may ever come to pass, you realize. But the Pontifex feels that we need to look into it even so. Therefore he's asked Dinitak and me to head out to Alaisor and—"

"Dinitak also?" Fulkari said, her eyebrows shooting upward.

"Dinitak will be traveling with us, yes. Doing special government research, using certain detecting equipment that—" No, he could hardly speak of that either. "Using certain special equipment," he finished lamely. "He'll be reporting to me on a daily basis. You do like Dinitak, don't you? You won't have any problem about his accompanying us."

"Of course not. —And Keltryn?" she asked. "What about her?"

"I don't understand," Dekkeret said. "What in particular do you mean?"

"Is she going to be coming with us too?"

He felt lost. "I'm not following you, Fulkari. Are you saying that whenever we take a trip anywhere, you'll want Keltryn to come along with us?"

"Hardly. But we'll be gone several months at the very least, won't we, Dekkeret?"

"At the very least, yes."

"Don't you think they'll miss each other, having to be apart as long as that?"

This was utterly incomprehensible. "Dinitak and Keltryn, you mean? Miss each other? I don't at all understand what you're talking about. Do they even know each other, except in passing?"

"You mean you don't know?" Fulkari said, and laughed. "He hasn't said anything about it to you? And you honestly haven't noticed? Dinitak and Keltryn? Really, Dekkeret! Really!"

3
------

*K*eltryn was in the little bedroom of her apartment at the Setiphon Arcade, laying out the cards for what she thought must be her three thousandth game of solitaire since the Pontifex had summoned Dinitak to Muldemar House for Teotas's funeral.

Four of Comets. Six of Starbursts. Ten of Moons.

Why was it necessary for Dinitak to be at Teotas's funeral? Dinitak had no official place in the government nor was he a member of the Castle Mount aristocracy. His only role at the Castle was as Dekkeret's friend and occasional traveling companion. And, so far as Keltryn was aware, Teotas and Dinitak had been only nodding acquaintances, nothing more, until very recently. There wasn't any reason for him to be at the funeral. No one had said anything at all about Dinitak's going down to Muldemar House when the funeral arrangements were first being set up.

And then, right on the eve of the funeral itself, a courier in Pontifical uniform suddenly arriving to say that Prestimion requested the presence of Dinitak Barjazid immediately at Muldemar? Why? On such short notice, Keltryn thought, it was unlikely that Dinitak would have been able to get down there in time for the ceremony. So it must have had to do with something else. And why had the message summoning Dinitak come from the *Pontifex*, rather than from his own good friend Lord Dekkeret? Dekkeret was down there too, after all. The whole thing was very mysterious. And she wished that Dinitak would hurry back, now that the funeral was done with, she assumed, and Teotas safely deposited in his tomb.

Petulantly she dealt out the cards.

Pontifex of Nebulas. Damn! She had the Coronal of Nebulas on the table already. Couldn't the Pontifex have turned up five minutes ago? *Nine of Moons. Knave of Nebulas.* She slipped the Knave below the Coronal of Nebulas. *Three of Comets.* Keltryn scowled. Even when the cards turned up in the right order she took no pleasure from it. She was sick of solitaire. She wanted Dinitak. *Five of Moons. Queen of Starbursts. Seven of—*

A knock!

"Keltryn? Keltryn, are you in there!"

She swept the cards to the floor. "Dinitak! You're back at last!" She ran toward the door, remembered at the last moment that she was wearing nothing but her loinclout, and hastily snatched up a robe. Dinitak was so terribly fastidious about such things, so very *moral.* Despite everything that had passed between them since they had become lovers, he would be shocked if she were to come to the door virtually naked. The robe had to be on her before it came off: that was how he was. Besides, Dekkeret might be with him. Or the Pontifex Prestimion, for all she knew.

She opened the door. There he was: alone. She caught his wrist and tugged him inside, and then she was in his arms, at last, at last, at last. She covered him with kisses. It felt to her as though he had been gone at least six months.

"Well!" she said, releasing him, finally. "Are you glad to see me?"

"You know I am." His eyes gleamed fiercely, shining like beacons in his narrow, angular face. He moistened his lower lip with a quick movement of his tongue. Straitlaced and high-minded as he might sometimes be, he seemed quite thoroughly ready right now to pull the robe from her.

A roguish mood seized her. She decided to make him wait a little while. It would be a test of her own fortitude as much as his. "Did you and your friend the Pontifex have a lot of interesting things to talk about?" she asked, taking a couple of steps back from him.

Dinitak looked very uneasy. His eyelids flickered three or four times very rapidly in what seemed almost like a tic, and a muscle twitched in one of his lean, sun-darkened cheeks. "It's—not something I can really discuss," he said. "Not now, anyway." His voice sounded strained and hoarse. "We had meetings—the Pontifex and the Coronal and I—there are some problems, political problems, they want me to provide some technical assistance—" He was still staring at her hungrily all the while. Keltryn loved that, the fierce way he looked at her. Those dark gleaming eyes, that powerful gaze, that tremendous *intensity* of his, the powerful magnetic force that emanated from him, that coiled-spring tension: those aspects of him had fascinated her from the first moment.

"And the funeral?" she said, deliberately continuing to hold him at bay. "What was that like?"

"I got there too late for it. But that didn't matter. It wasn't for the funeral that they asked me down, you know. It was for the other thing, the technical assignment."

"The thing you won't tell me about."

"The thing I *can't* tell you about."

"All right, don't tell me. I don't care. It's probably enormously boring, anyway. Fulkari's told me about the official things that Lord Dekkeret does all day long, now that he's Coronal. They're *colossally* boring. I wouldn't be Coronal for anything in the world. They could wave the starburst crown in front of me and the Vildivar necklace and Lord Moazlimon's ring and all the rest of the crown jewels and I *still* wouldn't—" Abruptly she had had enough of this game. "Oh, Dinitak, Dinitak, I missed you so horribly all the time you were at Muldemar! And don't say that it was only a few days. It felt like centuries to me."

"And to me," he said. "Keltryn—Keltryn—"

He reached for her, and she went willingly to him. The robe fell away. His hands ran eagerly up and down her body as she tugged him to the carpeted floor.

They were still new enough as a couple so that the physical part of their intimacy had a ferocious, almost compulsive urgency about it. Keltryn, to whom all of this was entirely unfamiliar, felt not only the excitement that came with the release of pent-up desires but also a powerful sense of wanting to make up for lost time, now that she had at last allowed herself to experience this aspect of adult life.

There would be sufficient opportunity later on, she knew, for deep, searching conversations, long hand-in-hand strolls through quiet corridors of the Castle, dinners by candlelight, and such. Enough of the old tomboyish Keltryn still remained alive in her, the virginal student of swordsmanship who was so adept at holding boys at bay, that she would tell herself from time to time that they ought not to allow their relationship to be entirely one of sweaty grappling and hot, wild copulation; but yet, now that she had had her first taste of sweaty grappling and hot, wild copulation, she found herself quite willing to postpone those deep, searching conversations and long hand-in-hand strolls for some future phase of the affair.

Dinitak, for all the asceticism that seemed to be an inherent part of his makeup, appeared to feel the same way. His own appetite for lovemaking, unleashed now after who knew how long a period of restraint, was at the very least as strong as hers. Gladly they pushed each other again and again to the edge of exhaustion, and beyond the edge.

But establishing that kind of relationship had not been at all simple to achieve. For the first two weeks after their initial accidental meeting outside Lord Haspar's Rotunda they had seen each other practically every day, but he never even came near to offering anything like a physical approach, and Keltryn had no idea how to elicit one. She had become only too well accustomed to the unwanted attentions of classmates like Polliex and Toraman Kanna; but how did one go about inviting *wanted* attentions? She began to wonder whether Dinitak might be the same sort of man as Septach Melayn, and whether it would be her peculiar destiny to fall in love only with men who were by innate nature unavailable to her.

She had no doubt that she *was* in love with him. Dinitak was unlike anyone else she had ever known, both in her girlhood in Sipermit and at the Castle. His dark, brooding good looks, that lean, taut Suvraelinu look that came from having grown up under the harsh, unforgiving sun of the desert continent, held a powerful, almost irresistible, appeal for her. That he was slender, almost flimsy, of build and hardly an inch taller than she was herself made no difference to her. When she looked at him she felt—in her knees, in her breast, in her loins—a sense of overpowering attraction of a sort she had never experienced before.

He was unusual in other ways, too. There was a bluntness, even a roughness, about his way of dealing with people that must have come, Keltryn thought, from his upbringing in Suvrael. He was a commoner, for one thing: that made him different right there from the boys she had grown up with. But there was something else. She knew very little about his background, but there were rumors that his father had been a criminal of some sort, that the father had tried to play some sort of ugly trick on Dekkeret when Dekkeret was a young man traveling in Suvrael, and that Dinitak, appalled at his father's schemings, had turned against him and helped Dekkeret take him prisoner.

Whether that was true or not, Keltryn had no idea, but it *felt* true. From various things Dinitak had said, to her and to other people around the Castle, she knew that he held a hard, austere view of things, that he had no patience with any sort of irregular behavior along a range that ran from mere laziness and sloppiness at one end of the scale to criminality at the other. He seemed driven by a powerful moral imperative: a reaction, someone said, against the lawlessness of his father. He was an idealist, honest to the point sometimes of brutality. He was quick to denounce lapses of virtue in others, and, to his great credit, he did not seem to commit any such lapses himself.

Such a person, Keltryn knew, could all too easily seem prudish and preachy and self-righteous. Yet, strangely, Dinitak did not strike her that way. He was good company, lively, entertaining, graceful in his manner, capable of a certain sharp-edged wit. No wonder that Lord Dekkeret was so fond of him. As for Dinitak's powerful sense of right and wrong, one had to admit that he lived by his own strictures: he was as hard on himself as he was on anyone else, and asked for no praise for that. He seemed naturally upright and incorruptible. It was simply the way he was. One had to take a person like that as he came.

But was a person like that, she wondered, too high-minded to indulge in the bodily passions? Because she herself had finally decided it was time to indulge in those passions herself, and she finally had found someone with whom she would like to indulge, and he seemed utterly unaware that she felt that way.

In her desperation it occurred to her, at length, that she had an expert in such matters right within her own family. And so she consulted her sister Fulkari.

"You might try putting him in a situation where he really has very little choice, and see what he does," Fulkari suggested.

Of *course* Fulkari would know how to go about it! And so one afternoon Keltryn invited Dinitak to join her for a swim in the Setiphon Arcade's pool that evening. Hardly anyone seemed to be using the pool these days, and no one at all—Keltryn had checked—went there in the evening. Just to be certain, though, she took the trouble to lock the door to the pool from within once she and Dinitak arrived.

He had brought a swimsuit with him, naturally.

Now or never, Keltryn thought. As he started off to one of the dressing rooms she said, "Oh, we don't really need to wear suits here, do we? I never bring one. I haven't brought one tonight." And she slipped quickly out of the few garments she was wearing, trotted blithely past him with her heart thundering so violently that she thought it would crack her ribs, and executed a perfect dive into the pink porphyry tank. Dinitak hesitated only a moment. Then he stripped also—she looked up from the pool, staring in wonder and awe at the beauty of his trim, narrow-waisted body—and leaped in after her.

They splashed around for a while in the warm, cinnamon-scented water. She challenged him to a race, and they streaked side by side from one end of the pool to the other, ending in what they could only call a tie. Then she hauled herself up out of the pool, found some towels to spread out on the tiled margin, and beckoned to him to join her.

"What if someone comes?" he asked.

She made no attempt to conceal the mischievous mirth she felt. "Nobody will. I locked the door."

She could not have made it more plain, lying there naked on this pile of soft towels in this warm, humid room that they had entirely to themselves, that she had brought him here to give herself to him. If he disdained her now, it would be the clearest possible message that he had no interest in being her lover—that he found her physically unattractive, or that he was not a man who responded to women, or else that his own hyperdeveloped moral sensibility would not permit him to enjoy the pleasures of the body in any free and easy way.

None of those things were true. Dinitak lay down alongside her, and easily and capably gathered her into his arms and put his lips to hers and sent one of his hands roving over her firm little breasts and downward then to the juncture of her thighs, and Keltryn knew that it was going to happen to her at last, that she was about to cross the great boundary that separated girls from women, that Dinitak would initiate her this evening into the mysteries that she had never dared to experience before.

She wondered if it would hurt. She wondered if she would do things the right way.

But it turned out that there was no need to think about right ways and wrong ways. Dinitak obviously knew what he was doing, and she followed his lead easily and after a time she was able just to let her own instincts take charge. As for pain, there was only a moment of it, nothing like what she had feared, though it was a bit startling for an instant and she did let a little gasp escape her lips. After that there were no problems. What had happened felt strange, yes. But very fine. Fantastic. Unforgettable. It seemed to her that she had stepped just now through a doorway which had admitted her to some altogether unfamiliar new world where everything glowed with bright auras of delight.

That one little gasp led to difficulties afterward, though. When it was over, Keltryn lay back in a dazed haze of pleasure and astonishment, and only gradually did she realize that Dinitak was staring at her with a stunned look on his face that could almost have been one of horror.

"Is something wrong?" she whispered, close to tears. "Was I displeasing to you?"

"Oh, no, no, no! You were wonderful!" he said. "More than wonderful. But why didn't you tell me it was your first time?" His forehead was knotted with anguish.

So that was it! His damned morals again!

"It never would have occurred to me. If you were wondering about it, I suppose you always could have asked."

"One doesn't ask about things like that," he said sternly. It was as if she had done something dreadfully improper, she thought. How had this become *her* fault? "Anyway," he went on, "I had no reason to suspect it. Not when you inveigled me down to this pool like this, and flung your clothes aside so shamelessly—and—" He struggled for words, did not seem to be able to find the right ones, and finally blurted, "You should have said something, Keltryn! You should have told me!"

This was bewildering. She began to feel anger rising. "Why? What possible difference could knowing it have made?"

"Because I feel so guilty for what's happened, now. Unknowingly or not, I've done something that I can't forgive myself for. To take a young woman's virginity, Keltryn—it's a kind of theft, in a way—"

This was getting farther and farther from anything that made sense to her. "You didn't take anything. I gave."

"Even so—one simply doesn't *do* such things."

"*One* doesn't? You mean, *you* don't. You sound positively prehistoric, Dinitak. Do you think the Castle is some sacred sanctuary of purity? I've spent months in the midst of a pack of silly boys who were absolutely slavering to do the very thing with me that you and I just did, and I said no to them all, and the first time I decide to say yes I get blamed for not having informed you in advance that I—that—"

Tears were surging up again, but this time they were tears of rage, not of fear. The idiot! How could he dare feel *guilty* in such a wonderful moment? What right did he have to expect her to give him details of her past sexual history?

But she knew that she had to put her anger aside and do something to repair this, and fast, or their friendship would never survive it.

In the gentlest tone she could find Keltryn said, "I don't want you to think you did anything wrong, Dinitak. So far as I'm concerned what you did was one hundred percent right. Yes, I was a virgin—and I can't tell you how tired I was of continuing to be one, and I think I would have gone right out of my mind if I had gone on being one an hour longer."

But that only made things worse. Now he was the angry one. "I see. You wanted to get rid of that tiresome innocence of yours, and therefore you found a convenient implement to help you dispose of it. Well, I'm glad to have been of use."

"*Implement?* No! No! What an awful thing to say. You don't understand anything, do you?"

"Don't I?"

"Please. You're spoiling everything. All this pious outrage of yours. This blustering righteous indignation. I know that you can't help it, that you take all these issues of morality tremendously seriously. But look at the mess you're making between us! It's all so terribly stupid and unnecessary."

He started to reply, but she put her hand over his mouth.

"Don't you realize I *love* you, Dinitak? That that's the reason why you're here with me tonight, and not Polliex, or Toraman Kanna, or some other boy from Septach Melayn's fencing class? All these weeks we were together, and you never once made a move, and I sat there praying desperately that you would, but you were either too shy or too pure or too something else to do it, and so, finally—finally—tonight, the two of us at the swimming pool, I thought—I'll put him in a position where he *can't* resist me, and see what happens—"

At last he understood.

"I love you, Keltryn. That's the only reason I was waiting. What I thought was that the time for that part of things hasn't come yet. I didn't want to cheapen our friendship by behaving like all those others. And I'm very sorry now that I miscalculated everything so badly."

Keltryn grinned. "Don't be. All that's over and done with. And now—"

"Now—"

He reached for her. She eluded his grasp, rolled past him to the side of the pool, threw herself in with a resounding splash. He came splash-

ing after her. She swam down the middle of the pool with all the speed
at her command, a pink streak cutting a line through the pink water,
and Dinitak came barreling after her. At the far end she pulled herself
up to the tiles again, laughing, and held out her arms to him.

That was the beginning. It was all much less complicated for them after
that. Keltryn began to comprehend that that odd puritanical side of
him had its own set of boundaries, that the harsh code of values by
which he lived was not something that could be delineated in simple
tones of black and white. Dinitak was no ascetic. Far from it; passion
and lust were certainly no strangers to his makeup. But things had to
happen in accordance with his unique sense of what was proper, and
Keltryn realized that she would not always be able to anticipate what
that was.

In the weeks that followed, they spent night after night in each
other's arms, until it actually began to seem desirable to have some
time off to get some sleep. Dinitak's trip to Muldemar provided that.
Provided rather too much of it, Keltryn thought, by the second day of
his absence. She could not get enough of him—nor, it seemed, he of
her.

She continued her twice-weekly fencing sessions with Audhari of
Stoienzar. After Septach Melayn's departure for the Labyrinth the fencing class had dissolved, but she and Audhari went on meeting, even so.
Fulkari, for a while, had been convinced that a romance was budding
there; but Fulkari had been wrong about that. Keltryn had never regarded big, good-natured Audhari as anything but a friend.

He guessed right away that something had changed in her life. Perhaps it was the dark semicircles under her eyes, or perhaps a certain
slowing of her reflexes that had set in, now that she was getting so little
sleep. Or, Keltryn thought, maybe there's some kind of emanation given
off by girls who have begun going to bed with men, a visible aura of un-
chastity, that every man is easily able to detect.

And finally he mentioned it. "There's something different about you
these days," Audhari observed, as they went at each other with their foils.

"Is there? And what would that be, then?"

He laughed. "I couldn't really say."

They dropped the subject there. He appeared to regret having brought it up, and she certainly was not eager to pursue the conversation.

She wondered, though, about his ambiguous words. *Why* couldn't he say? Was it because he genuinely didn't know what it was that had changed about her? Or did he feel uncomfortable about talking to her about it? Though he made no further references to it, it seemed to her, though, that a more personal tone had begun to steal into his remarks to her: a flirtatious one, even. He noted that she seemed not to be getting as much sleep as she needed. He observed that there was a new sexiness in the way she walked. He had never said things like that to her before.

She asked Fulkari about it. Fulkari replied that men often changed their way of speaking to a woman once they decided that she had become more available than she had been before.

"But I'm *not* available!" she said, indignant. "Not to him, anyway."

"Even so. Your whole manner's different, now. He may be picking that up."

Keltryn didn't much like the idea that all the men of the Castle might be able to figure out at a glance that she was sleeping with somebody. She was still too new to the world of mature men and women to feel entirely at home in it; she wanted to clutch her affair with Dinitak close to herself, sharing the knowledge of her transition into adulthood with no one except, perhaps, her sister. The idea that Audhari, or just about anyone else, could look at her and know right away that she had been Doing It with someone, and therefore she might somehow be interested in doing it with him as well, was offensive and disturbing to her.

Possibly, Keltryn thought, she was misunderstanding things. She hoped that she was. The last thing she wanted, now, was for her kind, earnest friend Audhari to begin making romantic overtures to her.

At a suggestion from her serving-maid, though, she went down one Starday into the lower reaches of the Castle, the market area, and bought from a purveyor of wizard-goods a tiny amulet of fine knitted wire known as a focalo, that had the property of warding off the unwanted attentions of men. She pinned it to the collar of her fencing jacket the next time she met with Audhari.

He noticed it at once, and laughed. "What's that thing for, Keltryn?"

She flushed a flaming scarlet. "It's just something I've started wearing, that's all."

"Has somebody been bothering you? That's why girls usually wear focalos, isn't it? To send a keep-away message."

"Well—"

"Come on. It can't be me you're worried about, Keltryn!"

"As a matter of fact," she said, feeling unutterably embarrassed now, but realizing that she had no choice but to tell him, "I've been starting to think that things have been getting a little peculiar between us lately. Or so it seems to me. Your telling me that I walk in a sexier way now, and things like that. Maybe I'm completely wrong, but—oh, Audhari, I don't know what I'm trying to say—"

He was more amused than annoyed. "I don't think I do either, actually. But one thing I'm sure of: you don't need that focalo around me. I could tell right from the start that you weren't interested in me."

"As a friend, I am. And as a fencing partner."

"Yes. But not anything beyond that. That was very easy to tell. —Anyway, you've got a lover now, don't you? So why would you want to get involved with me?"

"You can tell that too?"

"It's written all over your face, Keltryn. A ten-year-old could see it. Well, good for you, is what I say! He's a very lucky fellow, whoever he is." Audhari slipped his fencing mask into place. "But we really ought to get down to work now, I think. On your guard, Keltryn! One! Two! Three!"

Dekkeret said, "I don't mean to intrude on your personal life, Dinitak. But Fulkari tells me that you've been seeing a great deal of her sister in recent weeks."

"This is true. Keltryn and I have been spending a great deal of time together lately. A *very* great deal of time."

"She's a lovely girl, Keltryn is."

"Yes. Yes. I confess that I find her extremely fascinating."

They were dining together at Dekkeret's invitation, just the two of them, in the Coronal's private chambers. Dekkeret's steward had laid a magnificent meal before them, bowls of spiced fish, and the sweet pastel-hued fungi of Kajith Kabulon, and roast leg of bilantoon cooked in thokka-berries from far-off Narabal, accompanied by a rich, earthy wine of the Sandaraina region. Dekkeret ate robustly; Dinitak, restless and edgy, scarcely seemed hungry at all. He did little more than pick at his food and did not taste his wine at all.

Dekkeret studied him closely. From time to time over the years, he knew, Dinitak had struck up some casual relationship with this woman or that one, but they had never come to anything. He had the feeling that Dinitak did not want them to, that he was a man who had little need of ongoing feminine companionship. But from what Fulkari had told him, something quite different appeared to be going on now.

"As a matter of fact," said Dinitak, "I expect to be seeing her this very evening, after I leave you. So if you have business to discuss with me, Dekkeret—"

"I do. But I promise not to keep you here very late. I wouldn't want business matters to get in the way of true love."

"Such sarcasm isn't worthy of you, my lord."

"Was I being sarcastic? I thought I was speaking the simple truth. But let's get on to our business, at any rate. Which involves Keltryn, in fact."

Dinitak responded with a puzzled frown. "It does? In what way?"

Dekkeret said, "The plan now, as I understand it, is for us to depart for the western provinces on Threeday next. Since we'll be away for a few months or even more, maybe a good deal more, what I asked you here tonight to discuss was whether you'd like to invite Keltryn to accompany us on the trip."

Dinitak looked astounded. He rose halfway out of his seat and his face turned a blazing crimson beneath his dark Suvraelinu tan. "I can't do that, Dekkeret!"

"I don't think I understand you. What do you mean, you can't?"

"I mean it's completely out of the question. The idea's outrageous!"

"Outrageous?" Dekkeret repeated, narrowing his eyes to a mystified squint. After more than twenty years of their friendship, he still was unable to tell when he was likely to strike some odd vein of moral fastidiousness in Dinitak. "Why is that? What am I failing to see here? According to Fulkari, you and Keltryn are absolutely mesmerized by each other. But when I offer you a way of avoiding a long and undoubtedly painful separation from her, you flare up at me as though I've suggested something hideously obscene."

Dinitak seemed to grow calmer, but he was still visibly upset. "Consider what you're saying, Dekkeret. How can I possibly bring Keltryn along with me on this trip? It would say to everyone that I look upon her as nothing more than a concubine."

Dekkeret had never seen him as obtuse as this. He wanted to reach across the table and shake him. "As a companion, Dinitak. Not a concubine. I'm going to be bringing Fulkari with me, you know. Do you think I regard her as a concubine too?"

"Everyone understands that you will marry Fulkari after the mourning period for Teotas is over. For all intents and purposes she is already your consort. But Keltryn and I—nothing is established between us. I'm twice her age, Dekkeret. I'm not even sure that it's proper for us to have been doing what we're doing now. There's no way I could countenance taking an extended trip across the continent in the company of a young single girl."

Dekkeret shook his head. "You astound me, Dinitak."

"Do I? Well, then, I astound you. So be it. She can't come with us. I won't allow it."

This was not in any way what Dekkeret had expected. Indeed at the outset of the meal he had been wondering whether Dinitak, in some hesitant, awkward way, would eventually bring the conversation around to a request for permission to have Keltryn join them on the journey. Having her come with them made perfectly good sense to him. The girl *was* very young, yes, but by all accounts she was levelheaded beyond her years and growing up fast. Besides, she and Fulkari were not only sisters but the closest of friends, and it would be useful to have Keltryn keeping Fulkari company while he and Dinitak were occupied in the real tasks of the mission. And one would assume that Dinitak would relish the prospect of having her close at hand while they traveled. But he could not have been more wrong about that.

Beyond all doubt Dinitak was serious about this concubine business, crazy as it sounded. Dekkeret knew better than to try to argue with him in the area of moral niceties. Where matters of that sort were concerned, Dinitak inhabited a world of his own.

Dekkeret sighed.

"As you wish," he said. "The girl stays home."

The job of breaking the news to Keltryn became Fulkari's responsibility. She and Dekkeret agreed that if they left the matter to Dinitak, his clumsy explanations would infuriate Keltryn to the point where the relationship could not survive.

But she became infuriated anyway. "The fool!" she cried. "The preposterous little prig! So holy that I can't travel with him, is that it? Well, then. I'll spare him the shame of it. I never want to see him again!"

"You will," Fulkari said.

4

This would be Prestimion's fifth visit to the Isle of Sleep. That was unusual in itself, and more so because he was Pontifex now. But Prestimion had been an unusual monarch since the earliest days of his reign.

A Coronal might visit the Isle once or twice during his reign, generally in the course of making a grand processional: the post of Lady of the Isle, after all, was normally held by the mother of the Coronal, and it was reasonable for the Coronal to want to visit his mother now and then.

But for him to go to the Isle once he had become Pontifex was a very different matter. The Pontifex normally would have no official reason for going there. Pontifexes did relatively little traveling in general, and such as they did do was usually confined to the continent of Alhanroel.

If the Pontifex's prior reign as Coronal had been a lengthy one, his mother might well not have survived to the end of it: that had been the case with Lord Confalume, whose elder sister Kunigarda had served as Lady of the Isle during the latter half of his incumbency at the Castle. Any Lady who did live long enough to see her son's ascent to the senior throne customarily would remain on the Isle even after she had retired from her duties to make room for the new Coronal's mother. Former Ladies of the Isle dwelled at the capacious estate that was provided for them in the Terrace of Shadows on the Isle's Third Cliff.

Perhaps her son the Pontifex might choose to pay a call on her there once he had settled fully into the responsibilities of his new post. But more often than not he would neglect to make the journey until it was too late: his mother died before he could find an opportunity to go, or he himself grew too old to want to travel. Whole centuries had gone by without a visit by a Pontifex to the Isle.

Prestimion, who had always had the closest and warmest of relationships with his mother the Lady Therissa, had journeyed to the Isle of Sleep in his early years as Coronal Lord in order to introduce his bride Varaile to her, and to enlist his mother's aid in the struggle against the rebellious Dantirya Sambail. He had gone there again in the fifth year of his reign, having decided then to make his first grand processional for the sake of presenting himself to the world in the aftermath of the chaos that had been engendered by the Procurator Dantirya Sambail's two insurrections. That time he had crossed Alhanroel by land, just as he had done now, and had taken ship at Alaisor for the Isle, and gone on from there to Zimroel, making stops at Piliplok on the eastern coast and at Ni-moya inland.

In his eleventh year Prestimion had chosen to make a second processional, this one following a similar route, but carrying him onward beyond Ni-moya, clear across Zimroel to the crystalline city of Dulorn and beyond it to the remote western cities of Pidruid and Narabal and Til-omon, where visits from a Coronal were few and far between. Prestimion had found occasion on that trip for still another visit to his mother. And in the sixteenth year of his reign as Coronal he had undertaken the third and last of his grand processionals, this one a truly extraordinary one that had taken him across the bottom of Alhanroel to Stoien, thence to the Isle yet again, and from there, to the astonishment of all the world, southward to the forbidding desert continent of Suvrael, that had not seen a Coronal's face in three hundred years.

Now here he was arriving at the Isle once again. There before him in the sea reared the familiar colossal bulk of the place, that phenomenal wall of glittering white chalk rising high above the water, its three great tiers going up and up in diminishing circles to the holy sanctuary at the top, Inner Temple, where the Lady and her millions of acolytes dwelled. The sun, at this time of day, lay nearly overhead, and the smooth face of the Isle gleamed with an almost unbearable reflected brilliance in its intense light.

Large as the Isle was—and on any planet but Majipoor it would have been deemed a continent, not an island—it was accessible to shipping only at two harbors, Taleis on the western side facing Zimroel, and Nu-minor, in the Isle's northeastern corner, looking toward Alhanroel. Prestimion had always come to the Isle by the Numinor entrance. Taleis port was a place he had never seen. He realized now, standing on the deck of the swift vessel that had brought him here this time and peering out yet again at the brilliant white rampart that surrounded the harbor at Numinor, that he probably never would.

This, so Prestimion expected, would be the last visit he would ever make to the Isle of Sleep. Nor would he go on to Zimroel when he was finished here, which might have justified a brief stop at Taleis to satisfy his curiosity. The world was Dekkeret's now; Pontifexes did not undertake grand processionals; in years to come, as he aged, he would settle ever more deeply into his life at the Labyrinth.

A warm, sweet breeze blew toward them as their ship glided toward Numinor. Eternal summer was the rule in these latitudes. The Isle was forever in bloom: even from this distance Prestimion fancied that he could make out the bright colors of the groves of eldirons and tanigales and purple-blooming thwales that grew so profusely on its multitude of chalky terraces.

As they neared the Isle Varaile stood at Prestimion's side, with Septach Melayn and Gialaurys, who had accompanied the Pontifex on this voyage, nearby. The princes Taradath and Akbalik and Simbilon flanked their father and mother on the deck. The young Lady Tuanelys, who had no liking for ocean travel, had remained below in her cabin, as she had for most of the journey.

The ship's captain, a massive Skandar with grayish-purple fur, called out for the anchor to be lowered.

"Why are we dropping anchor all the way out here?" Prince Simbilon asked.

Prestimion began to reply; but Taradath, who had made the journey to the Isle with his father on Prestimion's last processional, spoke first: "Because any ship that's fast enough to get us across from Alaisor to here in any decent time is going to be too big to fit into the harbor," he said, a bit too patronizingly for Prestimion's taste. "Numinor port's a tiny little place, and they'll have to take us in by ferry. You'll see."

The protocol for a visiting Coronal upon landing at Numinor was for him to stop first at the royal guesthouse known as Seven Walls, a single-story building of gray-black stone situated right on the seawall at the rampart of the port. There he was required to perform various rituals of purification before beginning the ascent to the uppermost of the three terraces, where the Lady would be waiting for him. It was generally the custom for the Coronal to go upward to the Lady, rarely for the Lady to come down to the shore to meet him.

But Prestimion was Pontifex now, not Coronal, and he had no idea what kind of arrangements would be made. Nor had he asked. Perhaps Seven Walls was reserved only for Coronals, and Pontifexes were taken elsewhere. It made no difference. Let it come as a surprise, he thought.

Everything seemed to be going as usual, at first. The transfer to the ferry was carried out smoothly; the ferry pilot steered them efficiently through the reefs and shallows of the channel to their landing at Numinor port; a little group of the Lady's hierarchs, solemn in their golden robes with red trim, was waiting as always to greet him. They made the spiraling Labyrinth sign of reverence to him, formally greeted the Lady Varaile and the High Spokesman Septach Melayn and the Grand Admiral Gialaurys, and led them ashore, conducting Prestimion and his family in the customary fashion to Seven Walls, and the others to a hostelry off in the opposite direction.

Then things began to vary from the old routine. "The Lady herself awaits you in the guesthouse, your majesty," one of the hierarchs told him, as they drew near the building.

Prestimion's first response was surprise that his mother, who on his last visit had seemed at last to be beginning to succumb to the inevitabilities of age, would have subjected herself to the effort of descending from her sanctuary high up atop this mountainous island when it would be so much easier on her for him to go upward to her. Then he reminded himself that his mother was no longer Lady of the Isle. The person who was waiting for him at Seven Walls would be the new incumbent, Dekkeret's mother, the Lady Taliesme.

Why, he wondered, had Taliesme come here to him? Perhaps she did not yet feel firmly established in the grandeur that now was hers, and found herself, when confronted here with the arrival of a visiting Pontifex, impelled by the awe his office inspired to go down the mountain to him rather than require him to go up to her. But then another possibility, a much more troublesome one, leaped into Prestimion's mind as he saw Taliesme coming toward him through the courtyard of Seven Walls.

His mother Therissa had always been a woman of unconquerable strength of spirit. But the years were doubtless taking their toll. She must surely have found Teotas's death a mighty blow. Perhaps her health had given way beneath it. Perhaps, hard as it was to believe, she had undergone some kind of emotional collapse, or a even a physical one. She might be seriously ill—dying, maybe. Or possibly already dead. And Taliesme had not wanted him to make the ascent to Inner Temple unaware of the Lady Therissa's condition. So she had come to him here for the sake of breaking the news to him.

Yet Prestimion did not sense any atmosphere of stark calamity about Taliesme as she came forward to greet him. She moved with quick bird-like steps: a small, energetic woman robed in white, with the silver circlet of her office about her forehead. Her eyes were bright and sparkling, her hands readily outstretched.

"Your majesty," she said. "I offer you and your family the warmest welcome to our island."

"For that we thank you, your ladyship."

"And you have, of course, my deepest sympathies on your great loss."

He could not wait any longer. "My mother, I hope, has borne it well?"

"As well as could be expected, I should say. She looks forward eagerly to seeing you."

"I'll find her in good health, then?" Prestimion asked tensely.

There was just the tiniest moment of hesitation. "You'll find her not as strong as you remember her, your majesty. The death of Prince Teotas has been hard on her. I will not pretend otherwise. And there have been other troublesome little difficulties, of which we should speak before you ascend to Inner Temple. But first, I think, perhaps some refreshment is in order. —Will you come within, your majesty?"

A light meal had been laid out for them in Seven Walls: flasks of golden wine, trays of oysters and smoked fish, bowls of fruit. It seemed to Prestimion that Taliesme was as comfortable playing hostess to the Pontifex as she might have been entertaining some longtime neighbors in her old home in Normork, which Dinitak had told him once was a very humble little place indeed.

He was fascinated by the way she had been transformed, and yet not transformed at all, in the course of her elevation to the Ladyship.

She could not have been more different in her manner from her predecessor at the Isle. There was a world of contrast between Taliesme's simplicity and unassuming modesty and the aristocratic stateliness of the Lady Therissa. Yet an undeniable nobility had settled over her since she had assumed her duties here.

From the moment of her first visits to the Castle in the days when Dekkeret was merely Coronal-designate, Prestimion had been impressed by Taliesme's confidence, her poise, her serenity. Now that she was Lady of the Isle, a certain aura of grace and assurance of the sort that almost invariably came to typify every woman who held the post of Lady had been added to those qualities. But her essential self seemed fundamentally unchanged, not in any way overwhelmed by the greatness that had come to her with Dekkeret's ascent to the throne.

Prestimion felt his judgment of her son confirmed anew in her. Once again, as so often in the past, it had proved to be the case that the mother of the man who was deemed worthy of the title of Coronal Lord of Majipoor was herself a fitting candidate for the role of Lady of the Isle.

The conversation, which Prestimion allowed her to lead, traveled easily through a wide range of topics. They spoke first of all of the tragic death of Teotas: how startling, how mystifying, that a man of his abilities and character should undergo such a breakdown. "All the world mourns your brother, your majesty, and feels great sadness on your behalf and on your family's," Taliesme assured him. "I sense their grief and sorrow constantly." She touched the circlet that kept her in contact with the dreaming minds of Majipoor's billions, night after night.

Then, when it was appropriate to change the subject, she turned it deftly to her son Dekkeret, asking for news of him in his new role as Coronal. "He will be one of the greatest of our kings," Prestimion told her, and offered a sketchy summary of the plans Dekkeret had made, as much of them as he had revealed thus far, for his reign. He touched also—lightly, very lightly—on the matter of Dekkeret and the Lady Fulkari, indicating only that their often complex and sometimes stormy relationship appeared to be entering a new and sunnier period.

Finally, after Taliesme had taken the opportunity to praise the handsomeness of Prestimion's three sons and the blossoming beauty of his pretty young daughter, Prestimion judged it was time to return to the topic that was of the greatest interest to him.

A quick sidelong glance at Taradath was sufficient to convey to the boy that this would be a good moment for him and his brothers and sister to go outside for a stroll along the Numinor seawall. When they were gone he said, "You mentioned, when we arrived, certain troublesome little difficulties that my mother has been having. I would like to speak of those now, if we may."

"Indeed I think we should, your majesty." Taliesme drew herself up in her seat as though fortifying herself for what was to be said. —"I regret to tell you that your mother has been afflicted, for some months now, by dreams. Very bad dreams: dreams that I can only describe as nightmares. Which have had a fairly serious effect on her general well-being."

Prestimion caught his breath in shock and amazement. His mother too? There was no limit to Mandralisca's audacity. He had already shown himself willing to strike almost anywhere in the royal family.

But now his mother also? His *mother*? She who for twenty years had been the world's beloved Lady, and now wanted to live only in peaceful retirement? This was intolerable.

Before he could reply, though, Varaile said, breaking a long silence, "My daughter Tuanelys has had troubled dreams recently as well, your ladyship." Though she had addressed the Lady Taliesme, she was looking at no one in particular. She was hollow-eyed and haggard, having had yet another bleak dream herself in the night just past. "She cries out, she shivers in fright, she bursts into sweat. It was dreams of this sort, night after night, that drove Prince Teotas to take his life. And even I—I, too—"

Varaile was trembling. Taliesme looked toward her in shock and surprise. "Oh—my dear woman—my dear—"

Prestimion went to his wife and rested his hands gently on her shoulders to soothe her. But he maintained a calm tone of voice as he said, as though musing over the irony of it, "The Lady of the Isle receiving dreams instead of sending them? The *former* Lady, I mean. But even so: it seems so strange. —Has my mother described these dreams to you?"

"Not very clearly, majesty. Either she is unable to be specific, or unwilling. All I get from her is vague talk of demons, monsters, dark images—and something else, something deeper and more subtle and powerfully distressing, which she absolutely will not describe at all." Taliesme touched the tips of her fingers to her silver circlet. "I've offered to enter her mind and probe for the source, or to have one of the more experienced hierarchs of the Isle do it. But she will not allow it. She says that one who was once the Lady of the Isle must not open herself to the circlet of the Lady. Is that true, majesty? Is there some prohibition against doing that?"

"Not that I know of," said Prestimion. "But the Isle has its own customs, and few outside it know anything about them. I'll speak of this with her when I get to see her."

"You should," Taliesme said. "I'll mince no words, majesty. She suffers terribly. She should avail herself of whatever aid can be had, and she of all people should know that we stand ready here to help her."

"Yes. Absolutely."

"And another thing, majesty. These dreams, which have entered your family so freely—they are widespread throughout the world. Again and again I'm told by my acolytes that as they monitor the minds of sleeping people they detect pain, shock, torment. I tell you, your majesty, we spend nearly all of our time now with such people, seeking them out, trying through sendings to heal their suffering—"

So it was even worse than he had expected. Prestimion let his eyelids drift shut, and sat in silence for a time.

When he spoke again, it was in the quietest of voices. "It is almost like an epidemic of madness, would you not say, your ladyship?"

"An epidemic indeed," said Taliesme.

"We've had such a thing on Majipoor before. In the early years of my reign as Coronal, it was. I found out what was causing it, and I took steps to bring an end to it. This is, I think, a plague of a somewhat different sort, but I think I know what is causing this one too, and I tell you in the most solemn way that I'll bring an end to this one as well. An old enemy of mine is loose in the land. He will be dealt with. —When will I be able to see my mother, your ladyship?"

"It is too late in the day now to make the ascent to Third Cliff," Taliesme answered. Her face was set and somber and there was no sparkle in her eyes now. She and he had passed far beyond the pleasant courtesies of an hour before. Each now understood that a serious challenge lay ahead for them all. The note of fierce determination in Prestimion's tone seemed to have had a powerful effect on her. With just a few words he had conveyed a sense of present crisis, of impending large events that would require her participation at a time when she had only begun to take command of the great powers of the Isle. "I will escort you to her in the morning."

5

*P*restimion had dreams himself, that night.

Not nightmares, not him, for he was certain that the scheming poison-taster in Zimroel would not dare to approach the mind of Prestimion Pontifex. These were dreams of his own mind's devising. But they were wearisome dreams all the same, for in them he went up and up the white cliffs of the Isle of Sleep over and over again, forever ascending, never reaching the summit, an endless frustrating daylong journey past terrace after terrace that invariably culminated in his finding himself, at the end, at the very place from which he had set out. By morning Prestimion felt as though he had been climbing the wall of this island all his life. But he concealed his night of uneasy sleep from Varaile. She was preoccupied with Tuanelys: had gone to the little girl's bedroom more than once during the night, although it had turned out, each time, that Varaile had been imagining Tuanelys's cries, and the child had been sleeping soundly.

And now it was time for them to begin the upward journey in earnest. May the Divine grant us an easier trip, Prestimion prayed, than the ones I have been making all night.

He held the Lady Tuanelys on his lap aboard the floater-sled that would take them up the vertical wall that was the face of First Cliff. Varaile sat to one side of him, the Lady Taliesme to the other, and the boys in back. When the sled began its giddy climb, Tuanelys, frightened, wriggled about so that her face was buried in her father's chest; but Prestimion heard a whistle of appreciation from Prince Akbalik as they shot silently and swiftly upward against gravity's pull. He smiled at that: Akbalik was usually so restrained and serious. But perhaps the boy was beginning to change as he entered adolescence.

At the landing pad at the summit, Prestimion pointed out Numinor port far below, and the jutting arms of the breakwater where the ferry had delivered them to land. Tuanelys did not want to look. The two younger boys were wonderstruck, though, at the height of the ascent they had made. "That's nothing," Taradath said scornfully. "We've only begun to go up."

Prestimion found that the children were a welcome distraction during the long journey. It worried him that Taliesme might have held back some of the most disquieting details of the Lady Therissa's health, and he did not want to think too deeply about what waited for him above. So he derived great pleasure from watching Taradath, who had seen all this before, don the role of tour guide to his brothers and sister, loftily telling them, whether they wanted to know or not, that this was the Terrace of Assessment, where all pilgrims to the Isle were brought first, and this was the Terrace of Inception, and this the Terrace of Mirrors, and so on and so on throughout the day. It was amusing, too, to observe how little the other three cared to be instructed by their know-it-all oldest brother.

"We always stop for the night here at the Terrace of Mirrors," said Taradath grandly, as if this were a trip he made every six months or so. "First thing in the morning we go up to Second Cliff. It makes you dizzy, you do it so fast. But the view from up there is fantastic. Just you wait."

Out of the corner of his eye Prestimion caught sight of Prince Simbilon making a face at Taradath behind Taradath's back, and smiled.

Taradath would be seventeen soon, Prestimion thought. He made a mental note to talk with Varaile about sending him back to the Castle next year, enrolled as a knight-initiate. There was no reason why the grown son of a Pontifex had to remain with his family at the Labyrinth; and it would probably do Taradath some good to have the other young men of the Castle take him down a peg or two. Prestimion had done his best to teach Taradath that once he had entered adult life he would enjoy no special privileges or deferences simply because he was the Pontifex's son, but perhaps that was a lesson better learned at the hands of one's own peers.

Floaters were waiting to transport them from the Second Cliff landing stage to the final sled station at the base of Third Cliff. Quickly they traversed the Second Cliff terraces, where the pilgrims completed their training so that they could move on as acolytes to the highest level of the Isle and aid the Lady in her task. Up there on Third Cliff the Lady's vast staff of acolytes nightly donned the silver circlets that permitted one mind to touch another across any distance, and sent their spirits forth to heal through benign dreams those whose souls were in pain: to guide, to counsel, to console. On previous visits Prestimion, wonderstruck, had watched the Lady's legions at their work. But there would be no time for such diversions now.

The travelers reached the last of the floater-sled depots by mid-morning. Now came the final upward leap, to the flat summit of the Isle, thousands of feet above their starting point down at sea level.

The younger boys were excited by the astonishing clarity of the air of Third Cliff and the brilliance of the sunlight, which made everything take on a strange unworldly glow. As soon as the sled had landed they came rushing out and began to chase each other around the sled depot, while Taradath called out to them, "Hey, careful, you two! The air is really thin, up this high!" They paid no attention. The summit of Castle Mount was ever so much higher than this, after all. But the air of Castle Mount was artificial; what they were breathing here was the real thing, depleted of oxygen by the altitude, and before long Simbilon and Akbalik were feeling the effect of it, slowing down, panting hard now, staggering dizzily about.

Prestimion, who was standing beside Taradath, leaned close and whispered, "Don't say it."

Taradath did not seem to understand at all. "Don't say what, father?"

" 'I told you so.' Just don't say it." Prestimion put a little crackle into his voice. "All right? They know now that the air is different up here. No need for you to rub it in."

Taradath blinked a couple of times. "Oh," he said, and his cheeks reddened as he began to grasp Prestimion's meaning. "Of course I won't, father."

"Good."

Prestimion turned away, covering his mouth with his hand to hide his grin. Another small step in the boy's education, he thought. But there was still a long way to go.

The Terrace of Shadows, where the Lady Therissa had made her home since giving up the powers that had been hers, lay within the wall that separated the sheltered sanctuary that was Inner Temple from the rest of Third Cliff. Varaile and the children remained behind at the Third Cliff guesthouse. "Your mother's house is on the far side of Inner Temple," Taliesme told Prestimion. She led him through the immaculate garden that surrounded the lovely eight-sided marble building that was now her home, across a close-cut grassy lawn, and into a forested zone beyond that Prestimion had never entered before.

No buildings were visible here: only a curving row of smallish trees of a sort he did not recognize, rising directly in front of him. They had thick, smooth, reddish-brown trunks that bulged oddly in the middle, and bushy crowns of shining blue-green leaves that were lobed so that they looked almost like upturned hands. The trees had been planted so closely, one fat swelling trunk nuzzling up against the next, that they constituted what amounted to a wall. Only in a single place had a narrow space been left, marked by white marble flagstones, by means of which one could enter the very private sector that lay behind the grove.

"Come, majesty," Taliesme said, and beckoned Prestimion to follow her through.

It was dark and mysterious within. Prestimion found himself in another garden, less regular in form and not as carefully manicured as the one surrounding Inner Temple. It was planted mainly with what looked like palm trees—they had slender, ribbed trunks that rose to a phenomenal height without branching—that exploded far overhead into tremendous clusters of fan-shaped leaves so huge that it seemed they would prevent any sunlight from breaking through the shield that they formed. Yet these gigantic leaves were attached to wiry, tremulous stems that moved about freely in the slightest breeze, so that openings constantly were made in the leafy roof overhead, and bright shimmering shafts of light did penetrate in quickly darting bursts, creating a shifting pattern of shadows beneath.

"There is your mother's home," Taliesme said, pointing to a low, sprawling villa directly ahead. It was a handsome flat-roofed structure that had been fashioned of the same smooth white stone as had been used in the making of Inner Temple. Secondary buildings, similar in design, flanked it: servants' homes, Prestimion supposed. Other houses were dimly visible farther in. Those were the homes of senior hierarchs, Taliesme told him. "The Lady Therissa is expecting you. The hierarch Zenianthe, who is her companion, will take you to her."

Zenianthe, a slim, dignified white-haired woman who seemed to be of about his mother's age, was waiting for him on a portico lined with potted ferns. She made the Labyrinth symbol to Prestimion and gracefully signalled for him to enter.

The house was smaller within than it appeared from outside, and modestly furnished: the home of someone who has put aside the outer glories of life. The hierarch took Prestimion down a starkly simple corridor, past several little rooms that appeared at a quick glance to be virtually empty, and into a kind of conservatory at the heart of the house, glass-roofed, with a small round pool at its center and pots of greenery arranged along its margin. Prestimion's mother stood quietly to one side of the pool.

His eyes met hers. The jolt he got at his first sight of her was a far greater shock than he was expecting.

He had done as much as he could to prepare himself for this meeting. The Lady Therissa was five years older now than she had been at their last meeting; she had suffered a crushing loss in the death of her youngest son; and she had been assailed besides by whatever sort of diabolical torments Mandralisca had been sending against her by night. Prestimion knew that the effects of all that would surely be a doleful thing to behold.

He thought, though, that he had succeeded in fortifying himself against the worst of surprises; but now that he was in her presence at last, struggling with the impact of what he was seeing, he realized that no degree of preparation, perhaps, could have been sufficient.

The curious thing was that her great beauty appeared to have survived despite everything. She had always seemed much younger than her years: a slender, regal woman of superb grace and elegance, famous for her pale smooth skin, her dark gleaming hair, her calm unshakable spirit.

Those things, Prestimion knew, were the outward manifestations of the perfection of her soul. Other women might maintain eternal youthfulness with the aid of sorcerers' incantations and potions, but never the Lady Therissa. She looked the way she looked, over the years, because she was who she was. Neither her early widowhood nor the civil war that had nearly denied her eldest son Prestimion the crown that was rightfully his, nor the death of her second son Taradath in that same war, nor the great responsibilities that had devolved upon her when she had become Lady of the Isle, nor the later convulsion that had come over the world during the time of the plague of madness, had been able in any way to leave any sort of external mark on her.

Now, wondrous to behold, her hair was nearly as dark as ever—and naturally so, Prestimion was certain. Her face, though the lines of age had begun to enter it years ago, was still unwithered: the face of the most beautiful of women, rendered even more lovely, if that was possible, by the work of time. And as he moved around the side of the pool and went forward to greet her, her posture as she awaited him was as erect as ever, her entire bearing as queenly. In all ways the Lady Therissa seemed to be a woman twenty or thirty years younger than she actually was.

Then, looking close into her eyes, he saw where the real change had occurred.

Her eyes. That was the only place: nowhere else but her eyes. Another person, not ever having looked into those eyes before, might not have noticed anything amiss at all. But to Prestimion the transformation of his mother's eyes was a thing of such stunning, overwhelming magnitude that he was scarcely able to believe what he saw.

In that still-beautiful face her eyes had taken on a blazing, frightful strangeness that contradicted the very beauty in which they were set. They were the eyes of a woman who had lived a hundred years, or a thousand. Deeply sunken now, rimmed by an intricate webwork of fine lines, those transformed eyes stared out at him in a cold, rigid, unblinking way, unnaturally bright, weirdly intense, the eyes of someone who had seen the walls of the world peel back to reveal some realm of unimaginable horrors that lay behind them.

Gone now was that incredible look of serenity, the marvelous radiance that was the outer display of the inner perfection that had been, for him, her most significant characteristic. Prestimion saw the most terrible anguish in his mother's eyes now. He saw enormous pain in them: pain that was unbearable, but which was being borne nonetheless. It took all the force of will he could muster to keep himself from flinching away from the dreadful gleaming stare of those appalling eyes.

He took her hands in his. There was a tremor in her fingers that had never been there before. Her hands were cold to the touch. He realized fully now how old she was, how worn.

This weakness of hers stunned him. He had always looked to her to be his ultimate reservoir of strength. It had been that way in the time of the war against Korsibar; it had been that way when he had crushed the rebellion of Dantirya Sambail. Now he understood that that strength was exhausted.

I will have vengeance for this, Prestimion told himself.

"Mother—" His voice was hoarse, muffled, indistinct.

"Do I frighten you, Prestimion?"

Determined to give her no sign of the consternation he felt, he forced an unnaturally hearty tone, and a sort of grin. "Of course you don't, mother." Leaning forward, he kissed her lightly. "How could you ever frighten me?"

She was not deceived. "I could see it in your face as soon as you came near enough to get a good look at me. A quick little movement at the side of your mouth, it was: it told me everything."

"Perhaps I was a bit surprised," he conceded. "But *frightened*? No. No. You look a little older, I suppose. Well, so do I. So does everyone. It happens. It's not an important thing."

She smiled, and the icy harshness of her gaze softened just a little. "Oh, Prestimion, Prestimion, Prestimion, is this any time of your life or mine for you to begin lying to your mother? Don't you think there are mirrors in this house? I frighten myself, sometimes, when I look into them."

"Mother—oh, mother—" He gave up all pretense, and drew her close against him, folded her in his arms, held her in a gentle embrace, sending to her whatever he could of comfort.

She had become very thin, Prestimion realized. Almost brittle, as though she were all bones: he was afraid of holding her too tightly for fear that he would injure her in some way. But she pressed herself gladly against him. He heard something that almost might have been a sob, a sound that he had not heard from her before in all the years of his life; but perhaps it had only been an intake of breath, he thought.

When he released her and stepped back he was pleased to see that the fixed hard stare had relaxed a little further, and something of the old warm glow had come back into her eyes.

She nodded to him to follow her, and led him into a simple antechamber nearby, where a flask of wine and two bowls were waiting on a small stone table with an inlaid border of bright mother-of-pearl. Prestimion noticed that her hand quivered just a little as she poured the wine for them.

They took their first sips in silence. He looked straight at her and made no attempt now to avert his eyes, painful as that was for him.

"Was it losing Teotas that did this to you, mother?"

The tone of her reply was a steady, unwavering one. "I've lost a son before, Prestimion. There's nothing worse for a mother than to outlive her child; but I know how to handle grief." She shook her head. "No, Prestimion. No. It wasn't Teotas alone that aged me like this."

"I know something about the dreams you've been having. Taliesme told me."

"You know nothing about those dreams, Prestimion. *Nothing.*" Her face had darkened, and her voice seemed an octave deeper now. "Until you've directly experienced one yourself, you can't possibly know. And I pray that the Divine will spare you from anything of the kind. —You've not had one, have you?" ·

"I don't think so. I dream of Thismet, sometimes. Or that I'm wandering around lost in some strange part of the Castle. A couple of nights ago I dreamed that I was traveling up and up and up to Third Cliff in a floater-sled, without ever getting there. But everybody has dreams of that sort, mother. Just ordinary irritating dreams that you'd rather not be having, but you know you'll forget them five minutes after you awake."

"My dreams are of a different kind. They cut deep; and they linger. Let me tell you about my dreams, Prestimion. And then perhaps you'll understand."

She took a slow sip of her wine and stared down into the bowl, swirling it slowly. Prestimion waited, saying nothing. He knew a little of what Teotas's deadly dreams must have been like, and Varaile's, and even, to some degree, Tuanelys's. But he wanted to hear what his mother had to say of her own dreams, first, before he spoke to her of those other ones.

She was silent for a time. Then at last the Lady Therissa looked across at him again. Her eyes had taken on once more the cold, hard, ferocious glare they had had when he had first stared into them. But that he knew better, he might have thought those eyes were the eyes of a madwoman.

"Here is how it happens, Prestimion. I lie down, I close my eyes, I let myself slide off into sleep as I have done every night for more years than I care to think about." She spoke quietly, calmly, impersonally, as though she were telling a mere story, some fable about a person who had lived five thousand years before. "And—it happens once a week, perhaps, or twice, sometimes three—not long after sleep comes, I feel an odd warmth behind my forehead, a warmth that grows and grows and grows until I think my brain must be on fire. There is a throbbing in my head, here, here—" She touched her temples and the roof of her skull. "A sensation, also, as of a bright, hot beam of light cutting into my forehead and going deep within. Going into my *soul*, Prestimion."

"Oh—mother—how dreadful, mother—"

"What I've told you so far is the easy part. After the heat, the pain, comes the dream itself. —I am in court. I am on trial before a shouting mob. I stand accused of the most loathsome betrayals of trust, of the filthiest of lies, of treachery against those I was chosen to serve. It is an impeachment, Prestimion. I am being removed from my post as Lady of the Isle for having been negligent in my tasks."

She paused, then, and took some more wine, and sipped it unhurriedly. The effort of telling him these things was obviously a drain on her energies.

Prestimion was all but certain, now, that what was afflicting her had to be sendings from Mandralisca. But some part of him wanted not to believe that: wanted to cling to the wan hope that the poison-taster had not succeeded in making contact with his mother's mind.

Grasping at shadows, he said, "Forgive me for this, mother, but I see little difference here between this dream and any of mine in which I chase Thismet down a corridor of a thousand slamming doors. Our sleeping minds generate ridiculous absurdities to torture us. But when I awaken from the Thismet dream I know that she's long dead, and the dream evaporates like the empty thing it was; and when you awaken from your dream of being placed on trial you should know that you were never—"

"No." The single syllable cut through his words like a knife. "Your dream, I agree, is nothing more than the floating upward of the crumbling debris of the past, like something drifting on the tide. You awaken and it's gone, leaving only a troubling residue that remains just a little while. Mine is something quite other, Prestimion. It carries the force of reality. I awaken convinced of my own guilt and shame, utterly and unshakably convinced. And that feeling lingers on and on. It penetrates me like the venom of a serpent. I lie there sweating, shivering, *knowing* that I have failed the people of Majipoor, that in my term as Lady of the Isle I did nothing that was good, but only incalculable harm, to millions of people."

"You are convinced of this."

"Beyond all possibility of argument. It becomes more than a dream. It becomes a fact of my existence, as real to me as your father's name and face. A basic part of me that nothing could eradicate."

Prestimion's last doubts of the nature and source of his mother's dark dreams fell away from him. How could he resist the truth any longer? He had heard things much like this before, from Dekkeret, speaking of Teotas's dreams. *Guilt—shame—an overriding sense of unworthiness, of failure, of having betrayed those whom one had sworn to serve—*

She was watching him. Those eyes—those eyes—!

"You aren't saying anything, Prestimion. Do you understand in any way what I'm telling you?"

He nodded wearily. "Yes. Yes, I do. I understand very well. These are sendings that you're receiving, mother. A malevolent force is reaching into your mind from without and implanting things, more or less the way the Lady of the Isle implants dreams in those she serves. But the Lady brings only benevolent dreams that have no more than the force of suggestion. These dreams of yours carry far greater power. They have the force of reality. They are something that you have no choice but to believe is true."

The Lady Therissa seemed a little surprised. "So you know these things already, then!"

Again he nodded. "And I know who's sending them, too."

"As do I." She touched her fingertips to her forehead. "I still have the circlet I wore when I was Lady of the Isle. I used it to reach out toward the source of my dreams and identify it. It is Mandralisca, back at his evil work again."

"I know."

"He has killed Teotas, I think, by sending him dreams that were beyond his power to endure."

"I know that too," Prestimion said. "Dekkeret has worked it out, bit by bit, with the help of his friend Dinitak Barjazid. There is another Barjazid loose in the land, the brother of the one I killed at Stoienzar. He has allied himself with the poison-taster, who himself is in league with the kinsmen of Dantirya Sambail, and these hellish thought-control helmets are being made again. They have been used against Teotas, and against you, and also, I think, Varaile, and even, it may be, against my little daughter Tuanelys."

"But not, so far, against you."

"No. Nor do I expect that. I think he may be afraid to challenge me outright. To attack the Pontifex is to attack Majipoor itself: the people will not follow him there. No, mother, what he wants is to intimidate me by striking at those who are closest to me, I think, hoping that he can force me into making a deal of some kind with him and the people he serves. To grant them political control in Zimroel, perhaps. To restore to them the authority that I took away from the Procurator Dantirya Sambail."

"He will kill you, if he can," the Lady Therissa said.

Prestimion rejected that idea with a sweeping gesture of his hand. "That's something that I don't fear at all. I doubt that he would attempt it; I know that if he tried, he would not succeed." He left his seat and crouched at her side, resting one hand lightly over her forearm and staring up into her ravaged eyes. Tautly he said, "The one who will die, mother, is Mandralisca. You can be certain of that. I would slay him for what he did to Teotas, alone. But now that I know what he has done to you—"

"It's your plan to make war against him, then," she said, stating it, not asking.

"Yes."

"And raise an army and invade Zimroel and destroy this man with your own hand? I hear it in your voice. Is that what you mean to do, Prestimion?"

"Not I myself," Prestimion said quickly, for he could see where she was heading with this. The patterns of conflict crossing her features were obvious, her fierce loathing for Mandralisca and all he represented playing against her fears for her eldest son's life. "Oh, what I would give to be the one who cuts him down! I won't attempt to deceive you about that. But my days on the battlefield, I'm afraid, have been over for a very long time, mother. Dekkeret is my sword now."

6

It was the sixteenth day of Dekkeret's journey across the broad central plain of Alhanroel to the great city of the northwestern coast, Alaisor. He had arrived now at the city of Shabikant on the River Haggito, a muddy southward-flowing stream that came down from the Iyann. The one and only thing Dekkeret knew about Shabikant was that it was the place where the famous Trees of the Sun and the Moon grew.

"We should visit them while we have the chance," he told Fulkari. "We may never pass this way again."

As Prestimion had suggested, the Coronal and his party had taken the land route to Alaisor. It would have been far quicker to go by river-boat down Castle Mount via the Uivendak and its tributaries to the swift River Iyann, which would carry them onward to the shores of the Inner Sea. But there was no need for haste, since Prestimion would be making the long trip to the Isle before returning to Alhanroel, and he and Dekkeret were both agreed that there were advantages to be gained in having the new Coronal present himself formally at various major cities while on his way west, rather than hurrying by them by riverboat, with no more than a wave and a smile for the millions of people whom he would pass.

Therefore he had gone by way of the Great Western Highway to the grim mercantile center of Sisivondal in the midst of the dusty Cama-ganda drylands, a journey that was exceedingly ugly but spared them the troublesome crossing of the rugged Trikkala Mountains, and from Sisivondal across the great curving bosom of Majipoor through Skeil and

Kessilroge and Gannamunda and Hunzimar into the grassy Vale of Gloyn, where enormous herds of bizarre animals grazed placidly in huge savannas of copper-colored gattaga-grass, and onward beyond Gloyn, the halfway point between Castle Mount and Alaisor, in a gently north-northwesterly direction, stopping here and there to confer the honor of the new Coronal's presence on this provincial duke and that rural mayor. With not a word said to anyone along the way, of course, of the growing disturbance in Zimroel. That was no one's business except the Coronal's, thus far. Certainly these good people of west-central Alhanroel had no need to know about the minor unrest on the other continent.

Dinitak, by donning his helmet daily, was keeping Dekkeret apprised of what was going on over there. The five nephews of Dantirya Sambail had returned from their wanderings in the desert and set up a headquarters in the city of Ni-moya, something that they were not exactly forbidden to do, but provocative all the same. And it appeared that they had taken control of Ni-moya and the region immediately surrounding it, which, if the reports that Dinitak's mind-trollings had brought back were correct, was definitely a violation of Prestimion's twenty-year-old decree stripping Dantirya Sambail and his heirs forever of any and all political power in Zimroel.

Dekkeret did not feel that any of this required an immediate governmental response. He expected that he soon would have confirmation of Dinitak's reports arriving by way of more orthodox channels, along with greater detail of what actually was taking place, and he would wait until those reports had come. Then he and Prestimion together, when they met as planned a month or two from now at the coastal city of Stoien, could work out a fitting strategy for dealing with these troublesome Ni-moyans.

The royal party reached Shabikant a short while past noon, when the city, spreading before them for many miles to the north and south on the broad sandy plain that bordered the eastern bank of the Haggito, lay basking in the warmth of the bright mid-country sunlight.

Shabikant was a city of four or five million people, evidently something of a metropolis as the cities of this region went—a pretty place of graceful buildings of pink or blue stucco topped with ornate roofs of green tile. The mayor and a party of municipal officials came riding out to greet Dekkeret and his companions, and much bowing and starburst-making and speechifying took place before they finally were escorted into town.

The mayor—his title was hereditary and largely ceremonial, one of Dekkeret's aides whispered to him—was a rotund, red-faced, green-eyed little man named Kriskinnin Durch, who appeared generally over-whelmed at finding himself playing host to the Coronal Lord of Majipoor. Apparently Lord Dekkeret was the first Coronal to have visited Shabikant in several centuries. Kriskinnin Durch seemed unable to get over the fact that this great event was taking place during his own administration.

But he nevertheless wasted no opportunity in letting Dekkeret know that he himself was descended on his mother's side from one of the younger brothers of the Pontifex Ammirato—a not very significant monarch of four hundred years before, as Dekkeret recalled. "Then you are of far more distinguished lineage than I am," Dekkeret told him amiably, amused rather than annoyed by the man's bare-faced pretentiousness. "For I am descended from no one in particular at all."

Kriskinnin Durch seemed not to have the slightest idea of how to respond to such a bland statement of humble origins coming from the Coronal Lord of Majipoor. He chose, therefore, to pretend that Dekkeret had not uttered it.

"You will, of course, pay a call on the Trees of the Sun and the Moon while you are among us?" the mayor went on.

"That was my very intention," said Dekkeret.

Fulkari, speaking so that only he could hear, said, "They all seem to be descended from the brothers of Pontifexes on their mother's side, these backwoods mayors. And from beggars and thieves and counter-feiters on their father's; but it all averages out, doesn't it?"

"Hush," said Dekkeret, with a quick wink and a light squeeze of her hand.

By way of a royal hostelry he and Fulkari were provided with a pleas-ant pink-walled lodge right at the river's edge, which probably was usu-ally employed to house the mayors of nearby cities and other such regional functionaries when they came calling on Kriskinnin Durch. Dinitak and the rest of Dekkeret's staff were taken off to lesser lodgings nearby.

"I most sincerely hope you will find everything here to your liking, my lord," said the mayor obsequiously, and, backing away, bowed him-self out of their presence.

His chambers, Dekkeret saw, were large but lacking in grace of de-sign. They were furnished in the overstuffed style that had been popu-

lar nearly a century ago in the early years of Lord Prankipin's reign—
everything covered with heavy brocaded upholstery and resting on
squat, ungainly legs. A scattering of drab crude paintings that surely had
to be the work of local artists decorated the walls, most of them hanging
slightly askew. The whole place was almost exactly as he would have expected. Quaint, Dekkeret thought: very quaint.

The mayor had tactfully given Lord Dekkeret and the Lady Fulkari
separate suites, since no reports of any royal marriage had reached the
city of Shabikant and people tended to be quite fastidious about such
matters out in these agricultural provinces. But the two suites were, at
least, adjacent, and there was a connecting door, bolted closed, that was
not at all difficult to open. Dekkeret began to think the mayor might not
be quite as stupid as he had seemed on first encounter.

"What are these Trees of the Sun and the Moon?" Fulkari asked
him, when they were finished installing themselves in their rooms and
their various chamberlains and ladies-in-waiting had gone off to their
own quarters. Dekkeret had thrown the bolt and come into her suite,
where he found Fulkari lolling in a great tub of blue stone, lazily scrub-
bing her back with a huge brush whose long handle was of such a
strange zigzag design that it might just as easily have been some kind of
implement of witchcraft.

"As I understand it," he said, "they're a pair of fantastically ancient
trees that are supposed to have the power of oracular speech. Not that
anyone's heard them say anything for the past three thousand years or
so, I hasten to add. But a Coronal named Kolkalli came here somewhere back then while making a grand processional and went to see the
trees, and precisely at sunset the male tree spoke, and said—"

"These trees have sexes?"

"The Tree of the Sun is male and the Tree of the Moon is female. I
don't know how they can tell. Anyway, the Coronal came to the trees at
sunset and demanded that they predict his future, and at the moment
the sun sank below the horizon the male tree said thirteen words in a
language that the Coronal couldn't understand. Kolkalli became very
excited and asked the priests of the trees if they would translate it for
him, but they claimed that nobody in Shabikant was able to speak the
language of the trees any more. In fact they did understand it, but they
were afraid to say anything, because what the tree had uttered was a
prophecy of the Coronal's imminent death. Which happened three days
later, when he was stung on the finger by a poisonous gijimong and died

in about five minutes, which is essentially the only thing that is remembered about the Coronal Lord Kolkalli."

"You believe this?" Fulkari asked.

"That the Coronal was stung on the finger by a gijimong and died? It's in the history books. One of the shortest reigns in Majipoor's history."

"That the tree actually spoke, and it was a prophecy of his death."

"Verkausi tells the story in one of his poems. I remember studying it in school. I confess I don't quite see how a tree would be capable of speech, but who are we to quarrel about plausibility with the peerless Verkausi? I take a neutral position on the subject, myself."

"Well, if the trees *do* say anything tonight, Dekkeret, you mustn't let the locals slither out of translating the message." Fulkari brandished her fists in a pose of mock ferocity. " 'Translate or else,' you'll tell them! 'Translate or die! Your Coronal commands it!' "

"And if they tell me that the tree has just said that I've got three days to live? What do I do then?"

"I'd keep away from gijimongs, just for a starter," Fulkari replied. She extended one long, slender arm toward him. "Help me out of the tub, will you? It's got such a slippery bottom."

He took her hand and she leaped lithely over the rim of the tub and into the huge towel that he held open for her. Gently, lovingly, he rubbed her dry as she nestled against him. Then he tossed the towel aside.

For the fiftieth time that day Dekkeret was struck by the luminous beauty of her, the radiance of her hair, the sparkle of her eyes, the strength and vigor of her features, the elegant compromise that her body had made between athletic trimness and feminine voluptuousness. And she was such a splendid companion, besides: clever, alert, perceptive, lively.

It amazed him constantly how close they had been to a parting of the ways. He still could hear, all too often, echoes of words that had once been spoken: *Dekkeret, I don't want to be the consort of a Coronal,* she had said to him in that forest grove on Castle Mount. And he to Prestimion, in the Court of Thrones of the Labyrinth: *It's very clear that she's the wrong woman for me.* It was hard now to believe that they had ever said such things. But they had. They had. No matter, Dekkeret thought: time had passed and things were different now. They would marry as soon as this annoying business of Mandralisca was behind them.

His eyes encountered hers, and he saw the mischief glinting in them.

"But there's no time now," he said plaintively. "We have to get dressed. His excellence the mayor is awaiting us for lunch, and the tour of the city, and at sunset we go to see the celebrated talking trees."

"You see? You see? It's business all the time, for the Coronal and his consort!"

"Not *all* the time," Dekkeret said, speaking very softly, burying his face in the hollow of her shoulder. She was warm and fragrant from the bath. He ran his hands lightly down her long lean back, across her smooth rump, along her flanks. She trembled against him. But she was holding herself in check just as he was. "When today's speechifying is over," he said, "there'll be just the two of us here, and we'll have all night to ourselves. You know that, don't you?"

"Yes. Oh, yes, Dekkeret, I know! But first—duty calls!" She brushed her lips lightly against his to tell him that she had made her peace with that, that she understood that a king's pleasure must wait until a king's work was done.

Then she slipped from his grasp and held the door between their suites open for him, grinning, making little shooing gestures to send him off to his own place while she went about the task of dressing for the public events that lay ahead. He blew her a kiss and went through to get dressed himself: the royal robes in the green and gold colors emblematic of his high status, the ring, the pendant, all the little outward signs and symbols that marked him as king of the world.

She has changed, he thought. *She has grown into her role. We will be very happy together.*

But first, as Fulkari had said, duty called.

It was late in the afternoon before all the public formalities of the royal visit to Shabikant were behind them—the mayor's lunch at the town hall had turned out to be, of course, an interminable banquet attended by all the city's notables, with speech after speech of welcome and expressions of hope for a long and glorious reign—and Dekkeret and Fulkari at last, accompanied by Dinitak and several of Dekkeret's aides, were being conducted back down to the river to view Shabikant's greatest attraction, the Trees of the Sun and the Moon.

Mayor Kriskinnin Durch, almost beside himself with excitement, trotted along beside them. With him came half a dozen of the dignitaries who had been at the banquet, now wearing broad purple ribbons across their breasts that marked them, so the mayor explained, as officials of the priesthood of the trees. It was strictly an honorary distinction nowadays, he added: since the trees had been silent for thousands of years and the cult of their worship had fallen into disuse, the "priest-hood" had in fact become a social society for the leading men of Sham-bikant.

Fulkari, letting a little flash of wickedness go flickering across her face, claimed now to be having second thoughts about the visit. "Do you think this is so wise, Dekkeret? What if they decide to speak again, after all this time, and they tell you something you'd just as soon not have heard?"

"I think the language of the trees has probably been forgotten by now, don't you? But we can always opt not to hear the translation, if it hasn't been. And if it's a really bad prophecy the priests will surely pre-tend they can't understand what the tree is saying, just as they did for Kolkalli."

Twilight was not far off now. The sun, bronzy green at this hour, hung low over the Haggito, and in these latitudes gave the illusion of being oddly broadened and flattened in the final moment of its nightly descent through the western sky.

The trees were contained in a small oblong park at the river's edge. A palisade of black metal posts terminating in sharp spikes protected them. They stood side by side, two solitary figures outlined against the darkening sky in an otherwise empty field.

The mayor made a great show of unlocking the gate and ushering the guests from Castle Mount inside.

"The Tree of the Sun is on the left," he declared, in a tone throbbing with pride. "The Tree of the Moon is the one on the right."

The trees were myrobolans, Dekkeret realized, but they were by far the biggest ones he had ever seen, titans of their kind, and must surely be very ancient indeed. Very likely they had been strikingly impressive, too, back in Lord Kolkalli's time.

But it was easy to see that the two great trees were finally coming to the end of their days.

The vivid, distinctive patterns of alternating green-and-white stripes that marked the trunks of healthy myrobolans had faded and collapsed on these two into blurry formless blotches, and the tall thick trunks themselves had developed alarming curvatures, the Tree of the Sun leaning distressingly off to the south, the Tree of the Moon going the other way. Their many-branched crowns were nearly bare, with only a scattering of crescent-shaped gray leaves to cover them. Soil erosion at the two trees' bases had exposed their gnarled brown roots, though an attempt had been made to hide that by strewing the region around each tree with little banners and ribbons and heaps of talismans. The entire look of the place seemed sad, even pathetic, to Dekkeret.

He and Fulkari had been provided with talismans of their own to contribute to the pile. Precisely at the moment of sunset they were supposed to go forward and offer them to the trees, which might then respond—here the mayor winked broadly—with oracular statements. Or, he said, they might not.

The sun's lower rim was just touching the river, now. It began to sink slowly into it. Dekkeret waited, picturing in his mind the immense mass of the world as it rolled ponderously onward along its axis, carrying this district inexorably into darkness. Now the sun was half-gone. And now nothing but the copper glint of its upper curve remained. Dekkeret held his breath. All conversation among the townsmen had ceased. The air suddenly seemed strangely still. There was a certain drama about all this, he had to admit.

The mayor indicated with a nod that they should get ready to go forward in another moment.

Dekkeret glanced at Fulkari and they advanced solemnly to the trees, he to the female tree, she to the male one, and knelt and added their talismans to the mounds just as the last glimmer of the sun vanished in the west. Dekkeret bowed his head. The mayor had instructed him to speak to the trees in the privacy of his heart and ask them for guidance.

An intense silence ensued as the last light of day disappeared from the sky. No one in the group of townspeople standing behind them seemed even to be breathing.

And in that silence Dekkeret, in astonishment, thought that he did indeed hear something—a rusty, grinding sound, so faint that it scarcely crossed the threshold of his hearing, a sound that might have been rising from the ground out of the roots of the tree before which he knelt. Was it the huge old tree swaying in the first breeze of evening? Or had the oracle—how could it be possible?—actually spoken, offering the new Coronal a couple of groaning syllables of unintelligible wisdom?

He glanced again toward Fulkari. There was a strange look in her eyes, as if she had heard something too.

But then Kriskinnin Durch broke the spell with a cheerful, robust clapping of his hands. "Well done, my lord, well done! The trees have welcomed your gifts, and have, I hope, imparted their wisdom to you! What an honor for us this is, after all these years, a Coronal paying homage to our marvelous trees! What a wonderful honor!"

"You didn't really hear anything, did you?" asked Fulkari in a low voice, as she and Dekkeret moved away.

Had he? No. No. Of course not, he decided.

"The murmuring of the wind is what I heard," he said. "And maybe some shifting of the roots. But it's all very dramatic, isn't it? And spooky, even."

"Yes," said Fulkari. "Spooky."

7

"Sabers today?" Audhari asked, surprised, as he entered the gymnasium room where he and Keltryn held their twice-weekly fencing session. "You and I haven't ever dueled with sabers before."

"We will today," said Keltryn, in a voice tight and hard with anger.

She had arrived at the fencing-hall five minutes early to select her weapon and make herself familiar with its greater length and heft. Septach Melayn had thought she was too light-framed to work with the saber. Probably he was right about that. She had tried it a couple of times without much show of aptitude, and he had excused her from saber drills thereafter.

But she had no desire today for the elegant posing and prinking of rapier-work. Today she wanted the big weapon. She wanted to slash and bash and crash, to inflict damage and if necessary to be damaged herself. None of this had anything to do with Audhari. It was her boiling fury over Dinitak, mounting up and mounting up and mounting up until it overflowed within her, that drove her actions today.

Keltryn had lost track by now of how many weeks it was since Dinitak had gone off into the west-country with the Coronal and Fulkari. Four weeks, was it? Five? She could not say. It seemed like an eternity and a half. However long it was, it felt like a far longer span of time than her entire little romance with Dinitak had covered.

It all seemed like nothing more than a dream, now, those few strange weeks with Dinitak. Before he came along she had guarded her body as though it were a temple and she were its high priestess. Then—she was not even sure why; had it been real physical attraction, or the impatience of her own maturing body, or even something as trivial as wanting to step forward finally into the kind of existence that her sister had had so long?—she had opened herself to Dinitak, and permitted him to penetrate in more senses than one the sanctuary of her self, and he had led her into realms of pleasure and excitement far beyond anything she had imagined in her virginal fantasies.

But there had been more to it than sex, or so she had thought. For those few weeks she had ceased at last to think of herself as *I* and had begun to be a *we*.

And then—as casually as though she were a worn-out garment—he had discarded her. *Discarded.* No other word applied, so far as she was concerned. To go jaunting off into the west-country like that with Dekkeret and Fulkari, and to leave her behind because it was—what had Fulkari told her?—because it was "politically inappropriate" for him to be accompanied by an unmarried woman while he was traveling in the Coronal's entourage—

It was hard to believe that any man in the early throes of a passionate love affair would take such a position. Dinitak was famous for his bluntness, for his rugged honesty: he was surely capable of speaking up even to Lord Dekkeret, telling him, "I'm sorry, your lordship, but if Keltryn doesn't go, I don't go either."

But he hadn't said any such thing. She doubted that the Coronal would have been troubled in the slightest by her presence on the journey. It had been Dinitak's idea to leave her behind, Dinitak's, Dinitak's, Dinitak's. How could he do such a thing? Keltryn asked herself. And the ugly answer came too fast: *Because he's grown tired of me already. I must be too eager, too demanding, too—young. And this is his way of dumping me.*

"You've got it all wrong," Fulkari had said. "He's crazy about you, Keltryn. I assure you, he *hates* leaving you at the Castle like this. But he's just too prim to bring a young woman like you along with him on an official journey. He said it would be degrading to you, that it would make you seem like a concubine."

"A concubine!"

"You know he has some extremely old-fashioned ideas."

"Not so old-fashioned that he wouldn't sleep with me, Fulkari."

"You told me yourself that he seemed pretty hesitant even about that."

"Well—"

Keltryn had to admit that Fulkari was right on that score. She had practically had to throw herself at Dinitak, that day at the pool, before he was willing at last to accept what she was offering. And even then there had been that odd reaction of dismay and chagrin, afterward, when he realized that she had given him her virginity. He is just too complicated for me, Keltryn had decided. But that did not help her get over her fury at being excluded from the west-country trip, or at being separated for so many weeks from the man she loved while their romance was still in its full early heat.

In the days that followed her anger with him came and went. Sometimes she thought that she had ceased to care, that Dinitak had merely been a phase in her late adolescence that she would look back toward eventually with amusement and nostalgia. At such times she would feel entirely calm for hours at a stretch. But then she grew furious with him for having wrecked her life. She had given him more than her innocence, she told herself: she had given him her *love*. And he had thrown it mockingly back in her face.

This was one of the angry days, today. Keltryn had dreamed a vivid dream of him, of the two of them together; she had imagined that he was in her bed beside her; she had reached hungrily for him, only to find herself alone. And had awakened in a red haze of frustration and rage.

She would be fencing with Audhari this day. Sabers, she thought. Yes. Slash and bash and crash. Work the anger out of her system with some heavyweight swordplay.

The tall freckle-faced young man from Stoienzar seemed baffled and bemused by her desire to use the big weapon. Not only was she inexperienced with it, but his advantage of height and strength would be enormously more significant with sabers than it was with rapiers or batons, where technique and quick reaction time mattered as much as simple force. But she would not be gainsaid.

"On your guard!" she cried.

"Remember, Keltryn, the saber uses the cutting edge as well as the point. And you have to protect your arm against—"

She lowered her mask and let her eyes blaze at him. "Don't condescend to me, Audhari. On your guard, I said!"

It was an impossible match, though. The saber *was* a little too heavy for her slender arm. And she had only the sketchiest idea of the correct technique. She knew that the fencers had to keep farther apart than they did when using rapiers, but that meant it was impossible for her to reach him with a simple lunge. She had to resort to crude inelegant back-alley lateral swings that would surely have brought yelps of outrage from Septach Melayn had he been there to witness her performance.

It was satisfying, in its way. It did allow her to vent some of her wrath. But what she was doing was not fencing at all. It had no style, no manner, no form. She would have accomplished just as much by grabbing up a hatchet and hacking up some firewood. Audhari, perplexed by her frantic assaults, had to abandon his own well-developed technique and parry whatever way he could. Whenever he intercepted the attack of her blade with his own, the collision sent an agonizing shiver of pain through Keltryn's hand and arm. And finally he blocked one onslaught of hers so ringingly that her saber flew clattering to the floor.

She knelt to pick her saber up and remained kneeling for a moment more, struggling to catch her breath.

"What's going on here today?" Audhari asked. He tossed his fencing mask aside and went closer to her. "You seem all worked up over something. Is it anything I've done?"

"You? No—no, Audhari—"

"Then what is it? You've chosen a weapon that's obviously too heavy for you, and you're swinging it around like a battle-axe instead of trying to fence properly with me. The best saber men deploy it almost like a rapier, you know. They go for lightness and speed, not for brute power."

"I suppose I'll never be a good saber man, then," she said sullenly, accenting the *man*. She was maskless now too.

"That's hardly anything to be ashamed of, though. Look, Keltryn, let's forget this saber business and start over with something lighter, and—"

"No. Wait." She shut him up with an impatient wave of her hand. A new and strange thought was coming into her mind.

It's time to move on beyond Dinitak.

Dinitak had served his purpose in her life. Whatever had existed between them was over and done with, as he was going to find out whenever he returned from his trip to the west-country. She didn't need him any more. She would be a fool to go on pining as she had for a man who could abandon her so lightheartedly.

To Audhari she said, "Maybe we should just forget about fencing this morning. There are other things we could be doing."

Her tone was sly but not ambiguous. Audhari looked at her uncomprehendingly, blinking as though she had spoken in the tongue of some other world. Keltryn stared straight into his eyes and gave him a hot, intense smile that she was certain he could interpret in only one way. Now it seemed that understanding was dawning in him.

Her own boldness amazed her. But it was very pleasing to be doing this, and doing it all on her own initiative, without relying for once on Fulkari's advice. She was glad now that Fulkari was away from the Castle. The time had come, she knew, for her to learn to make her own way through the whirlpools of life.

"Come on, Audhari!" she cried. "Let's go upstairs!"

"Keltryn—"

Audhari appeared totally astounded. He was bright red from the collar of his fencing jacket to the roots of his hair. His lips moved, but no reply emerged.

"What's wrong?" she asked, finally. "You don't want to, is that it?"

He shook his head. "How weird you are this morning, Keltryn!"

"I'm not attractive, is that it? Do you think I'm ugly? Do you, Audhari? I wouldn't want to impose myself on a man who thinks I'm unattractive, you know."

All too obviously Audhari felt as though he would rather be in the depths of the Labyrinth right now than having this conversation. "You're one of the most beautiful girls I've ever seen, Keltryn."

"Then what's the problem?"

"The problem is that that's not enough. Whatever we did upstairs would be completely meaningless. You've never shown the slightest interest in me, *that* way, and I've known it and I've respected it. Now you change your mind just like that? That isn't right. It doesn't make sense. It feels like you just want to *use* me."

"And if I do, what of it? You can use me too. Would that be so terrible?"

"I'm not like that, Keltryn. And it wouldn't be any good. Any more than your trying to fence with a saber was."

Now it was her turn to look astounded. After all that she had heard while she was growing up about how men were nothing but mere monsters of lust, why was it her bad luck to keep running into ones who worried so much about morality and respectability and propriety? Why was it so difficult to find simple uncomplicated debauchery when she wanted some?

Audhari, still red-faced, went on: "Please, can we just drop this talk, all right? Please. If you want to fence, let's fence, and if not, not. But we've been such good friends for so long, and now—what you're doing now is so damned confusing, Keltryn! I beg you, stop it. Just stop it."

She glowered at him. This was the last thing she would have expected. "Oh, I'm confusing you, am I? Well, then. I humbly beg you to forgive me for that," she said frostily. "I'd never want to feel that I was guilty of having confused my dear sweet friend Audhari."

Putting her saber back in the weapons rack, she went from the room without another word.

She knew that she was being cruel, and that *she* was the confused one. It didn't matter. She hated him for having refused her in a moment of—

Need? Spite? She didn't know what it was. What she knew was that she understood a great deal less about men than she had thought a few months ago.

She was still simmering with rage half an hour later when she was crossing the Pinitor Court and caught sight of Polliex of Estotilaup, her former fencing-class partner, coming from the opposite direction. As he drew near he smiled at her in a mechanical, impersonal way, but showed no sign of wanting to stop to talk. Since her last and most emphatic refusal of his invitations to her to join him for a weekend of fun and frolic at the pleasure-city of High Morpin, he had maintained an attitude of the most rigorous properness in such sporadic contact as they had had. He was, after all, a duke's son, and knew how to behave once he had been turned down.

But Polliex also knew how to behave when an attractive young woman, even one that had treated him earlier with disdain, indicated at some later time that his attentions would not be unwelcome. Keltryn greeted him with a warmth that she doubted he would misinterpret, and he very smoothly responded without revealing the faintest trace of surprise when she began to speak of High Morpin, its power-tunnels and mirror-slides and juggernauts, and expressed regret that she had never found time to go there even once since coming to Castle Mount.

Polliex was remarkably good-looking and his courtly, polished manners were extremely pleasing in comparison with Audhari's awkward boyishness and Dinitak's stern rigorous virtue. Her three days and nights with him at High Morpin were filled with delight. But why, she wondered, was she holding herself back, as she found herself again and again doing, from full enjoyment of all that Polliex offered? And why did thoughts of Dinitak keep stealing into her mind, even now, even here, even when she was with someone else? She was finished with Dinitak. And yet— Oh, damn him! she thought. Damn him!

8

In Thilambaluc, a medium-sized city four hundred miles farther along the road to Alaisor, Dekkeret, remembering something that Prestimion had told him he had done in the first months of his own reign, went out at midday into the marketplace in the gray clothes of an ordinary wayfaring man to hear what might be heard. It is useful, Prestimion had said, for the Coronal sometimes to learn at first hand what people were saying in the marketplace. The Castle atop its Mount was too far up in the sky to provide a clear enough view of the real world.

Dinitak was the only one who went with him. They slipped away in a quiet moment of the morning, Dekkeret saying nothing about what he had in mind to anyone on his staff. As for Fulkari, she had been feeling slightly ill that day, and had retired to her room at their hostelry. He did not mention his journey to her either.

Although Prestimion had told him that he had gone in disguise on these excursions, even to the extent of wigs and false mustaches, Dekkeret saw no need for any such intricate subterfuges. Prestimion, because he was such a distinctive-looking man, easily identifiable by the curious contrast between his surprisingly unprepossessing stature and his overwhelmingly kingly, commanding presence, would have run some risk of being recognized even among people who had not yet had a chance to see his portrait. The look in his eyes alone marked him for what he was.

But Dekkeret believed he was less likely to be discovered out here so far from the Castle. The new coinage showing his features had not yet been released, and in any case who would be able to identify a Coronal from his stylized face on a coin? Nor were the portraits of the new Coronal that hung in every shop-window particularly realistic; Dekkeret barely recognized his own image in them himself. Wearing rough casual garb that he had borrowed from one of the grooms traveling with the royal party, and with a shapeless cloth cap slouching across his head, he would seem like nothing more than just another brawny itinerant laborer, a big simple man who had come to town looking for work as a road-mender or a logger or something else equally fit for a man of his size and strength. He'd not get a second glance. And no one would have any reason to recognize Dinitak Barjazid at all.

The marketplace in Thilambaluc was a double-lobed oval with a cobbled roadway running up the middle between the two sectors. Everything within was crowded together higgledy-piggledy, each booth jammed up against its neighbor. In the eastern half of the market were dozens of stalls devoted to vegetables and fruits, and the butchers' tables, fresh red meat piled everywhere and streams of blood running off. A zone given over to the sale of little sweet cakes and mild frothy beverages led to one where the tables were heaped with mounds of cheap clothing, and that was fronted by a row of rickety little cooking-stoves tended by the ubiquitous Liiman sausage-sellers.

Across the way, on the far side of the center roadway, the merchandise was of an even more varied sort: barrels and sacks of spices and dried meats; tanks of live fish; booths hung with simple glittery necklaces and bracelets; stacks of secondhand books and pamphlets, worn and frayed; mounds of wickerwork chairs and flimsy lacquered tables of the same sort, piled ten or twelve feet high; pots and pans and other kitchen implements of every kind; a corner where jugglers and other entertainers were performing; another where public scribes had their tables set out; another advertising the wares of sorcerers and wizards. Both the marketfolk and buyers were of a wide mixture of races other than human—a good many scaly Ghayrogs here, a sprinkling of ashen-hued Hjorts, the occasional towering Skandar or Su-Suheris moving through the throng.

Dekkeret could not remember the last time he had been in a public marketplace. The richly cluttered texture of this place fascinated him. It was so full, so busy. He vaguely remembered the one in Normork from his childhood as having been more spacious, the merchandise generally finer, the customers better dressed, but of course Normork was a city of

Castle Mount and this was a nondescript provincial town in the middle of nowhere.

"Well, shall we go in?" he said to Dinitak.

As he expected, nobody showed any sign of knowing who he was. He moved casually through the place, pausing at this stand to examine a cunningly arranged pyramid of smooth-skinned blue melons, at this one to sniff at some unfamiliar custardy-looking yellow fruit, at this to accept a sample pinch of savory smoked meat from its vendor. Where the crowds were particularly dense, they opened for him as crowds ordinarily will when a man of Dekkeret's height and mass is coming through, but without any sort of deference except to his superior bulk.

He listened wherever he went, hoping to pick up someone's opinions of the new Coronal, or some reference to having had unusually unpleasant dreams lately, or complaints about high taxation, or anything else at all that might guide him to a better understanding of daily life in the world over which he now ruled. But these people had not gone to the market for the sake of holding conversations. Aside from the constant interchanges between buyer and seller having to do with the price and quality of the merchandise, they said very little.

On the far side from where he and Dinitak had entered, where the various entertainers were performing, they saw fifteen or twenty people gathered around a gaunt, gray-bearded man in red-and-green robes who seemed to be a professional storyteller, judging by his clear, firm voice and the conspicuously placed begging-plate full of coins sitting on the ground beside him. "This man's servants," he was saying as Dekkeret and Dinitak approached, "would set out fine golden bowls filled to the brim with good wine, and at a signal from the great wizard the bowls would fly through the air, and offer themselves to all the passersby, and anyone who chose could drink of them at will. I saw also that the wizard was able to make statues walk, and could leap into the fire without being burned, and assume two faces at once, and sit in the air many minutes at a time with his legs folded beneath him without falling, and do many another thing that defied my understanding."

A stocky red-haired man with a tanned, seamed face stood just to Dekkeret's left, listening in slack-jawed awe. Dekkeret turned to him and asked, "Who is he speaking of, friend?"

"The master magus Gominik Halvor of the city of Triggoin, master. Has just come back from Triggoin himself, that one has, and is telling tales of the wondrous things he saw there."

"Ah," said Dekkeret. He knew that name, Gominik Halvor: from Triggoin indeed, he was, an adept of adepts among sorcerers, who had served as a magus at Prestimion's court at the Castle long ago, before Dekkeret's own time there. But to the best of Dekkeret's knowledge Gominik Halvor had been dead ten years or more. Well, Dekkeret thought, a good storyteller does not have to worry about such petty factual details, so long as he pleases his audience. And the steady clink of copper coins into the man's plate, even the occasional flashing glint of a silver piece, testified that he was doing just that.

"One day I stood in the marketplace of Triggoin, just as you are standing here with me," the storyteller went on, "and a sorcerer appeared, a blue-furred Skandar half the size of a mountain, and took a wooden ball with several holes in it, and long ropes of sturdy twine passing through the holes, and threw it up so high that it went out of sight altogether, while he stood holding the end of the rope. Then he beckoned to a boy of twelve years who was his assistant, and ordered him to climb the rope; and up the boy went, higher and higher until he too was gone from view.

"The Skandar then called out three times to the boy to return, but the boy did not reappear. So the Skandar took from his waistband a keen-edged knife of a size like this"—and the storyteller indicated with his hands a blade that was more like a sword—"and slashed fiercely through the air with it, once, twice, three times, four, five. On the fifth slash one of the boy's severed arms fell to the ground in front of him, and a moment later a leg, and then the other arm, and the other leg, and then, as we all gasped in amazement and horror, the head of the boy. The Skandar put the knife aside then and clapped his hands, and the boy's torso came plummeting down out of the sky: and as we watched, the severed limbs and head at once reattached themselves to the trunk, and the boy stood up and bowed! And we were so astounded by this that we rushed forward to press whatever coins we had upon this sorcerer, not just weights or crowns, but some of us contributed five-royal pieces, even, which was the least we could offer for such a remarkable performance."

"I think he may be giving us a subtle hint," said Dinitak. "But five royals would be too ostentatious, perhaps. Let's see if I have something smaller." He scooped a handful of coins from his purse, selected a bright one-royal coin, and tossed it into the bowl. There was a little round of applause from the other onlookers. Here in the provinces, even a single royal had substantial purchasing power.

"On another day," the storyteller continued, with a grateful look toward Dinitak, "I saw a demonstration of a related kind performed by the great magus Wiszmon Klemt, who produced a thick bronze chain of fifty yards in length and hurled it into the air as easily as you would toss your hat aloft. It remained standingly rigidly upright, as though fastened to something invisible overhead. Then animals were brought forward: a jakkabole, a morven, a kempile, a gleft, even a haigus. One by one they scrambled up the chain until they came to the very top, and there they immediately disappeared. When the last of the beasts had vanished, the magus snapped his fingers and the chain came tumbling down to land neatly coiled at his feet; but of the animals that had disappeared, nothing was seen again."

"This is very entertaining," said Dekkeret, "but not, I think, particularly useful. Shall we move on?"

"I suppose we should," Dinitak agreed.

As they started up the pathway that ran past the aisle of entertainers a plump, oily-skinned man in a soiled crimson robe detached himself from the crowd and stepped in front of them. Dekkeret saw that he had a little astrological amulet of the kind called a rohilla pinned to his breast, strands of blue gold wound around a lump of pink jade. Confalume, that superstitious man, had worn one of those constantly. Around this man's throat was an amulet of some other sort that Dekkeret could not name. A flat triangular ivory pendant inscribed with mysterious runes dangled below it. That he was a professional magus was a reasonable guess.

Which was swiftly confirmed. "Tell you your future, my master?" the man said, looking up at Dekkeret.

"Nay, I think not," Dekkeret replied, affecting a coarse east-country inflection. The last thing he wanted in this place was a magus, even one who, like this one, was most likely a charlatan, peering into his soul. "I have me no more than a few coppers to my name, and you'd want more than that of me, eh, master?"

"Perhaps your rich friend, then. I saw him throw that big coin in the pot."

"Nay, he is na' interested neither," said Dekkeret. And, to Dinitak: "Come along now, will ye?"

But the magus was not so easily put off. "The two of you for fifty weights! A mere half a crown, a third my usual price, because the fees have been so slow today. What do you say, my masters? Fifty weights, the two of you? A trifle. A pittance. And I will sketch for you a map of the road that lies ahead."

Again Dekkeret shook his head.

Dinitak, though, laughed and said, "Why not? Let's see what's in our stars, Dekkeret!" And before Dekkeret could protest further Dinitak pulled out his purse again, plucked five square copper coins, ten-weight pieces, from it, and pressed them into the sorcerer's hand. The magus, grinning triumphantly, clamped his hand around Dinitak's wrist, peered close into Dinitak's eyes, and began to murmur something intended to pass for a formula of divination.

Despite his misgivings Dekkeret found himself wondering what the man was going to tell them. Given his own skepticism toward all things magical and the general look of disreputability about this marketplace magus, he had no expectation at all of anything of value coming forth. But the degree of inaccuracy in the man's predictions might be amusing. If he saw Dinitak opening a shop in Alaisor and becoming a successful merchant, say. Or undertaking a journey to some fabulous place that he had always dreamed of seeing, like Castle Mount.

The baffling thing that happened next was not amusing in the slightest, though. Halfway through the mumbled recitation of the formula the grin disappeared, and the magus abruptly halted his chant and clapped a hand over his mouth as though he were about to be sick. His bulging eyes stared out at Dinitak in an expression of absolute shock and horror and fear. It was the way one might look at someone who has just revealed himself to be the carrier of a deadly plague.

"Here," the astrologer said. His voice was thick with dread. "Keep your fifty weights, my master! I am unable to perceive your horoscope. I have no choice but to return your money." From a pocket of his robe he drew Dinitak's five coins. Then, seizing Dinitak's wrist, the magus dumped the coins back into his palm and went scuttling hastily away, glancing back a couple of times in that same horrified way before losing himself in the crowd.

Dinitak's swarthy face was weirdly pale, and he was biting down hard on his lower lip. His eyes were wide with amazement. Dekkeret had never seen him as rattled as this. Dinitak looked stunned by the consultation's abrupt end. "I don't understand," he said. "Am I so frightening? What did he see?"

9

"Thastain, with someone who's here to meet with Count Mandralisca," Thastain announced to the cold-eyed Ghayrog guard who stood in front of the building that once had been the procuratorial palace.

The Ghayrog gave him only the most perfunctory of flickering glances. "Enter," he said automatically, and stepped aside.

After all this time Thastain still could not fully accept the fact that all he needed to do was speak his name and he would be admitted to the fabulous palace that once had been the home of the Procurator Dantirya Sambail. It was hard enough for him to believe that he was actually living in the city of Ni-moya at all. For a boy who had grown up in an unimportant little provincial town like Sennec, merely to *visit* Ni-moya was the ambition of a lifetime. "See Ni-moya and die," the proverb went, in the part of the country that he came from. To find himself right in the heart of that greatest of all cities, living just a few hundred yards from the palace and able to walk in and out of that extraordinary building unchallenged, was a stunning thing.

"Have you ever been in Ni-moya before?" he asked the stranger that he was escorting to the Count.

"This is my first time," the man said. He had an odd thick-tongued accent that Thastain was unable to place: *Zies eesz may vfeerst tiyme.* His documents listed his place of residence as Uulisaan. Thastain had no idea where that might be. Perhaps it was in some remote district on the southern coast, far down below Piliplok. Thastain knew that people from Piliplok spoke with a strange accent, and maybe those who lived even farther down the coast spoke even more strangely.

But there was very little about this visitor that Thastain did not find strange. In recent months a whole procession of curious characters had come here on business with Mandralisca. It was Thastain's responsibility to meet them at the hostelry where most such visitors were put, conduct them to the official headquarters of the Movement on Gambineran Way, check out their appointment documents there, and lead them into the palace for their meetings with the Count. He had grown accustomed to seeing all sorts of marginal types pass through, an odd assortment of individuals who all too plainly moved along the weirder, more dimly lit edges of society. Mandralisca seemed to have a great appetite for people of that sort. This one, though, was perhaps the most curious of them all.

He was very tall and thin, almost flimsy-looking, and dressed in a peculiar way, a coarse and heavy black overjacket thickly padded with down above a light tunic of faded green silk. The look in his eyes, somehow both arrogant and uneasy at the same time, was peculiar. The eyes themselves were peculiar too, almost yellowish where they ought to have been white, and an eerie purple at their centers. Peculiar also was his face, broad and pale with small features all jammed together in the middle. The way he held his shoulders, hunched up against his ears. The way he walked, as if he suspected that his head might be in imminent danger of coming loose at the neck. Even his name: Viitheysp Uuvitheysp Aavitheysp. What kind of name was that? Everything about this man was mystifying. But it was not Thastain's job to pass judgment on Mandralisca's visitors, only to show them to the Count's office.

"Is an excellent city, Ni-moya," Viitheysp Uuvitheysp Aavitheysp remarked, as Thastain led him down the inland side of the palace. They were passing through a gallery linking one wing and the next that had one long window of clear quartz, affording a stunning view of the metropolitan core that rose in level upon level up into the hills. "Much have I heard concerning it. Is one of best cities in world, I think."

Thastain nodded. "The best, they say. Nothing to rival it even on Castle Mount." He slipped easily into his tour-guide mode. Somehow that eased the tensions that this unsettling stranger had evoked in him. "—Have you had much of a chance to see the place yet? That's the Museum of Worlds, over on that hill up there. And the Gossamer Galleria, down there to the left. You can just barely make out the dome of the Grand Bazaar from here, with the beginning of the Crystal Boulevard beyond it."

He felt almost like a native, casually pointing out the great attractions like that to this visitor from afar. In truth Thastain was as much in awe of Ni-moya and its wonders now as when the Five Lords had moved their capital here from the Gornevon desert many months before. But in his heart he liked to pretend that he was a genuine child of the great city, quick-witted and worldly-wise and sophisticated.

When they came to the end of the quartz gallery Thastain turned left and headed out onto the covered walkway that would bring them to the riverfront side of the palace, which was Mandralisca's sector of the building. "We go this way," Thastain said, as the visitor started to stray off into the private quarters of the Lord Gaviral. Officially the procuratorial palace now was Gaviral's residence, but Mandralisca had taken half the southern wing, with the best river views, for his own uses. There had been a time when the Five Lords had treated Mandralisca more or less as they treated their servants, but that time was over now. It seemed to Thastain that these days Mandralisca gave the orders and the Five Lords did pretty much as he said.

Another guard waited at the end of the walkway: a Skandar, he was, none other than Thastain's old nemesis Sudvik Gorn, who had made such a nuisance out of himself long ago when they had gone up north to burn the keep of the Vorthinar lord. Thastain gave him the merest glance, now. The course of time had raised Thastain up to become a member of Count Mandralisca's inner circle of aides, and Sudvik Gorn was nothing but a hallway guard.

"Visitor for the Count," Thastain told the Skandar. And, to Viitheysp Uuvitheysp Aavitheysp, once again: "We go this way." He indicated a spiral ramp leading toward a dizzying series of elbow-bend staircases that went up and up and up.

At the beginning Thastain had feared he would never learn his way around inside the procuratorial palace. But, huge though it was, he had taken the measure of it by this time.

The first time he saw it from the river it had seemed as immense as he imagined the Coronal's castle to be, but he knew now that much of the palace's height came from the shining white pedestal that lifted it far above the riverfront level. The host of external galleries and staircases that one viewed from below gave the place the appearance of a formidable maze, but that was misleading. The building itself, a complex series of interlocking pavilions and balconies and porches, was certainly a vast one, but its interior plan was strikingly logical and Thastain had quickly mastered the routes that traversed its interior.

Mandralisca had taken for his office the magnificent chamber in which the Procurator Dantirya Sambail had lorded it in the days when he ruled with almost regal splendor over the continent of Zimroel. Dantirya Sambail had been dead more than twenty years now—longer than Thastain had been alive—but the presence of that larger-than-life man still seemed to linger in the enormous room. The splendor of its gleaming floor, a burnished slab of pink marble inlaid with crisscrossing swirling slashes of some dazzling jet-black stone, and the shining crescent arc of the great curving desk of crimson jade, and the brilliant white wall-hangings of thick rich steetmoy fur, all spoke eloquently of the Procurator's fabled taste for luxury.

The entire wall of the chamber on its riverfront side was a single great bubble of quartz of the finest quality, as clear as air itself. Through it one had a view of the great sweeping curve of the River Zimr, which at this point was so wide that one was just barely able to see all the way across to the green suburbs on the farther bank. A string of huge brightly painted riverboats laden with passengers and freight coursed serenely along the river's main channel. Directly below the window, a long row of low buildings with brilliantly tiled roofs and ornate mosaic ornaments on their walls lined the river quay for a considerable distance, glittering in the midday sun: humble customs-houses, they were, which Dantirya Sambail had had redecorated at a cost of many thousands of royals so that they would be more pleasing to his eye as he looked out on them from high overhead.

The Count Mandralisca was behind his desk when Thastain entered. The little helmet of bright metal mesh that he always kept close by him was at the Count's elbow. His other two constant companions were beside him: to his left, sorting through a pile of documents, the little bandy-legged aide-de-camp Jacomin Halefice, and to his right that shifty-eyed Suvraelinu, Khaymak Barjazid, he who designed and built Mandralisca's thought-helmets for him.

We three, Thastain told himself, are the only people in the world that Count Mandralisca trusts—as much as he trusts anyone at all.

"Well," Mandralisca said, with the false joviality that he often liked to affect. "It is Duke Thastain. And who have you brought me this time, my good duke?"

Back in the earliest weeks of Thastain's time in the service of Count Mandralisca, when he was nothing more than a green boy up from the provinces, the Count, in that darkly playful way of his that could sometimes seem so threatening, had arbitrarily bestowed an honorary title of nobility on him: Count of Sennec and Horvenar. And thereafter he would often address Thastain as "Count Thastain." It was a meaningless thing, just another example of Mandralisca's mocking, sardonic sense of humor. Thastain knew better than to be offended by it. That was simply Mandralisca's style, cold and often cruel, and always capricious. Thastain had quickly come to see that for the Count, coldness and cruelty and capriciousness were simply useful ways of sustaining his power and authority. There was no way he could make people love him, but engendering fear through unpredictability could be just about as effective.

Lately, though, Mandralisca had taken to calling Thastain "duke" instead. More of his capriciousness, Thastain wondered, or was it something else? Perhaps it could be a sign that he was advancing in Mandralisca's favor. Or maybe it was simply an indication that Mandralisca remembered only that once upon a time he had amused himself by giving the boy from Sennec a make-believe title, but had forgotten which title it was.

More likely the latter, Thastain decided: though he had reason to regard himself as one of Mandralisca's special favorites, he knew it was foolish to believe that he had any more real significance for the Count than his leather boots or the cutlery he used at dinner. Thastain understood quite well by now that he was here simply as something for Mandralisca to use. The only person whose existence held any sustained importance in Mandralisca's mind was Mandralisca himself.

"This is Viitheysp Uuvitheysp Aavitheysp," declared Thastain, stumbling over the difficult name, though he tried his best to prolong and roll the double letters as the visitor had done. "Of Uulisaan."

"Ah. From Uulisaan," Mandralisca repeated, savoring the word with real delight. He seemed to disappear into a mood of meditative contemplation for a moment or two. Then, to Thastain: —"Do you know where Uulisaan happens to be, dear duke?"

Thastain kept his face expressionless. This *duke* thing was beginning to annoy him now.

"Not at all, your excellence."

Mandralisca glanced toward Viitheysp Uuvitheysp Aavitheysp, who had remained just within the arching doorway, standing hunched up against the wall in that weird awkward stiff-bodied way of his. "It is in Piurifayne, is it not, my friend? The southwestern part of the province, over on the Gonghar side?"

"That is correct, milord Mandralisca," said Viitheysp Uuvitheysp Aavitheysp.

Piurifayne?

The word ran through Thastain's mind like a fiery sword. Piurifayne was the province of the Metamorphs, the Shapeshifters, the race that had ruled the planet before the first human settlers arrived. Piurifayne, yes. Nobody ever went there; but everyone knew about it, that wild primordial rain forest in central Zimroel, lying between the mountains of the interior and the swift River Steiche, where the Shapeshifters had been compelled to live for the past seven thousand years. Lord Stiamot had ordered them to be penned up in there after completing his conquest of them in the Shapeshifter War; and there they remained, mysterious and aloof, dwelling completely apart from the other races that had come to colonize the planet that once had been theirs, and generally feared by them.

How could this man be from Piurifayne? No one but Shapeshifters lived in Piurifayne. And Shapeshifters were forbidden by ancient law to leave it, although it was common knowledge that from time to time they did, disguised as humans or sometimes as Ghayrogs, to move surreptitiously on shadowy errands through the cities of the settled world.

So that could only mean—

"Now do you understand, my good duke?" said Mandralisca, giving Thastain his most icy smile. And, to Viitheysp Uuvitheysp Aavitheysp: "Perhaps it would be more comfortable for you to take another form, my friend—"

"If it would be safe to do so here—" said the Metamorph, with quick glances toward Thastain, toward Jacomin Halefice, toward Khaymak Barjazid.

"They are my colleagues," said Mandralisca grandly. "Have no fear." And with that assurance Viitheysp Uuvitheysp Aavitheysp at once began to undertake the shift out of human guise.

It was something that Thastain had never seen before. He had never even dreamed that he would. Like nearly everyone he knew, he looked upon the Shapeshifters with horror and a kind of dread: terrifying, archaic creatures, unfathomable, unknowable, lurking out there in their jungles full of poisonous resentment of the people who had displaced them from their world, plotting who knew what ultimate revenge for that displacement. The thought of actually being in the same room with one made his flesh creep.

But he watched in astonishment, unable to turn his eyes away, as the Metamorph writhed and shivered within his odd, ill-fitting clothing like a creature preparing to molt its skin, and the features of his curious face seemed to grow soft and blurry and indistinct—they were actually *flowing*—and his hunched-up shoulders commenced a weird dance of their own, jerking and twisting about as though trying to turn at right angles to his spine—

A few moments more and the transformation was finished. The man whom Thastain had brought to this room was gone, and in his place was a different being, frail-looking, elongated and angular, with sallow, faintly greenish skin and inward-sloping eyes that had no pupils and knife-sharp cheekbones and slitlike lips and a tiny, almost invisible nose.

A Metamorph. A Shapeshifter.

Thastain still had trouble believing it: a creature out of forbidden Piurifayne, standing no more than a dozen feet away from him. Here in the office of Count Mandralisca, by express invitation of the Count himself.

The Vorthinar lord, up there in the north, had been in league with Shapeshifters—Thastain had seen one up there himself, walking patrol in front of the keep, the first and only time before this that he had. But that was one of the reasons, so he thought, that the Five Lords had deemed it desirable to break the Vorthinar lord's power. One did not consort with Metamorphs. It was like allying oneself with demons. But now—Mandralisca himself—a Shapeshifter right here in the procuratorial palace—

Thastain looked toward Jacomin Halefice, and then toward Khaymak Barjazid. But they betrayed no signs of surprise or dismay. Either they had mastered the art of concealing such feelings in the presence of the Count, or they had already been aware of the identity of the mysterious visitor.

Mandralisca gathered the Barjazid helmet into his two cupped hands, the way one might gather up a little pile of treasured coins, and held it out in front of him. "This is our little weapon," he said to the Metamorph, "the device with which we will free our continent from the grip of our Alhanroel masters. Our experiments with it have been quite

fruitful so far." He nodded across at Khaymak Barjazid. "We are indebted to this man for making it available to us."

"And with this small device," said Viitheysp Uuvitheysp Aavitheysp,
"it is possible to reach into any mind in the world, you say?" The thick,
contorted accent was gone, now that the Metamorph had resumed his
own form. His voice had become silken-smooth. "And to wield power
over that mind?"

"So it would appear."

"The Coronal's mind? The Pontifex's?" The Metamorph paused.
"Or the Danipiur's, say?"

"It seemed to me altogether too dangerous, too provocative, to meddle with the minds of the Coronal or the Pontifex," Mandralisca replied
smoothly. "I assure you that I could do it if I chose; but I have not so
chosen. I will tell you, though, that I've successfully reached the minds
of certain members of the Pontifex's family: his brother, his mother, his
wife, his child. By way of letting him know our capabilities, so to speak.
—You understand that this is in the strictest confidence, to be shared
with no one other than the Danipiur herself. And as for the Danipiur—
no, no, of course, I would never attempt to tamper with the mind of the
great queen whose ambassador you are."

"But you could, if you wanted to?"

"Very likely I could. But to what purpose? It would only offend and
repel. The Piurivars are our friends. As you know, we regard you as allies in our great struggle."

Thastain was as thunderstruck by that calm statement as he had
been by the first revelation of the Shapeshifter's identity. *Allies?* Was that
what Mandralisca had in mind? Human and Metamorph, fighting side
by side against the forces of the Pontifex and the Coronal?

He must, Thastain thought. Why else was this creature here? And
why else would Mandralisca be speaking so respectfully of the
Shapeshifter queen, or so politely calling the Shapeshifters by their own
name for themselves?

"Would you like to see a little demonstration of our helmet?" Mandralisca asked pleasantly. He dangled the device in Thastain's direction.
"Here, Duke Thastain. Suppose you slip this over your head and show
our friend how it functions."

"Me?"

"Why not? You're a quick-witted lad. You'll pick up the trick of it in
no time whatever. Here. Here."

Thastain was aghast. He had never so much as touched the helmet. So far as he knew, no one but Mandralisca himself, and, he supposed, Khaymak Barjazid, was allowed to go near it. Using it required special training, and was said to be difficult and exhausting besides, and very risky for anyone inexperienced in its handling. He held up both his hands, palms facing outward, and said numbly, "I beg that you excuse me from this, your grace. I have no skill for such things."

But Mandralisca was insistent. Once more he extended the hand holding the helmet toward Thastain. There was a chilly determination in his eyes that Thastain had seen all too many times before, but never aimed at him. "Here, my little duke," Mandralisca said again. "*Here.*"

It would be suicide for him to put the helmet on. Was that what the Count was trying to achieve? Or was this merely one more of those little capricious games that he so very much enjoyed playing?

Thastain was still debating how to handle the situation when Khaymak Barjazid leaned toward Mandralisca and said, in a quiet, almost murmuring tone, "If I may interject something here, your grace, allow me to point out that it could be possible for a user unfamiliar with the helmet's functions to damage it if he uses it improperly."

That seemed to come as news to the Count. "Indeed, is that so? Well, then: we wouldn't want to do any harm to our helmet, would we?" He caressed the little device in that fondling, loving way he had with it. "Perhaps we'll skip the demonstration. I'm not in the mood for working with the helmet just now myself. Unless you, Barjazid—no, never mind. No demonstration." To the Metamorph he said, "I'll gratify your curiosity about our helmet another time. What I've asked you here to discuss today is the precise nature of the alliance I've proposed to the Danipiur."

"She is eager to hear your offer," said Viitheysp Uuvitheysp Aavitheysp.

Thastain listened in amazement verging on disbelief as Mandralisca swiftly set forth his plan for establishing the independence of the continent of Zimroel. He meant very shortly to issue a proclamation in the name of the Lord Gaviral, he said, dissolving the ancient bonds that linked Zimroel to the dominant eastern continent. At the same time a new constitution would be promulgated under which Zimroel would become a separate entity with Ni-moya as its capital and the heirs of the Procurator Dantirya Sambail as its monarchs. The Lord Gaviral would take the title of Pontifex of Zimroel, and one of his brothers, yet to be chosen, would be designated as Zimroel's Coronal. The continent of

Suvrael, Mandralisca added, would proclaim its own independence at the same time, and would institute a separate government for itself with Khaymak Barjazid as its first king.

It was, said Mandralisca, the Lord Gaviral's great hope that the new governments of Zimroel and Suvrael would be swiftly recognized by the leaders of Alhanroel, and that peaceful relationships among the three continents would continue as they had since time immemorial. But the Lord Gaviral was not so naive as to think that men like Prestimion and Lord Dekkeret would greet the secession with any such benign response. On the contrary, Mandralisca continued: it was much more probable that the Alhanroel government would launch a military invasion of Zimroel and attempt to restore its supremacy by force.

"That could never succeed," Viitheysp Uuvitheysp Aavitheysp said unhesitatingly. "The supply-line distances are too great. It would take every crown in the imperial treasury to cover the cost of sending an army here big enough to do the job."

"Precisely," said Mandralisca. "And even if they tried it anyway, that army would find itself confronting the angry opposition of the billions of patriotic citizens of Zimroel. Who are loyal to the family of the Procurator Dantirya Sambail and unalterably hostile to the exploitative rule of the Pontifex. The armies of Prestimion would have to battle every step of the way, from the moment of their landing on our coast onward."

"Ah," said the Metamorph reflectively. "So the traditional allegiance of the people of Zimroel to the Pontifical government will melt away overnight, then. You are certain of that, Count Mandralisca?"

"Completely."

"Perhaps you are correct." The Metamorph indicated by his tone that such things as the loyalties of the people of Zimroel were a matter of complete indifference to him. "But in what way, I must ask, does all this concern the Danipiur and her subjects?"

"In this way," replied Mandralisca. He leaned forward intently and pressed the tips of his fingers together. "What is the most likely place for an invading force from Alhanroel to land here? Piliplok, of course: the main port on our eastern coast. It's the gateway to all of Zimroel, as everyone is well aware. Therefore Prestimion and Dekkeret will expect us to fortify it against an attack. And for the same reason, they'll not choose to make their landfall at Piliplok at all."

"There is no other place for an army to come ashore," said the Metamorph.

"There is Gihorna."

An inflection that Thastain interpreted as surprise entered Viitheysp Uuvitheysp Aavitheysp's voice. "Gihorna? There are no first-class ports anywhere along the whole Gihorna coast."

"But there are some third-class ones," said Mandralisca. "Prestimion has never been known for doing things the easy way, or the expected way. I think they'll land at five or six places in Gihorna at once, and begin marching toward Ni-moya. They will have two possible routes. One lies straight up the coast, via Piliplok, and up the Zimr from there to the capital. But that will bring them into confrontation with the armies that they must know will be waiting there to defend against just such a Piliplok landing. The only other route, as you surely already see, is by way of the River Steiche and its surrounding valley. Which would bring them up against the borders of the province of Piurifayne."

Viitheysp Uuvitheysp Aavitheysp received that statement with the same show of indifference as before. The slitted eyes displayed a look of what could almost have been boredom.

"I ask you again, what is that to us?" said the Shapeshifter. "Not even Prestimion would dare cross into Piurifayne for the sake of making war against Ni-moya."

"Who knows what Prestimion would or would not do? But this I do know: that any incursion into the jungles of Piurifayne, a difficult proposition at best for any army no matter how well equipped, would be made fifty times harder if the Piurivars were to engage in a campaign of guerilla warfare to keep the imperial forces away from their villages. Indeed a line of Piurivar warriors positioned up and down the Steiche itself would quite probably be able to succeed in preventing the imperial army from entering Piurifayne at all. Eh, my friend? What do you think."

Viitheysp Uuvitheysp Aavitheysp responded with a silence so long and intense that Thastain, listening to the colloquy in mounting disbelief, felt his ears ringing with it. Was Mandralisca serious? Was the Count actually telling an ambassador from the Danipiur that he wanted Metamorphs to go into battle in the service of the Five Lords against the Alhanroel government? Thastain's mind was reeling. This was all like some very strange dream.

Then at last the Shapeshifter said calmly, "If Prestimion or Dekkeret were to send an army marching through our province, that would, of course, concern us greatly. But I tell you once more, I think that they would not do that. And for us to fortify our Steiche boundary for the sake of preventing them from coming across it would be an act of war against the imperial government that would have serious consequences for my people. Why should we risk it? What interest do we have in taking sides in a struggle between the Pontifex of Alhanroel and the Pontifex of Zimroel? They are equally detestable to us. Let them fight it out to their hearts' content. We will go on living our own lives in Piurifayne, which your Lord Stiamot kindly granted to us long ago as our little sanctuary."

"Piurifayne is in Zimroel, my friend. An independent government of Zimroel, grateful for Piurivar assistance in the war of liberation, might show its gratitude in interesting ways."

"Such as?"

"Full citizenship for your people? The right to move freely wherever you please, to hold property outside Piurifayne, to engage in any form of commerce? —An end to all forms of discrimination against your race, is what I'm offering. Complete equality throughout the continent. Does that interest you, Viitheysp Uuvitheysp Aavitheysp? Would it be worth putting troops along the Steiche for?"

"It would be if we could trust your promise, Count Mandralisca. But can we? Ah, can we, Count Mandralisca?"

"You will have my oath on it," said Mandralisca piously. "And as my good friends here will testify, my oath is my sacred bond. Is that not so, Jacomin? Khaymak? Duke Thastain, I call upon you to speak on my behalf. I am a man of honor. Is that not so, my friends?"

10

At Kesmakuran, a neat little city of perhaps half a million souls five hundred miles deeper into the west-country, with row upon row of low square-roofed houses built mainly of a handsome pinkish-gold stone, Dekkeret halted to perform an act of homage at the tomb of Dvorn, the first Pontifex. Visiting the tomb was Zeldor Luudwid's idea. "Dvorn is greatly venerated in these parts," the chamberlain said. "It might well be taken as sacrilege, or at the very least a serious insult, if the Coronal were to come this way and not lay a wreath on his tomb."

"The tomb of Dvorn," Dekkeret repeated in wonder. "Can it really be? I've always thought of Dvorn as a purely mythical character."

"*Someone* had to be the first Pontifex," Fulkari pointed out.

"I grant you that. He may even have been named Dvorn, I suppose. That still doesn't mean that anything we think we know about him has any foundation in reality, though. Not after thirteen thousand years. We're talking about someone who lived almost as long before Lord Stiamot's time as Stiamot is before ours."

But Zeldor Luudwid was a persuasive person in his quiet, self-effacing way, and Dekkeret knew better than to ignore his advice. As the prime carryover from Lord Prestimion's administration, he was better versed in the minutiae of the realm than anyone else in the new Coronal's entourage.

And, according to Zeldor Luudwid, the Pontifex Dvorn was worshipped practically as a god in this region, the alleged place of his birth. The cult of Dvorn had adherents for a thousand miles in all directions.

It was right here in Kesmakuran, so it was claimed, that Dvorn had launched his uprising against whatever chaotic pre-Pontifical government had existed in the earliest days of the occupation of Majipoor by human settlers; and here he had been buried after a distinguished reign of nearly a hundred years. Pilgrims came constantly to his tomb, said Zeldor Luudwid, and knelt before the sacred vessels in which some of his hair and even one of his teeth were preserved, and begged the great Pontifex to intercede with the Divine for the continued welfare and security of the citizens of Majipoor.

Dekkeret had heard nothing about any of that before. But it was impossible for any Coronal to make himself familiar with all the multitudinous cults that had sprung up in the world since Prankipin had first begun his policy of encouraging superstitions of every variety.

What Dekkeret did know were the legendary tales: how in a troubled time, five or six hundred years after the first human colonists had arrived on Majipoor, a provincial leader named Dvorn had assembled an army somewhere in the west-country and marched across province after province, preaching a gospel of world unity and stability and gaining the allegiance of all those who had wearied of the strife between one district and another, until he was the master of the entire continent of Alhanroel. He had given himself the title of Pontifex, using a word that had meant "bridge-builder" in one of the languages of Old Earth, and had chosen Barhold, a young army officer, to govern the world in association with him, with the title of Coronal Lord. It was Dvorn who had decreed that upon the death of each Pontifex the Coronal Lord would succeed to that title and would select a new Coronal to take his own place. Thus he saw to it that the monarchy would never become hereditary: each Pontifex would pick the best qualified member of his staff as his successor, ensuring that the world would remain in capable hands from generation to generation.

All of that was told in the third canto of the vast epic poem that was every schoolchild's bane, Aithin Furvain's *The Book of Changes*. But it was significant that Dvorn was merely a name even to Furvain. Nowhere in the third canto or anywhere else did the poet make the slightest attempt to depict him as a person. He provided no hint of what Dvorn might have looked like; he told no anecdotes that gave insight into Dvorn's character; Dvorn existed in the poem only in his function as founder of the government and primordial giver of laws.

So far as Dekkeret was concerned, Dvorn was entirely mythical, a traditional culture-hero, a symbolic figure that someone had invented to explain the origins of the Pontifical system. Dekkeret suspected that the medieval historians, feeling a need to attach a name to that otherwise unknown warrior who had helped to bring that system into being, and whose life and deeds and even identity had long since been lost in the mists of early history, had chosen to call him Dvorn.

As Fulkari had suggested, *someone* had to be the first Pontifex. Let him, then, be called Dvorn. It would never have occurred to Dekkeret that an actual tomb of Dvorn might exist in some remote part of west-central Alhanroel, complete with actual physical relics of the first Pontifex (several of his teeth, they said, a knucklebone or two, and also—after thirteen thousand years!—some of his hair), or that he was worshipped in a quasi-godlike fashion by the people of the area.

Yet here was the Coronal Lord Dekkeret in Kesmakuran, standing just outside the veritable tomb of the Pontifex Dvorn, making ready to present himself before the statue of the ancient monarch and humbly ask for Dvorn's blessing on his reign.

He felt incredibly foolish. Prestimion had never warned him that being Coronal might involve his traveling around the land kneeling before provincial idols and sacred oracular trees and all manner of other fantastic idiocies, begging for the mercy of inanimate things. He was annoyed with Zeldor Luudwid for having pushed him into this thing. But there was no backing out of it now: it was his duty as Coronal, he supposed, to participate in the beliefs and observances of his people whenever he chose to leave the tranquility of Castle Mount and come out here among them; and it did not matter how inane those beliefs and observances might be.

The tomb was a deep artificial cave that had been carved, no one seemed to know how long ago, into the side of a good-sized mountain of black basalt just outside town. A pair of odd wooden structures that looked very much like cages were affixed to the cave wall on either side of the entrance to the tomb, high off the ground and reachable only by a narrow ladder of wooden struts connected by ropes. Each cage contained a vertically mounted wooden wheel, much like the water-wheel that a miller might use.

Two young women wearing only loincloths were marching constantly upward on the paddles of these wheels, causing them to revolve without cease. Their slender naked bodies gleamed with perspiration, but they moved tirelessly, keeping a steady rhythmic pace, as though

they were mere parts of the machinery about them. Their faces showed
the fixed expressions of sleepwalkers; their eyes stared far off into other
worlds.

Two other women dressed just as skimpily stood below, near the
rope-ladders, looking up vigilantly at the pair toiling on the wheels.
Dekkeret had been told earlier that a corps of consecrated women,
numbering eight all told, labored here day and night to keep these
wheels eternally in motion. Each of the operators of the wheel walked
a shift that was many hours in length, never pausing for meals or even
a sip of water. The two at the ladders were the women of the next
team, waiting here ready to jump into service ahead of time in case
one of the women in the cages should tire and falter even for a
moment.

Dekkeret understood that it was a matter of the highest honor in
Kesmakuran to serve on the wheel. Every young woman of the city as-
pired to be one of those chosen for a one-year term inside the wooden
cages. The rite was, so he had learned, an ongoing prayer to the Pontifex
Dvorn, imploring him to maintain the continuing tranquility of the
commonwealth that he had created. Even the smallest interruption in
their unending climb, the most trivial alteration in the rhythm of their
steps, might jeopardize the survival of the world.

Dekkeret could not linger long to observe this remarkable performance, though. The time had come for him to enter the tomb. The six
Guardians of the Tomb—they did not call themselves priests—stood
flanking him, three to his right, three to his left. The Guardians were big
men, nearly as big as Dekkeret himself, who wore black robes with scarlet trim, the Pontifical colors. They were brothers, apparently, ranging
from fifty to sixty years in age, resembling one another so closely that
Dekkeret had trouble remembering which one was which. He was able
to tell the Chief Guardian from the others only because he was the one
holding the ornately woven wreath that Dekkeret was going to place before the statue of Dvorn.

He himself had donned his robes of office for the occasion, and he
was wearing the little golden circlet that was serving him in lieu of the
full version of the starburst crown on this journey. Fulkari and Dinitak
would not be accompanying him into the tomb; he gave them each a
glance as he made ready to enter, and was grateful to them both for
keeping their faces frozen in expressions of the highest seriousness. One
sly little wink from Fulkari, or a quick grimace of skepticism from Dini-

tak, would instantly destroy the high solemnity of bearing that Dekkeret was working so hard to sustain.

He entered the tomb by way of an imposing rectangular entrance-way some twenty feet high and at least thirty feet wide. A thick carpet of sweet-smelling red petals had been laid down underfoot. Dozens of glowfloats drifting overhead provided a gentle greenish light that illuminated the elaborate pictorial reliefs that had been cut into the walls from floor to ceiling. Scenes from Dvorn's life, Dekkeret guessed: depictions of the great monarch's military triumphs, of his coronation as Pontifex, of his raising of Barhold to the rank of Coronal. They seemed quite well done and Dekkeret wished he could get a closer look at them. But the six Guardians were marching in a steady lockstep alongside him, faces turned rigidly forward, and it seemed best to him to do the same, so that all he saw of the reliefs was what he could glimpse out of the corners of his eyes.

And then Dvorn himself in all his grandeur and royal magnificence rose before him, a colossal figure of mellow cream-colored marble set in a great niche at the back of the cave.

The seated image of the Pontifex was ten feet high, or even more, a noble statue with its left hand resting on its knee and the right hand raised and extended toward the mouth of the cave. The expression on Dvorn's carved face was one of great placidity and benevolence: not merely a regal face but a downright godlike one, the serene smiling features perfectly composed, calm, reassuring, all-consoling.

It was, thought Dekkeret, an utterly magnificent piece of sculpture. He was surprised that such a masterpiece was so little known beyond its own district.

This was the way one might portray the face of the Divine, he told himself—provided some artist had decided to regard the Divine as a human being rather than as the abstract and forever unknowable spirit of creation. But no one ever attempted to depict the Divine in such a literal guise. Was something like that what the unknown maker of this great work had had in mind—to show Dvorn as an actual deity? Certainly there was something almost sacrilegious about the godlike serenity with which the sculptor had endowed the face of the Pontifex Dvorn.

To the right and left of the immense statue were two smaller niches, set high on the wall of the cave, that contained large round mirror-bright bowls of polished agate. These, Dekkeret suspected, were the vessels in which the relics of the Pontifex Dvorn were kept, the hair and the teeth and the knucklebones and the rest. He did not propose to inquire about those things, though.

The Chief Guardian handed Dekkeret the wreath. It was fashioned of dried reeds of several colors and textures, braided together in a bewilderingly complex pattern that must have taken the weaver many hours to achieve, and bound every four inches or so by thin metal bands inscribed with lettering of an antique kind that was unintelligible to Dekkeret. He was supposed to place the wreath in a shallow pit that had been carved in the cave floor directly in front of the statue and set fire to it with a torch that the Chief Guardian would hand him. Then, while it smoldered, he was instructed to kneel, enter a state of contemplation, and place his soul in the care of the great founding Pontifex.

That would be an odd thing for him to do, a man who put no faith in supernatural things. But Prestimion's words of months ago, as the two of them stood together in the vastness of the Pontifical throne-chamber in the depths of the Labyrinth, came drifting back to him now:

To the fifteen billion people over whom we rule we are the embodiment of all that is sacred here. And so they put us up on these thrones and bow down to us, and who are we to say no to that, if it makes our job of running this immense planet any easier? Think of them, Dekkeret, whenever you find yourself performing some absurd ritual or clambering up onto some overdecorated seat. We are not provincial justices of the peace, you know. We are the essential mainsprings of the world.

So be it, Dekkeret thought. This was the task that faced the Coronal Lord of Majipoor today. He would not question it.

He laid the wreath in its pit, accepted the torch from the Chief Guardian, and touched the tip of the flame to the edge of the reeds.

Knelt, then. Bowed his head before the statue.

The Guardians stepped back, disappearing into the shadows behind him. Quickly Dekkeret lost all awareness of their presence. Even the endless click-clack of the turning prayer-wheels outside the cave, which he still had been noticing only moments before, faded from the screen of his perceptions.

He was alone with the Pontifex Dvorn.

Now what, though? Pray to Dvorn? How could he do that? Dvorn was a myth, a creature of fable, a vague figure out of the early cantos of *The Book of Changes.* Even in the privacy of his own thoughts Dekkeret was unable to bring himself to pray to a myth. He was not really accustomed to prayer at all.

He had faith in the Divine, yes. How could he not? He was his mother's son. But it was not a faith that ran very deep. Like everyone else—even Mandralisca, perhaps—he would make small requests of the Divine in casual conversation, and give thanks to the Divine for this or that favor granted. But all of that was just in the ordinary manner of speaking. To Dekkeret the Divine was the great creative force of the universe, a distant and incomprehensible power, hardly likely to pay attention to the trifling individual requests of any one creature of that universe. Neither the urgent prayers of the Coronal Lord of Majipoor nor the panicky cries of a frightened bilantoon pursued by a ravening haigus in the forests would stir the special mercy of the Divine, who had brought all creatures into being for purposes beyond the knowing of mortal beings, and had left them to make their own way throughout their lives, until the hour had come for them to be recalled to the Source.

But still—he felt that something was happening here—something strange—

The wreath was burning now, sending up flickering bluish-purple flames and twisting coils of dark smoke. A sweet fragrance that reminded Dekkeret of the aroma of the pale golden wine of Stoienzar filled his nostrils. He breathed deeply of it. It seemed the proper thing to do. And as it flooded down into his lungs a potent dizziness came over him.

He stared for an endless timeless time at the serene stone face that loomed there before him. Stared at that wondrous face, stared, stared, *stared*. And suddenly it seemed necessary for him to close his eyes.

And now it seemed to him that he heard a voice within his head, one that spoke not with words but with abstract patterns of sensation. Dekkeret could not have translated any of it into specific phrases; but he was certain that there was some sort of conceptual meaning there even so, and a definite sense of oracular power. Whoever, *what*ever, was speaking to his mind had recognized him as Dekkeret of Normork, Coronal Lord of Majipoor, who one day would be Pontifex in the direct line of succession from Dvorn.

And it was telling him that great labors lay before him, and at the end of those labors he was destined to bring about a transformation of the commonwealth, a change in the world nearly as great as the one that Dvorn himself had worked when he brought into being the system of Pontifical government. The nature of that change was not made clear. But it would be he himself, the voice seemed to indicate, he, Dekkeret of Normork, who would work that great transformation.

What was streaming into his mind had the force of true revelation. Its force was overwhelming. Dekkeret remained motionless for what might have been weeks or months or years, bowed down before the statue, letting it fill his soul.

After a time the power of it began to ebb. He no longer sensed any substance to what he felt. He was still in contact, somehow, with the statue, but what was emanating from it now had become nothing more than a far-off inchoate reverberation that went echoing off into the recesses of his mind, *boum, boum, boum,* a sound that was emphatic and powerful and somehow significant, but which carried with it no meaning that he could understand. It came less and less frequently and then not at all.

He opened his eyes.

The wreath was nearly burned, now. The slim metal rings that once had bound it lay scattered amidst a thin, acrid-smelling sprinkling of ash.

Boum, once again. And after a time, again, *boum.* And then no more. But Dekkeret remained where he was, kneeling before the statue of Dvorn, unable or perhaps just unwilling to rise just yet.

It was all very strange, he thought: coming in here feeling like an idiot for taking part in such mummery, and then, as the event unfolded, finding himself overcome by something very close to religious awe.

As his mind began to clear he found himself reflecting on what a weird journey this trip across the continent had been. The oracle trees of Shabikant that had spoken to him, perhaps, at the moment of sunset. The astrologer in the marketplace of Thilambaluc who had taken that single look into Dinitak's eyes and fled in horror. And now this. Mystery upon mystery upon mystery, a procession of puzzling omens and forebodings. He was out of his depth here. Suddenly Dekkeret longed to leave this place, to move onward to the coast and join up with Prestimion, good sturdy skeptical Prestimion, who would explain all this to him in rational terms. But still—still—he was held spellbound by what he had just experienced, that feeling of overwhelming awe, that eerie silent wordless voice tolling in his brain.

When he emerged from the cave it was obvious that Fulkari and Dinitak were able to tell at a glance that something unusual had happened to him in there. They came quickly to his side the way one goes to a man who seems to be about to topple to the ground. Dekkeret shook them away, insisting that he was all right. Fulkari, looking worried, asked him what had happened in the cave, but his only response was a shrug. It was not anything he wanted to talk about so soon, not with her, not with anyone. What was there to say? How could he explain something that he barely understood himself? And even that, he thought, was inaccurate. It had been, in fact, something that he had not understood at all.

11

"This very room," said Prestimion bleakly, looking out over the sea, "was our battle headquarters in the campaign against Dantirya Sambail. Dekkeret, Dinitak, Maundigand-Klimd and my mother and I right here, with the Barjazid helmet, while you two were out in the jungle, closing in on his camp. But we were still young then, eh? Now we are these many years older, and we must fight that war all over again, it seems. How my soul rebels against the thought! How I boil with anger at those mischievous monstrous men who refuse to let the world dwell in peace!"

From behind him came the flat, broad, Piliplok-accented voice of Gialaurys: "We destroyed the master, my lord, and we will destroy the lackeys as well."

"Yes. Yes. Of course we will. But what a filthy waste, fighting yet another war! How wearisome! How needless!" Then Prestimion managed a thin smile. —"And you really must stop calling me 'my lord,' Gialaurys. I know it's an old habit, but I remind you I am Coronal no longer. The title is 'your majesty,' if you must. Everyone else seems to have learned that by now. Or simply 'Prestimion' will do, between you and me."

"It is very hard for me to remember these courtly niceties," Gialaurys said in a sour growling tone. His wide meaty-jowled face, ever innocent of deception of any kind, showed his annoyance plainly. "My mind is not as keen as it once was, you know, Prestimion." And from another corner of the room came the sly chuckle of Septach Melayn.

It was a week, now, since the Pontifical party had made the ocean crossing from the Isle of Sleep to the Alhanroel mainland for Prestimion's intended rendezvous with Lord Dekkeret. The Coronal himself was still well up the coast, according to the latest word—somewhere a little way south of Alaisor, in the vicinity of Kikil or Kimoise—but was heading toward Stoien city as quickly as possible. Another day or two, perhaps, and he would be here.

The three of them had gathered this afternoon in one of the lesser chambers of the royal suite atop the Crystal Pavilion, which was the tallest building in Stoien city, rising high up above the heart of that lovely tropical port. A two-hundred-foot-long wall of continuous windows afforded spectacular views from every room, the city and all its startling multitude of pedestals and towers on one side, the immense glass-blue breast of the Gulf of Stoien on the other.

This was one of the gulfside rooms. For the past ten minutes Prestimion had stood by that great window, staring fiercely out to sea as though he could reach all the way to Zimroel and strike Mandralisca and his Five Lords dead with his glaring eyes alone. But of course Zimroel, unthinkably far off in the west, was beyond the range of even the most terrible of glances. He wondered how high this building would have to be in order to let him actually see that far. As high as Castle Mount, he suspected. Higher.

All he could see from here was water and more water, curving away into infinity. That distant point of brightness on the horizon—could it be, Prestimion wondered, the Isle of the Lady, from which he had so recently come? Probably not. Probably even the Isle was too far to glimpse from here.

Once again he found it a burden to contemplate the vast size of Majipoor. The mere thought of it was a weight on his spirit. What madness it was to pretend that a planet so huge could be governed by just a couple of men in fancy robes sitting on splendid thrones! The thing that held the world together was the consent of the governed, who by voluntary choice yielded themselves up to the authority of the Pontifex and the Coronal. And that consent seemed to be breaking down now, at least in Zimroel. It would, apparently, need to be restored by military force. And, Prestimion asked himself, just what sort of consent was that?

Prestimion's mood had been prevailingly dark for days, a darkness that rarely left him more than moments at a time. He could not tell how much of that he owed to the strain of so much recent travel, he who was finally being forced to admit that he was no longer young, and how much to the despair that he felt over the inevitability of a new war.

For there *would* be a war.

So he had told his mother weeks ago at the Isle of Sleep, and so he believed with every atom of his being. Mandralisca and his faction had to be eliminated, or the world would split asunder. The great final battle against the villainy that those people represented would be fought, if he had to lead the march on Ni-moya himself. But Prestimion hoped it would not come to that. *Dekkeret is my sword now,* is what he had told the Lady Therissa, and that was true enough. He himself longed for the peace of the Labyrinth. That thought astonished him even as it formed in his mind. But it was the truth, the Divine's own truth.

A hand touched his shoulder from behind, the lightest and quickest of touches. "Prestimion—?"

"What is it, Septach Melayn?"

"Is time, I would like to suggest, for you to stop staring at the sea and come away from that window. Is time for a little wine, perhaps. A game of dice, even?"

Prestimion grinned. So many times, over the years, had Septach Melayn's well-timed frivolity pulled him back from the brink of despondency!

"Dice! How fine that would be," he said: "The Pontifex of Majipoor and his High Spokesman down on their knees on the floor of the royal suite like boys, rolling for the triple eyes, or the hand and the forks! Would anyone believe it?"

"I remember a time," said Gialaurys, speaking as though to the empty air, "when Septach Melayn and I were playing tavern dice on the deck of the riverboat that was taking us up the Glayge from the Labyrinth after Korsibar had stolen the throne, and just as he rolled the double ten I looked up and there was the new star blazing in the sky, the blue-white one, so very bright, that for a time people called it Lord Kor-sibar's Star. And Duke Svor came out on deck—ah, he was a slippery one, that little Svor!—and saw the star, and said, 'That star is our salvation. It means the death of Korsibar and the rising of Prestimion.' Which was the Divine's own truth. That star is still shining brightly to this very time. I saw it just last night, high above, between Thorius and Xavial. Prestimion's star! The star of your ascendance, it is, and it still shines! Look you for it tonight, your majesty, and it will speak to you and lift your heart." Now he was facing directly toward the Pontifex. "I pray you, put all this gloom of yours aside, Prestimion. Your star is still there."

"You are very kind," said Prestimion gently.

He was more deeply touched than he could say. In the thirty years of his friendship with the massive, slow-moving, inarticulate Gialaurys he had never heard anything like such eloquence out of him.

But of course Septach Melayn had to puncture the moment. "Only a moment ago, Gialaurys, you told us your fine mind was losing its keen edge," the swordsman said. "And yet here you are recalling a game of dice we played half a lifetime ago, and accurately quoting to us the exact words Duke Svor spoke that evening. Is this not most inconsistent of you, dear Gialaurys?"

"I remember what is important to me, Septach Melayn," Gialaurys replied. "And so I recall things of half a lifetime ago more clearly than I do what I was served last night at dinner, or the color of the robe I wore." And he glared at Septach Melayn as though, after all these decades of having been on the receiving end of the quicker man's banter, he would gladly catch Septach Melayn up in his huge hands and snap his slender body in half. But it had ever been thus with those two.

Prestimion said, laughing now for the first time in much too long, "The wine is a good idea, Septach Melayn. But not, I think, the game of dice." He crossed the room to the sideboard, where a few wine-flasks sat, and after a moment's inner deliberation chose the creamy young golden wine of Stoien, that grew so old so fast it was never exported beyond the city of its manufacture. He poured out three bowls' full, and they sat quietly for a while, slowly drinking that thick, rich, strong wine.

"If there *is* to be a war," said Septach Melayn after a time, and there was an odd tension in his voice, "then I have a favor to ask of you, Prestimion."

"There will be a war. We have no alternative but to eradicate those creatures."

"Well, then, when the war begins," Septach Melayn went on, "I trust you will permit me to play a part in it."

"And me as well," said Gialaurys quickly.

Prestimion did not find these requests at all surprising.

Of course he had no intention of granting them; but it pleased him that the fires of valor still burned so strongly in these two. Did they not understand, he wondered, that their fighting days were over?

Gialaurys, like so many big-bodied men of enormous physical

strength, had never been famous for his suppleness or agility, though that had not mattered in his years as a warrior. But, as also tends to happen to many men of his build, he had thickened greatly with age, and he moved now in a terribly slow and careful way.

Septach Melayn, whip-thin and eternally limber, seemed as quick and lithe as he had been long ago, essentially unchanged by the years. But the network of fine lines around his penetrating blue eyes told a different story, and Prestimion suspected that that famous cascade of tumbling ringlets had more than a little white hair mixed now with the gold. It was hardly possible that he still could have the lightning-swift reflexes that had made him invincible in hand-to-hand combat.

Prestimion knew that the battlefield was no place for either of them these days, any more than it was for him.

Delicately he said, "The war, as I know you understand, will be Dekkeret's to fight, not mine or yours. But he'll be apprised of your offers. I know that he'll want to draw on your skill and experience."

Gialaurys chuckled heavily. "I can see us entering into Ni-moya now, sweeping all opposition aside. What a day that will be, when we go marching six abreast up Rodamaunt Promenade! And it will have been my great pleasure personally to lead the troops north from Piliplok. The invasion army *will* land in Piliplok, of course. —And you know, Prestimion, what we rough men from Piliplok think of those soft Ni-moyans and their eternal pursuit of pleasure. What joy it will be for us to knock down their flimsy gates and march into their pretty city!" He rose and walked about the room, making such effeminate mincing gestures that a roar of delighted laughter came from Septach Melayn. " 'Shall we go to the Gossamer Galleria today to buy a fine robe, my dear?' " said Gialaurys in a high-pitched strangled voice. " 'And then, I think, dinner at the Narabal Island. The breast of gammigammil with thognis sauce, how I *adore* it! The Pidruid oysters! Oh, my dear—!' "

Prestimion too was holding his sides. This sort of performance was nothing that he would ever have expected from the gruff Gialaurys.

Septach Melayn said in a more serious way, when the merriment had subsided a little, "What do you think, Prestimion? Will Dekkeret really choose to land in Piliplok, as Gialaurys says? I think there are some difficulties in that."

"There are difficulties in anything we do," said Prestimion, and his mood grew grim again as he contemplated the realities of the war he was so passionately determined to launch.

It was a fine brave thing to cry out for an end, at long last, to the iniquities of the Sambailids and their venomous chief minister. But he had no idea of the true depth of the Five Lords' support in Zimroel. Suppose it was already possible for Mandralisca to assemble an army of a million soldiers to defend the western continent against an attack by the Coronal? Or five million? How would Dekkeret raise an army big enough to meet such a force? How would the troops be transported to Zimroel? Would transporting that many men even be possible? And, if so, at what a cost? The armaments needed, the ships, the provisions—

And then, the invasion itself—the glint in Gialaurys's eyes as he spoke of rough men of Piliplok knocking down the flimsy gates of Nimoya brought no corresponding thrills of delight to Prestimion. Nimoya was one of the wonders of the world. Was it worth putting that incomparable city to the torch merely for the sake of maintaining the world's present system of laws and rulers?

He would not let himself waver from his belief that it was necessary and inevitable to go to war. Mandralisca was a blight upon the world, a blight that could only spread and spread and spread if it were left unchecked. He could not be tolerated; he could not be appeased; he must be destroyed.

But, Prestimion thought gloomily, would the people of future times ever forgive him for it? He had wanted his reign to be known as a golden age. He had bent every effort toward that goal. And yet, somehow, the years of his ascendance had been marked by catastrophe upon catastrophe—the Korsibar war, the plague of insanity that followed it, the rebellion of Dantirya Sambail—and now it seemed certain that the final achievement of his reign would be either the destruction of Nimoya or else the partition of what had been a peaceful world into a pair of mutually hostile independent kingdoms.

Both choices seemed equally hateful. But then Prestimion reminded himself of his brother Teotas, terror-stricken to the point of suicidal madness and scrambling about in a panicky haze atop some precarious parapet of the Castle. His little daughter Tuanelys, writhing in fear in her own bed. And how many other innocent people across the world, random victims of Mandralisca's malevolence?

No. The thing had to be done, no matter the cost. He forced himself to harden his soul around that thought.

As for Gialaurys and Septach Melayn, they were already caught up in the anticipation of the glorious military campaign that they hoped would cap their years. And were, as usual, disagreeing: Prestimion heard Septach Melayn, his eyes agleam, saying, "Is utterly idiotic, my dear friend, the whole idea of landing at Piliplok. Don't you think Mandralisca can figure out that that's where we'd have to come ashore? Piliplok's the easiest port in the world to defend. He'll have half a million armed men waiting for us at the harbor, and the river behind them blockaded by a thousand ships. No, sweet Gialaurys, we'll have to put our troops ashore well south of there. Gihorna's the place, say I. Gihorna!"

Gialaurys screwed his face into a mask of contempt. "Gihorna's a wasteland, a dismal swamp, uninhabitable, altogether abominable. The Shapeshifters themselves won't go near the place. Mandralisca won't even need to fortify it. Our men will sink into the mud and vanish as soon as they step out of their landing-craft."

"On the contrary, my dear Gialaurys. It's precisely *because* the Gihorna coast is so unappealing that Mandralisca is unlikely to think we'll land there. But we can, and will. And then—"

"—And then we march north for thousands of miles up the side of the continent to Piliplok, which according to you we should avoid doing because it is the easiest port in the world to defend and Mandralisca's army will be waiting for us there, or else we have to turn west right into the dark jungles of the Shapeshifter reservation and head for Ni-moya that way. Do you really want that, Septach Melayn? To send the whole army into the perils of unknown Piurifayne on its way north? What kind of insanity is that? I'd rather take my chances on a straightforward Piliplok landing and fight whatever battle we have to fight there. If we follow the jungle route the filthy Metamorphs will pounce on us and—"

"Stop it, both of you!" Prestimion said, in a tone of such vehement insistence that Septach Melayn and Gialaurys both turned toward him wide-eyed. "All this arguing is completely pointless. *Dekkeret* is the commanding general who will fight this war. Not you. Not me. These matters of strategy are for him to decide."

They continued to stare at him. They both looked shaken; and not only, Prestimion thought, on account of the harshness with which he had just spoken to them. It was his abdication of command, he suspected, that amazed them so. That was not at all like the Prestimion they had known all these years, to cut off this kind of debate by saying that such a matter of high policy was outside his jurisdiction. He was amazed at it himself.

But Dekkeret was Coronal now, not Prestimion; Dekkeret was the one who would have to prosecute this war; it was up to Dekkeret to devise the best way to go about it. Prestimion, as the senior monarch, could offer advice, and would. But it was Dekkeret to whom the ultimate responsibility for the war's success must fall, and the final word on strategy had to be his.

Prestimion told himself that he was content with that. The system of government to which he was dedicated, the age-old system that had worked so well since Dvorn the Pontifex had devised it, required it of him. So long as Dekkeret, his chosen successor as Coronal, conducted the war bravely and effectively, it was right and proper for Prestimion himself, as Pontifex, to retire to a secondary role in the conflict. And Prestimion had no doubt that Dekkeret would.

In a quieter tone he said, "A little more wine, gentlemen?"

Someone was knocking at the door, though. Septach Melayn went to open it.

It was the Lady Varaile, who had gone off for a time to be with the children. Tuanelys was still troubled by dreams; and Varaile herself looked careworn and weary, suddenly older than her years. Merely to see her in this condition was enough to inflame Prestimion's wrath all over again: he would kill Mandralisca with his own hands, if ever he had the chance.

She was holding a slip of paper. "There's been a message from Dekkeret," she said. "He's in Klai, less than a day's journey away. And hopes to be here tomorrow."

"Good," Prestimion said. "Excellent. Did he have anything else to say?"

"Only that he sends the Pontifex his love and respect, and looks forward to his reunion with him."

"As do I," said Prestimion warmly.

He realized, suddenly, how very tired he was of the responsibilities of great power, and how much he had come to depend on Dekkeret's youthful vigor and strength. It would be good to see him, yes. And especially good to discover how he, Dekkeret, planned to cope with this crisis. For that is not my task but his, thought Prestimion, and how glad I am of that!

A time will come when you'll be eager to be Pontifex, Confalume had told him once, in the old Pontifex's rooms in the Labyrinth just a few days before his death. Yes. And now it had. For the first time Prestimion understood to the depths of his spirit what the old man had been talking about that day.

12

*T*he last time Dekkeret had been in Stoien city had been in the second or third year of Prestimion's reign as Coronal, a time when he was merely an earnest young newcomer to the inner circles of Castle Mount without the faintest expectation of becoming Coronal himself. Stoien awakened old memories for him, and not all of them were fond ones.

The eerie, unforgettable beauty of the city, matchlessly situated along a hundred miles of lovely white beaches here on the rim of the Stoienzar Peninsula: that had remained fresh in his mind all these years. Nor had Stoien changed in any way. Its skies were still cloudless. Its curious buildings, rising from the peninsula's flat terrain on artificial platforms anywhere from ten feet in height to hundreds, still dazzled the eye as they had before; its lush vegetation, the omnipresent denseness of bushes with leaves brilliant with irregular bursts of indigo and topaz and sapphire, of cobalt and claret and vermilion, still set the soul ablaze with delight. Such damage as had been done by the fires that madmen had set during the chaos of the insanity plague had long since been repaired.

But it was in Stoien that Dekkeret had taken leave for the last time of his dear friend and mentor Akbalik of Samivole, Akbalik who had been his guide in his earliest years in Prestimion's service at the Castle. Akbalik whom Dekkeret had loved more than any other man, even Prestimion—Akbalik who in all probability would be Coronal now, if he had lived—it was here to Stoien that Akbalik had come, limping and in pain from the swamp-crab bite that he had suffered while hunting for the fugitive Dantirya Sambail in the steaming jungles east of the city, and which would kill him not long afterward. "The wound is nothing," Akbalik told Dekkeret when Dekkeret arrived in Stoien after a voyage to the Isle, to which he had gone bearing urgent messages for Lord Prestimion. "The wound will heal."

But perhaps Akbalik had already known that it would not, for he had also exacted from Dekkeret an oath promising that he would speak out against anything that Lord Prestimion might want to do that would put his life at risk, such as chasing after Dantirya Sambail into the same jungles where Akbalik had been bitten: "No matter how angry you make him, no matter what risks to your own career you run, you must keep him from doing anything so rash." Which Dekkeret had sworn, though inwardly he felt it should be Akbalik's task, not his, to say such things to the Coronal; and then Akbalik had set out eastward from Stoien across Alhanroel, escorting the Lady Varaile—pregnant then with the future Prince Taradath—back to Castle Mount. But he made it no farther than Sisivondal on the inland plateau before the poison in his wound killed him.

All that was long ago. Now the winds of fortune had made Dekkeret Coronal. Prince Akbalik of Samivole was remembered only by middle-aged folk. The only Prince Akbalik of whom most people were aware was Prestimion's second son, named in the other Akbalik's honor. But the sight of Stoien's strange and wondrous myriad of towers brought that first Akbalik, that calm, wise, gray-eyed man who had meant so much to Dekkeret, vividly back to life in his memory, and a great sadness came over him at the recollection.

To make it even worse, Prestimion and his family were settled in the very same lodgings they had had on that earlier occasion, the royal suite of the Crystal Pavilion, and they had put Dekkeret and his companions up there also. Nothing could have been better designed to force him to relive the final exhausting moments of the war against Dantirya Sambail, when Prestimion, making use of the Barjazid helmet, had struck against the Procurator from this very building, aided wherever possible by Dinitak and Maundigand-Klimd and the Lady Therissa and Dekkeret himself.

But there was no other choice, really. The Crystal Pavilion was Stoien's premier building, the only place in the city suitable to house a visiting monarch. —Or, in this case, a pair of monarchs: for here were Coronal and Pontifex both in Stoien at the same time, a thing that never had happened before, and that had, so Dekkeret learned before he had been in Stoien more than ten minutes, thrown the city administration into such a state of panicky confusion that they would need the rest of their lives to recover from it.

It was fairly late in the evening when Dekkeret and his party arrived. He was caught a little off balance by the discovery that Prestimion wanted to meet with him at once. Dekkeret had had a hectic journey down the coast from Alaisor—he had not anticipated that Prestimion would come so quickly from the Isle to the mainland—and he begged an hour's respite, or two, to rest and cleanse himself from the dust of the road before seeing the Pontifex.

Fulkari wondered why it was necessary to have such an immediate conference. "Is it really so urgent? Can't we be allowed some time for dinner first, and a night's sleep?"

"Perhaps there have been developments in Zimroel that I don't know about," Dekkeret said. "But I think not. This is simply his nature, love. Everything is urgent to Prestimion. He is the most impatient man alive."

She accepted that grudgingly, and when he had bathed he went upstairs to Prestimion's rooms. Septach Melayn and Gialaurys were there with him, which Dekkeret had not expected.

Nor did he expect the swiftness with which the Pontifex swept him toward the point of the meeting. Prestimion embraced him warmly, as a father might embrace a long-lost son, but almost at once they were deep into a discussion of the matter of Zimroel. Prestimion cared hardly at all to hear about Dekkeret's journey across the continent, his odd adventures in Shabikant and Thilambaluc and the other obscure stops along his westward route. Two or three brusque questions, followed by quick interruptions of Dekkeret's replies, and then they were talking of Mandralisca and the Five Lords, and how Prestimion believed the crisis in Zimroel must be resolved.

Which was, Dekkeret rapidly learned, by sending a great army across the sea—an army led in person by the Coronal Lord Dekkeret—to set things to rights there by force, if need be.

"At long last we must break this Mandralisca, and break him so that he can never recover from it," said Prestimion. As he uttered those words his features underwent an extraordinary transformation, his intense sea-green eyes now strangely aflame with a cold fury that Dekkeret had never seen in them before, his thin lips tightening into a taut grimace, his nostrils flaring with an astonishing vindictive rage. "Let there be no mistake about it: we have to destroy him, regardless of the cost, and all those who follow his banner as well. There is no hope of peace in the world so long as that man continues to breathe."

Prestimion's tone was an extraordinarily belligerent one, uncompromising, fierce. Dekkeret was taken aback by that, though he did his best to hide his surprise and dismay from the Pontifex. Surely Prestimion knew, better than any man alive, what it meant for there to be civil war on Majipoor. Yet here he was, trembling with barely contained wrath, instructing his Coronal to set all of Zimroel ablaze, if necessary, for the sake of ending the Sambailid rebellion!

Perhaps I am misunderstanding him, Dekkeret thought, hoping against all probability.

Perhaps he is not advocating actual warfare at all, but only a grand show of imperial pomp and force, under cover of which Mandralisca can be peacefully encircled and removed.

It was Dekkeret himself who had first suggested, some months earlier, that it might be necessary for him to go to Zimroel and make an end to such unrest as was brewing there. And Prestimion had agreed that that might be a good idea. But it was Dekkeret's impression that they had both been thinking of something along the lines of a grand processional: the Coronal making a formal state visit to the western continent, with all the pageantry that a visit of that sort entailed, and thereby reminding the people of Zimroel of the ancient covenant under which all regions of the world lived together in peace. During that visit Dekkeret would be able to determine the strength of Mandralisca's insurrection and, through the power and authority of his mere presence, take steps—*political* steps, *diplomatic* steps—to bring it to a halt.

But Prestimion had spoken just now of sending an army—a *great* army—to Zimroel to deal with Mandralisca.

There had never been any talk, so far as Dekkeret recalled, of his undertaking the Zimroel journey at the head of any sort of military force. When had Prestimion's thinking shifted from the use of peaceful means against the rebels to one of all-out war? Dekkeret wondered what had turned the Pontifex so suddenly into such a fire-breather. No one had greater reason to hate war than Prestimion, and yet—yet—that look in his eyes—the angry crackle of his voice—could there be any doubt of his meaning? *There must be war*, was the essence of what Prestimion was saying. *And you are the one who will wage it for us.* It sounded very much like an order: a direct command from the senior monarch.

Dekkeret wondered how he was going to cope with that.

Certainly Mandralisca had to be removed: no question of that. But was war really the only way? Suddenly Dekkeret found his mind aswirl with a torrent of roiling conflicts. War was as repugnant a concept to him as it was to any sensible being. It had never occurred to him that his reign might begin, as Prestimion's had, on the battlefield.

He glanced quickly about for guidance toward Septach Melayn, toward Gialaurys. But Gialaurys's jowly face was rigidly set, a bleak, stony mask of icy determination, and even the flippant and sportive Septach Melayn had a strange look of seriousness about him just now. They were both of them resolved on war, Dekkeret realized. Perhaps these two, Prestimion's oldest friends, were the very ones who had turned the Pontifex onto that course.

Cautiously Dekkeret said, hoping Prestimion would not notice the ambiguity of his phrasing, "I give you my pledge, your majesty, that I will do whatever must be done to restore the rule of law in Zimroel."

Prestimion nodded. He looked calmer now, his face less flushed than it had been a moment before, some of the tension gone from it. "I'm confident that you will, Dekkeret. And so far as a specific plan of action goes—?"

"As soon as possible, majesty." More ambiguity, but Prestimion did not appear to find that troublesome. "It would be unwise for me to rush toward decisions just now. Your brother's death deprived me of my High Counsellor, and I've had no opportunity to choose another. And therefore, your majesty—"

"You are being very formal with me today, Dekkeret."

"If I am, it is because we are discussing great matters of war and peace. You have been my friend for many years; but you are also my Pontifex, Prestimion. And"—he gestured toward Septach Melayn—"we are in the presence of your High Spokesman as well."

"Yes. Yes, of course. This is serious business, and calls for a serious tone. —By all means, Dekkeret, take a few days to think things over." Prestimion smiled for the first time in the course of the meeting. "Just so long as the path that you choose is one that will rid me of Mandralisca."

Fulkari must have seen at once, when Dekkeret returned to their rooms on the floor just below Prestimion's, what an effect his meeting with the

Pontifex had had on him. Quickly she drew a bowl of wine for him and waited without speaking while he drank it down.

Then she said, "There's trouble, isn't there?"

"Apparently so."

He could barely bring himself to speak. He felt a little dizzy from weariness, from hunger, from the strain of the strange, tense encounter.

"In Zimroel?"

"In Zimroel, yes."

Fulkari was staring at him oddly. He had never seen such a look of profound concern in those lovely gray eyes of hers. Dekkeret knew that he must be a terrible sight. His whole body felt clenched. A throbbing had begun behind his eyes. His jaw muscles were aching: too much insincere smiling, he supposed. He accepted a second bowl of wine from her and drank it nearly as swiftly as he had the first.

"Do you want to talk about it at all?" she asked gently, when some time had gone by in silence.

"No. I can't. I *can't*, Fulkari. These are high matters of state."

Dekkeret had moved to the window now, and stood with his back to her, looking out into the night. All the mysterious beauty of Stoien city lay spread out before him, the slender buildings on their lofty brick pedestals, the variations of high and low, the artificial hills rising in the distance, the dazzling abundance of tropical vegetation. Fulkari, somewhere on the other side of the room, said nothing. He knew that he had wounded her with the sharpness of his words. She was his life's companion, after all. She was not yet his wife, but she would be, whenever the pressures of this unexpected crisis relented long enough for a royal wedding to take place. And yet he had spoken to her as though she were some casual amusement of the evening, with whom it would be unthinkable to share the slightest detail of what had passed between the Pontifex and the Coronal. He realized that he was asking her to bear all the burdens of being the royal consort without making her privy to any of the daily challenges of his task.

He let a couple of moments go by.

Then he said, "All right. There's really no sense in hiding it from you. Prestimion is so upset about this Mandralisca affair—this *rebellion*—that he intends to put it down by force. He's talking about sending an army into Zimroel to crush it. Not even an ultimatum first, if I understood him correctly: just invade and attack."

"And you disagree, is that it?"

Dekkeret swung around to face her. "Of course I disagree! Who would lead that army, do you think? Who'd be in charge of putting troops down in Piliplok and heading up the river to Ni-moya? It isn't Prestimion who'll be doing that, Fulkari. It isn't Prestimion who'll stand in front of the gates of Ni-moya and demand that they be thrown open, and who will have to smash them down if they're not."

She was regarding him now in a steady, level way. Her voice was calm as she said, "Of course. Such things would be the Coronal's responsibility. I understand that."

"And do you think the people of Zimroel are going to greet an invading army with open arms, and love and kisses?"

"It would be an ugly business, I agree, Dekkeret. But what choice is there? I know a little of what Dinitak's been telling you—the helmet that this man Mandralisca uses, the things he does with it, the way he's stirred up those five ghastly brothers to proclaim the independence of Zimroel. What else can the Pontifex do, in the face of open rebellion, but send an army in to straighten things out? And if there are casualties—well, how can that be helped? The commonwealth must be preserved."

Now it was his turn to stare.

What he saw was a Fulkari that he had never fully seen before, the Lady Fulkari of Sipermit, a woman of high aristocratic pedigree, who traced her ancestry back through the generations to Lord Makhario. Of *course* she would see nothing wrong with putting down the Sambailid rebellion by the use of armed might. It came to him with the sudden force of revelation that after all these years of life at the Castle, even after having become Coronal himself, he was seeing for the first time, really seeing, the essential difference between the aristocrats of the Mount and a commoner like himself.

But he said nothing of that. He replied simply, "I don't want to make war on Zimroel. I don't want to kill innocent people, I don't want to burn towns and villages, I don't want to knock down the gates of Ni-moya."

"And Mandralisca?"

"Must be stopped. *Destroyed*, to use Prestimion's word. I have no quarrel with that. But I want to find some other way to bring it about, something short of waging total war against the people of Zimroel." Dekkeret looked toward the sideboard and the remaining wine, but decided against taking a third bowl. "I'm going to send for Dinitak. I need to talk with him."

"Now?" Fulkari asked, giving him a look of mock horror.

"He'll have valuable things to say. He's as close to a High Counsellor as anyone I have right now, Fulkari."

"You also have me. And I give you this bit of high counsel: it's two and a half hours now since we arrived in this place, or a little more, and we haven't managed to find time to have anything to eat yet. Food is a good thing when one is hungry. Food is important. Food is a pleasing concept."

"We'll invite him in to join us, then."

"No, Dekkeret! No."

"What's this? Do we have open defiance here?" he said, more amused by her audacity than annoyed.

Fulkari's eyes also were flickering with a gleam of amusement. "That might be the word for it. Outside this room you are my Coronal Lord, yes, but in here—here—oh, Dekkeret, don't be so foolish! You can't be Coronal your every waking moment. Even a Coronal needs some rest, and we've been traveling all day. You're too tired to think usefully about these things now, or to discuss them with Dinitak. I say let's have dinner sent in, at long last. And then let's go to bed." A different sort of gleam entered her eye now. "Sleep on all this. Pray for a useful dream. You can talk to Dinitak in the morning."

"But Prestimion is expecting—"

"Shush." Her hand covered his mouth. She pressed herself close against him, and despite himself he slipped his arms around her and let himself melt into her embrace. Her lips rose to meet his. His hands traveled down the length of her smooth, slender back.

Fulkari is right, he thought. Nothing requires me to be Coronal my every waking moment.

Dinitak can wait. Prestimion can wait. And Mandralisca can wait as well.

In the night, as Dekkeret slept, fragments of memory came floating up out of the deep well of his spirit and went dancing about in his mind, stray bits and pieces out of the recent past that seemed to be trying to assemble themselves into some coherent whole.

*   *   *

—He is in Shabikant, kneeling before the two oracular trees, the ancient Trees of the Sun and the Moon. And from those trees comes the faintest of sounds, a far-off rusty grinding sound, as though the trees after the silence of ages are trying to muster their powers once more and speak out to the newly crowned king and tell him something he must know.

—He is in Kesmakuran, at the tomb of Dvorn the first Pontifex, this time kneeling before the ancient monarch's great smiling statue, and the sweet hazy smoke of the herbs burning in the pit before him fills his lungs and invades his mind, and he closes his eyes and hears a voice within his head speaking in some strange wordless way, telling him, until it all dissolves into a meaningless *boum, boum, boum,* that he is destined to bring about great change, that he will work a transformation in the world nearly as great as that which was worked by Dvorn himself when he created the Pontificate.

—He is in the marketplace at Thilambaluc, he and Dinitak, and a tawdry marketplace astrologer is telling Dinitak's fortune for a price of fifty weights, but the fortune-telling has hardly begun when the man's eyes bulge with shock and alarm and he thrusts Dinitak's coins back into his hands, claiming that he is unable to offer a prediction of his future and will not take his money, and runs swiftly away. "I don't understand," Dinitak says. "Am I so frightening? What did he see?"

—He has been wandering the Castle alone in the first days of his reign, and he is standing outside the judgment-hall that Lord Prestimion built, and the Su-Suheris magus Maundigand-Klimd comes upon him and asks for a private audience, and tells him that he has had a mysterious revelation in which he saw the Powers of the Realm gathered before the Confalume Throne to perform some ritual of high importance, but a mysterious fourth Power was present in the Su-Suheris's vision along with the Pontifex and the Coronal and the Lady of the Isle. Dekkeret is perplexed by that, for how can there be a fourth Power of the Realm? And Maundigand-Klimd says, "I have one other detail to add, my lord." The aura of that unknown fourth, the Su-Suheris declares, carries the imprint of a member of the Barjazid family.

In Dekkeret's dreaming mind these fragments of memory drifted round and round and round again, until suddenly they were united into a single strand and the pattern came clear—the mysterious distant sound coming from the shifting roots of the oracular trees, the wordless words of the statue of the first Pontifex, the fear in the eyes of the marketplace astrologer, the revelation that had been visited upon Maundigand-Klimd—

Yes.

He sat upright, wide awake, as awake as he had ever been, heart pounding, sweat streaming from every pore.

"A fourth Power!" he cried. "A King of Dreams! Yes! Yes!"

Fulkari, lying beside him, stirred and opened her eyes. "Dekkeret?" she asked foggily. "What is it, Dekkeret? Is something wrong?"

"Up! Bathe yourself, dress, Fulkari! I need to speak with Dinitak immediately."

"But it's the middle of the night. You promised, Dekkeret—"

"I promised to sleep on it, and to pray for a useful dream. And so I have, and the dream has come. And brought me something that can't wait until morning." He was out of bed and searching for his robe. Fulkari was sitting up, now, blinking, rubbing her eyes, muttering to herself. He kissed her lightly on the tip of the nose and went out into the hall to find the steward of the night.

"Get me Dinitak Barjazid," Dekkeret called. "I want him right away!"

It seemed to take no time at all for Dinitak to arrive. He was fully dressed and entirely awake. Dekkeret wondered whether he had been to sleep at all. Dinitak was such an ascetic in so many ways: sleep must seem a waste of time to him.

"I would have summoned you right after I met with Prestimion," Dekkeret began, "but Fulkari was able to talk me into waiting until I had had a chance to rest a little while. It was just as well I did."

Quickly he sketched for Dinitak a summary of his conference with

Prestimion the night before. Dinitak seemed surprised at none of it, neither Prestimion's unconcealed hatred for Mandralisca nor the Pontifex's fierce desire to destroy the Sambailid rebellion by force of arms. It was, he said, exactly what one would expect of a man who had been tried by the Sambailid clan as the Pontifex Prestimion had been tried.

"I tell you bluntly, I detest the idea of going to war against Zimroel," Dekkeret said. "The Lady Taliesme surely will be opposed to it also. I think Prestimion secretly feels the same way."

"I suspect you may be right there. He has no love for war."

"But he's so troubled by the attacks on his own family that obliterating Mandralisca is his highest priority and he doesn't care how the job gets done. *Go to Zimroel, Dekkeret,* he said to me. *Take the biggest army you can. Set things to rights there. And destroy Mandralisca.* War is what he means, Dinitak. It's my hope that I can get him to soften his mind on this."

"You will have a struggle there, I think."

"I think so too. The Pontifex is not famous for his patience. He feels that his reign as Coronal was stained by the scheming of his enemies, and he believes, probably rightly, that this man Mandralisca has been behind most or perhaps all of the trouble. Now that trouble has burst out again, he wants to be rid of Mandralisca, once and for all. Well, who doesn't? But war, to me, is a last resort. And I'd be the one who would have to command the troops, after all, not Prestimion."

"That would not matter to him. You are the Coronal. The Pontifex decrees policy, and the Coronal carries out the decrees. It has always been thus."

Dekkeret shrugged. "Nevertheless, if I can avoid this war, I will, Dinitak. I'll go into Zimroel, yes. And I'll see to it that Mandralisca's days of troublemaking are brought to an end, just as Prestimion wants. It's what happens *after* Mandralisca's out of the picture that I want to discuss with you now."

The bedroom door opened and Fulkari emerged, dressed in a handsome green morning robe. She gave Dinitak an amiable smile, as if to say that she saw nothing wrong with Dekkeret's holding a policy conference at this hour of the night. Dekkeret threw her a grateful wink. Quietly she took a seat by the window. The first faint purplish streaks of dawn were visible in the east.

"Peacefully or otherwise," Dekkeret said, "the Mandralisca problem has been solved, let us assume. The uprising of the five Sambailids has been curbed, and they've been made to see that they had better not get such ideas again. Without Mandralisca to do their thinking for them, they probably won't. All right. The question that will remain, Dinitak, is this: what can we do to prevent future Mandraliscas from arising? He and his master Dantirya Sambail have given the world an entire generation of trouble. We can't let anything like that happen again. And so— an idea, a very strange idea, in the middle of the night—"

13

"You are a duke?" the Shapeshifter asked, as Thastain led him from Mandralisca's office. "Truly, a duke? You are so young to be a duke."

Thastain grinned. "It amuses him to call me that. Or count, sometimes: he calls me that too. I'm not a duke or a count of anything, though. My father was a farmer in a place called Sennec, west of here. He died and we couldn't pay the debts and we lost the farm, and I went into the service of the Five Lords."

"But he calls you a duke," said Viitheysp Uuvitheysp Aavitheysp. "You are a farmer's son, and he calls you a duke. It is only a joke, you say. A strange joke, is what I think. It seems almost to be a kind of mockery. I do not understand human jokes. But, then, why should I? Am I in any way human?"

"Only in your appearance right now," Thastain replied. "But of course that can change. —Come this way, sir. Down these steps, if you will."

I am having a polite conversation with a Metamorph, he thought, astounded. I just called him 'sir'. Life held no end of amazements, it seemed.

As his meeting with Mandralisca ended, the ambassador from the Danipiur—for that was what he was, Thastain realized, the ambassador from the Shapeshifter queen—had reverted to his assumed human form for the journey back to his lodgings. So now he was a peculiar-looking long-legged man once again, who walked as though he had learned how to walk only last week and spoke with a thick buzzing accent that was a struggle for Thastain to penetrate. It seemed to him that Viitheysp Uuvitheysp Aavistheyp was almost as strange in pseudo-human guise as when he was wearing his own form.

Like any farm boy of northern Zimroel, Thastain had been raised to fear and loathe the Shapeshifters. They were the dread alien beings of the Piurifayne jungles to the southeast, who seethed with hatred over the loss of their world to human invaders thirteen thousand years before, and would never rest until they had somehow recaptured control of it. Though Lord Stiamot had confined them to their rain-forest reservation, everyone knew that their form-changing abilities made it possible for them to slip out of Piurifayne at will and go secretly among humans, working every manner of mischief: poisoning wells, stealing mounts and blaves, kidnapping babies to be raised as slaves in their jungle villages. Or so Thastain had grown up believing.

He had never spoken to a Metamorph before, not knowingly. He had never so much as seen one at close range. And now—*Come this way, sir. Down these steps, if you will.* Wonder of wonders. *Come this way, sir.*

They emerged from the procuratorial palace into the clear, bright light of another perfect Ni-moyan day. The hostelry where Mandralisca kept his out-of-town visitors was a ten-minute walk away from the river—up the hill past the Movement headquarters and the apartment building where Thastain himself lived, turn left, enter an underground passageway that quickly turned into a broad stone staircase going up to the next level inland. And there was the hostelry, a great white tower, as most of the buildings of this sector of Ni-moya were, standing in a row of similar towers that formed a solid phalanx along the street known as Nissimorn Boulevard. Four of the Five Lords had mansions farther down Nissimorn Boulevard, where the apartment towers gave way to the private dwellings of the very wealthy. Everyone knew Nissimorn Boulevard. It was such a famous street that when he first saw it Thastain wondered if his feet would begin tingling as they came in contact with its pavement.

"The Count Mandralisca makes jokes of you," the Metamorph went on as they ascended the stone staircase, "but even so you are one of his most important people. Is that not so, that you are a close aide?"

"One of the closest. You saw the other two just now. Jacomin Halefice, Khaymak Barjazid, and I: we are his inner circle, the people he most trusts." It was the truth, more or less, Thastain thought. The Count was more at ease with Halefice and Barjazid and him than with anyone else. He had told them things that he had kept secret from everyone all his life, about his childhood, his father, his service with Dantirya Sambail. That had to signify a certain closeness.

But Viitheysp Uuvitheysp Aavitheysp said, startling Thastain with the accuracy of his perception, "You are the people he most trusts, yes, but how much does he trust you? Or anyone? And how much do you trust him?"

"I can't speak to any of that, sir."

"He is a difficult man, I think, your Count Mandralisca. Proud, suspicious, dangerous. He offers us an alliance. He makes us promises."

Thastain saw what was going on now. He maintained an uneasy silence.

The Shapeshifter said, "We have not done well by the promises of your people in the past. There were Pontifexes and Coronals who swore to make our lives better, to grant us this privilege and that one that had been taken from us by Lord Stiamot, to permit us to come forth freely from our lands. You see how we live now."

"Count Mandralisca is neither a Pontifex nor a Coronal. The thing that he seeks is to free the people of this continent from the rule of such kings as those. He means *all* the people of this continent, your people included."

"Perhaps so," the Shapeshifter said. "And he is an honorable man, would you say, your Count Mandralisca?"

Honorable?

That word was not, thought Thastain, the first one that would come to mind in describing Mandralisca. Cold-hearted, yes. Cruel, maybe. Frightening. Fierce. Determined. Ruthless. But honorable? Honorable? Thastain had known a few unquestionably honorable men in his Sennec days, good, strong, uncomplicated men, whose word was their bond. Liaprand Strume, for one, the storekeeper, who would always allow more credit to someone in trouble. Safiar Syamilak, his father's bailiff, the devoted guardian of their lands. And the big red-bearded man with the farm just upriver from theirs, the one who had cracked his back lifting the wagon that had fallen on that little boy—Gheivir Maglisk, that was his name. Three honorable men, no doubt of that. It was hard to see what Count Mandralisca had in common with those three.

On the other hand it was not his business to be speaking harshly of Count Mandralisca to this Metamorph, or to anyone else. It was Mandralisca whom he served, not the Metamorphs. If this creature wanted to find out how trustworthy Mandralisca might or might not be, he would have to do it on his own.

"The Count is an extraordinary man," Thastain replied finally. No lie, that. "When this land of ours is freed at last from the oppression of the Pontifexes, you'll see how well Count Mandralisca keeps his promises." Which was also the truth, for what it was worth. — "Look there, sir," Thastain said, desperately searching for some distraction. "How the early-afternoon light strikes the Crystal Boulevard."

"Is so very beautiful, yes," said Viitheysp Uuvitheysp Aavitheysp thickly, shading his strange eyes against the brilliant stream of radiance that batteries of revolving reflectors summoned from the Crystal Boulevard's shining paving-stones. "Is the greatest of cities, your Ni-moya. I am thankful to your Count for permitting me to come here. Is my hope someday to bring my clansfolk here to see it as well, when your Count has won his war against the Pontifex and the Coronal. For such his promise is, that we will be allowed to come."

"Such his promise is, yes," Thastain agreed.

Jacomin Halefice was in the Movement headquarters building when Thastain returned to it after delivering the Shapeshifter to his hostelry. Thastain was glad to see him. Lately a friendship of sorts had come into being between Thastain and the aide-de-camp, based, apparently, on Halefice's fears that Khaymak Barjazid was supplanting him in Mandralisca's affections. Halefice, Thastain knew, went a long way back with Mandralisca — back to the days when the two of them had been in the service of Dantirya Sambail. They had fought together against the army of Prestimion in the Procurator's rebellion.

But it was Barjazid, whom Mandralisca had known only a short while, who controlled the all-important helmets. Often, nowadays, the Count seemed to favor the little man from Suvrael over Halefice; and so, evidently, Halefice had decided to cultivate the friendship of the young and swiftly rising Thastain, forming an unstated alliance against a further increase in Khaymak Barjazid's influence with Mandralisca.

Thastain, young as he was, was clever enough to know that Halefice was being foolish. There was no need for anyone to worry about the place he held in Mandralisca's "affections." Mandralisca *had* no affections, only schemes, desires, goals; he kept people about him who would help him in the fulfillment of those things, saw them entirely as instruments toward his intended purposes, discarded them if they were no longer useful. You were deluding yourself if you imagined that you were any kind of friend to Mandralisca, or he to you.

Even so, Thastain welcomed Halefice's overtures. It was a nerve-wracking business, working for Count Mandralisca. You never knew when you would make some critical mistake, or even a minor one, and he would turn on you with all his terrible ferocity. Thastain had not really anticipated being thrust into such proximity with the terrifying Count when he had chosen to enter the service of the Five Lords. Jacomin Halefice softened that proximity for him. The aide-de-camp was a genial, easy-natured man, whose company was a pleasant relief after an hour or two with the Count. And perhaps Jacomin Halefice might even be able to protect him against Mandralisca's wrath should he someday become its target. Sooner or later, after all, everyone did.

"Took the Shapeshifter home, did you?" Halefice asked. "That was a surprise, eh, seeing the Count invite one of those in for a conference! But he'll ally himself with anyone and anything, will our Count, if he thinks it'll serve his needs."

"And will it serve his needs, do you think, to bring in the Shapeshifters in the struggle against Alhanroel? How can you trust such creatures?"

"They are a bunch of slippery serpents, yes," Halefice said, with a grin and a nod. "I love them no more than you do, boy. But I see why Mandralisca would attempt to make common cause with them, just the same. They have much more reason to hate the Pontificate than he does, you know. And the enemy of your enemy, remember, is your friend. Mandralisca believes that when the time comes, the Piurifayne folk will do everything they can to make life difficult for Prestimion and Dekkeret."

"So we have Metamorphs as our friends, now!" Thastain shuddered. "Stranger and stranger every day. —The Metamorph doesn't trust the Count very much, by the way. Doesn't entirely think he's going to keep his promises about granting them equality once the war is won."

"He told you that, did he? Very confiding of him. I wouldn't pass that word along to Mandralisca, though, if I were you."

"Why not?"

"What good will it do? If Mandralisca's planning to doublecross the Shapeshifters when he no longer has any use for them, he'll do it regardless of what they might suspect. He doesn't expect anyone to trust him anyway, does Mandralisca. And if you tell him that the Shapeshifter's been pouring things such as you've just told me into *your* ears, the Count'll start worrying about how chummy you're getting with his new Metamorph friends. Keep it to yourself, is what I say. Don't even tell me. You *haven't* told me. Understood?"

"Understood," Thastain said.

"What about going out on the Promenade for some sausages and beer, now?" Halefice suggested.

Thastain welcomed the return to the bright warm sunlight. His head was spinning. He had not been expecting any sort of conversational intimacy with that Shapeshifter, and the fact that Viitheysp Uuvitheysp Aavitheysp had appeared to want to use him as a confidant was disturbing and unsettling. If the Metamorphs mistrusted Mandralisca's promises, let them take that up with Mandralisca himself, he thought, not whisper it in the ear of his youngest and least surefooted aide.

And, though he had not found his brief moments of contact with the Shapeshifter as horrifying and repugnant as he had expected—had, indeed, begun in that brief conversation to look upon the Shapeshifters as actual people with actual grievances, rather than dread monsters—he still resented the fact that Mandralisca had thrust him so blithely into that contact. It had not been right to ask that of him. His old conditioning was still powerful. He did not crave the companionship of Metamorphs. He was not at all sure that he cared to be in the service of a man who thought it would be desirable to form an alliance with them.

Thastain was, in fact, getting weary of Mandralisca and his icy-souled ways. Mandralisca treated him reasonably well, even seemed to find his company somewhat amusing, but he knew how little that really meant. Even the Metamorph had been able to see the contempt behind the Count's use of the mock title of "duke" for him.

"Do you notice," Jacomin Halefice said, as they stood by the riverfront walk eating their sausages, "how tense the Count has become these days? Not that he was ever a man of easy spirit. But the slightest provocation now is enough to set him twanging like a tightly strung harp-string."

"Indeed," said Thastain noncommittally. He had learned long ago the great value of listening and nodding and saying very little of his own when Count Mandralisca was the subject of the discussion.

"Khaymak thinks he is overusing the helmet," Halefice went on. "Night after night he roves the world with it, entering people's minds and doing what he does to them. Barjazid says that the helmet is a wearying thing to use, when one uses it as much as that. And who would know better?"

"Who, indeed," said Thastain.

"But I think more than the helmet is involved. This is no trifling thing, proposing to make war against the Coronal. I think the Count sometimes fears he may have overreached himself. He must do all the planning himself, you know. The Five Lords are worthless creatures. And now, this business of enlisting the Metamorphs in our cause—it is always dangerous, dealing with *them*, of course. You must watch your back at every moment. The Count knows that. And, I think, the Danipiur's ambassador knows he must look to the Count in the same fashion. A wondrous pair, they are! —Another round of sausages, eh, Thastain?"

"What a good idea," Thastain said.

"Of course," said Halefice, "the important question is not whether the Count intends to doublecross the Shapeshifters, but whether they will doublecross *us*. If the Count has not convinced the Shapeshifter that his promises are sincere, how likely are they to help our cause, when the day of action comes? Suppose they decide that his talk of civil equality is no more to be believed than anything else the Unchanging Ones have said over the years, and abandon us to fight our own battles among ourselves."

"Unchanging Ones?"

"Their term for us. The Count may be making a grievous error if he places overmuch reliance on the goodwill of his new Metamorph friends. —But of course we are not having this discussion, Thastain. We are simply standing here enjoying our sausages."

"Indeed," said Thastain.

And thought: So Halefice also thinks they mistrust each other, do Mandralisca and Viitheysp Uuvitheysp Aavitheysp? Surely he is right about that. They are of the same kind, in a sense: slippery treacherous serpents, just as Halefice says. Well, they deserve each other.

But do I really deserve either one of them?

14

"*A* breakfast meeting is what he wants," Prestimion said. "A discussion of the highest priority, he says, just the two of us, Pontifex and Coronal together. Not Septach Melayn, not Gialaurys, not even you, Varaile. And only last evening he was asking for more time to prepare his invasion plan, because he's operating without a High Counsellor. What could have come over him in the night, do you think?"

Varaile smiled. "He knows you very well, Prestimion. How little you enjoy any sort of delay."

"I don't think that's it. *I* may be an impatient, impulsive man, but Dekkeret certainly isn't. And this time I wasn't rushing him, for once. I agreed yesterday that it would be all right for him to take three or four days to think things over. Instead he's coming back at me the very next morning. There has to be a reason for that. And I'm not sure I'm going to like it when I discover what it is."

The meeting took place in a private dining room adjacent to the Pontifex's quarters, on the eastern side of the building facing into glorious golden-green morning sunlight. At Prestimion's orders the meal was served all at once, plates of fruit, steamed fish, a stack of sweet brown stajja-cakes, some light breakfast wine. Neither of them touched much of it. Dekkeret seemed to be in a very strange mood, tense, wound up very tight, and yet with a glowing, oddly exalted look in his eyes, as though he had had some rapturous vision in the night.

"Let me tell you my plan," he said, when the brief social pleasantries were done with. "With the alterations that I've made in it as a result of a night's thinking."

There was something almost theatrical about the way Dekkeret had said that. Prestimion was mystified by it.

"Go on," he said.

"What I intend," Dekkeret said, "is at once to undertake the first grand processional of my reign. That will give me a convenient and un-controversial pretext for visiting Zimroel. Since I'm already here on the west coast, I'll announce that that will be my first stop. I'll set out as soon as possible. Sail right across to Piliplok, journey up the Zimr to Ni-moya, continue on into the far western lands, stopping at Dulorn, Pidruid, Narabal, Til-omon, all those cities of the west where 'Lord Dekkeret' is nothing more than a name."

He paused then, as though to give Prestimion a chance to express his approval.

Prestimion, growing more and more bewildered by his Coronal's words and manner, said, "I remind you, Dekkeret, there's an insurrec-tion going on over there. What we spoke of yesterday was your invading Zimroel with a major army, in order that the uprising can be put down. A campaign of war against the rebels who defy our authority. *War.* That's something quite different from a grand processional."

Serenely Dekkeret said, "Prestimion, *you* were the one who spoke of an invasion. I never did. Invading Zimroel, raising my hand in war against its people, who are my own people: these are not policies with which I can agree."

"So you oppose the idea of dealing with the rebellion by force?"

"Most emphatically, majesty."

Prestimion felt the blood beginning to leap in his veins. He was as-tounded as much by Dekkeret's air of bland calm assurance as by the outright insubordination embodied in his words.

He controlled himself with some effort. "I think you have no choice in this, my lord. How can you even think of a grand proces-sional of the usual sort at a time like this? For all you know, you'll ar-rive in Piliplok and find that they've sworn allegiance to one of these Sambailid brothers, hailing him as their Procurator or even, maybe, as their Pontifex, and won't even let you land. Imagine that: the Coronal of Majipoor turned away at the harbor! What will you do then, Dekkeret? Or you'll get to Ni-moya and the river will be blockaded by a hostile fleet, and you'll be told that this is Sambailid territory and you're not welcome in it. What then? Won't you regard that as a cause of war?"

"Not necessarily. I'll remind them of the covenant that binds them in loyalty."

Prestimion stared. "And if they laugh at you, what course of action will you take?"

"I promised you, Prestimion, that I would do whatever needs to be done to restore the rule of law in Zimroel. I intend to keep that promise."

"By measures that nevertheless fall short of outright war."

"I've never said that. I'll have troops with me. I'd use them if I had to. But I don't think a war will be necessary."

"If I tell you that I see it as the only solution, that will put us in direct conflict, you and me, won't it?" Prestimion still spoke in a measured tone, but his anger was rising from moment to moment. This was a development he had never envisioned. In all the years since Dekkeret had first emerged as the obvious choice to become the next Coronal, Prestimion not once had imagined that he and Dekkeret would ever find themselves differing on any great matter of state. This seemed the final betrayal, to have his own protégé rise up against him in a time of such crisis. "I urge you, Dekkeret, rethink what you've just said."

"You are Pontifex, majesty. I obey you in all things and always will. But I tell you, Prestimion, I oppose this war of yours with all my soul."

"Ah," said Prestimion. "With all your soul."

Prestimion had not felt so baffled since the moment long ago when he had watched Confalume's son Korsibar placing the starburst crown on his own head with his own hands and proclaiming himself king. What is the Pontifex to do, he asked himself, when his Coronal throws his orders back in his face? Confalume had never prepared him for something like this. Prestimion saw the relationship between himself as Pontifex and Dekkeret as Coronal, suddenly, much as the aging and increasingly ineffectual Confalume, grudgingly yielding power to the young firebrand Coronal Lord Prestimion, must once have seen it in his own day.

He fought to contain his surging temper. In another moment he would be shouting and snarling. That must not be allowed to happen. To win time for himself he broke a stajja-cake in half, nibbled at it without interest, washed it down with cool golden wine.

"Very well," Prestimion said at last. "You think you can avoid war. No doubt you can, if you're resolved not to start one. But that still leaves the problem of Mandralisca and his uprising. You've pledged to bring both of them under control. Just how do you plan to do that if not by military force?"

"The same way we did in the campaign against the Procurator. Mandralisca has a helmet. We have helmets also. He has a Barjazid: I have a Barjazid. My Barjazid will outmaneuver his Barjazid and take him out of the picture; and that will leave Mandralisca at my mercy."

"I think this is naive of you, Dekkeret."

Now anger flared for an instant in the younger man's eyes. "And I think your thirst for war against your own citizens is an unbecoming thing for one who fancies himself a great monarch, Prestimion. Especially when it's a war you'll be waging by proxy, many thousands of miles from the battlefield."

It was difficult for Prestimion to believe that Dekkeret had actually said such a thing. "No!" he roared, slamming his open hand against the table so that the cutlery jumped high and the wine-flask went flying over the edge. "Unfair! Unfair! Wrongheaded and unfair!"

"Prestimion—"

"Let me speak, Dekkeret. This must be answered." Prestimion realized that his hands were clenched into fists. He put them out of sight. "I have no thirst for war," he said, as calmly as he could manage it. "You know that. But in this case I think war is unavoidable. And I will wage it myself, Dekkeret, if you have no stomach for it. Do you think I've forgotten how to fight? Oh, no, no: you get yourself back to the Castle, my lord, and I will take the troops to Zimroel, and I'll take my place proudly in the front lines with Gialaurys and Septach Melayn, as we did in the old days." His voice was rising again. "Who was it who broke Korsibar's armies that day at Thegomar Edge, when you were not much more than a boy? Who was it who put the thought-helmet on his own head in this very building and reached out to smash Venghenar Barjazid with it in the Stoienzar jungles? Who was it who—"

Dekkeret raised both his hands in appeal. "Gently, your majesty. Gently. If there is to be another war, and may the Divine spare us from that, you know I will lead it, and I will win it. But let this rest a moment, I pray you. There's more to tell you, and it has implications that reach far beyond the problems of the moment."

"Speak, then," Prestimion said in a hollow voice. His furious outburst had left him numb. He wished he had not knocked the wine over, now.

Dekkeret said, "Do you remember, Prestimion, when we spoke in the tasting-room at Muldemar House, just the two of us as we are this morning, and you reminded me of that strange prophecy of Maundigand-Klimd's that a Barjazid would become the fourth Power of the Realm? Neither of us could make any sense of that then, and we put it aside as an impossibility. But in this night just past I understood its meaning. A fourth Power is needed. And with your consent I will create Dinitak Barjazid as that Power, once the matter of Mandralisca and the five Sambailids is behind us."

"I see that you have gone mad," said Prestimion, all rancor gone, only sadness in his tone now.

"Hear me out, I pray. Judge my madness for yourself when I've spoken."

Prestimion's only response was a resigned shrug.

"We have never known such prosperity on Majipoor as we have in the modern era," said Dekkeret. "The era of Prankipin and Lord Confalume—of Confalume and Lord Prestimion—of Prestimion and Lord Dekkeret, if you will. But we have never known such turbulence, either. The coming of the mages and sorcerers, the rise of the strange new cults, the troublemaking of Dantirya Sambail and Mandralisca—all these things are new to us. Perhaps the one thing goes with the other, prosperity and turbulence, the uncertainties of new wealth and the mysteries of magic. Or perhaps we have simply grown too populous, now—with fifteen billion people on one world, huge though it is, perhaps there must inevitably be some discord, even strife."

Prestimion sat quietly, waiting to see where this was going. It was evident that Dekkeret had rehearsed this speech over and over in his mind for half the night: it behooved him, especially after his angry outburst of a few moments before, to give it some show of attention before rejecting whatever demented irrational idea it was that his chosen Coronal had managed to spawn.

Dekkeret went on: "In the earlier time of troubles that we speak of as the time of Dvorn, the first two Powers were created, with joint command: the Pontifex the older, wiser monarch to whom the responsibility for devising policy was given, and the Coronal the younger, more vigorous man who had the task of executing those policies. Later, when a wonderful new invention made it possible, came the third Power, the Lady of the Isle, who with her multitude of associates enters the minds of great numbers of people each night and offers them solace and guidance and healing. But the equipment the Lady uses has its limitations. She can speak with minds, but she is unable to direct or control them. Whereas these helmets that the Barjazids have invented—"

"Have stolen, rather. A sniveling treacherous little Vroon named Thalnap Zelifor invented the things. One of the many errors for which I will be someday called to account is that I put that Vroon and his helmets into the hands of Venghenar Barjazid, to our great injury ever since."

"The Barjazids, especially Khaymak Barjazid, have built upon that Vroon's designs and greatly increased their abilities. I was one of the first, you will recall, to feel the force of the helmet, long ago when I was traveling in Suvrael. But what I felt then, strong as it was, was nothing like the power available in the later version of the helmet you used to strike down Venghenar Barjazid in the Stoienzar those many years ago. And the helmet that drove your brother into insanity, and has harmed so many others lately up and down the land, is far stronger yet. It is a formidable weapon indeed."

Dekkeret leaned forward, his gaze intently focused on Prestimion.

"The world," he said, "needs more stringent government than it had in years gone by, or else we will have new Mandraliscas all the time. What I propose is this: that we take the helmets into the government, giving them over to Dinitak Barjazid and making it his responsibility to search out malefactors, and to control and punish them by using his helmet to transmit powerful mental sendings. He will monitor the minds of the world, and keep the wicked in check. For this he will require the status and authority of a Power of the Realm. We will call him, let us say, the King of Dreams. His rank will be equal to our own. Dinitak will be the first of that title; and it will descend through the generations to his descendants thereafter. —There you have it, your majesty."

Astonishing, Prestimion thought. Unbelievable.

"Dinitak, as I understand it, has no descendants at present," he replied at once. "But that's the least of the things I see wrong with this scheme of yours."

"And the others?"

"It's tyranny, Dekkeret. We rule now by the consent of the people, who freely make us their kings. But if we have a weapon that permits us to control their minds—"

"To *guide* their minds. Only the wicked need fear it. And the weapon is already loose in the land. Better that we make it exclusively ours, forbidden to anyone else, than to leave it out there for future Mandraliscas. We, at least, can be trusted. Or so I prefer to think."

"And your Dinitak? Can *he*? He's a Barjazid, I remind you."

"Of the same blood," said Dekkeret, "but not of the same nature. I saw that in Suvrael, when he urged his father Venghenar to go with me to the Castle and show you the first helmet. Later we saw that again when he came to us at Stoien, bringing a helmet we could use against his father in the rebellion. You were suspicious of him then, do you remember? You said, 'How can we trust him?' when he showed up bearing the helmet. You thought it might be all some intricate new scheme of Dantirya Sambail's. 'Trust him, my lord,' is what I said to you then. 'Trust him!' And you did. Were we wrong?"

"Not then," Prestimion said.

"Nor will we be now. He is my closest friend, Prestimion. I know him as I've never known anyone else. He's driven by a set of moral beliefs that make the rest of us seem like pickpockets. You said it yourself at Muldemar, remember, that time when he gave you an answer that was truthful, but a little too blunt? 'You are no diplomat, Dinitak, but you are an honest man,' or words to that effect. —Did you notice that although he came with me on this trip, Keltryn didn't?"

"Keltryn?"

"Fulkari's younger sister. She and Dinitak have had a little romance—but why would you know that, Prestimion? You were off at the Labyrinth when it started. Anyway, he wouldn't take Keltryn with him. Said it was improper to be traveling with an unmarried woman. *Improper!* When did you last hear a word like that?"

"A very holy young man, I agree. Too holy, perhaps."

"Better that than otherwise. We'll marry him off to Keltryn sooner or later—if she'll have him, that is; Fulkari tells me she's furious with him for leaving her behind—and they'll begin a tribe of holy young Barjazids who can succeed their great ancestor as Kings of Dreams in the centuries ahead. And fear of the harsh dreams that the King of Dreams can send will maintain peace in the land forever after."

"A nice fantasy, isn't it? But it makes me very uneasy, Dekkeret. I once took it upon myself to meddle with the minds of everyone on Majipoor in one great swoop, at Thegomar Edge, when I had my mages wipe out all memory of the Korsibar uprising. I thought then it was a good thing to do, but I was wrong, and I paid a bitter price for it. Now you propose a new kind of mind-meddling, a constant ongoing monitoring. —I won't allow it, Dekkeret, and that ends it. You would need to have the approval of the Pontifex to establish any such system, and that approval is herewith withheld. Now, if we can return to the problem of Mandralisca—"

"You doom us all to chaos, Prestimion."

"Do I, now?"

"The world has become too complicated to be governed from the Labyrinth and the Castle any longer. Zimroel has grown wealthy and restless under Prankipin and Confalume and you. And they know how long it takes to ship troops from Alhanroel to deal with any sort of trouble there. The rise of the Procurator Dantirya Sambail as a sort of quasiking in Zimroel was the beginning of a secessionist movement there. Now it's gone another step. There'll be the constant threat of divisiveness and insurrection across the sea unless we have some direct and immediate way of intervening. The whole structure will come apart."

"And you actually think that using the Barjazid helmet is the only way we have of holding the world government together?"

"I do. The only way short of turning Zimroel into an armed camp with imperial garrisons stationed in every city, that is. Do you think that would be better? Do you, Prestimion?"

Abruptly Prestimion rose and went to the window. He yearned for nothing more than to bring this maddening discussion to an end. Why would Dekkeret not yield, even in the face of a Pontifical refusal? Why would he not see the impossibility of his great idea?

Or am I, Prestimion wondered, the one who refuses to see?

For a long time he stared out silently into the streets of Stoien city. He remembered a time when he had stared out another window of this very building at pillars of smoke rising from the fires set by lunatics at the time of the plague of madness, a plague that he had, however indirectly he had done it, brought upon the world himself.

Did he, he asked himself, want to see fires such as those in the cities of Majipoor again? In Zimroel: in wondrous Ni-moya, and magical crystalline Dulorn, and tropic Narabal of the sweet sea breezes?

You doom us all to chaos, Prestimion—

A fourth Power of the Realm.

A King of Dreams.

Young Barjazid wearing the helmet, roving the night to seek out those who threatened to break the peace, and warning them sternly of the consequences, and punishing them if they disobeyed.

Of the same blood but not of the same nature—

It would be a mighty transformation. Did he dare? How much less risky it would be simply to apply the Pontifical veto to this wild scheme and put it away, and send Dekkeret off to Zimroel to crush this new uprising and hurl Mandralisca finally into his grave. While he himself returned to the Labyrinth and lived out the rest of his days pleasantly there amid imperial pomp and ceremony, as Confalume had done for so long, never needing to grapple with the hard questions of governance, for he had a Coronal who could grapple with such things for him.

A constant threat of divisiveness and insurrection across the sea. The whole structure will come apart—

From somewhere behind him Dekkeret said, "I want to point out, your majesty, that we have that vision of Maundigand-Klimd's to take into account here. And also, on my journey here across Alhanroel, there were several occasions when I had visionary experiences of my own, to my great surprise, that seemed to indicate—"

"Hush," Prestimion said softly, without turning. "You know what I think of visions and oracles and thaumaturgy and all the rest of that. Be quiet and let me think, Dekkeret. I pray you, man, just let me think."

A King of Dreams. A King of Dreams. A King of Dreams.

And finally he said, "The first step, I think, is to speak with Dinitak. Send him to me, Dekkeret. The powers you want to entrust to him are greater even than our own, do you realize that? You say we can trust him, and very likely you're right, but I can't act just on your say-so. I suspect that I need to find out just how holy he is. What if he's *too* holy, eh? What if he thinks that even you and I are miserable sinners who need to be brought in check? What would we be loosing on the world, in that case? Send him to me for a little chat."

"Now, you mean?" Dekkeret asked.

"Now."

15

"The plan is this," Dekkeret told Fulkari, two hours later. "We are to call it simply a grand processional. It won't be labeled in any way as a military expedition. But it'll be a grand processional that *looks* a lot like a military expedition. The Coronal will be accompanied not only by his own guardsmen, but by a contingent of Pontifical troops—a *substantial* number of Pontifical troops. Which gives the whole enterprise something of the aspect of a peacekeeping mission, since a grand processional would normally involve Castle personnel only, and the forces of the Pontifex would have no role in it. The message we'll be sending, then, is this: 'Here is your new Coronal, and hail him as your king. But if anyone among you has treasonous thoughts of insurrection, you are warned that there is an army standing here behind him that will bring you to your senses.'"

"Was this Prestimion's idea, or yours?"

"Mine. Based on his suggestion long ago that one good way I could investigate the situation in Zimroel at first hand was to go there under the guise of making a grand processional. I managed to convince him just now that we'd do best by holding back the option of actual warfare to be our last resort, one that we can always call upon if I get the wrong sort of reception when I'm over there."

"Zimroel!" Fulkari said, shaking her head in wonder. "That's a place I never dreamed I'd see." There was no mistaking the sheen of excitement in her eyes. It was as though she had not heard him mention the prospect of becoming embroiled in warfare at all. "We'll go to Ni-moya,

of course. And Dulorn? They say that Dulorn looks like something out
of a fairy tale, an entire city built out of white crystal. What about
Pidruid? Til-omon? —Oh, Dekkeret, when do we sail?"

"Not for some while, I'm afraid."

"But if it's such an urgent situation—"

"Even so. Alaisor's where the ships bound for Zimroel embark, so
we'll need to go back up there first. The fleet will have to be assembled,
the imperial troops mustered. That'll take time, all the rest of the summer, perhaps. Meanwhile the official proclamations of a processional
have to be drawn up and shipped to every city of Zimroel that I'll be visiting, so that they'll be on notice to receive me with the splendor that
Coronals are customarily received when they come to town." He
smiled. "Oh, one more thing: you and I have to get married, also.
Toward the end of this week, is probably the best time. Prestimion himself has agreed to perform—"

"*Married?* Oh, Dekkeret—!" There was mingled delight and perplexity in her tone. But it was the perplexity that predominated. Her
lower lip trembled a little. "Here, in Stoien? We aren't going to have a
Castle wedding? You know I'll do it wherever you want. But why such
short notice, though?"

He took her hands between his. "They tend to be very conventional
people over in Zimroel, I understand. It simply won't look right to them
if the Coronal shows up on his first grand processional accompanied
by—by a—"

"A concubine? Is that the word you want?" Fulkari stepped back and
laughed. "Dekkeret, you sound exactly like Dinitak now! Improper! Unseemly! Shameful!"

"Let's say 'awkward,' then. The situation in Zimroel's so delicate that
I can't risk any sort of political embarrassment when I'm over there. But
if the answer's no, Fulkari, you'd better tell me now."

"The answer's yes, Dekkeret," she replied unhesitatingly. "Yes, yes,
yes! You knew that." Then the jubilant gleam went from her eyes and
she looked away from him, and in quite a different tone she went on,
"But still—I always thought—the way these things are done, you know,
at the Castle, in Lord Apsimar's Chapel, where Coronals are supposed
to get married, and then the reception afterward in the courtyard by Vildivar Close—"

Dekkeret understood. This was Lord Makhario's many-times-great-
granddaughter speaking, Lady Fulkari of Sipermit, to whom the ways of

the Castle aristocracy were second nature. Fearing now that she would be inexplicably cheated of the grand and glorious wedding ceremony that she had assumed would be hers ever since the moment of their betrothal.

Gently he said, "We can get married again at the Castle later on. The full business, I promise you, Fulkari, the total grand event, with your sister as your bridesmaid and Dinitak my best man, and the whole court watching, and a second honeymoon in High Morpin at the lodge the Coronal keeps there for his private holidays. But we'll have our *first* honeymoon in Ni-moya. And a wedding performed by the Pontifex himself, right here and now, before he sets off back to the Labyrinth. —What do you say?"

"Well, of course, we can't have the Coronal Lord of Majipoor making the grand processional in the company of some little tart, can we? By all means, let's make it official, then. I'll marry you wherever, whenever you want, whatever you think is best." There was that lovely sparkle of delight and mischief in her eyes again. "But afterward, my lord, when we are home at the Castle again—satin and velvet, and Lord Apsimar's Chapel, and the courtyard by Vildivar Close—"

It was a simple ceremony, almost perfunctory, absurdly so for so solemn a rite of state as a Coronal's wedding: held in Prestimion's suite, the Pontifex presiding, Varaile and Dinitak as witnesses, Septach Melayn and Gialaurys looking on.

The whole thing took no more than five minutes. Prestimion did wear his scarlet-and-black robes of office, and the starburst crown was on Dekkeret's brow, but otherwise it could just as well have been the wedding of a shopkeeper and his pretty young clerk at the office of the municipal Justiciar. All those who were present understood the reasons for this haste. A proper royal wedding would follow in the fullness of time, yes—once the challenge of the Five Lords of Zimroel had been met. But for now the basic proprieties would be satisfied. Lord Dekkeret and the Lady Fulkari would go off to Zimroel with wedding bands on their fingers, and let no one in the western continent breathe a word about the wickedness of Castle morality.

The wedding feast, at any rate, was a properly luxurious affair, with wines of five colors, and plate upon plate of Stoienzar oysters and smoked meats and the pungent pickled fruits that they doted on here in the tropical lands. Septach Melayn sang the ancient wedding anthem in a creditable if reedy tenor, and Fulkari, a little tipsy, gave Prestimion so unexpectedly passionate a kiss that the Pontifex's eyes went wide and the Lady Varaile clapped her hands in mock admiration; and at the appropriate moment Dekkeret gathered up his bride and carried her off to their suite on the floor below, making such a lively show of boyish eagerness that one might readily think this would be the first night that she and he had ever spent together.

A few days later the Pontifical party set out on the return journey to the Labyrinth: by ship along the north shore of the Stoienzar Peninsula to Treymone of the famous tree-houses, and overland from there through the Velalisier Valley and the Desert of the Labyrinth to the imperial capital. Dekkeret stood with Prestimion at the royal quay on the Stoien waterfront for a brief farewell as Varaile and the Pontifex's children boarded their vessel. Septach Melayn and Gialaurys remained tactfully to one side. At Dekkeret's request, they would be accompanying him into Zimroel on the grand processional.

Dekkeret spoke briefly of his regrets over the harsh words that had passed between them not long before; but Prestimion brushed that aside, saying that he regretted his own anger at that breakfast meeting at least as much, and that the whole episode was best put out of mind. Out of it, he pointed out, had come a general agreement between them on some of the greatest matters of state that any Coronal and Pontifex had ever had to contemplate.

Prestimion did not need to add that the specific set of tactics to use in handling the Zimroel problem was something he was leaving in Dekkeret's hands. They both knew that: this was a Coronal's task, not a Pontifex's.

As for the advent of the fourth Power of the Realm and Dinitak's designation as King of Dreams, they left any recapitulation of that unsaid also. Dekkeret knew that Prestimion was still uncomfortable with the concept, but that he would not stand in the way of implementing it— eventually. Prestimion had had his conference with Dinitak, although neither man chose to discuss with Dekkeret what had taken place. Evidently all had gone well, Dekkeret concluded. The campaign against Mandralisca came first, though.

At the end they embraced, and it was a warm one, though it was, as always, an awkward business on account of the difference in their heights. Prestimion bade Dekkeret farewell, and congratulated him once more on his marriage, and wished him well in his grand processional, and told him they would meet again at the Castle once the work at hand had been consummated. Then he turned and walked in all imperial dignity aboard the vessel that would carry him to Treymone, without looking back.

Dekkeret himself, his bride, his companions Dinitak Barjazid and Septach Melayn and Gialaurys, and the rest of the royal entourage were on their way five days later. They too began their journey by ship, sailing northward from Stoien across the Gulf to the quiet little port of Kimoise on the western coast. Fast floaters were waiting there that took them up the coast to Alaisor via Klai and Kikil and Steenorp, a retracement in reverse of the route they had followed down to Stoien for Dekkeret's rendezvous with the Pontifex. But there would be a long wait in Alaisor while the fleet was assembled and the troops mobilized.

For it *was* a mobilization. Dekkeret had no illusions about that. He knew he had to go across to Zimroel prepared to fight a war. But the great test of his reign would lie in whether he could succeed in sidestepping that war. Would that be possible? He profoundly hoped so. He was the Coronal Lord of Zimroel as well as that of Alhanroel, but he did not want to win the loyalty of the citizens of the western continent by the sword.

This was Dekkeret's fourth visit to Alaisor, the major metropolitan center of the western coast. But he had never had time on the other three journeys to see the great city properly.

On his first visit, traveling to Zimroel with Akbalik of Samivole years ago when he was still just a young knight-initiate, he had stopped there only long enough to catch the ship that would take them across the Inner Sea. He had passed through Alaisor again a couple of years later, this time an even shorter visit, for that was the frenzied time when he was racing across the world to the Isle of Sleep to bring word to Lord Prestimion that Venghenar Barjazid had escaped from prison at the Castle and intended to turn his thought-control helmets over to the rebel Dantirya Sambail. And on this most recent visit, just a few months before, Dekkeret had been there only a couple of days before receiving word that Prestimion had arrived in Stoien and requested his immediate presence. He had barely had an opportunity to place a wreath on the tomb of Lord Stiamot before it was necessary to move onward.

Now, though, there was more than ample time to experience the marvels of Alaisor. Dekkeret would gladly have been on his way to Zimroel without delay. But there were ships to call in from other ports, new ones to construct, soldiers to levy from the surrounding provinces. Like it or not, his stay in Alaisor was going to be an extended one this time.

It was a superbly located city, an ideal seaport. The River Iyann, running westward through upper Alhanroel, reached the sea here. By carving a deep track through the lofty palisade of black granite cliffs that ran parallel to the shore, the river had created a link between the districts of the interior and the great crescent bay at the base of the mountains. That bay at the mouth of the Iyann had become the harbor of Alaisor. The city itself had sprung up primarily along the coastal strip, with tendrils of urban settlement reaching behind it into the hills to form the spectacularly situated suburb of Alaisor Heights.

Dekkeret and Fulkari were housed in the four-level penthouse suite atop the thirty-story Alaisor Mercantile Exchange where visiting royalty usually stayed. From their windows they could see the dark spokes of the grand boulevards that ran toward the waterfront from all corners of the city, converging just below them in the circle marked by six colossal black stone obelisks that was the site of Lord Stiamot's tomb. Stiamot had been en route to Zimroel in his old age, the story went, to ask the pardon of the Danipiur of the Metamorphs for the war he had waged against her people, when he fell mortally ill in Alaisor. He had asked to be buried facing the sea. Or so the story went.

"I wonder if he's really buried there," Dekkeret said, as they looked down on the ancient tomb. Some people of Alaisor were moving among the obelisks, strewing handfuls of bright flowers. The tomb was freshly bedecked with blossoms every day. "For that matter, did he ever exist at all?"

"So you doubt him too, the way you doubted Dvorn, when we were at *his* tomb."

"It's the same thing. I agreed that someone whose name was Dvorn probably was Pontifex at some time or other long ago. But was he the one who founded the Pontificate? Who knows? It was thirteen thousand years ago, and at that distance in time do we have any good way of distinguishing history from myth? Likewise with Lord Stiamot: so ancient that we can't be sure of a thing."

"How can you say that? He lived only *seven* thousand years ago. Seven's very different from thirteen. Compared with Dvorn, he's practically our contemporary!"

"Is he? Seven thousand years—thirteen thousand—these are incredible numbers, Fulkari."

"So there never was a Lord Stiamot at all?"

Dekkeret smiled. "Oh, there was a Lord Stiamot, all right. And either he or somebody else of the same name probably was the one who conquered the Metamorphs and sent them off to live in Piurifayne, I suppose. But is he the man who's buried under those black obelisks? Or did they just bury *someone* there, five or six thousand years ago, someone important at that time, and gradually the idea took hold that the person in that tomb is Lord Stiamot?"

"You're terrible, Dekkeret!"

"Simply realistic. Do you believe that the real Stiamot was anything like the man the poets tell us about? That superhuman hero, striding from one end of the world to the other the way you or I would walk across the street? My guess is that the Lord Stiamot of *The Book of Changes* is ninety-five percent fable."

"And will the same thing happen to you, do you think? Will the Lord Dekkeret of the poems that will be written five thousand years from now be ninety-five percent fable too?"

"Of course. Lord Dekkeret and Lady Fulkari both. Somewhere right in *The Book of Changes* Aithin Furvain himself tells us that Stiamot once heard someone singing a ballad about one of his victories over the Metamorphs, and wept because everything they were saying about him in that song was wrong. And even *that* is probably a fable too. Varaile once told me that they were singing songs in the marketplace about Prestimion's struggle with Dantirya Sambail, and the Prestimion they sang about was nothing like the Prestimion she knew. It'll be the same with us someday, Fulkari. Trust me on that."

Fulkari's eyes were glistening. "Imagine it: poems about us, Dekkeret, five thousand years from now! The heroic saga of your great campaign against Mandralisca and the Five Lords! I'd love to read one of those—wouldn't you?"

"I'd love to know what the poet tells us about how things turned out for Lord Dekkeret, anyway," said Dekkeret, staring down somberly at the ancient tomb in the plaza below. "Does the saga finish with a happy ending for the gallant Coronal, I wonder? Or is it a tragedy?" He shrugged. "Well, at least we won't have to wait five thousand years to find out."

There was no escaping a second ceremony at the tomb this time, and a visit to the temple of the Lady atop Alaisor Heights, the second holiest shrine to the Lady in the world, and a formal dinner at the celebrated Hall of Topaz in the palace of the Lord Mayor of Alaisor, Manganan Esheriz. And as the weeks went by there were other official events as well, a numbing succession of them, as Alaisor took full advantage of the unusual fact of a Coronal's extended presence in the city.

But Dekkeret spent as much of his time as possible planning his tour of Zimroel: the landing at Piliplok, the journey up the Zimr, the entry into Ni-moya. He learned the names of local officials, he studied maps, he sought to identify potential trouble spots along the way. The trick would be to arrive at the head of a huge army while still managing to carry off the pretense that this was only a peaceful grand processional undertaken for the purpose of introducing the new Coronal to his western subjects. Of course, if he should find a rebel army waiting for him when he landed at Piliplok, or if Mandralisca had gone so far as to blockade the sea against him, he would have no choice but to meet force with force. But that remained to be seen.

The summer ticked along. The time soon would come, Dekkeret knew, when the season changed and the winds turned contrary, blowing so vigorously out of the west that departure would have to be postponed for many months. He wondered if he had misjudged the timing, had spent so much time assembling his fleet that the invasion must be delayed until spring, and his enemies given that much more time to dig themselves in.

But at last everything seemed propitious for departure, and the winds still were favorable.

His flagship was called the *Lord Stiamot*. Of course: the local hero, the Coronal whose name was a synonym for triumph. Dekkeret suspected the ship had formerly borne some less resounding name and had hastily been renamed on his behalf, but he saw no harm in that. "Let that name be an omen of our coming success," Gialaurys said with gruff exuberance, pointing to the golden lettering on the hull as they went aboard. "The conqueror! The greatest of warriors!"

"Indeed," said Dekkeret.

Gialaurys was exuberant also—indeed, he was the only one—when Piliplok harbor finally came into view, many weeks later, after a slow and windy crossing of the Inner Sea made notable by the presence of a great band of sea-dragons that stayed close at hand much of the way. The huge aquatic beasts frisked and frolicked about Dekkeret's fleet with alarming playfulness day after day, lashing the choppy blue-green sea with their immense fluked tails and sometimes rising from the water, tail first, to display nearly their entire awesome bodies. The sight of them was exhilarating and frightening at the same time. But at last the dragons vanished to starboard, disappearing into the next phase of whatever mysterious journeys the sea-dragons were wont to make in the course of their endless circlings of the world.

Then the sea changed color, darkening to a muddy gray, for the voyagers had reached the point off shore where the first traces of the silt and debris carried into the ocean by the Zimr could be detected. The huge river, in its seven-thousand-mile journey across Zimroel, transported untold tons of such stuff eastward. At its gigantic mouth, sixty miles across and wider, all that tremendous load was swept into the sea, staining it for hundreds of miles out from shore. The sight of that stain meant that Piliplok city could not be far away.

And then, finally, the shore of Zimroel came into view. The chalky mile-high headland just north of Piliplok that marked the place where the great mouth of the Zimr met the sea stood out brightly against the horizon.

Gialaurys was the first to spy the actual city. "Piliplok ho!" he bellowed. "Piliplok! Piliplok!"

Piliplok, yes. Was a hostile fleet waiting there for him, Dekkeret wondered?

It did not appear that way. The only vessels in view were mercantile ones, moving about their business as though nothing at all were amiss. Evidently Mandralisca—unless he had some surprise up his sleeve—did not intend to deny the Coronal of Majipoor the right to land on Zimroel's soil. To defend the continent's entire perimeter against invasion was, after all, an enormous task, possibly beyond the rebels' resources.

Mandralisca must be drawing a line somewhere closer to Ni-moya, Dekkeret decided.

Gialaurys could barely contain his delight as his birthplace came into view. Joyfully he clapped his hands. "Ah, there's a city for you, Dekkeret! Take a good look, my lord! Is that a city, or isn't it, eh, my lord?"

Well, he had every reason to smile at the sight of his native city. But Dekkeret, who had been to Piliplok before on his trip with Akbalik, knew what to expect of it, and he greeted the place with none of the old Grand Admiral's glee. Piliplok was not his idea of urban beauty. It was a city that only its natives could love.

And Fulkari gasped in outright shock at her first glimpse of it as they entered the harbor. "I knew it wasn't supposed to be beautiful, but even so, Dekkeret—even so—could it have been some lunatic who laid this place out? Some crazed mathematician in love with his own insane plan?"

That had been Dekkeret's reaction too, that other time, and the city had grown no lovelier in the twenty-odd years of his absence. From the central point of its splendid harbor its eleven great highways fanned out in rigidly straight spokes, crossed with unerring precision by curving bands of streets. Each band delimited a district of different function—the marine warehouses, the commercial quarter, the zone of light industry, the residential areas, and so forth—and within each district every building was of an architectural style unique to that district, every structure looking precisely like its neighbor. Each district's prevailing style had only one thing in common with the styles of its neighbors, which was that they all were characterized by a singular heaviness and brutality of design that oppressed the eye and burdened the heart.

"In Suvrael, where hardly any trees or shrubs of the northern continents can survive our heat and powerful sunlight," said Dinitak, "we plant what we can, palms, tough succulents, even the poor scrawny things of the desert, for the sake of giving our cities some beauty. But here in this benevolent coastal climate, where anything at all will grow, the good folk of Piliplok seem to choose to grow nothing at all!" Shaking his head, he pointed toward shore. "Do you see a stem anywhere, Dekkeret, a branch, a leaf, a flower? Nothing. Nothing!"

"It is all like that," said Dekkeret. "Pavement, pavement, pavement. Buildings, buildings, buildings. Concrete, concrete, concrete. I remember seeing a shrub or two, last time. No doubt they've had those removed by now."

"Well, we aren't coming here as settlers, are we?" said Septach Melayn lightly. "So let us pretend that we adore the place, if they should ask us, and then let us get ourselves far from it as soon as we can."

"I second the motion," Fulkari said.

"Look," said Dekkeret. "Here comes our reception committee."

Half a dozen vessels had put out from the harbor. Dekkeret, still uneasy, was relieved to see that they did not have the look of military ships—he recognized them as the strange-looking fishing vessels of Piliplok that were known as dragon-ships, lavishly ornamented with bizarre fanged figureheads and sinister spiky tails, with garish painted rows of white teeth and scarlet-and-yellow eyes along their sides, and intricate many-pronged masts carrying their black-and-crimson sails—and that they flew ensigns of welcome that showed the green-and-gold colors symbolic of the power and authority of the Coronal.

It could, of course, all be some deceptive maneuver of Mandralisca's, Dekkeret supposed. But he doubted that. And he felt further reassurance when a huge voice came booming across the waters to him through a speaking-tube, crying out the traditional salute: "Dekkeret! Dekkeret! All hail Lord Dekkeret!" It was the unmistakable deep rumble of a Skandar's voice. There was a greater concentration of the giant four-armed beings in Piliplok than anywhere else in the world. The Lord Mayor of Piliplok himself, Kelmag Volvol by name, was a Skandar, Dekkeret knew.

And that was unquestionably Kelmag Volvol now, an immense shaggy figure nearly nine feet high in the red robes of mayoralty, standing in the bow of the lead dragon-ship making clusters of starburst signs, four at a time, and then signalling that he wished to come aboard the *Lord Stiamot* for a parley. If this were a trap, Dekkeret thought, would the mayor of the city have been willing to bait it with his own person?

The two flagships lined up broadside. Kelmag Volvol clambered into a wickerwork transport basket. A thick rope that culminated in a massive curved blubber-hook, normally used in the butchering of sea-dragons, was lowered from the rigging and the hook was fastened to the basket. The rope then was hoisted by pulleys so that the basket containing Lord

Mayor Kelmag Volvol was lifted aloft and swung outward over the rail of the ship. Slowly and steadily it traveled through the gap separating the vessels, Kelmag Volvol standing solemnly upright all the while, and neatly deposited him beside the capstan head on the deck of the *Lord Stiamot*.

Dekkeret lifted both his hands in greeting. The towering Skandar, nearly half again as tall as the Coronal, knelt before him and saluted once more.

"My lord, you are welcome to Piliplok. Our city rejoices at your presence."

Protocol now called for an exchange of small gifts. The Skandar had brought a surprisingly delicate necklace fashioned from finely interwoven sea-dragon bones, which Dekkeret placed around Fulkari's neck, and Dekkeret offered him a rich brocaded mantle of Makroposopos manufacture, purple and green with the royal starburst and monogram at its center.

The ceremonial sharing of food in the Coronal's cabin was the next order of ritual. This posed certain technical difficulties, since the *Lord Stiamot* had not been designed with Skandars in mind, and Kelmag Volvol could barely manage to negotiate the companionway that led belowdecks. And he had to stoop and crane his neck to fit within the royal cabin itself, which was roomy enough for Dekkeret and Fulkari but which the Lord Mayor Kelmag Volvol filled practically to overflowing. Septach Melayn and Gialaurys, who had accompanied them below, were forced to stand in the passage outside.

"I must begin this meeting with troublesome news, my lord," the Skandar said as soon as the formalities were over.

"Concerning Ni-moya, is it?"

"Concerning Ni-moya, yes," said Kelmag Volvol. He threw an uneasy glance toward the two men outside. — "It is a highly sensitive matter, my lord."

"Nothing that needs to be hidden from the Grand Admiral Gialaurys and the High Spokesman Septach Melayn, I think," Dekkeret replied.

"Well, then." Kelmag Volvol looked acutely uncomfortable. "It is this, and I regret to be the bearer of such tidings. Your journey onward to Ni-moya: I must advise you against it. A cordon has been placed around the city and the territory immediately surrounding it, to a distance of some three hundred miles in all directions."

Dekkeret nodded. It was as he had guessed: Mandralisca had reined in his original grandiose plans to claim all of Zimroel at the outset, and was limiting the sphere of his rebellion to an area he was easily capable of defending. But a rebellion was still a rebellion, even so.

"A cordon," Dekkeret repeated thoughtfully, as though it were a mere nonsensical sound that conveyed nothing to him. "And what, I pray, does that mean, a cordon around Ni-moya?"

The pain in Kelmag Volvol's great red-rimmed eyes was unmistakable. His four shoulders shifted about in keen embarrassment. "A zone, my lord, protected by military force, which officials of the imperial government are forbidden to enter, because it is now under the administration of the Lord Gaviral, Pontifex of Zimroel."

A snort of astonishment came from Septach Melayn. "Pontifex, is he! Of Zimroel!"

And from Gialaurys: "We will flay him and nail his hide to the door of his own palace, my lord! We will—"

Dekkeret motioned to them both to be still.

"Pontifex," he said, in the same wondering tone. "Not merely Procurator, the title his uncle Dantirya Sambail was content to hold, but Pontifex? *Pontifex!* Ah, very fine! Very bold! —He makes no claim to Prestimion's own throne, does he? He is content only to rule over the western continent, our new Pontifex, beginning with the territory around Ni-moya? Why, then, I applaud his restraint!"

Skandars, Dekkeret remembered a moment too late, had virtually no capacity for irony. Kelmag Volvol reacted to Dekkeret's lighthearted words with such a sputtering display of astonishment and distress that it was immediately necessary to assure him that the Coronal did indeed regard the developments in Ni-moya with the greatest concern.

"Which brother is this, this Gaviral?" Dekkeret said to Septach Melayn, who had lately been gathering information concerning these nephews of Dantirya Sambail.

"The eldest one. A small scheming man, with a certain rudimentary intelligence. The other four are little more than drunken beasts."

"Yes," said Dekkeret. "Like their father Gaviundar, the Procurator's brother. I met him once, when he came to the Castle in Prestimion's time as Coronal, sniveling after some favor having to do with land. An animal, he was. A great huge coarse vile-smelling hideous animal."

"Who betrayed us at the battle of Stymphinor in the Korsibar war," said Gialaurys darkly, "when Navigorn nearly cut our army to pieces and Gaviundar and his other brother Gaviad, our allies then, shamefully held back their troops. And his seed comes back to haunt us now!"

Dekkeret turned again to the Skandar, who looked baffled by all this talk of unknown battles, but was struggling to hide his confusion. "Tell me the rest of it. What territorial claims is this Gaviral actually making? Just Ni-moya, or is that only the beginning?"

"As we understand it down here," Kelmag Volvol went on, "the Lord Gaviral—that is the title he uses, the Lord Gaviral—has decreed this entire continent independent of the imperial government. Ni-moya is apparently already under his control. Now he has sent ambassadors to the surrounding districts, explaining his purposes and asking for oaths of allegiance. A new constitution will shortly be announced. The Lord Gaviral soon will select the first Coronal of Zimroel. It is believed that he will name one of his brothers to the post."

"Has the name of a certain Mandralisca been mentioned?" Dekkeret asked. "Does he figure in this in any way?"

"His signature was on the proclamation we received," said Kelmag Volvol. "Count Mandralisca of Zimroel, yes, as privy counsellor to his majesty the Lord Gaviral."

"*Count*, no less," muttered Septach Melayn. "Count Mandralisca! Privy counsellor to his majesty the Pontifex Lord Gaviral! Has come a long way from the days when he was tasting the Procurator's wine to see if it'd been poisoned, that one has!"

16

"You asked for me, your grace?" Thastain said.

Mandralisca nodded curtly. "Bring me the Shapeshifter, if you will, my good duke."

"But he is gone, sir."

"Gone? *Gone?*"

Mandralisca felt a momentary surge of fury and dismay so wildly intense that it astounded him with its force. Only for a moment; but in that moment it had seemed to him that he was being swept through the air in the teeth of a hurricane. It was a frightening overreaction, and not the first of its kind in recent days.

He hated these spells of soul-vertigo that had begun coming over him lately. He hated himself for succumbing to them. They were a mark of weakness.

The boy must see it, too. He was staring.

Mandralisca forced himself to say more calmly, "Gone where, Thastain?"

"Back to Piurifayne, I think, sir. Summoned home by the Danipiur to deliver his report, I believe."

Stunning news. Mandralisca felt another whirlwind go roaring through his mind.

He groped for the riding crop that always lay on his desk, gripped its handle until his knuckles were white, shoved it aside. To quiet himself he went to the window and stared out. But that only made things worse, for he found himself looking into the rain. For the past three

days Ni-moya had been pelted by surprising rains, a deluge beyond all
expectation this late in the summer, when the long dry season of autumn and winter should be coming on. Everything beyond the window was a blank gray wall. The river, though it lay just below, could
not be seen at all. Nothing there but gray, gray, gray. And the unending drumming of the rainfall against the great quartz window of his office had already begun to be maddening. Another day and it would
have him screaming.

Calm. Stay calm.

But how? Dekkeret—the word had just come in—had landed safely
in Piliplok, with many troops. And Viitheysp Uuvitheysp Aavitheysp had
taken himself back to Piurifayne for a chat with his queen.

"He *left*," Mandralisca said, "and I wasn't told? Why not? We had an
important meeting scheduled for today, he and I." The red tide of anger
was mounting again. "The Metamorph ambassador unexpectedly sets
out for home without troubling to stop in at my office to take his leave
of the privy counsellor, and no one says anything to me!"

"I had—no idea, sir—I never thought—"

"You never thought! You never thought! Exactly, Thastain: you
never thought."

He had wanted the words to sound icy-cold, but they came out as a
kind of throttled screech. Mandralisca thought his head was going to ex-
plode. Khaymak Barjazid had told him just the other day that it was risky
to be using the helmet as much as he was. Perhaps that might be so; perhaps it could be making him just a little unstable, he thought. Or maybe
it was simply the tension he felt now that the hour of the long-dreamed-
of war of independence was at hand. But he had never had so much difficulty maintaining his self-control. And this was no moment to be
losing control.

Not with Dekkeret in Piliplok. And the Metamorph ambassador
gone.

For the second time in a minute and a half Mandralisca fought back
his own overloaded emotions and struggled to think things through.

The plan to fortify the entire coast against the Coronal had long
since been scrapped. In the end Mandralisca had abandoned the idea
on the grounds that it was one thing to invite the people of Zimroel to
join the rulers of Ni-moya in a general declaration of independence,
and something else again to ask them, this early in the uprising, actually
to lift their hands against an anointed Coronal. Better to let the

vengeance-hungry Shapeshifters handle Dekkeret, Mandralisca had decided, finally, after weeks of inner debate. But suddenly that decision
was beginning to look like a significant strategic error, a gamble that had
gone wrong. The force of Shapeshifter guerillas that Mandralisca had
been negotiating to place in the forests along Dekkeret's likely route
north did not yet exist. And now the Shapeshifter ambassador himself
had vanished. His essential ally. His secret weapon against the Alhanroel
government.

The Danipiur had already been told the essence of Mandralisca's
proposal, civil freedom for her people in return for their military aid
against Dekkeret. Perhaps Viitheysp Uuvitheysp Aavitheysp had simply
gone home to discuss with the Danipiur the final details involved in de-
ploying the troops Mandralisca had requested.

Perhaps.

Why, though, had the Shapeshifter not said anything about that to
him first? Possibly something much more disquieting was going on:
something more like a Shapeshifter change of heart about the entire enterprise. What had seemed so simple earlier was now beginning to present unexpected challenges.

But anger was the wrong response, he knew. Fear, despair, anxiety—
all useless. It was much too early in the campaign to give panic a
foothold. There were always going to be surprises, setbacks, miscalcula-
tions.

In the softest tone he could manage Mandralisca said, "I should have
been informed right away, Thastain. I regret that I wasn't. But there's
nothing that can be done about that now, is there? —Is there, Thastain?"

"No, your grace." The merest whisper.

The boy was white-faced and trembling. It seemed to be all he could
do to meet Mandralisca's gaze. Was he expecting to be beaten for his
negligence? The riding crop, maybe? Mandralisca had not seen Thastain so fear-stricken since the early days at the desert headquarters out
by the Plain of Whips.

But terrorizing the underlings would serve no useful purpose now.
The sudden departure of Viitheysp Uuvitheysp Aavitheysp might or
might not be a serious development, though at the very least it raised the
possibility of major complications and confusions. But, no matter what
the Shapeshifter might be up to, Mandralisca told himself, it was far
from sensible just now to be alienating valuable members of his own

staff. And Thastain was valuable. The boy was loyal; the boy was helpful; the boy was intelligent.

Mandralisca said, "What I want you to do now, Thastain, is to get
yourself out into the Grand Bazaar, talk to one of the shopkeepers, tell
him that I want him to put you in contact with some senior member of
the Guild of Thieves. —You know about the guild of official thieves of
Ni-moya, Thastain? How they operate in the bazaar in cooperation with
the merchants, taking a certain regulated percentage of goods for themselves in return for guarding the place against greedy free-lance thieves
who don't understand when enough is enough?"

"Yes, sir."

"Good. Talk to the thieves, then. They have connections with the
local Shapeshifter community. This city's swarming with Shapeshifters,
you know. There are more of them here than you'd ever believe, lurking all around the place. Get in touch with them. Use my name. If you
have to throw money around, then throw it freely. Tell them that I have
urgent need to send a message via one of them to the Danipiur—*urgent
need*, Thastain—and when you find someone who's willing to carry that
message, bring him here to me. Is that clear, Thastain?"

Thastain nodded. But there was an odd look on the boy's face.

Mandralisca said, "You don't much care for Shapeshifters, do you,
Thastain? Well, who does? But we need them. We need them, you understand? Their cooperation is necessary to the cause. So hold your nose
and get yourself off to the bazaar, and don't waste any time about it." He
smiled. The inner storm seemed to be passing; he felt almost like himself again. "—Oh, and on your way out tell Khaymak Barjazid that I
want to see him in here, right away."

Barjazid looked at the bunched-up mass of metal mesh in Mandralisca's
hand that was the thought-control helmet, then at Mandralisca, then at
the helmet again. He had not replied at all to the request Mandralisca
had just made.

"Well, Khaymak? You aren't saying anything, and I'm waiting. Here:
take the helmet. Get to work."

"A direct attack on the mind of Lord Dekkeret? Do you think this is
wise, excellence?"

"Would I have asked you to do it if I didn't?"

"This is a considerable change of plan. We had agreed, I thought, that there would be no attempts undertaken against the Powers themselves."

"There've been several considerable changes of plan lately," Mandralisca said. "Certain concessions to financial and political realities have had to be made. We didn't blockade the sea to keep the Coronal's fleet from landing, though at one time we were talking about that. We didn't set up military outposts up and down the coast, either. And we assumed we would be getting valuable help from Shapeshifter troops, but suddenly that seems to be in doubt also. And so Dekkeret is now in Piliplok and very soon will be heading this way. He's brought an army with him."

"May I remind you, your grace, we have an army too."

"Ah, and will it fight? That's the question, Khaymak: will it fight? What if Dekkeret comes marching up to our borders and says, 'Here I am, your Coronal Lord,' and our men fall down and start making starbursts to him? That's a risk I don't feel comfortable taking. Not while we have *this*." He opened his clenched hand and held the helmet forth. "By the use of this I drove Prestimion's brother over the edge of madness, and many another also. It's time to go to work on Dekkeret. Take it, Khaymak. Put it on. Send your mind down to Piliplok and latch it onto Dekkeret's, and begin taking him apart. It may be our only hope."

Once more Khaymak Barjazid looked at the helmet in Mandralisca's hand, but he made no move to reach out for it. Mildly he said, "It has been very clear for a long time, excellence, that your own powers of operating the helmet are superior to mine. Your greater intensity of spirit— your stronger force of character—"

"Are you telling me that you won't do it, Khaymak?"

"Against such a powerful center of energy as the mind of Lord Dekkeret surely must be, it would perhaps be desirable that you be the one who—"

Mandralisca felt the whirlwinds starting up again within him. I must not allow that, he thought, clamping down. Stay calm. Calm. Calm.

Coldly, cuttingly, he said, "You told me only a few days ago that I may be using the helmet too much. And I do see certain signs of strain in myself that may very well be the result of just that." His hand strayed toward the riding crop. "Don't waste any more of my energy in discussing this, Khaymak. Take the helmet. Now. And go to work on Dekkeret with it."

"Yes, your grace," Barjazid said, looking very unhappy indeed.

Carefully he affixed the helmet, closed his eyes, seemed to enter the trancelike state with which one operated the device. Mandralisca watched, fascinated. Even now the Barjazid helmet still seemed like a miraculous thing to him: such a flimsy little webwork of golden wires, and yet one could use it to reach out over thousands of miles, enter other minds, any minds, even those of a Pontifex or a Coronal, and impress one's will—take control—

Several minutes had passed, now. Barjazid was perspiring. His face had grown flushed beneath its heavy Suvrael tan. His head was bowed, his shoulders hunched together in a sign of obvious stress. Had he reached Dekkeret? Was he sending beams of red fury into the Coronal's helpless mind?

Another minute—another—

Barjazid looked up. With trembling hands he lifted the helmet from his brow.

"Well?" Mandralisca demanded.

"Very strange, your grace. *Very.*" His voice was hoarse and ragged. "I did reach Dekkeret. I'm sure I did. A Coronal's mind—surely it's like no other. But it was—*defended.* That's the only term I can use. It was as if he was shielding himself in some way against my entry."

"Is this possible, technically speaking?"

"Yes, of course—if he's wearing a helmet too, and knows how to use it. And he does, of course, have access to helmets, the ones confiscated from my brother long ago, that have been locked away at the Castle. It's certainly possible that Dekkeret has brought one of those with him. But that he could use it with such mastery—that he would so much as know how to use it at all—"

"And that he would happen to be wearing it at the exact moment when you tried to attack him," Mandralisca said. "Yes. A coincidence like that is the most unlikely thing of all. Maybe you were right, just now, that you simply don't have enough inner force, mental strength, whatever it is, to break through Dekkeret's defenses. Let me try, I suppose."

Barjazid surrendered the helmet only too gladly.

Mandralisca held it cupped in both his hands for a moment, wondering whether this was really a good idea. It had been obvious all day that the pressures of this campaign had begun significantly to deplete his vitality. Using the helmet involved a great drain on one's energies. A further expenditure of spirit at this time could well be damaging.

But it could be even more damaging to let Barjazid see how weary he was. And if he could manage, in one great stroke of mental force, to shatter the mind of the enemy who would otherwise soon be coming toward him out of Piliplok—

He put the helmet on. Closed his eyes. Entered the trance.

Sent his mind roving, southward, eastward, Piliplokward.

Dekkeret.

Surely that was he. A fiery red globe of power, like a second sun, out there by the coast.

Dekkeret. Dekkeret. Dekkeret.

And now—to strike—

Mandralisca summoned every bit of strength within him. This was the act from which he had held back so long, the direct attack on his primary foe, the outright onslaught against the single man who held the royal forces together. For reasons that had never been clear even to him—caution, strategy, perhaps even fear?—he had not struck at Prestimion when he was Coronal, and he had not struck at Dekkeret, either. He had sought to win his goals by more indirect means, gradually, rather than through one outrageous coup. It was, he supposed, his nature: silence, patience, cunning. But all those hesitations dropped away now. This was the moment to reach Dekkeret and destroy him—

The moment—

To—strike—

The moment—the moment—

He was striking, but nothing was happening. That fiery red globe was impossible to hit. It was not a matter of insufficient force, of that he was sure. But his angry lightning-bolts were glancing aside like feeble darts striking stone. Again, again, again he thrust; and each time he was rebuffed.

And then his last reservoir of energy was empty. He swept the helmet from his forehead and leaned forward against his desk, taut, quivering, resting his head on his arms.

After a moment he glanced up. The look on Khaymak Barjazid's face was frightful. The little man was staring at him with eyes bulging with shock and horror.

"Your grace—are you all right, your grace?"

Mandralisca nodded. He was numb with exhaustion.

"What happened, your grace?"

"Shielded—just as you said. Impossible to get near him. Completely defended." He pressed his fingertips to his aching eyes. "Can he be some kind of superman, do you think? I know this Dekkeret, this Coronal, only by repute—we have never met—but nothing I've ever heard about him would lead me to think he has any special powers of mind. And yet—the way he deflected me—the ease of it—"

Khaymak Barjazid shook his head. "I know of no power of the human mind that would let it fend off the thrust of the helmet. More likely they have come up with some new form of the device. My nephew Dinitak, you know, is with the Coronal's party. He understands the helmets. And may have modified one in such a way that he can use it to protect his master."

"Of course," said Mandralisca. It was all completely clear now. "Dinitak, who sold his own father out to Prestimion by bringing him the helmets, and who has done it again these twenty years afterward. He has ever been a thorn in my side, that nephew of yours. Great is the mischief he's done: and great will be his suffering, Khaymak, when I finally begin to pay him back for it!"

Thastain returned toward nightfall, rumpled and soiled from his day in the maze of tunnels and galleries and narrow arcades that was the Grand Bazaar of Ni-moya, and soaked through and through by the inexorable rain. Mandralisca could see at once that the boy must have failed in his mission, for he looked both glum and fearful, and he had returned alone, instead of bringing some Shapeshifter with him as Mandralisca had ordered. But he listened with a sort of weary patience to Thastain's long recitation: his tour of the vast labyrinthine market, his conversations with this merchant and that one until finally he had won the cooperation of a certain Gaziri Venemm, a dealer in cheeses and oils, who after much hesitation and circumlocution agreed, upon payment of a purse full of royals, to arrange for Thastain to be conducted to one of his fellow merchants who was believed—*believed*—to be a Shapeshifter masquerading as a man of the city of Narabal.

And indeed, Thastain reported, the supposed man of Narabal did appear, from his shifty ways and uncertain accent, to be a Metamorph in disguise. But he would not, not for any price, agree to undertake a mission to the Danipiur.

"I mentioned your name, your grace. He was indifferent. I mentioned the name of Viitheysp Uuvitheysp Aavitheysp. He tried to pretend that he had never heard that name before. I showed him a purse of royals. It was all no use."

"And is he the only Shapeshifter in the bazaar?" asked Mandralisca.

"I spoke with four more of them all told," said Thastain, and from the look of distaste on his face Mandralisca knew that it was true, and that it had not been a pleasant task. "They will not do it. Two denied, very indignant, that they were Metamorphs at all; and I could see that they were lying, and that they knew I knew they were lying, and that they did not care. A third pleaded poor health. A fourth simply refused, before I had spoken six words. I can go back to the bazaar tomorrow, excellence, and perhaps then I can find—"

"No," Mandralisca said. "There's no point in that. Something has happened. The Danipiur's ambassador has decided not to help us, and has returned to Piurifayne to tell her that. I'm certain of it." He was surprised at his own composure. Perhaps he had passed beyond the whirlwind zone, now. "Get me Halefice," he said.

When the aide-de-camp arrived Mandralisca said at once, "There are some new difficulties, Jacomin."

"Other than the arrival of Dekkeret and the disappearance of the Metamorph, excellence?"

"Other than those, yes." Mandralisca provided a crisp summary of his own thwarted attempts against Dekkeret with the helmet and Thastain's fruitless search in the bazaar for a cooperative Metamorph. "Very soon, I suppose, the Coronal will be marching this way. The Shapeshifter aid I had counted on will evidently not materialize. As for the military forces we've been able to raise ourselves, they are sufficient to defend Ni-moya, I suppose, but not to permit us to go beyond the perimeter of the lands we already hold."

There was a stricken look on Halefice's face. "Then what will we do, your grace?"

"I have a new plan." Mandralisca looked from Halefice to Barjazid, from Barjazid to Thastain, letting his gaze linger on each of them, assaying them carefully, seeking to measure their trustworthiness. "You three are the first to hear it, and you will also be the last. The scheme is this: the Lord Gaviral will invite Dekkeret to a parley at a place midway between Piliplok and Ni-moya, telling him that we want to arrive at a peaceful solution to our disputes, a compromise that will treat the grievances of Zimroel without damaging the structure of the imperial government. I know that that will appeal to him. We'll sit down at a table together and try to work things out. We'll offer our terms. We'll listen to his."

"And then?" Halefice asked.

"And then," said Mandralisca, "just when the talks are going as smoothly as can be, Jacomin, we'll kill him."

17

"*A* parley," Dekkeret said, fascinated by the strangeness of the idea. "We are asked to a parley!"

"First he tries to strike at you with his helmet, and then he asks you to a parley?" Septach Melayn said, laughing. "I see that the man will try anything. You will refuse, of course."

"I think not," said Dekkeret. "He has been testing us. And now that we've shown him that Dinitak can beat back his attacks, I think he's found out what we are made of, and wants to change his tune for a new and sweeter one. We should listen to it, and see what it sounds like, eh?"

"But a parley? A *parley*? My lord, the Coronal does not negotiate peace terms with those who deny his sacred authority," said Gialaurys in his deepest, most sternly ponderous tone. "He simply destroys them. He sweeps them aside like gnats. He does not enter into discussions with them concerning the concessions he is being asked to make, the territory he is expected to yield, or anything else. A Coronal can concede nothing at all, ever, to any such creatures as these."

"Nor will I," said Dekkeret, smiling a little at the old Grand Admiral's staunch and earnest rigor. "But to refuse outright to hear the virtuous Count Mandralisca's proposals—or, rather, those of the great and mighty Pontifex Gaviral, since I see that it's Gaviral who invites us to this meeting—no, I think it would be wrong to take that position. We should listen, at least. This parley will draw them out of Ni-moya, which will spare us the need to lay siege to that city, and perhaps to do harm to it. We will talk with them; and then, if we must, we will fight; but all the advantage lies on our side."

"Does it?" Dinitak asked. "We have an army, yes. But I remind you, Dekkeret, we are on enemy soil, very far from home. If Mandralisca has been able to collect forces anywhere near the size of our own—"

"Enemy soil?" Gialaurys cried. "No! No! What are you saying? We are in Zimroel, where his majesty the Pontifex's coinage still is legal tender, and I mean the Pontifex Prestimion, not this foolish puppet of Mandralisca's. The imperial writ is law here still, Dinitak. Lord Dekkeret here is king of this land. And also I was born here, no more than fifty miles from this spot that you call enemy soil. How can you even speak such words? How—"

"Peace, good Gialaurys," said Dekkeret, close to laughter now. "There's a certain truth to what Dinitak says. This may not be enemy soil right here, but we don't know how far upriver we can go before that changes. Ni-moya has proclaimed its independence: by the Lady, has named its own Pontifex! Has begun striking its own coins with Gaviral's silly face on them, for all we know. Until we have put things to rights, we need to think of Ni-moya as an enemy city, and the lands surrounding it as hostile territory."

They were camped on the northern bank of the Zimr, not far inland from Piliplok, in a pleasant, unspectacular countryside of rolling hills and well-tended farms. The air was warm here, a dry wind blowing from the south, and from the tawny look of the vegetation it was clear that in this district the rains of spring and early summer had long since ended. A host of small thriving cities lined both sides of the river in this district, and in each of them, so far, Dekkeret had been greeted with pleasure and excitement by the populace. Of whatever strange thing was going on in Ni-moya, the local officials seemed to have only the faintest idea, and they spoke of it to Dekkeret with obvious embarrassment and uneasiness. Ni-moya was thousands of miles away, in another province; Ni-moya, to these country people, was sophisticated to the point of decadence; if Ni-moya had decided to involve itself in some sort of peculiar political upheaval, that was a matter between Ni-moya and the Coronal, and no doubt the Coronal would very quickly take steps to restore the natural order of things there.

Septach Melayn said, "Read me the Sambailid lord's demands again, will you, my lord?"

Dekkeret riffled through the elegantly lettered parchment sheets. "Mmmm . . . here it is. Not demands, exactly. Proposals. The Lord Gaviral—an interesting title; who ever made him lord of anything?— deplores the possibility that armed conflict might break out between the forces of the people of Zimroel and those of the Coronal Lord Dekkeret of Alhanroel—notice, I am Coronal of Alhanroel, here, not of Majipoor—and calls for peaceful negotiations to resolve the conflict between the legitimate aspirations of the people of Zimroel and the equally legitimate authority of the imperial government of Alhanroel."

"At least he concedes that it's a legitimate government," said Septach Melayn. "Even if he does keep talking about it as Alhanroel's government, and not Majipoor's."

"Be that as it may," Dekkeret said, with a shrug. "He's taking the approach that this is to be a discussion between powers of equal standing, and that, of course, we can't allow. But let me go on: he wants—ah—here, yes—the primary thing that he wants to discuss at our meeting is the restoration of the title of Procurator of Zimroel, hereditary to his family. Hopes we can come to a peaceful agreement concerning the powers of said Procurator. Implies that his current title of Pontifex of Zimroel is merely provisional, and that he would be willing to abandon all claim to a separate Pontificate, in return for a constitutional compromise granting greater autonomy to Zimroel in general and the province of Ni-moya in particular, all of this under a Sambailid procuratorship."

"Well, then," Septach Melayn said, "is somewhat less fuss here than at first report. Sounds to me as though he'd be willing simply to settle for the name of Procurator and political control over Ni-moya and its surroundings. Which is more or less what Dantirya Sambail had."

"A title which Prestimion stripped him of," said Gialaurys. "And vowed there would never be Procurators in Zimroel again." The Grand Admiral's jowly face reddened, and growling sounds came from somewhere deep within him. He had the look, Dekkeret thought, of some great volcano preparing to erupt. "Are we to hand to the worthless nephew that which Prestimion took from the uncle, just on the nephew's say-so? Dantirya Sambail, at least, was a great man in his way. This one's a stupid pig and nothing more."

"Dantirya Sambail a great man?" Dinitak said, startled. "From all I heard, he was a monster of monsters!"

"That too," said Dekkeret. "But a shrewd and brilliant leader. He was no small instrument in the bringing of Zimroel into the modern world, in the days when Prankipin and Confalume ruled, and this continent was a patchwork of little principalities. He worked well with Castle and Labyrinth for forty years, until the time came when he took it into his head to be the one who named the new Coronal, and after that nothing was ever the same." And, to Gialaurys: "You know better than to think that we'd actually be handing power to this Gaviral any-way, my lord Admiral. This letter's Mandralisca's work. Is Mandralisca who'd be the real Procurator, if ever we let the title come back into being."

"And neverthless you intend to parley, my lord, knowing you are in fact parleying with the serpent Mandralisca, who has tried once already to take your life?" Gialaurys asked.

Septach Melayn stroked his little curling beard and laughed. "Do you remember, Gialaurys, when we were all of us drawn up at Thego-mar Edge just before the final battle of the Korsibar war, and a herald under a white flag came out from Prince Gonivaul, who was Grand Admiral then, saying that Lord Korsibar still had hope of a peaceful resolution of all disputes and was calling for a parley?"

"Yes, and suggested that Duke Svor should be the one we send out to discuss terms with him?" said Gialaurys, grinning at the memory.

To Dinitak Septach Melayn said, "Svor was the least warlike of us all, and the trickiest. And had been a good friend of Korsibar's before the factions divided. We saw no purpose in the parley, but Prestimion said, 'It does no harm to listen,' just as Dekkeret has said here today. And so Svor rode forth and met with Gonivaul in the middle of the open field, and Gonivaul made his proposal, which was that Svor wait until the battle had begun and at that time go among Prestimion's captains to say that Lord Korsibar would make them all dukes and princes if they would abandon Prestimion in mid-struggle and defect to the usurper. And also he offered little Svor Korsibar's own sister, the beautiful This-met, to be his wife, as the fee for his treason. That was Korsibar's idea of a parley."

"And what did Svor do?" Dekkeret asked.

"Rode back to our camp and told us what had been offered, and we all had a good laugh, and then the battle began. In which Svor died bravely, as it happened, fighting well on Prestimion's behalf, though the sly little man had never been much known for his valor before that day."

"And will we all have a good laugh also," said Dinitak, "when we find out what Mandralisca's idea of a parley is?"

"That do I hope," said Dekkeret.

"So you are resolved to go through with this thing?" Gialaurys asked.

"Indeed I am," Dekkeret said. "Where's the herald from the Lord Gaviral? Tell him I accept the invitation. We will set out at once for the appointed place."

*   *   *

The appointed place was three thousand miles up the Zimr near a town called Salvamot, where in the old days the Procurator Dantirya Sambail had maintained a country retreat, Mereminene Hall by name. The domain had remained in the family after the Procurator's downfall, and was now, apparently, the property of the Sambailid who called himself the Lord Gavahaud.

"Which one is that?" Dekkeret asked Septach Melayn. "Their names all sound alike to me. Is he the big drunken one?"

"That is Gavinius, my lord. Gavahaud is the popinjay, the pompous paragon of style and taste, a veritable Castle Mount of vanity and foolish arrogance. I look forward to taking instruction from him in the niceties of fashion."

Dekkeret chuckled. "We all have much to learn from these people, I think."

"And they will learn a little from us, my lord," said Gialaurys.

It was not a usual thing for seagoing vessels to engage in river travel, but there would not have been riverboats enough to carry all of Dekkeret's force, and the Zimr was so deep and wide it could handle the larger ships of the Coronal's maritime fleet without difficulty. The only problem had to do with the regular commercial shipping on the Zimr, which was unprepared to find such a host of huge ocean-craft taking up the preponderance of the channel. They scattered this way and that as the great phalanx of Lord Dekkeret's armada moved northward.

It was virtually a changeless landscape here, a broad riparian plain, low rolling hills beyond, and a succession of little bustling agricultural towns strung along both banks, with day after day of bright skies and warm sunlight. There were reports of heavy rains in Ni-moya, unseasonal downpours, but Ni-moya was far away, and here in the Zimr's lower valley there was only dry weather and unending warmth.

This was, in theory, Dekkeret's inaugural grand processional, but he paid no visits to any of the river towns, merely stood in the bow of the *Lord Stiamot* and waved to the assembled populace as he went sailing by. Even on a grand processional it was impossible for the Coronal to call at any but the most major cities, or else he would spend all the rest of his days going from place to place, growing fat on mayors' banquets, and never see the Castle again. And the business of Mandralisca and the Five Lords was too pressing to permit any such stops now, even at such relatively important places as Port Saikforge, Stenwamp, or Gablemorn.

On and on they went, town after town, through the placid Zimr valley: Dambmuir, Orgeliuse, Impemond, Haunfort Major; Cerinor and
Semirod and Molagat; Thibbildorn, Coranderk, Maccathar. Septach
Melayn, who had appointed himself the keeper of the maps, called off
each name as the towns came into view. But they all looked alike,
anyway—the waterfront promenade, the pier where throngs of riverboat
passengers waited for the next vessel, the warehouses and bazaars, the
dense plantings of palms and alabandinas and tanigales. As one place
after another flowed by him in a pleasant blur, Dekkeret found himself
reflecting yet again on the sheer immensity of the great world that was
Majipoor: the multitude of its provinces, its myriad cities, its billions of
people, spread out over three great continents so huge that it would be
a lifetime's task, and then some, to traverse them all. Here in this
densely populated valley, what did Ni-moya matter, or the Fifty Cities of
Castle Mount? To these people, the lower Zimr valley was a world unto
itself, a little universe, even, swarming with life and activity. And yet
there were dozens, scores, hundreds of such little universes everywhere
in the world.

It was a miracle, he thought, that a planet so vast and populous had
managed so well to live at peace with itself, at least until these troublesome recent times. And would live peacefully again, he swore, once the
poisonous irruption of evil into the world that Mandralisca and his ilk
represented had been contained and cauterized away.

"This is Gourkaine," said Septach Melayn one bright cloudless
morning, as yet another river town came into view.

"And of what significance is Gourkaine, then?" Dekkeret asked, for
Septach Melayn had uttered the name with a certain emphasis and
flourish.

"Of none at all, my lord, except that it is the town just downriver
from Salvamot, and Salvamot is where our friends the Five Lords of
Zimroel await us. So we are almost at our goal."

Salvamot was a town just like all the others, except that no throngs of
eager citizens had gathered at the piers to hail the Coronal when his armada was nearing their city, as had been the case everywhere else thus
far, even at nearby Gourkaine. Nor were there any banners flying that
bore Lord Dekkeret's portrait on them and the royal colors. Only a small

group of municipal officials could be seen, collected in a tight and uneasy-looking knot by the main quay.

"It is as though we have crossed some sort of border," said Dekkeret. "But we are still thousands of miles from Ni-moya. Does the power of the Five Lords reach all the way down to here, I wonder?"

"Bear in mind, my lord, that Dantirya Sambail was a frequent visitor to his lands here," Septach Melayn said, "and his kinsmen also, I'd wager. These people here must feel a special loyalty to that tribe now. And also, look you there—"

He indicated a quay just upriver from the town. A dozen or more big riverboats were docked there, and from their masts fluttered the long crimson banners of the Sambailid clan, with their blood-red crescent-moon emblem emblazoned upon them. It appeared that other such ships lay just to the north, around a slight bend that the Zimr made here. So the Five Lords, or some of them, at any rate, were already on the scene here in Salvamot, and with an armada of their own. Small wonder that the local citizenry would greet the arriving Coronal with some degree of restraint.

A detachment of the Coronal's guard preceded Lord Dekkeret ashore. Soon the guard-captain returned accompanied by a short, thick-necked man in black robes and a golden chain of office, who announced himself to be Veroalk Timaran, the Chief Justiciar of the Municipality of Salvamot—"I would hold the title of mayor, in another place, my lord," he informed Dekkeret gravely—and expressed his great delight and satisfaction that his city had been chosen as the site of this historic meeting. He bowed so extravagantly to the Lady Fulkari that veins bulged out on the broad column of his neck and his face turned red. He would, he said, escort the Coronal and his companions to the estate of the Lord Gavahaud in person. The Lord Gavahaud had provided floaters for the royal party, said the Justiciar Veroalk Timaran, and they were waiting a little way beyond.

There were just three small vehicles, with a capacity of perhaps fifteen occupants, and scarcely any room for the Coronal's bodyguard.

Dekkeret said amiably, "We have brought our own floaters, your honor. We prefer to travel in those. I would be pleased to have you ride beside me in my own."

The Chief Justiciar had not been prepared for this, and he seemed flustered, perhaps not so much at the distinction of being asked to ride in the Coronal's personal floater as at the realization that the day was already departing from the script that had been provided him. But he was in no position to place himself in opposition to the Coronal's wishes, and he watched in what seemed to be mounting consternation as Dekkeret's men proceeded to unload a score of floaters from the flagship, and as many more from the second vessel, and went on to unload still more from the third: enough vehicles to transport the Coronal's entire corps of guardsmen, and a good many of the imperial troops as well.

"If you will, your honor," said Dekkeret, beckoning the Chief Justiciar Veroalk Timaran toward a floater bearing the starburst crest.

Salvamot—city, town, whatever it was—thinned out swiftly once they were away from the river, and very shortly Dekkeret found himself riding through flat open country studded with sparse stands of slender trees that had russet trunks and purple leaves, and then making a winding ascent in more heavily forested terrain toward a low plateau to the east. The domain of the Lord Gavahaud, said the Justiciar, lay up there.

Fulkari rode at Dekkeret's side, and Dinitak also. Dekkeret would gladly have left her behind to wait for him at Piliplok, for he had no idea what danger awaited him at this conference, or whether it would end in some sort of armed conflict. But she would not hear of it. The Five Lords, she said, would not dare touch an anointed Coronal. And even if they attempted any violence, she said—and it was clear that she saw the peril too—what sort of royal consort would she be, to shrink back into safety while her lord was at risk? She would rather die bravely with him, she said, than carry a cowardly widowhood back with her to the Castle.

"There will be no widowhoods for you just yet," Dekkeret told her. "These are men who lack all courage, and we will quickly have them kneeling to us."

Privately he was not so certain of that. But that made no difference. Fulkari would not be denied, and, come what may, she would be with him to the end of this.

Septach Melayn was in the second floater, and Gialaurys in the third, and the others followed close behind. It was a considerable force, hundreds of armed men, and others ready at the pier should any signal of distress go up. If we are riding into ambush, Dekkeret thought, we will make them pay a good price for their treachery.

But all seemed peaceful enough as the floaters entered the great arched gateway of Mereminene Hall. There were crescent-moon banners galore here, and a host of men in the green Sambailid livery, some of them armed, but only in the ordinary way of men-at-arms who guard a great estate. Dekkeret saw no lurking battalions, no cache of waiting weaponry.

A tall thickset red-haired man, strikingly ugly, a preening strutting figure in sweeping maroon cloak and foppish yellow tights that were much too tight, came forward with a clanking of golden spurs. He made a grand excessive bow to Dekkeret and Fulkari, culminating in exaggerated starburst salutes as he straightened up. "My lord—my lady—you do us great honor. I am the Lord Gavahaud, whose pleasure it is to show you to the accommodations that will be yours during this your stay. My lordly brother will be pleased to greet you afterward, when you are installed."

"What kind of accent is that?" Fulkari asked, under her breath. "He utters everything through his nose. Is that the Ni-moyan way of speech? I've never heard the like."

"False grandeur is what they speak here," said Dekkeret. "We must be careful not to snicker, whatever the provocation."

The guest-lodge of Mereminene Hall was a place of shining adamantine floors and vermilion-tiled walls and faceted windows intricately set in lead, easily worthy of housing a visiting Coronal. The main house must surely be even grander, Dekkeret thought. And this was a mere country estate. Old Dantirya Sambail had not been one to stint, it seemed. But why would he? In his time he had been king of Zimroel, effectively, and no doubt had wanted to equal in a single generation all that the Coronals of Castle Mount had built for themselves over thousands of years.

Nor was there any stinting of hospitality by this Gavahaud, either. The lodge swarmed with platoons of bowing servants; rare wines and exotic fruits aplenty were supplied for the delectation of the guests if they cared to refresh themselves upon arrival; their bed-linens were of the finest manufacture, glowing warm-hued silks and satins.

A chamberlain came within an hour with word that there would be a formal dinner that evening, adding that it was the wish of the Lord Gaviral that no discussions of serious matters should be expected until the following day.

The Lord Gaviral—he who styled himself Pontifex of Zimroel—came to the guest-lodge an hour after that, alone, simply dressed, unarmed, and on foot. Dekkeret was surprised at how small a man this Gaviral was, no taller than Prestimion and much less solidly built: flimsy-framed, in fact, with the constantly moving eyes and twitching lips of a man who is uneasy in his spirit. He had heard that these Sam-bailids were massive hulking ugly men as the old Procurator and his brothers had been, and certainly Gavahaud fit that description, but not this one, who had some of the ugliness but none of the size. Only by his rank plume of orange-red hair and his broad, wide-nostriled nose was his kinship with the tribe of Dantirya Sambail confirmed.

But he was courtly enough, speaking well and making every show of respect for his royal visitor, and behaving not in any way like one who has proclaimed himself to be a lord and even a Pontifex in defiance of all the natural order of things. He inquired merely whether the Coronal found his lodgings suitable, and hoped that his lordship's appetite would be equal to the feast that awaited him. "I regret that two of my brothers have been unable to join us for this meeting," said Gaviral. "The Lord Gavinius is unwell, and could not leave Ni-moya. The Lord Gavdat, who practices the study of magery, has remained behind as well, because he is in the midst of important prognosticatory calcula-tions that he feels must not be interrupted even for so important a gath-ering as this."

"I regret their absence," said Dekkeret courteously, although Sep-tach Melayn had already told him that Gavinius was a revolting drunken fool, and the other one, Gavdat, evidently was a fool of a dif-ferent kind, forever lost in the claptrap of geomantic studies. But cour-tesy would cost him nothing; and he was only too well aware that it made no difference whether he met with one Sambailid brother, or five, or five hundred. Mandralisca was the force to reckon with. And of Man-dralisca nothing at all so far had been said.

It was evening, now. Banquet time.

As Dekkeret had suspected, the late Procurator had indeed lived here on a truly regal scale. The main house was a massive stone pile with some seven or ten great-windowed halls radiating from its core, and the banquet hall was the greatest of all, a tremendous gallery of rugged antique design, with bare red beams of bright thembar-wood, and rough heavy walls of mortared boulders piled to an astounding height. And this at the country estate of a provincial lordling; what was the procuratorial palace at Ni-moya like, Dekkeret wondered, if Dantirya Sambail's mere country retreat had been a place of this sort?

The big room was full: the entire court of the Five Lords must be here, Dekkeret thought. Protocol was somewhat strained at the high-table seating. Dekkeret, as Coronal, was entitled to the center position,

with Fulkari at his side. But the Lord Gaviral claimed at least for the
time being to be the Pontifex of this continent, whatever that meant,
and the Lord Gavahaud his brother, as the actual owner of Mereminene
Hall, was the putative host of the meeting. Which one of them would
sit at the Coronal's right hand? There was much murmuring, and in the
end Gavahaud deferred to Gaviral, and let him take the seat of honor
beside Dekkeret, but not before some further confusion involving the
third brother, the Lord Gavilomarin, who had appeared now also, a
blinking, watery-eyed lump of a man with a blithering smile and a general air of witlessness about him. He took the central seat without asking, apparently choosing it at random, and had to be moved along
toward the end of the dais, down by Septach Melayn and Gialaurys.
Dinitak was seated at the opposite end.

Where, Dekkeret asked himself, was the infamous Mandralisca?

His name had not so much as been mentioned thus far. That seemed
very odd. In the awkward first moments after taking his seat Dekkeret
said to Gaviral, by way of having anything to say at all, "And your privy
counsellor, of whom I've heard so much? Surely he is here tonight, but
where?"

"He dislikes the prominence of the dais," said Gaviral. "You will find
him over there on the left, against the wall."

Dekkeret glanced in the direction Gaviral indicated, far across the
room to an ordinary table set amidst many others. Though he had never
seen Mandralisca, he recognized him at once. He stood out from all
those around him like death at a wedding feast: a pallid, somber, harsh-
faced, thin-lipped man garbed in a tight-fitting suit of shining black
leather that was altogether without ornament except for some large,
bright pendant of gold, no doubt an emblem of office, on a chain
around his neck. His hard, glittering eyes were trained directly on
Dekkeret, nor did he flinch away as the Coronal's gaze came to rest on
him.

So that is Mandralisca, Dekkeret thought. After all this time, he and
I are no more than a hundred feet apart.

He found himself fascinated by the man's chilly, repellent face and
sinister aura. There was an unquestionable magnetism about him, a diabolical force. Tremendous demonic power of will was evident in his
features. Dekkeret understood now how this man, the embodiment of
all that had bedeviled Prestimion throughout the years of his otherwise
glorious reign, could have caused so much trouble in the world for so

many years. Here was a truly dark soul; here was one whose very existence made one wonder about the Divine's purpose in creating him.

After a long moment the contact between Majipoor's Coronal and
the Lord of Zimroel's privy counsellor broke, and it was Mandralisca
who was the first to look away, in order to make some remark to his
table-companions. There were three of those: a round-faced common-
looking man of middle years or a little more, a handsome, open-faced
lad with golden-white hair who could not have been more than eighteen or nineteen, and a small, swarthy-skinned, squinch-eyed fellow who
beyond any question had to be Dinitak's despised helmet-making uncle,
Khaymak Barjazid of Suvrael.

Servitors brought wine around, and filled all their bowls. Dekkeret
wondered idly whether Dantirya Sambail's old custom of taking a
poison-taster with him wherever he went might not have been appropriate here. Though it seemed absurd, he put his hand over Fulkari's
when she reached in an automatic way for her wine-bowl, and held her
back.

She gave him a questioning look.

"We must wait for the toast," he whispered, not knowing what else to
say.

"Oh. Of course," she said, looking a little abashed.

The Lord Gaviral was on his feet, now, wine-bowl in his hand. The
hall grew silent. "To amity," he said. "To harmony. To concord. To the
eternal friendship of the continents."

He looked toward Dekkeret and drank. Dekkeret, realizing now that
his wine had been poured from the same flask as Gaviral's, rose and returned the toast with equally empty generalities, and drank also. It was
superb wine. Whatever else would happen here at Mereminene Hall,
they were not going to be poisoned this evening, he decided.

All around the room, the Sambailid folk were on their feet—all of
them men, Dekkeret noted—holding high their bowls and calling out,
"To amity! To harmony! To concord!" Even Mandralisca had joined the
toast, although what he held in his hand was a water-glass, not a wine-
bowl.

"Your privy counsellor doesn't care for wine, eh?" Dekkeret said to
Gaviral.

"Abhors it, in fact. Will not touch the stuff. Had to drink too much
of it, I suppose, when he was taster to my uncle the Procurator."

"I take your point. If I thought there might be poison in every wine-bowl that was handed me, I might lose my taste for drink myself, after a year or two," said Dekkeret, and laughed, and took another sip of his own.

It still seemed very odd to him that Mandralisca had not come up to be introduced. The merest provincial mayor was ever eager to force his name and pedigree on a visiting Coronal; and here was a man who held the rank of privy counsellor to someone who gave himself the title of lord, and claimed authority over all of Zimroel, and he chose instead to nest among his own companions at a far table. But that was Mandralisca's style, apparently: to lurk in the background and allow someone else the visible glory. That was how he had operated in Dantira Sambail's time, and that seemed to be how he operated now.

Dekkeret did remark again on Mandralisca's evident shyness to Gaviral at one point in the evening, saying that it was strange that he was not at the high table.

"He is a man of very humble birth, you know," Gaviral said piously. "He feels it is not his place to be up here with those of us whose ancestry is so splendid. But you will meet him tomorrow, my lord, when we all gather in the meadow to explore the details of the treaty we wish to propose."

18
---

*I*t was midday, bright and warm, when the summons came to gather in the meadow for the conference that had brought the Coronal to this place. When Dekkeret reached the site, a broad grassy plain far from the main houses that was bordered on three sides by a dark, dense forest and on the fourth by a pleasant stream, he saw that a meeting-table made of broad planks of polished black wood, mounted on a foundation of thick yellowish beams that tapered to a point, had been erected parallel to the stream. A neat array of paper and parchment was set out on it, weighed down by crystal globes to keep them from blowing away in the gentle breeze, and also inkpots, milufta-feather pens, and various other writing gear. Dekkeret saw also an assortment of wine-flasks, wine of half a dozen different colors, and a row of bowls waiting to be filled. Once the treaty had been presented and—as Gaviral so plainly hoped—agreed upon, the signatory parties would no doubt be expected to celebrate the event right here upon the spot.

The Lord Gaviral, resplendent in a metallic jerkin that seemed almost like a suit of armor and richly tooled scarlet leggings piped with golden thread, was already at the site, standing beside the table. His brothers Gavahaud and Gavilomarin, splendidly dressed also, flanked him.

As for Mandralisca, he stood just at his master's elbow, clad now not in last night's skin-tight black leathers but in a far gaudier costume: a knee-length red-and-green jacket with a wide, flat collar decked with white steetmoy fur and hanging sleeves that were slashed to allow his arms to come through, over dark gray hose of the finest weave, and a broad meshwork belt at his waist supporting a fancy tasseled pouch. It was the sort of dandyish costume that Septach Melayn might have chosen, though the sight of Mandralisca's pale, hard, sinister face rising above that flaring collar muted the outfit's flamboyance more than somewhat. Mandralisca's own threesome of companions, the pudgy little bandy-legged aide-de-camp and the tall fair-haired youth and the scrawny, evil-looking Barjazid, were only a short distance behind him.

Dekkeret had worn his green-and-gold robes of state to the meeting, and the slender golden circlet that he often used in the place of the starburst crown. Gialaurys, beside him, was in full armor, but without a helm. Septach Melayn was content with a doublet and bright leggings. The spiral Labyrinth symbol on his breast was his only ornament. Dinitak wore his usual simple tunic, and Fulkari had chosen simple garb also. A row of Dekkeret's hand-picked guardsmen stood some distance to the rear. Gaviral had an honor guard behind him as well, at the same distance.

"An auspicious day, my lord!" cried Gaviral, as Dekkeret approached. "A day when harmony is to be attained!"

His voice was cheery, but sounded forced and strained; and there was a generally edgy look about him, a fidgeting of his lips, a flickering instability of his gaze. Well, thought Dekkeret, he has a great deal at stake here: he has brought the Coronal Lord far into this unfamiliar territory to demand unheard-of concessions from him, and the Coronal has given every indication that he will listen to the Sambailid demands seriously and perhaps even to accede to them, but he has no certain assurance of what the Coronal actually has in mind. Nor do I of him, Dekkeret thought. We are both playing here with closely guarded hands.

"Harmony, yes. Let us hope that that is what we fashion here today," said Dekkeret, giving Gaviral the warmest of smiles.

As he spoke he allowed his eyes to rest steadily on Gaviral's, which were bloodshot and uneasy; but the Sambailid looked quickly away, and busied himself fussing among the papers and writing apparatus laid out on the table, as though he were some sort of amanuensis rather than the self-styled Pontifex of Zimroel. Dekkeret's gaze moved onward toward Mandralisca, who offered an altogether different response, a cold, unwavering stare, full of menace and loathing, which Dekkeret admired for its unconcealed sincerity if for nothing else.

"Shall we drink to a successful conclusion to our talks, lordship, before we get to the work of setting forth our proposals and hearing your response?" Gaviral said.

"I see no reason why not," replied Dekkeret, and the wine-bowls were filled. Once again—he could not help himself—Dekkeret kept surreptitious watch to see whether his bowl and Gaviral's were filled from the same flask, which once again they were. Indeed, the bowls were being filled so indiscriminately up and down the table that there was no way that poison could be involved, not unless Gaviral cared to take some of his own men down with the visitors.

Gaviral offered the same toast to amity and concord as he had the night before, and they all took light sips of their wine, mere symbolic tastes. Mandralisca, as before, did not drink.

Then Gaviral said, "We have prepared this document for your examination, my lord. —This is our privy counsellor, as you know, the Count Mandralisca. He will show you the text, of which he is the author, and he will deal with any questions that may arise, clause by clause."

Dekkeret nodded. Mandralisca, followed as ever by his three minions, marched ostentatiously around the end of the long table and up Dekkeret's side of it. Dekkeret saw now that the aide-de-camp was carrying tucked under his arm a rolled parchment scroll, which he brought forth and handed to Mandralisca. The privy counsellor, opening it, held it out in front of himself and studied it as if wishing to ascertain that the aide-de-camp had indeed brought the right one; and finally, seemingly satisfied, leaned forward and laid it down on the table in front of Dekkeret.

"If you will, my lord," said Mandralisca, with an odd tone in his voice that was a mixture, Dekkeret thought, of willed obsequiousness and barely throttled rage.

There was a great silence all around as Dekkeret began to read the document through.

It was not an easy business, reading that scroll. The text was close-packed and verbose, and the calligraphy was ornate and of an antiquarian sort, with many an irritating curlicue and decorative swirl. It called for close concentration, verging almost on decipherment. Dekkeret, struggling with it, soon discovered that it opened with a lengthy and circumlocutory preamble, implying, perhaps, that the Sambailids were asking for nothing more than provincial autonomy and a revival of the procuratorial title. But it was followed by other clauses that contradicted that, clauses seeming to assert that what they actually wanted was a good deal more—in fact an end to all imperial rule everywhere in the continent of Zimroel, complete independence, total withdrawal of the existing regime.

"Is there a problem, my lord?" asked Mandralisca, hovering by Dekkeret's shoulder and leaning close.

"A problem? No. But I find a certain lack of clarity in your opening statements. I'll look at them again, I think."

Frowning, he went back to the beginning, sought to disentangle clause from clause, separating each statement from its carefully mated opposite. It was a task that called for the deepest concentration, and deep concentration was what Dekkeret endeavored to give it.

Not so deep, though, that he failed to see from the corner of his eye the bright flash of the blade that Mandralisca had suddenly pulled from that tasseled pouch at his waist, nor heard Fulkari's immediate gasp of alarm. But it was all happening so swiftly that he could do nothing more than lean backward, away from the thrust that was heading his way from the rear.

But then in one split second the long-haired boy, Mandralisca's own aide, reached his hand forward, swooped up the wine-bowl at Dekkeret's elbow, and hurled its contents into his master's eyes. At the same time with his other hand he made a grab at Mandralisca's descending arm. Mandralisca, eluding the boy's grasping hand, whirled about blindly and swept the dagger-blade in a furious gesture across the boy's throat, drawing a spurt of red. The boy seemed to crumple and disappear. And then, amid the general uproar, Septach Melayn appeared at Dekkeret's side, his drawn sword in his hand, ordering Mandralisca in a terrible roaring cry to stand back from the Coronal's presence.

Mandralisca, half blinded, his face streaming with wine, did back away, but only as far as the place where the Lord Gavahaud stood gaping in astonishment and terror. From Gavahaud's scabbard he yanked the elaborately chased dress-sword with which the vain Sambailid had furnished his outfit, and swung quickly around, still trying to blink the wine out of his eyes as he confronted the onrushing Septach Melayn.

"Here," said Septach Melayn coldly, halting and tossing to Mandralisca a kerchief that he was carrying tucked in his sleeve. "Wipe your face. I will not kill a man who is unable to see." He gave the surprised Mandralisca a moment to blot away the wine; and then he came forward again, his rapier in swift motion.

Dekkeret, still stunned and bewildered by all that had taken place, half rose from his seat at the conference table. But no intervention was possible. Septach Melayn and Mandralisca were already hard at it, moving steadily out in the meadow as they fought. Dekkeret had never seen two swords moving so swiftly. Septach Melayn was the swiftest man alive with a sword; but Mandralisca met him thrust for thrust, parry for parry, a wild display of virtuoso swordsmanship, feinting, pivoting, moving always with lightning speed. There was no stroke that Septach Melayn could not deal with and deflect, but still — still — to see Septach Melayn held at a standstill, unable to break through the other's defense —

And then Mandralisca, turning abruptly away from Septach Melayn, reached down and snatched up a handful of the soft, loose meadow soil and flung it into Septach Melayn's face. Unlike Septach Melayn, he had no compunctions about fighting with a man who could not see. The earthen clod broke up as it struck Septach Melayn, some going to his eyes, some to his nostrils, some to his mouth; and as he stood baffled for a moment, coughing and spitting and wiping at his eyes, Mandralisca rushed forward in a furious frenzied onslaught, driving his blade toward the center of Septach Melayn's chest.

Dekkeret watched in horror. Mandralisca's sword and Septach Melayn's moved with blurring speed. For an instant it was impossible to see what was happening. Then Dekkeret caught sight of Septach Melayn parrying Mandralisca's desperate attack, sweeping Mandralisca's sword aside with a grand upstroke of his own. An instant later Septach Melayn lunged and thrust, and took Mandralisca through the throat with his stroke.

The two men stood frozen for an instant.

There was an utterly weird look, a strange thing that was almost a look of triumph, on Mandralisca's face as he died. Septach Melayn pulled his blade free of the toppling Mandralisca and swung about so that he was facing toward the conference table and Dekkeret. But then Dekkeret realized that somewhere in the final melee Septach Melayn had been wounded also. Blood was streaming down the front of his doublet, a trickle at first, then more, so much that the little golden Labyrinth emblem was completely hidden in the weltering flow.

The whole meadow was in chaos now, concealed Sambailid troops emerging from their hiding places in the forest, Dekkeret's own guard rushing forward to protect him, and the rest of Dekkeret's soldiers, coming in now from the outskirts of the field where they had been waiting for a signal from their king, joining the fray also when they heard the bellowed command that came from Dekkeret. In the midst of all this the Coronal ran toward Septach Melayn, who was staggering and lurching, but still contriving somehow to remain on his feet.

"My lord—" Septach Melayn began. And halted, for some spasm of pain seemed to overtake him; but then he recovered himself a little and said, smiling, "The beast is dead, is he not? How glad I am of that."

"Oh, Septach Melayn—"

Dekkeret would have caught him then, for it seemed that he was about to fall. But Septach Melayn waved him away. "Take this, my lord," he said, handing Dekkeret his sword. "Use it to defend yourself against these barbarians. I will not need it again." And added, with a glance at the fallen Mandralisca: "I have achieved what I was put into this world to do."

Now Septach Melayn tottered and began to topple. Dekkeret seized him by the shoulders and held him upright in a tender embrace. It seemed to him that Septach Melayn weighed next to nothing, tall as he was. Dekkeret held him that way long enough to hear a quiet little sigh come from him, and then the death rattle. And then he eased him gently to the ground.

Swinging about, now, Dekkeret took in the madness all around him in a single glance. One swarm of his guardsmen stood in a circle of swords about Fulkari; she was safe. A second group had formed a wall around his own self. Gialaurys loomed like a mountain beside the conference table, clutching the Lord Gaviral by the throat with one huge hand, and the Lord Galahaud the same way with the other. Dinitak had found a poniard somewhere and was brandishing it at his uncle's breast, and Khaymak Barjazid had his hands raised high to show that he was his nephew's prisoner. All over the field the Sambailid warriors, realizing now that their leaders were taken, were throwing down their weapons and lifting their hands in similar gestures of surrender.

Then Dekkeret looked down and saw the boy who had thrown the wine in Mandralisca's face, lying practically at his feet, with Mandralisca's plump little aide-de-camp kneeling over him. He was streaming with blood from that terrible wound to the throat.

"Is he alive?" Dekkeret asked.

"Barely, my lord. He has only moments left."

"He saved me from death," said Dekkeret, and an eerie chill came over him as there entered into his mind the recollection of another day long ago, in Normork, and another Coronal faced with an assassin's blade, and the casual unthinking swipe of that blade that had taken his cousin Sithelle's life and in a strange way simultaneously set him on his path to the throne. So it had all happened again, a life sacrificed so that a Coronal might live. Dekkeret, looking across to Fulkari, saw the ghost of Sithelle instead, and trembled and came close to weeping.

But the boy was still alive, more or less. His eyes were open and he was staring at Dekkeret. Why, Dekkeret wondered, had he mysteriously turned against his master in this fatal way in that decisve moment? And had his answer at once, exactly as if he had asked his question aloud. For in the softest of voices the boy said, "I could not bear it any longer, my lord. Knowing that he meant to kill you here today—to kill the lord of the world—"

"Hush, boy," Dekkeret said. "Don't try to speak. You need to rest."

But he did not appear to have heard. "And knowing also that I had taken the wrong turn in life, that I had foolishly given myself to the most evil of masters—"

Dekkeret knelt by him and told him again to rest; but it was no use, now, for the faint voice had trickled off into silence, and the staring eyes were unseeing. Dekkeret glanced up at the aide-de-camp and said, "What was his name?"

"Thastain, my lord. He came from a place called Sennec."

"Thastain of Sennec. And yours?"

"Jacomin Halefice, lordship."

"Take him to the lodge, then, Halefice, and have his body laid out for burial. We'll give him a hero's funeral, this Thastain of Sennec. The sort one would give a duke or a prince who fell fighting for his lord. And there will be a great monument in his name erected in Ni-moya, that I vow."

He walked across then to the place where Septach Melayn lay. Gialaurys, still gripping the two Sambailids as though they were mere sacks of grain, had gone there too, dragging his captives with him, and stood looking down at his friend's body. He was weeping great terrible silent tears that flowed in rivers down his broad fleshy face.

Quietly Dekkeret said, "We will take him away from this loathsome place, Gialaurys, and return him to the Castle, where he belongs. You will carry his body there, and see to it that he is given a tomb to match those of Dvorn and Lord Stiamot, with an inscription on it saying, 'Here lies Septach Melayn, who was the equal in nobility of any king that ever lived.'"

"That I will do, my lord," said Gialaurys, in a voice that itself seemed to come from beyond the grave.

"And also we will find some bard of the court—I charge you with this task too, Gialaurys—to write the epic of his life, which schoolchildren ten thousand years from now will know by heart."

Gialaurys nodded. He gestured to a pair of guardsmen to take charge of his two prisoners, and dropped to his knees, and scooped up Septach Melayn and slowly carried him from the field.

Dekkeret pointed next at the body of Mandralisca, face down in the grass. "Take this away," he said to his captain of guards, "and see that it is burned, in whatever place the kitchen trash of this place is burned, and have the ashes turned under in the forest, where no one will ever find them."

"I will, my lord."

Dekkeret went at last to Fulkari, who stood white-faced and stunned beside the conference table. "We are done here, my lady," he said quietly. "A sad day this has been, too. But we will never know a sadder one, I think, until we come to the end of our own days." He slipped his arm around her. She was trembling like one who stands in an icy wind. He held her until the trembling had abated somewhat, and then he said, "Come, love. Our business here is done, and I have important messages to send to Prestimion."

19

*F*rom her many-windowed room high up atop the Alaisor Mercantile Exchange, Keltryn stood staring out to sea, watching the great red-sailed ship from Zimroel as it entered the harbor. Dinitak was aboard that ship. They had hurried her by swift royal floater in a breathless chase across the width of Alhanroel so that she would be here in Alaisor when he arrived, and they had installed her in royal magnificence in this huge suite that they said was ordinarily reserved only for Powers of the Realm; and now here she was, and there *he* was, aboard that majestic vessel just off shore and coming closer to her with every passing moment.

It still amazed her that she was here at all.

Not just that she was in the fabled city of Alaisor, so far from Castle Mount, with those extraordinary black cliffs behind her and the gigantic monument to Lord Stiamot in the plaza just below her room. Sooner or later, she supposed, she would have found some reason to see the world, and her travels might well have brought her to this beautiful place.

But that she had come running here at Dinitak's behest, after all that had passed between them—

She could remember only too well saying to Fulkari, upon learning that he was leaving her behind when he went to Zimroel, "I never want to see him again!"

And Fulkari smugly saying, "You will."

She had thought then that Fulkari was wrong, simply wrong. She could never swallow such humiliation. But time had passed, days and weeks and months, time in which she had the leisure to dwell in memory on those hand-in-hand strolls in the hallways of the Castle, those candlelit dinners, those nights of astounding passion. Time to reflect, also, on Dinitak's unique nature, his strangely intense sense of right and wrong. Time to think that perhaps she could almost comprehend his reasons for going to Zimroel without her.

And then, by special courier, those two messages from abroad—

Dinitak Barjazid, to Keltryn of Sipermit, saying, in that odd formal manner of his, *I am returning by way of Alaisor, and I beg you most urgently to be there when I arrive, my dearest one, for we have things of the greatest importance to discuss, and they will be best discussed there.* "I beg you most urgently!" That did not sound much like Dinitak, to beg at all, and most urgently at that. "My dearest one." Yes.

The second message, in the same pouch, was from Fulkari, and what Fulkari said was, *He will ask you to meet him at Alaisor. Go to him there, sister. He loves you. He loves you more than you could possibly believe.*

She could not repress the instantaneous flare of anger that was her first reaction. How dare he? How dare *she*? Why fall into the same old trap again? Go all the way to *Alaisor*, no less, at his behest, for his convenience? Why? Why? Why?

He loves you.

He loves you more than you could possibly believe.

And Dinitak:

I beg you most urgently.

My dearest one. My dearest one. My dearest one.

A knock at her door. "My lady?" It was Ekkamoor, the chamberlain from the Castle who had looked after her on this frantic journey to the continent's edge. "The ship is about to dock, my lady. Is it your wish to be at the pier when it does?"

"Yes," she said. "Yes, of course!"

It flew the Coronal's green-and-gold banner, and the Coronal's starburst emblem was on its prow. But there was a yellow flag of mourning flying from its mast as well, and Keltryn, watching from the waiting-room as the gangplank was fixed in place, stared frowning as a solemn-faced honor guard came from the vessel first, bearing a coffin, by the looks of it a coffin of the most costly make. Walking behind it was a heavy-shouldered, powerfully built man whom she recognized, after a moment, as the Grand Admiral Gialaurys, Septach Melayn's old friend and companion-in-arms, but a Gialaurys who seemed to have aged a hundred years since she last had seen him at the Castle at the time of Lord Dekkeret's coronation. His head was bowed, his face was dark and grim. As the procession bearing the coffin went past her, he did not appear to notice her at all. But why should he? If he knew her at all, it was only as one of the innumerable young ladies of the court. And he was obviously so preoccupied with his grief that he could spare no attention for those he passed while coming ashore.

But who is it that is dead? she wondered, looking back at the somber procession as it vanished from view.

And then a familiar voice cried, "Keltryn! Keltryn!"

"*Dinitak!*"

He had changed, somehow. Not outwardly: he was the same slender, compact man, with the same sun-darkened face and the same look of taut-coiled intensity. But something was different. There was—what?— a kind of grandeur about him now, an almost regal air of attainment and purpose. Keltryn saw it right away. She ran to him, and he opened his arms to her, and she pressed herself tight against him, and the sensation of contact brought warm, good memories to life in her, but there was also, even now, that puzzling sense of changes that had taken place within him.

Of course. He had gone to Zimroel with the Coronal. He had taken part in some kind of terrible struggle against the enemies of the throne.

After a time she stepped back from him and said, "Well, here I am, Dinitak!"

"Here you are, yes. How wonderful that is."

"And Zimroel—you'll tell me all about it—?"

"In time. It is a very long story. And there is so much else to tell too." A curious smile traveled like a flickering flame across his dark features. "I am to be a Power of the Realm, Keltryn. And if you will have me, you will be, like your sister, the consort of a Power."

The words made no sense at all to her. She stood there, saying them over and over in her mind, and in no way could she draw a meaning from them.

He said, "It is agreed, by Dekkeret and Prestimion and the Lady. I am to wear the helmet, and enter minds as the Lady does, and seek out those who would do harm to others. And with the helmet I am to warn them of the consequences of their actions, and to punish them if they proceed in spite of the warning. The King of Dreams is to be my title; and it will descend to my children, and to my children's children forever, who will be trained in the helmet's use. So there will be no more Mandraliscas in the world. You see, then, I am to be a Power. But will you be a Power's wife, Keltryn?"

"You're asking me to marry you?" she said, dumfounded.

"If the King of Dreams is to have children who will inherit his tasks, he must have a queen, is that not so? —We will live in Suvrael. That is Prestimion's decision, not mine, that the new Power must make his home far from those of the other three; but it is not the worst place in the world, Suvrael, and I think you will get used to it much quicker than you think. If you like, we can return to the Castle to be married, or go to the Labyrinth and have Prestimion perform the ceremony, but Dekkeret and I are agreed that it is best for me to go to Suvrael as quickly as I can, in order that I can—"

She was barely listening, and scarcely understanding at all. A Power of the Realm? King of Dreams? Suvrael? It was all whirling madly in her mind.

"Keltryn?" Dinitak said.

"So much—so strange—"

"Tell me this, at least: will you marry me, Keltryn?"

That much she could focus on. There would be time later to comprehend the rest of it, King of Dreams and Suvrael and all of that, and what had happened while he and Dekkeret and the others were over in Zimroel, and whose body it was that Gialaurys had escorted from the ship.

"Yes," she said, understanding that much. *He loves you. He loves you more than you could possibly believe.* "Yes, Dinitak, yes, yes, yes, yes!"

Prestimion said, glancing down at the despatch that had just been brought to him, "Gialaurys has come from Alaisor to Sisivondal with the body, and is setting out on his way back to the Mount. So we will have to set out ourselves for the Castle in a day or two also, Varaile."

She smiled. "I knew you'd have to find some excuse to get yourself away from the Labyrinth before much longer, Prestimion. I don't think we've ever spent as many consecutive months anywhere as we have since we got back here from Stoien."

"In truth I've grown quite accustomed to life in the Labyrinth, my love. Confalume said I would, sooner or later; and he was right in that, as he was in so many things. It's when you're Coronal that you're a rover. The blood is hot in you, then. The Pontifex prefers a quieter life, and the Labyrinth has a way of growing on one, don't you think?" He gestured about him with one hand and then the other, indicating all the familiar possessions of their Castle household, everything now comfortably installed in the apartments of the Labyrinth that once had been Confalume's and now were theirs, and looking as though they had been in place for decades rather than months. "—In any case, it wasn't my decision to bury Septach Melayn at the Castle. It was Dekkeret's. To which I gladly defer."

"He was your friend, Prestimion. And High Spokesman to the Pontifex, as well. Wouldn't it be more appropriate for him to be laid to rest here at the Labyrinth?"

Prestimion shook his head. "He was never a man of the Labyrinth, was Septach Melayn. He came here only out of loyalty to me. Castle Mount was his place, and there he will lie. I will not overrule Dekkeret on that. He died saving Dekkeret's life; that act alone gives Dekkeret claim on where to bury him."

He realized that he was speaking quite calmly of these details of Septach Melayn's burial, as though it were merely some ordinary piece of business of the realm, and for a moment Prestimion actually thought that the pain of his friend's death might be starting to heal. But then it all came sweeping back upon him, and he grimaced and turned away. His eyes were stinging. That Septach Melayn, of all men, should have been lost in the struggle against Mandralisca—that he should have given up his own life for the sake of ridding the world of that—that—

"Prestimion—" said Varaile, reaching a hand toward him.

He fought to regain his control, and succeeded. "We needn't discuss this, Varaile. Shouldn't. Dekkeret has decreed a Castle funeral and a Castle burial, and Gialaurys is bringing him there, and the monument is already being designed, and I will officiate at the ceremony, and so you and I should start packing for our trip up the Glayge. And so be it."

"I wonder what sort of burial Dekkeret decreed for Mandralisca."

"I'll ask him, if I think of it whenever he returns from his processional. I'd have fed the body to a pack of hungry jakkaboles, myself. Dekkeret's a kindlier man than I am, but I like to think he'd do the same."

"He is a kingly man, is Dekkeret."

"Yes. Yes, that he is," said Prestimion. "A king among kings. I have left the world in good hands, I think. He told me he would crush Mandralisca without going to war, and he has done that, and pushed those five ghastly brothers back into the box out of which they sprang, and all Zimroel sings Lord Dekkeret's praises, now, apparently." Prestimion laughed. The thought of Dekkeret's deeds in Zimroel had brightened his spirit. "Do you know, Varaile, what it is that I will be famous for, in the years ahead? The great thing that they will remember about me? It will be that I came upon the boy who was to become Lord Dekkeret, one day while I was in Normork, and that I had the good sense to gather him to me and make him my Coronal. Yes. What they will say of me is that I was the king who gave the world Lord Dekkeret. —And now let us get ourselves ready for this journey to the Castle, love, and for the one bit of sad business we must do there, before we enter into the happy times of our reign."

They had been traveling up the Zimr for weeks and weeks, city upon city, Flegit and Clarischanz, Belka and Larnimisculus and Verf, and now they were in Ni-moya at last, were Dekkeret and Fulkari, installed in the great palace that once had belonged to Dantirya Sambail, wandering in amazement through its multitude of rooms, exclaiming over the splendor of its design.

"He did indeed live like a king," Fulkari murmured. They had reached the westernmost wing of the building, where a colossal window of a single pane provided a sweeping view that ran from the waterfront on their left to the white towers of the Ni-moyan hills on the right, and the great bosom of the giant river rolling on before them far into the remote regions of the continent. "What will you do with this place now, Dekkeret? You aren't going to have it torn down, are you?"

"No. Never. I can't hold this building guilty of the crimes of Dantirya Sambail and his five pitiful nephews. Those crimes will be forgotten, sooner or later. But what a crime against beauty it would be to destroy the Procurator's palace."

"Yes. Quite so."

"I'll appoint a duke to reign over Ni-moya—I don't know who it will be, but he'll be someone without a drop of Sambailid blood in him—

and he and his heirs can live here, knowing they do so by grace of the Coronal's generosity."

"A duke. Not a procurator."

"There'll be no more procurators here, Fulkari. That was Prestimion's decree, which I will renew. We'll remake the government of Zimroel to decentralize it again: a single authority here's too dangerous, too threatening to the imperial government itself. Provincial dukes, loyalty to the crown, frequent grand processionals to underscore the allegiance of Zimroel to the constitution—that's how it will be, yes."

"And the Five Lords?" she asked.

"Lords no more, you can be sure of that. But it would be a sin to put such fools to death. When they've done enough penance for their little uprising, they can go back to their palaces in the desert, and there they'll stay forever. I doubt they'll make any further trouble. And if the thought of it even comes into their minds, the King of Dreams will take care of that."

"The King of Dreams," Fulkari said, smiling. "Our brother Dinitak. A brilliant scheme, that was. Although you've cost me a sister by sending him off to Suvrael."

"And cost myself a friend," said Dekkeret. "It can't be helped. Prestimion insisted: the King of Dreams must make his headquarters down there. We can't have three of the four Powers clustered in Alhanroel. He'll do the job well, I think. He was born for it. —Did you ever think, Fulkari, that your wild tomboy of a sister would marry a Power of the Realm?"

"Did I ever think I would?" she asked, and they laughed, and moved closer to each other by the great window. Dekkeret stared outward. Night was beginning to fall, now. Somewhere out there to the west was a further world of marvels that they were yet to visit: Khyntor of the great steaming geysers, and crystalline Dulorn where the Perpetual Circus offered its carnival of wonders night and day, day and night, and ancient cobblestoned Pidruid beyond it on the coast, and Narabal, Til-omon, Tjangalagala, Cibairil, Brunir, Banduk Marika, all those fabled cities of the distant west.

They would visit them all. He was determined to go everywhere. To stand before the people and say, *Here I am, Dekkeret your Coronal Lord, who will devote his life to your service.*

"What a beautiful sunset," Fulkari said softly. "So many colors: gold, purple, red, green, all swirling together."

"It is. Very beautiful."

"But it's still only the middle of the day in Khyntor, isn't it? And morning in Dulorn. And the middle of the night before, out in Pidruid. Oh, Dekkeret, the world is so very big! The Castle seems so far away, just now!"

"The Castle *is* far away, my sweet."

"How long will we be gone on this processional, do you think?"

Dekkeret shrugged. "I don't know. Five years? Ten? Forever?"

"Seriously, Dekkeret."

"I tell you, Fulkari: I don't know. As long as it takes. The Castle will get along without us, if it has to. I am the Coronal Lord wherever I happen to be on Majipoor. And we have an entire world to visit." The sky was changing as they watched, the colors deepening, red giving way to bronze, purple shading into a dark maroon. Soon it would be night here, and twilight in the west. The stars were beginning to appear. One of the lesser moons came into view and cast a silver strand of light on the waters of the river. Dekkeret's arm tightened around Fulkari's shoulders, and they stood silently for a time. "Look you there," he said then, when at last all the colors had faded to black. "There is Majipoor before us, and the night is as beautiful as the day."